The Little Antique Shop Under The Eiffel Tower

REBECCA RAISIN

ONE PLACE. MANY STORIES

HQ
An imprint of HarperCollins*Publishers* Ltd
1 London Bridge Street
London SE1 9GF

This paperback edition 2020

1

First published in Great Britain by
HQ, an imprint of HarperCollins*Publishers* Ltd 2020

ISBN: 9780008389178

MIX
Paper from
responsible sources
FSC
www.fsc.org   FSC™ C007454

This book is produced from independently certified FSC™ paper
to ensure responsible forest management.

For more information visit: www.harpercollins.co.uk/green

Printed and bound in Great Britain by
CPI Group (UK) Ltd, Croydon CR0 4YY

For my Mum, who went without so we could have it all

Chapter One

A forget-me-not-scented breeze ruffled the pages of my newspaper, obscuring the headline that had caught my eye. The fragrant sky blue flowers spilled from planters on the balcony above, perfuming the spring air sweetly. Impatiently, I snapped the pages taut, hoping I was mistaken, and there wasn't bad news on the horizon. For our foreign neighbors, at any rate.

"What is it?" Madame Dupont asked, holding a tiny cup of café noir to scarlet-painted lips. "You've practically got your nose pressed against the ink. It'll come off you know, and you'll walk around all day with the *French Enquirer* text written backward across your skin."

I shook my head ruefully. Only Madame Dupont could think of such a thing. She was a vivacious seventy-something woman who still wore a full face of heavy makeup, with rouged cheeks that were so pink they were almost purple. Her deep hazel eyes were outlined thickly with kohl, and framed by false lashes that looked like exotic ebony fans. Still the twinkle in her eyes was that of a woman half her age, and she had a vitality and spark that was hard to match. Plumes of smoke swirled around her carefully coiffed gray hair, which she pointedly didn't color, claiming the silvery streaks suited her skin tone. She was never without a lit cigarette encased in an ivory holder, a relic from another era. I'd found it for her at a flea market by the bank of the Seine, and she cherished it.

Of course, when I nagged her about her addiction she laughed high and loud, declaring her vices kept her young. Madame Dupont cast most people in the shade when it came to the business of living; with her beguiling charm, and French sophistication, she was an icon in Paris. In her youth she'd been a famous cabaret singer, and rubbed shoulders with artists around the world, and that glamor had never left her. Sought out by men and women alike who were desperate to be part of her life, and know her secrets. I found it amusing, the way people clamored for her attentions. However, our morning tête-à-têtes were taken on a quiet avenue in Paris, so we could gossip in private without a local spotting Madame Dupont and striking up conversation.

The black and white pages ruffled insistently once more as if reminding me about the article and the distressing headline. "There's been a spate of robberies in Sorrento, Italy," I said, handing Madame Dupont the newspaper. "The Dolce Auction House, and the Rocher Estate."

"What? But we were just there!" Madame Dupont said, donning her diamond-encrusted spectacles and skimming the article.

"Oui," I said. "Can you imagine?" We were well abreast of our Italian counterparts and what they traded in the antique world. I'd accompany Madame Dupont for an adventure in exotic locales; I couldn't resist the idea of stepping onto foreign soil and breathing in different air, sitting under different stars. We'd go on buying jaunts when a dazzling collection beckoned. More so, Madame, who owned the Time Emporium, and traveled extensively to source unique clock-work. I specialized in French antiques, and only bid for pieces that were from my native country but had lived elsewhere for a while. Between estate sales, auctions, flea markets, and my sources, I had enough in Paris alone to keep me busy, but a little wanderlust in my veins justified the travel.

Madame Dupont had invited me to join her for two days in the town of Sorrento. I'd accepted, but her stamina with work and play had worn me to the bone. In response I'd taken afternoon siestas to gather my strength for our evenings out. During the day we'd admired the antiques on display at those very same exclusive auction houses, and Madame Dupont had successfully bid for some exotic timepieces. There'd been no French antiques on offer so I'd happily perused the Italian lots but kept my bidding paddle down.

She frowned. "Oh no . . ." she said, mouthing the words silently as she continued to read. "Tragic for them to lose the *L'Amore di uno* and the *L'arte di romanticismo* collections." The exquisite jewels were well known because of their Italian heritage. Pink diamonds became synonymous with Coco Salvatore, the soprano singer, who was never seen without them, up until her death a few years before.

In Sorrento we'd been stunned silent when we came to the pink diamond collections on display. They'd pulsed with life, as if they'd absorbed some of the soprano's vivacity, some of her sound.

Madame Dupont put a hand to her chest. "Such horrible news. What if the thief had walked straight past us but we were too engrossed in the diamonds to notice?"

I nodded, sipping my café au lait. "Oui, imagine that. And we had no idea those beauties were about to be snatched."

Straightening her skirt, Madame Dupont remained quiet, until finally saying: "How those thieves can override technology that can detect the merest whisper is a mystery, though. They'd have to be experts on security systems, and all that goes with it these days. I can barely send email, so I do applaud their nous."

"Madame! You can't applaud thieves!" We paused while a tiny car parked sideways in a car space next to us. The mini car was prevalent in Paris, and expert drivers maneuvered the minuscule vehicles to fit in any size gap.

"Why? It's true, the facts are he's a jewel thief with a brain."

"*He?*" I asked.

With a look heavenward she said, "Of course it's a he. Or . . . maybe it's a team of he's. Women respect diamonds too much to steal them. Who knows, but it would be much easier if it *were* only one person. The more people who are in on the secret the more likely it is they'll be caught."

I wrinkled my forehead in mock consternation. "You sound like you're speaking from experience, Madame."

I couldn't help but tease her. Madame's past was full of salacious stories, yet it wasn't from her scarlet lips they spilled. Outrageous rumors still abounded about her glory days. The most infamous one was that she'd been the lover of the idolized Marquis Laurent back in the sixties. He was famous for his flamboyant lifestyle, obscene wealth, and ties with royalty. Their affair was scandalous for many reasons, but everyone remembered the split more than anything – she was the first woman to ever break his heart. No one walked away from the Marquis unless he said so, but Madame Dupont had, because his plan of settling down scared her silly. She hadn't settled then and wouldn't now. She craved her freedom, whether it be from man, child, or relative.

That meant she played by her rules, always.

"Are you suggesting in my long, rich history of living I've been a criminal of some sort?" A rash of youthful giggles erupted from her.

"I wouldn't put it past you, not that you'd ever tell." That was the thing about Madame's past: from the woman herself, little was said.

"Oui, my secrets are under lock and key unless I go senile, and even then I hope I'd have the good sense to lie." She smiled. Her gaze traveled just past me, as she considered something. "Have you thought about it though, Anouk, the work involved in being a criminal these days? What he would need to do in order to get in and out without detection defies belief. And then there's selling the loot. No one could ever *wear* the jewelry in case it was recognized."

I tore off the edge of my croissant. Flakes of pastry scattered over the table. "What a waste of such precious artifacts. It's not only the worth of the jewelry – there's a whole history attached to those diamonds. And now it's lost forever. And what for? To sit in someone's vault for a lifetime. What's the point of that?" I ate slowly, leaning back in my chair, and turned toward a glimpse of the Eiffel Tower, visible from the Boulangerie Fret-Co on the Avenue de la Bourdonnais. Madame Dupont and I had been breakfasting at the same place for years.

Regular customers strode in and promptly out with a fresh baguette. Nothing ever changed: the coffee was always strong, the croissants buttery, and the view of the tower partially obstructed by a leafy canopy of trees, which shimmied as the wind collected them. It was mostly quiet here in the mornings, with only the stooped man next door ambling about whistling as he dragged his postcard carousels to the footpath, giving them a light dusting with a rag.

Madame Dupont lived in a penthouse apartment on the Avenue Élisée Reclus one street over. A hop, skip, and a jump and she was practically at the Eiffel Tower. My little antique shop wasn't far from there, closer to the Avenue Gustave Eiffel, and surrounded by nature, leafy trees, and lush gardens, with flowers that changed with the seasons.

"Greed! That's what it is!" Madame Dupont said. "That's what drives these black market buyers. The collections won't be lost, not forever. I'm sure the Italian *Carabinieri* will catch those responsible. After all, they're just as well armed these days in technology – someone's always watching." Her words were meant to reassure, but her high-pitched musical tone gave her away. She knew as well as I did, if the jewels had left the country, they'd never be seen again.

"Maybe," I said not convinced. The avenue was slowly coming alive: cars zoomed along tooting their horns, tourists with sleepy expressions meandered by on the hunt for coffee, the usual

5

soundtrack to our morning, and a sign it was time to start our own jobs.

I finished the last of my coffee. "I suppose we should be thankful Paris hasn't been targeted."

Madame Dupont just lifted a brow and took a sip of her coffee.

Chapter Two

Just past noon, the shadow of the Eiffel Tower fell through the window of my little antique shop, casting a sepia light over the treasures sitting solemnly inside. Chestnut swirls and golden hues of dusty sunlight swept in, shimmering on the antiques and making them appear faded, like an old photograph. The space appeared otherworldly, as if we'd truly stepped back in time.

Instead of languishing in the filmy haze, I turned back to the matter at hand, unable to shake off the sensation all was not what it seemed.

"You have my word, Anouk," Oceane said, her china blue eyes fervent. She dropped her voice to a whisper. "I've known Agnes forever. She's trustworthy, I promise." With a wave she indicated a thin, raven-haired woman who stood a few paces back and blushed under my scrutiny. Agnes fiddled absently with the tassels on her handbag and wouldn't meet my gaze.

"She's French?" I whispered, still not convinced. I would only sell my precious antiques to those who had an introduction from a customer I trusted. A foible, but one I wouldn't change. If I sold to just anyone, who knew what would happen to our heritage? Even when times had been tough financially, I still made sure I was selling to someone reliable.

Every now and then Agnes's composure slipped, and she'd gaze at the antique jewelry with a type of hunger that made her features sharp. Those were the kind of people I said *non* to, because I didn't trust their motives. They weren't after a piece of history, or an heirloom to cherish – they were accumulating things with no regard to the past. Certain items with sentimental and historical value had to be protected, and I did my best to uphold those principles, despite the economic strain it sometimes caused.

However, Oceane from *Once Upon a Time*, a little bookshop on the Seine, was a loyal and trusted customer of mine, and would only introduce someone to me if she felt they were genuine. It was just the shiftiness in the woman's eyes that made me hesitate. Perhaps I was unsettled by the reports of the Italian robberies earlier that morning, and thus, analyzing the woman's motives too closely.

Still, antiques had to be treasured. Efforts taken to ascertain that the right match was made.

Sadly tradition was slowly slipping away as people looked to the future, rather than the past. Technology and the desire to have things instantaneously were pervading old values. My shoulders slumped just thinking of it.

"Of course she's French," Oceane said, pulling me back to her. "Her family have a boulangerie on Rue Saint-Antoine. She's after a small ruby pendant for her maman. Her parents are celebrating their fortieth wedding anniversary. I *promise*, she's legitimate."

The cagey demeanor of the woman changed at the mention of her parents' impending wedding anniversary. A ruby gift was tradition after forty years of marriage. Agnes smiled softly, her expression relaxed – she looked beyond me, as if she was thinking of them, and the memories they'd created in their years of matrimony. I watched her for a beat. She was unaware of my analysis, caught somewhere inside her mind, glassy-eyed, almost hypnotized, at wherever her reminisces were taking her.

A fine trail of goose bumps broke out over my skin, a surefire sign I could trust her with my exquisite jewelry. Sometimes, I relied on my own visceral reaction to a person more than any other sign.

Agnes's gaze darted to a simple solitaire ruby pendant in the display cabinet, and there it stayed. She wasn't greedy, she didn't want them all, only wanted one perfect piece – you could read it on her face as clearly as if the words were written on her skin.

The precious gem twinkled magnificently even in the shadow of noonday. Her fingers found the hem of her shirt, and she toyed with it as if she was trying to stop herself from reaching for the ruby. She had chosen well. Classic, timeless, and utterly captivating. Luscious red so deep you could get lost in it.

I prided myself on finding out the origins of any purchases I made, as I believed without that the piece lost some of its luster.

"Come closer." I gestured to Agnes. "I bought that pendant a few years ago from an estate sale in Provence. Would you like to know more about its past life?"

She nodded. "Oui, I'd like that very much. I've never seen anything so perfectly suited to my maman. Somehow the rest of the jewelry fades in comparison."

It was the right pendant; of that I was certain. I said quietly, "When I was at the sale a neighbor came to watch her late friend's belongings be auctioned, so I approached her and asked what she knew of the ruby pendant – what it had meant to its former owner. Like you, it had called to me amongst everything else on show. The neighbor told me the woman had found love as a young girl, and it had lasted a lifetime."

Agnes smiled, perhaps recognizing the same in her parents.

I continued: "Her husband had given her the ruby on their honeymoon, and she was always fumbling with it, touching it to make sure it was still there. Of all the pieces she'd owned, the neighbor said the ruby was what most represented their love, and its longevity."

Agnes cocked her head as she absorbed the story of the ruby.

"Did she live a good and long life?" When a customer bought something sacred like the ruby, they'd be carrying the previous owner's story forward too. The ruby absorbed fragments of the heart and soul of its owners, past and present, like osmosis, becoming part of the fabric of it for eternity.

I smiled. "She did. They both did. Octogenarians, until death came for him, and then soon after, her. The neighbor said it wasn't all lavender fields and laughter. They argued high and loud about his job, which took him all over the country, and left her alone at home. They fought about her hair: he liked it long, so she cropped it short. Once she threw all his clothes off the balcony in a fit of pique, and he laughed, which made her angrier. The neighbor said they were drawn to each other like magnets. The highs, and lows were many, but only because of their fierce love for one another." I paused, watching Agnes's face light up at their epic story. This was the best part of my job, knowing intuitively that the ruby was going to be prized not only because of its beauty but also because of its history.

I continued: "They were married for sixty-two years before he was summoned away. It was said she wrote him love letters every day until it was her time. I almost kept the ruby for myself, I was so taken with their love story." That day there had been antiques worth more and easily saleable but I was drawn to the ruby and knew I had to have it. And now I knew why – for Agnes's mother.

If I closed my eyes, I could see it as it had been, hanging brilliantly against her olive-skinned décolletage, the faint scent of lavender in the air, an olive grove in the distance. But perhaps that was just a daydream, a picture painted by my imagination.

Agnes gave me a wide smile. "My parents still hold hands walking to work. They bicker about whose baguette recipe is the best, and I mean really bicker in typical French style, hands on hips, red-faced, low steady growls, until someone intervenes, and placates them saying both recipes have their merits. Maman calls him a goat, and he says she's a mule, and they affect animal noises, until one of them starts howling with laughter, scaring the customers. Some days, they don't talk at all, because they've spent the day chatting to their regular clientele and they've run out of words. Other days she rests her head on his shoulder and he murmurs to her as if they're the only two people in the world. Their love still shines . . ."

"And now it will sparkle," I said with a grin.

Carefully, I took the pendant from its housing. It winked under the lights as though it was saying *yes*. "For your maman." I offered her a closer look.

With a slight quake in her hands, she took the proffered pendant and whispered, "It's perfect." She blanched when she saw the price tag, but admirably reined herself in. For such a unique and precious gift, it was worth every cent. Any fiscal talk set my teeth on edge, and I was glad she didn't mention it. It was poor taste, and I didn't negotiate, and neither did any of my self-respecting Parisian customers. "Can I take it . . .?"

I gave her a nod. "Let me wrap it for you."

Oceane smiled her thanks while Agnes watched me polish the pendant before I placed it in a satin-lined box, wrapped it, and tied an antique lace ribbon around to finish it off.

"May they have many more anniversaries as special as this one," I said. Agnes handed over a stack of well-thumbed Euros, her face bright like a child's on Christmas Eve. Times like this I realized how much I loved my little antique shop, and pairing something from a lifetime ago, to start over in a new home, with a new family. I knew Agnes would recount the story of the former owner of the pendant to her parents, and they'd know it was more than just a piece of jewelry. And when they passed it on, their love story would be remembered too.

"Merci," Agnes said, cradling the box in her open palms as if she held something as delicate as a baby bird.

Just then a rowdy tour group appeared by the window. I stiffened in response.

11

"*Merde*. There's so many of them," Oceane said, following my gaze to the tourists outside, led by a guide who was purposely bringing these people to me knowing I'd turn them away. Innocents, who just wanted to see what all the fuss was about.

"Ah, the ever-present legacy of Joshua, the American whose shadow is felt even when he's not here," Oceane said. I'd confided in her recently about my ex-boyfriend, Joshua, who spitefully informed the editor of *Solitary World*, one of the biggest guide books sold on the planet, about my little antique shop and the secret room. Since then, I'd been inundated by people wanting to take photos and mark off another stop on their to-see list in Paris.

My blood boiled each time I saw their faces fall, the groups expecting to clap eyes on something marvelous and instead told there was no such thing. But I had to protect the delicate objects in my care. If I opened the doors to just anyone I'd be overrun and things would be damaged. Or worse, stolen, and I couldn't face that again. I hadn't told Oceane the rest of the bitter breakup story because I didn't want any more pity, but his vindictiveness was the least of what Joshua had done in his efforts to ruin my life.

"Do you want me to tell the guide off? He shouldn't be bringing them here only to disappoint them," Oceane asked, glaring at the group forming at the front door, their noses pressed against the glass.

"Non, it's OK. The guide is well aware he isn't welcome, but he does it for their entertainment. *The French mademoiselle who won't let people shop*, he cries out like I'm a novelty. I suppose they think it's odd, and then they move to the next place and it's fodder for a funny travel story when they're home." I flounced over and turned the sign to Closed. Dusting my hands, I ignored the plaintive cries from the gaggle and gave the tour guide an icy stare.

"But what about the secret room!" one yelled out.

The secret room was just that – a secret – and no sugar-dusted fingers would pad at the treasures in there or snap pictures of what lay hidden in its depths.

The tour guide was gesticulating wildly and putting on a show for their benefit. "You have to know the secret handshake if you want to shop here," he said, turning and giving me a wolfish smile. "Anouk is unconventional – just like the dust gatherers she collects. The French mademoiselle who won't let people shop!"

"See?" I said to Oceane. "He's so predictable."

"A jerk," she countered.

The crowd were delighted by such an anomaly, and peered at me through the glass. I did my best to ignore the guide, knowing he'd eventually get bored and move on. A reaction is exactly what he wanted from me, so I was loath to give it.

Instead, I walked toward Agnes who was still staring at the box in her hands, unaware of anything else going on around her. "Next time," I told her, touching her arm. "You don't need an introduction. You may visit my shop alone."

Her eyes widened and she clapped a hand over her mouth, muffling, "Merci! Merci!"

There was something I trusted about Agnes now. Usually I wouldn't grant a first-time customer the ability to shop without returning with another loyal customer for months, sometimes years. But aside from the immediate bout of unease, I sensed Agnes was the type of person who appreciated old beauty, valued it; you could see it by the instinctive way she responded to the ruby story. She worked hard for what she had, as did her parents, and there was a sincerity about her. I liked the way she hadn't romanticized her parents' love; she told their tale warts and all. In my eyes, those attributes made a person whole, and utterly dependable with my treasures.

"Merci, Anouk," Oceane said. "You've made their anniversary very special. See you again soon." After a peck on each cheek, they stepped out into the splendor of the breezy spring day.

With the door swung open the chatter and merriment from outside drifted in. Paris was in full bloom, from the flowers to the influx of visitors and the radiance of the sunshine. The faint echo of boats gurgling along the Seine carried over, the wind sweeping up its earthy, fathomless scent and blowing it gently across the cornflower blue Parisian sky all the way into my little antique shop.

Distracted by the elements, I jumped when a camera flashed in my face. I hastily blinked away at the orb clouding my vision. The tour group were still mingling close. They held phones aloft, snapping pictures, edging closer to me saying, "Say cheese!"

Why did they always say that? *Say cheese?* It didn't make any sense.

"Au revoir," I said coolly to the tour guide, and closed the door tight.

Silently I cursed Joshua for betraying my trust and breaking my heart. With the number of malicious things he did, being published in the *Solitary World* travel guide and the havoc it created lingered long after he'd gone. Still, I'd learnt a valuable lesson, and steeled myself against men and strangers too, knowing I'd never make that mistake again.

One of the women from the group gave me an apologetic smile that I returned before nodding my thanks.

Chapter Three

"Bonjour, Anouk! What's new?" My little sister's lyrical voice bounced around the shop, after she flung herself through the door, and took two great lunges to wrap me in her arms, suffocating me in the peach-scented locks of her hair. She was a bubbly, zany girl with a zest for life that matched no other. Great in theory, but if you spent any longer than a day with her, you'd find yourself zapped by an exhaustion you couldn't shake, as though her reserves of energy pilfered your own. It was hard to keep up with her constant motion, and bevy of ideas about every little thing.

With her free spirit and flighty attitude my papa hoped she would follow my example, so sent her to study in Paris, and build the foundations she would need to make a life of *his* orchestrating, with me as a sort of chaperone.

Lilou flouted his rules, and snubbed his advice, though not to his face, or down the line of the phone. If she stopped long enough and he actually caught her on the telephone she lied, or she instructed me to lie about what was really going on. It was a game of cat and mouse, with me an unwilling participant.

Papa thought I'd steer her down the right path, but so far all that meant was bending the truth to him when she escaped the tediousness of her paralegal course and flitted off somewhere with the war cry, '*You only live once!*' It was enough to make me throw my hands in the air, and think of her as my wayward child, rather than younger sister.

So far I was having even less luck than Papa at getting her to focus. If he knew she was playing truant with her studies he'd be livid. But she was like a wrecking ball, impossible to stop once the momentum got going, and so very clever at manipulating the situation in her favor. Still, you had to give her credit – she certainly lived life on her terms.

"Lilou, where have you been? Papa's been calling every day," I said, trying to rearrange my expression to appear somber, which was hard when her dazzling face was beaming at me. How I loved her, craziness and all.

She shrugged. "Papa can call all he wants. I hate that paralegal course. I'm not doing it." She shook her head. "I don't want to work in a legal firm; the dullness would kill me." I stifled a smile, knowing it was true. Papa wanted Lilou to become a paralegal, had his heart set on it, after hearing a proud neighbor gush about his daughter and the executive life by proxy she was leading, but that wasn't Lilou. An office environment would make her wilt like a rose without sunlight.

Living for the moment was fine for now, but I did agree she should have something to fall back on. I worried she'd find herself lost one day, with no skills and no real ambition.

"He'll cut off your allowance if you don't study, and then how will you pay for your apartment?"

Typically, she ignored the crux of the issue and said, "I *am* working. I don't need to study. And luckily –" she flashed a grin "– my job allows me the freedom to travel. I just need to make more money, which'll take time! There's nothing wrong with making jewelry for a living . . . It *is* a career!"

It was obvious Lilou would not be swayed. "It's a fantastic hobby, and it might become a business if you work at it, but you don't earn anywhere near enough to even make your rent. An

Etsy store and eBay doesn't pay your bills, let alone the lifestyle you lead. He worries, that's all." Lilou's jewelry was spectacular but it sold for a pittance, and I couldn't see her building it up to a level she could comfortably live on because work was a foreign word to her.

With a flick of her long silky tresses, she rolled her eyes heavenward. "I have to start somewhere. Etsy and eBay are great stepping-stones for me. Sure I'm not at the 7th arrondissement stage . . ." She pulled a face, teasing me about the location, and exclusivity, of my shop. "But it's a start. Papa should focus on his own life, and so should you for that matter. Don't let him force you to be my keeper."

I smirked. "Good idea," I said, voice heavy with sarcasm. "Here's the phone." I lifted the receiver. "Give him a call and explain that to him."

She had the grace to color, the apples of her cheeks pinking up, only making her more beautiful. "Well . . . maybe we can leave it a few more weeks, Anouk? Just until I really build up my sales." Papa was set in his ways, and neither of us wanted to answer to him, gruff as he was. "Forget it for now," she said. "I saw the most magnificent sunset in Marseille. I'm going to create a whole range of orange jewelry in ode to it. Let's go to lunch and I can tell you everything. I've left Claude at your apartment so we don't have to rush." She leaned over the counter to grab my handbag, and in one swift movement took my elbow and barreled me out of the door. I halted and fumbled for my keys.

"Claude's at my apartment?"

"Yeah, you've made a very valid point, and I was thinking of it, even before your spiel. You're totally right – I can't support myself with what little Papa gives me, and what little income I make with my jewelry, so I've given up my apartment in favor of staying with you – to save money on rent. I knew you'd be supportive of my decision . . ." She frowned at my expression of abject horror.

"Lilou . . ."

"What? You said yourself I had to figure out my expenses and set some long-term goals. That's exactly what I've done! I'll miss my apartment but sacrifices have to be made. Living with you will be one *huge* sacrifice but I'm planning for the future – just like you wanted. And how happy will Papa and Maman be knowing you're keeping a close eye on little old me?"

I took a steadying breath, disarmed by her cunning, clever ways. Living with her would be a lesson in patience, tolerance, and cleanliness, to say the least. "It's just . . . I like my own space, as you well know."

She swung to face me. "Claude and I will use it as a landing base, that's all. Don't worry, you'll still have your freedom."

With the shop locked and the sign flicked to Closed, we let the debate drop and meandered away. In France we were accustomed to having long lunches, and sometimes ducking home for a nap before recommencing work. It was a way to relax and recharge. There was no race to get to the weekend because each day was a good day, with its own rhythms.

"Hang on, who's Claude?" I asked.

"My boyfriend!" She zoomed on, pinning my arm so I had no choice but to keep pace.

We zigzagged through throngs of people who were enjoying the spectacle of a lively Parisian spring day.

"What? What happened to Rainier?" I asked, trying to catch my breath as she propelled me forward.

Before Lilou had vanished three weeks ago, she'd been smitten with a gorgeous Frenchman whose broody nature intrigued her. Rainier was a wine-maker from Haut-Médoc who was taking a year to explore his native country to broaden his horizons, sipping Bordeaux along the way – an oenophile if I ever met one, as he supped, and swished, lamenting about the complexities of wine like he was reciting poetry. I thought he was perfect for her, mysterious enough to keep her guessing, and therefore interested.

"Oh," she hesitated, no doubt trying to formulate a lie to soften the fact she'd ditched him like an apple core. "We just weren't compatible. C'est la vie."

"C'est la vie *again*?" I couldn't hide the rebuke in my voice. It was one thing to take flight every time something shinier came along, but she'd left a trail of broken hearts in her wake, and I knew only too well what that felt like. I couldn't tell her how to care – she wouldn't listen anyway – but it grated that she could be so frivolous with other people's feelings. I blamed it on her youth, and hoped she'd grow out of it. There was a six-year age gap between us but sometimes it felt like twenty.

I mused. "I liked Rainier. He was soft on the inside."

She ignored me and winked at two young guys sitting on the grass nearby. Lilou was an incorrigible flirt who winked, waved, and whispered her way around Paris, just for fun.

Turning away from the guys, she said, "I could have set you and Rainier up. You should have told me!"

I gasped, and broke into a fit of giggles at the ridiculous idea. "Not for me, for you!"

We strolled along the fringes of the Champs de Mars. The 800-meter-long green space was once used as a market garden centuries ago. Once upon a time locals grew abundant crops to harvest and plied their wares. Now it was a verdant park for people to picnic on and gaze at the Eiffel Tower.

"Well you haven't met Claude yet. And . . ." she paused for effect ". . . his brother Didier lives in Paris, and just so happens to be an art critic. Art. He likes *art*. *You* like art!"

As if that was enough to jump into bed with someone, which is what she constantly nagged me to do. I shook my head in a vigorous no.

"Don't do that thing you do, not again, please." It was her mission to set me with up with a man, *any man*, the only prerequisite seemed to be that he was breathing. So far she'd introduced me to a sixty-year-old count with a handlebar moustache, a dreadlocked guitarist who spoke in tongues, and the last and most explosive no: a magician who kept threatening to make my clothing disappear. I shuddered at the thought of such paramours.

We walked in silence, enjoying the hazy sunlight on our faces. Twenty minutes later we arrived at one of our favorite restaurants, *Mille*, near Les Invalides. Inside the various buildings that made up Hôtel National des Invalides there were museums and monuments pertaining to the French military, and deep within its walls lay Napoléon Bonaparte's tomb. It was a hallowed place and steeped with history, a popular spot for tourists who could wander most of the expanse for free.

Mille served traditional French food, and a selection of fine wines, perfect for a slow lunch, and it was a good vantage point for people watching, which was one of my favorite things to do.

The maître d' recognized us and hurried over, motioning to a table by the window. We thanked him, taking proffered menus. Lilou ordered white wine without consulting me, and fluttered her lashes at the poor smitten man, as was her way. "Vin blanc, OK?" she asked, leaning her head on her hand, giving me a lazy smile.

"Well you've ordered it now, haven't you?" I furrowed my brow, trying to appear disapproving, but failing.

"Oui, I have." She laughed, and it lit up her blue eyes. We were similar in appearance, but Lilou had a playfulness to her that made her radiant, which I had never had, even in my teens. While our facial features were alike, our style was markedly different. I tended to wear vintage clothing, forties style, and Lilou was very a la mode, and kept up with the latest fashion trends even on her limited budget. Her hair was always loose, and shiny, like a shampoo model, and mine was curled or coiffed. She favored natural makeup, and I preferred the dramatic smoky-eyed, scarlet-lipped look. Though many a time she'd pilfer my wardrobe for scarves or dresses – a younger sister's rite of passage.

Perusing the menu I decided on the dish of the day – let it

be a surprise – and Lilou went for the beef fillet with béarnaise sauce and potato dauphinoise. For such a lithe specimen of a girl she could eat as heartily as any man. She'd have entrée first and finish the meal with a rich dessert, of which I would steal a bite, and then she'd order yet another bottle of wine. I had her measure, and knew without doubt I'd pay for the lunch, and its accoutrements. It was nice to be able to shut off for a few hours, with someone who knew me inside out.

I enjoyed our sisterly time together, and the fact we could be ourselves and relax into the afternoon. I wondered if that might change if we lived together. The thought of Lilou wreaking havoc inside my pristine apartment, where everything was just so, was enough to make me rue my choice not to say no to her – but how could I? Parisian apartments were expensive, and I knew she couldn't keep up paying for hers for any length of time. I calmed myself, promising there'd be rules she'd have to adhere to. She would be on her best behavior surely?

We ordered our meals, and the waiter filled our wineglasses. I sat back feeling my limbs loosen with the first sip of crisp white wine.

"As I was saying," she said, giving her hair a customary flick, "I know my match-making choices haven't been ideal but this Didier . . ." She pretended to pull her collar out as if she was hot, and waggled her eyebrows suggestively. "Whoa! Seriously, you have to meet him."

I clucked my tongue like my maman would do when Lilou was being *too* Lilou. "No thank you. Your choices have been downright hideous." I gave her a withering stare. "A magician? A sixty-year-old count? You might think I'm mature but I'm only twenty-eight for God's sake. I don't think we need to reach for the fringes of society just yet. And certainly not a man old enough to be my papa!"

She leaned forward and whispered, "Some women find silver foxes very attractive, I'll have you know."

It was like speaking another language with Lilou. "Silver foxes?"

"Oui," she said. "Silver foxes, you know, a man with a sprinkling of gray, a little mature but a whole *lot* of sex appeal." She slapped her hand on the table and let out a roar of delight.

"Hush, Lilou. Mon Dieu!" All eyes were cast toward us.

"What?" She blew out her cheeks. "You can't nurse a broken heart forever. Six months is enough grieving time, *too* much time for a man like him. You need to have a passionate affair!"

I shriveled in my seat, hoping no one could understand her fast-talking sentences. "I'm not grieving –" I scoffed "– far from it. I don't have time for it, that's all." Lilou knew the intimate details about Joshua because the *petit espion* had found my diary and read every single word. If not for that she'd know zero, because who would tell the world a horror story like that? "And if I did have time for a relationship, I wouldn't reserve it for the type of men you're suggesting. A silver fox, I mean . . .?"

Laughter burbled from her. "You said you wanted someone extraordinary! Gray is the new black, non?"

I arched a brow. "I don't think so, Lilou." Really, she was so adamant about the most ridiculous things.

Tugging her dress down as she sat back in her chair, she said, "Sister of mine, I hate to say it, but you are only *twenty-eight*. Not eighty-eight. Why can't you have a little fun while you're waiting for Mr. Right? Even Madame Dupont beds more men than you do, and she *is* almost eighty."

Madame Dupont took Lilou into her confidence when it came to matters of the boudoir. Lilou was a good secret-keeper *when she wanted to be*, and Madame Dupont trusted her. They recognized something in one another: a spark of similarity, of lives lived the same, only half a century apart.

I struggled not to roll my eyes at Lilou's disappointed expression. "For some of us, it's not all about sex you know. There's more to intimacy than that."

She sighed. "What do you want – flowers, chocolates? A sonnet

22

or two? Your name written in the sky?" She pretended to yawn as if she was bored. "A cookie-cutter romance? No, Anouk, no. You need to dust off your lingerie, and throw yourself at the first available debonair man, and let nature take its course. High octane, a helluva lot of adventure, and boom, you'll never remember what's-his-name."

It was impossible not to laugh. *Dust off my lingerie?* "Thanks for your input, Lilou, but I don't think that's very sage advice. Throw myself at just anyone as if I've been sex starved or something! What's the rush? What if Monsieur First Available is a raving sociopath? He could be married, or a misfit, or a gambler. What if he had a hairy back? A passion for flat-pack furniture?" I suppressed a giggle at Lilou's darkening expression. "What's wrong with taking time to get to know someone and then later expressing love with little gifts, especially a poem?"

"It's just so last century." She raised her hands up. "And let's be real, can we? You're not going to meet anyone stuck at work or holed up in your apartment, are you? I can see your tombstone already." She gazed over my shoulder, and scrunched her face up as if she was crying, with a faux sob she said, "Here lies Anouk LaRue. Born. Worked. Died. She leaves behind her beloved little antique shop, who'll miss her dearly." For effect she buried her face in her hands and faux wept, once again drawing attention from curious onlookers. If only they knew.

"There's nothing wrong with the amount I work. It's called," I enunciated slowly, "*being responsible*. Setting myself up for the future. A man would complicate all of that. When the time is right, I'll date again, but at the moment, the thought makes me want to scream. I just simply do not have a minute of the day left to worry about another person. You make it seem like we need men to survive! We don't!"

She took her hands from her face. "No time? You spend an age reading the newspaper. You play around on your laptop every evening! How much time do you need for love? Joshua was a nasty excuse for a boyfriend – I get that. Pure evil, and enough to break the steeliest of hearts, but so what? That was a million years ago, and it's time to forget it. If you hide away it means he's still winning. We don't *need* men? We don't *need* wine either, but how much sweeter is life with it?"

I shook my head. She didn't understand, and she never would. Lilou was a free spirit, and so utterly different to me. Yet here she was suggesting I missed love, but it just wasn't an issue for me. The thought of another man in my life was enough to make me recoil in horror. I just couldn't envisage it. Didn't need it. Didn't miss it. I'd choose the wine option any day.

"Lingerie aside, Lilou, it really is more complicated than that and you know it. I have to work doubly, even triply hard after Joshua sold the piano from under me. My savings were tied up in that piece, and without any help from the gendarmes, what could I do, except to scramble to sell antiques at a discount so my business wouldn't go bust. I'm still trying to get my finances stabilized and replenish the stock. And if *that's* what love does to you, forget it."

Even after all this time the memory of Joshua and what he'd done still stung. I was a fool to have believed a word that poured from his honeyed mouth. Every single sentence that fell from his lips, I listened to rapt. So exotic with his American accent and bright-eyed gaze. His declarations of love seemed so sincere and took me to a place I'd never been before.

"I don't have time to sift through their lies." I swished another mouthful of wine, glad for its numbing properties.

"Not all men lie," she said giving me a pointed look.

I scoffed. "And how do you know that? Your longest relationship has been three weeks, Lilou."

She shot me a glare. Joshua had taken a selection of antiques from the secret room, including a very rare piano, very *expensive* piano, promising me they were off to good homes, people he'd known forever. Payment to follow. The sale would fund our 'grand plan'.

And the buyers were French people, he said. Trustworthy.

In that flurry of love, I had believed him. Of course I had.

It was the greatest shock when I stumbled on them at an online auction and confronted him about it. *Non, non, non,* he mimicked my French accent, *remember your messages? The antiques are mine as you said so many times! Au revoir, Anouk. It was fun while it lasted.*

Ambushed.

And fraught, the gendarmerie couldn't help me. They said I'd gifted them to him. They had proof. Text messages that came from my cell phone, saying those exact words. Joshua was clever. He'd been ribbing me, he called it. Teasing me about 'gifting' my treasures and like the lovestruck idiot I was, I played along by text, waiting months for these so-called buyers to pay. By the time I realized what he'd done, he was on the arm of another woman. Antiques vanished. And those texts came back to taunt me.

The grand piano once owned by Fania Fénelon is yours! A gift from me to you. Love Anouk xxx

It was the cold, calculating way he did it that struck fear in me – the thought that a man could fake a love like ours broke something inside of me. I begged, yelled, pleaded for the gendarmes to listen to me, but they gave me a bored stare, and asked me to come back with more proof, like I should do their job for them.

Joshua and I had planned to pool our resources and were going to buy the best antiques, build a museum, so the world could clap eyes on such rare beauty, and not just people who could afford such luxuries. In order to do that, we had needed to sell some bigger pieces to fund it, and then source the most famous, the most illustrious of what France had to offer. Little did I know, he was selling them to amass *his* fortune . . . He'd played *me* like a piano, knowing instinctively I'd fall for it because it was a lifelong dream of mine to open a museum for cherishables.

The thing that hurt the most was that I did love him. When it all came to light I realized I had been in love with a ghost.

Joshua wasn't who he portrayed himself to be. The man I loved didn't exist. The one who held my hand as we slept, or woke me with butterfly kisses, was a charade. So if I held myself at arm's length from the world, that's why, and I wasn't going to be apologetic about it.

Sadly, Joshua was still working the antique circuit, so I ran into him often, which felt like a stab wound to the chest.

Lilou gave my hand a pat, dragging me back to the present moment. "Three weeks might be my limit with a guy, but that's because I haven't found anyone who makes me want more." She lifted a shoulder. "I know what that *crétin* did, and the fallout that remains. I'd strangle him if I knew I could bury his body and get away with it." Her eyes blazed at the thought. "All I'm suggesting is ease yourself back into the dating game with a few one-night stands. Pick a rugged type, one that has commitment-phobe written all over him, and go from there . . ."

"Lilou! I couldn't do that. Non. I need to know more about a man before I let him sprawl all over my cotton sheets . . ."

She wrinkled her nose. "Oh God, because they're some kind of special antique material? Fine, swap the sheets for a cheap supermarket brand for one night!" Her voice rose with every inflection.

A waiter hovered close by, refilling the wineglass of a woman at the table beside ours, and overfilled it as he concentrated hard on us out of the corner of his eye. Ruby red wine spilled over, staining the white tablecloth. The woman gasped, and the waiter wrenched his gaze away, apologizing profusely to her.

Lilou jerked a thumb in his direction. "Prime example: nice taut derrière, sleepy eyes, and sensual full lips. Just picture those buff arms tangled around you, the bed sheets . . ."

This time the waiter knocked over the woman's wineglass. Burgundy liquid spilled quick and fast into the woman's white-skirted lap. Lilou gave them a cursory glance. "OK, maybe not him, he's too clumsy." His face colored scarlet.

"Stop!" I hissed, struggling to remain composed. "I see your point and I'll take it under advisement."

She swallowed back half a glass of her wine. "I hate it when you say that."

* * *

Lilou and I stood out front of the little antique shop, languid after lunch, and hugged our goodbyes. "See you tonight," I said.

"Actually you won't." Lilou gave me an elfish grin. "I'm off to follow a musical festival around Normandy with Claude. I thought I might do a collection of jewelry based on sound. It's a research trip."

"What?" My big-sister instinct kicked in. "You've only just got back. You and Rainier were only going away for a week. It's been three and now Rainier is gone, and there's someone called Claude, and you're going to follow a *music festival*? I thought you were doing a line of sunset-inspired jewelry? No, Lilou! You're supposed to be studying. At least try and build up your online site so we have ammunition if Papa finds out."

She let out a long harrumph as if I was the veritable thorn in her side. I could guess what was coming next . . .

"Anouk, *you only live once!*"

Voila!

Once Lilou had her sights set on something, she was a force to be reckoned with. Even though her life lacked direction, I had a feeling she'd always be OK by using her charm and quick wit. She was irresistible when she flashed her radiant smile. Deep down she was a minx, but I loved her so, even though she added an element of drama to my already busy life and created the worry I carried in my heart when she was off on one of her adventures. I was desperate for anyone or anything to slow her down and keep her in one spot, long enough that she'd plant roots and stay.

I dreaded another call from my papa, asking after her. I'd have to cross my fingers, and lie yet again, knowing eventually it would all come crashing down around me.

A part of me envied her; I was never that frivolous, never had been. My days revolved around work, sourcing antiques, investigating their history, traveling near and far for estate sales and auctions, hunting through bric-a-brac for gems at flea markets and vintage fairs. That didn't leave much time for anything else. My heart and soul went into my business. I kept myself coiled tight against any uncertainty that came my way.

I shook the familiar feeling of angst away before it could settle, blackening my mood.

"When Papa phones me what do you suggest I say?"

With a groan, she said, "Tell him I'm at the library! Or at study club, or out with a lawyer . . . who cares." Typical flippant Lilou style.

"He's going to find out eventually and then we'll both be in trouble."

She laughed, high and loud. "What can he do?"

"He can cut off your allowance . . ."

Her face paled. "True, so lie good." She kissed me goodbye, and stole away. "I'll be back soon!" The words bubbled above, blowing toward me in the Seine-scented breeze.

I watched her retreating frame, heading off into the sunset like an actress from a movie, her long hair undulating and her step jaunty.

From the corner of my eye I sensed someone watching me. I turned, hoping it wasn't another uninvited customer. A man sat at one of the benches along the promenade. He was wearing chinos, with a tight white T-shirt. His lips curved into a smile when we made eye contact. He was double-take gorgeous with his blond hair swept back like he'd just stepped off a windblown boat, and his aviator sunglasses reflected my own surprised gaze back.

For one brief moment, I considered Lilou's advice: go out with a man, any man, and see what happened. He moved to stand, like he was going to approach me, and the idea suddenly seemed ridiculous. I bustled into my shop as quickly as possible and locked the door, peeking out through the lace curtain. He was still watching, an amused smirk on his face. In one swift movement he stood and waved, sending me scurrying back into the dark recesses of the shop. Mon Dieu, he knew I was spying on him!

For one unguarded minute the stranger with the athletic physique and gorgeous face had intrigued me. Perhaps I had too much wine at lunchtime. I bustled around keeping busy, and pushed any silly notions from my mind. There was work to do.

Chapter Four

In the Luxembourg Gardens tulips popped their yellow heads up as if to say hello. They were such happy flowers, and in abundance now spring had sprung. It was peak time in the park; tourists and locals alike perched on the side of fountains, reading, chatting, or staring off into space. Checkered picnic rugs were spread out, topped with baskets laden with lunchtime feasts.

Normally, I'd sit and people-watch, eavesdrop, and imagine who these strangers were and what brought them to Paris, but today I didn't have a moment to spare. I was meeting someone with some pertinent information about an upcoming auction, and I had to move fast. My sources were varied, some were a touch shady, and others were part of the traditional antique establishment. They confided in me, because they trusted me, and knew I only wanted the best for French antiques, and I paid them in return, in a multitude of ways.

Sitting under the shade of a chestnut tree was Dion. A sixty-something-year-old contact of mine who gave me information about antiques and my competitors. We'd become close over the years, and he treated me like a daughter in some ways. When he had arrived in France he had little more than the clothes he was

30

wearing, and now he had a nice apartment, and a steady income selling certain information.

His passion, though, was refugees. He gave a ton of money to charities, and often flitted off for aide work during the winter months. Dion had no idea I knew about his charity involvement but I'd done checks on him, like he'd done on me. It was the way the circuit worked. I knew he'd come from a war-torn country, and got out just in time to save his life, but sadly most of his family were unable to leave. It was why, I think, he was always chasing deals, something to keep the loneliness at bay. Something to help him forget at least for a little while.

"Anouk." He nodded solemnly, as was his way.

"Bonjour, Dion. What have you got for me?" We always got straight to the point; Dion wasn't a fan of small talk.

"An arcane scroll originally from Antibes. It's damaged because of its age, but still, it's so rare you could name your price if you sold it on. The seller just wants it gone. He inherited a bunch of antiques from his grandfather but doesn't hold them in any esteem. You know what the youth of today are like . . ."

Like Lilou, I thought with a smile. "Sure, sure. So what's the deal? Who's up against me?" You had to be quick in this business, or risk losing out. Everyone had their own ways and means of getting there first.

Dion shook his head, the thick black shock of hair not moving an inch, so weighed down with gel, which shone silver in the sunlight. His face was lined with fatigue. I often wondered if he pushed himself too far to the detriment of his own health in the business of gathering information. He veered away from society types, and old money, having little respect for those born with the so-called silver spoon in their mouths. "So far only Joshua is sniffing around. That guy has a nose like a bloodhound. He's always one step ahead."

My pulse sped up at the mention of Joshua who like a contagion seemed to spread far and wide, knocking people from

31

their perches. Dion knew my background with Joshua because I'd asked him for help trying to get the piano back from his clutches. To no avail. Still, Dion had tried hard and his loyalty had meant a lot in such a dark time. On the antique circuit, ruthlessness was a key characteristic, and emotion and affection was kept out of it, or very well hidden, so Dion's generosity of spirit had touched me. Around town I was known as the eccentric one because I often fell in love with a piece that had only sentimental value, and bid on objects other dealers deemed worthless.

I joined Dion on the wooden bench with a heavy sigh. "Joshua, again? I wish people weren't so easily fooled by his charm." But how could they not be? He was smooth, and suave and utterly beguiling. Lots of practice at wooing people to suit his needs.

Dion clasped his hands over his middle. "The problem with Joshua is that it's all a sport to him. He'll win, and use whatever cunning faculty he can. He will get bored eventually, and move on, Anouk. People like him always do."

In the distance a mother and child held hands, taking tiny steps across the grass. "I hope so. Somewhere far far away." I wished he wasn't a shadow everywhere I went. "So any tips on how I convince the grandson to sell to me?" Already my brain was spinning with ideas. How to secure the scroll, who I could get to value it – it'd have to be an expert in the field – and then finally who I could sell it to. I knew a woman who'd have the right provisions in place, a humidity-controlled room, the right kind of display case to prevent dust, to protect the delicate parchment. Madame Benoit, who lived near the Champs-Élysées, would love such a thing. She was a fifty-something Parisian who loved collecting rare pieces.

"The grandson is training as a classical musician. He plays the cello, amongst other things. It wouldn't be unreasonable to think he'd swap the scroll for the Mollier cello. Word is he's a fan of Mollier, God rest his soul."

I smiled. "The Mollier cello!" Dion had already half done the deal for me. He was like that: outwardly the tough guy, inwardly a teddy bear looking out for his closest clients. "My estimate for the cello was around ten thousand Euro. If he'd swap for the scroll, I'd be well in front. Time to visit our young musician and see what can be done." Dion shook my hand, slipping me a folded piece of paper. Without reading it I knew it would contain the man's phone number and address. "Let me know if you need a chauffeur," he said.

"Oui, I will."

Dion smiled, flashing his tobacco-stained teeth. "When you win it, don't forget your friends, will you?" He winked.

I smiled back. "Never. And until the deal is done, here's a little something to tide you over." From the depths of my handbag I took a bottle of Château Lafite Rothschild, a wine from Bordeaux, and handed it to Dion. I kept my cellar, which was only really a wine rack in the corner of my shop, stocked with fine wine in order to have something tangible to give thanks.

"Château Lafite Rothschild for me? This is worth a lot of money, Anouk." He inspected the label on the bottle. Dion knew a lot about everything, from wine to antiques, to people's secrets.

"It's the least I can do." I bent to kiss his still-stunned face.

"Merci," he said, collecting himself. "Call me if I can help with the grandson."

I smiled and managed a quick nod. "I will, same as always." Dion didn't believe in lengthy phone calls – thought the government was listening in, recording every single one of us. If I called him he automatically named a place to meet, and that was that.

I had a soft spot for Dion in a paternal way. Life had been a struggle for him, and he was doing his best to climb out of a black hole, by whatever means he could. It was the way sometimes his eyes clouded, the slump to his beefy shoulders, like his sadness hovered above him and pressed him down. Sometimes

I wanted to play Lilou's trick and be the matchmaker for him, but I knew well enough not to meddle. Who was I to help him find love when I'd been so spectacularly bad at it myself?

* * *

"I'm so sorry for the loss of your grandfather," I said softly after introducing myself. I tried very hard not to drop eye contact and exclaim over the sumptuous furniture surrounding me. Besides, it wasn't fitting in the circumstances.

The young man, Andre, nodded solemnly and stared out the bay window. I was just out of Paris in the town of Rocquencourt, on the family's lush sprawling estate. Not far from here was the Palace of Versailles, and while Andre's estate was on a much smaller scale, from what I had seen so far it was equally as opulent as the former royal château.

Andre had the serenity of an expansive garden with a small lake but was close enough to Paris, giving him the best of both worlds. There were stables on the property, and some dog kennels. Thick hedges and fat-trunked trees, standing close together like a row of gruff watchman protecting the property, surrounded the garden.

"Merci," he said eventually. His thin, drawn face appeared much older than Dion had thought him to be. "Were you close?" I wanted to kick myself for my nosiness, but something about him suggested he was angry, rather than grieving. It was just a feeling, the fleeting look of mutiny on his face when I mentioned his grandfather.

He let out a bitter laugh. "No we weren't close. Unless you were a wad of rolled-up Euros, he didn't have the time of day for you."

"Oh," I said lamely, unsure of what to say to such a thing.

"My grandfather was a cold man. Driven by money, and money only. Hence I have no desire to continue with his legacy of collecting things, which will never be appreciated. You've heard about the arcane scroll, I take it?"

I clasped my hands, feeling a wave of empathy for Andre. "I did." It struck me he'd invited me into his house without clarifying my reason for visiting, as if he knew I was coming. Dion, again, helping grease the wheel. "I was hoping to secure the late Monsieur Mollier's cello for you in return for the scroll, if that's something you'd consider."

"Mollier's music was the soundtrack to my youth, a way to block out the real world."

His cheeks pinked as if he'd said too much, so I hurried to reassure him. "Music has the ability to be a friend, an escape hatch when we most need one."

"Oui," he said, smiling.

"May I see the scroll?" I spoke quickly, not wanting to scare him off by getting too personal; instead I tried to be business-like and brisk.

He surveyed me for the longest time. I felt he was weighing up whether he could trust me. I only hoped I could afford any counter offer he made, like the cello for the scroll, and extra funds on top, if the scroll was in good shape. Because of Joshua's theft, my business was still teetering, so I didn't have the high reserve of funds I used to for deals like this.

Red-haired Andre took a key from his pocket, unlocking a drawer. From the vague scent wafting out I knew it was a humidity-controlled space. I was relieved that the scroll had been well cared for in its time here.

"Anouk, please come closer, but don't touch it. It's whisper thin, and will have to be handled correctly by experts if it's moved from here." While he wasn't keen on keeping his grandfather's collections at least he respected the antiques, which made me soften toward him even more.

I made my way over, a hand on my throat as my pulse beat a fast rhythm. It never waned, that first flush of excitement seeing something that was hundreds of years old. It was preserved as well as it could be for its age, though damaged in places, as if it had been set alight, and someone had snuffed the flame out in time to save the body of it. It resembled a fairy-tale treasure map, with its rough black edges. But instead of sketches of geography it contained text.

"It's a poem," he said, smiling. Andre's posture relaxed, and when grinning, he looked infinitely younger. What hate he must've held in his heart to transform his entire being when he recalled his grandfather, and how quickly it disappeared once he was distracted.

I leaned close and tried to read the tiny words, written in fancy flowery cursive that was difficult to translate. Goose bumps prickled my skin and I knew I couldn't simply swap the cello for the scroll. The scroll was worth far too much money, and I wouldn't be able to sleep at night if I wasn't honest with Andre. But would I have enough funds to make the deal?

"It's breathtaking," I said pulling my gaze away and meeting Andre's, whose expression was haunted once more. "A treasure."

"I'd like to take you up on your offer," he said abruptly. "The cello of Monsieur Mollier's in exchange for the scroll. *But* only if experts transport the scroll, and you vouch for its safety in transit and with its new owner. As much as I hate what it represents, it still has historical significance, and I'd hate to see it ruined by inappropriate handling."

"Oui, of course, I can have all of that arranged. But there is a problem," I said, fluttering my hands. "This scroll is worth more than I thought. While it has been slightly burnt at the edges, the writing is still well preserved. I'd have to get a specialist to investigate its origins and likely author, but I know from experience and by sight it's worth a lot of money. Much more than the cello."

Andre moved to the plush lounges and sat, motioning for me to do the same. "I have papers from numerous scholars who've studied the period. You can have those too. And I'm well aware of its value, Mademoiselle LaRue, but you see, this holds only bad memories for me. My grandfather manipulated the former owner, bullied him into selling it really, for far less than it was worth. He then had the gall to brag about it. Greed is a terrible thing; it can turn men into monsters." With a sad shrug he gazed out of the window into the distance. His grandfather sounded far too similar to Joshua for my liking. He continued, his voice soft: "This is a way to atone for what he did."

I could understand his motivations, and thought that Andre was the kind of man the world needed more of. Someone not driven purely by money, or greed.

Quietly, he said, "I made some enquiries about who I should sell it to, and your name kept popping up. I know you'll find the right home for it. And then it will be a chapter closed for me, and I would very much like that."

I didn't know what to say in the face of such generosity. "Merci, Andre, that's very kind of you, and you have my word I'll find it the perfect home. So, I'll secure the Mollier, and call you once it's done?" I was rendered silent once more by the fact people had spoken so highly of me, and that Andre was so pure of heart to make up for his grandfather's shady deals.

"Oui." His features softened. "Mollier was an inspiration to me. To own something as extraordinary as his very own concert cello would be an honor."

Outside an old fluffy dog gave a halfhearted bark before settling onto one of the benches under a row of acacia trees. I turned back to Andre. "Wait until you hold it. It hasn't lost its luster after all this time. There's magic inside, I'm sure."

Andre gave me a wide smile. "Let's hope it stays there when I play, and doesn't run away screaming." He made a self-deprecating face. Enquiries I made about Andre suggested his talent was astonishing, but I could tell he was the humble type.

The mood had lightened and I hoped Andre would have some closure in his life, and be able to move forward. "I'm sure you'll add another layer of magic too."

We made the deal on a handshake and said our goodbyes.

Andre walked me out into the fading light of the spring day to my waiting car. Dion was playing chauffeur today, and sat reading a newspaper, squinting against the gentle sun that shone through the windscreen.

I smiled, and gave Andre the customary French goodbye peck on both cheeks. "I'll be in touch. Au revoir."

Back in the car I briefed Dion on what had transpired with Andre, and the reason he was happy to see the scroll go.

"Life is such a complex thing." He started the engine. The car purred – it was Dion's pride and joy, and was polished to a shine. I'd never understand men and cars. "You *have* to secure that cello; don't lose it, Anouk."

"I will. I'll bid until they all fall away. I'm hoping the more popular showy instruments will woo the crowd, and they'll leave the Mollier to me." We drove sedately out of the estate, heading for the double-bronzed gates. As they creaked open a flashy red sports coupe careered sideways from the road, into the driveway and came to an abrupt stop, spraying gravel in its wake. Dust plumed up and straight into my open window.

"Who is this fool?" I spat between dusty mouthfuls.

I was ready to yell a volley of abuse to the dangerous driver when I clapped eyes on his face. It was the hot guy wearing the Aviator sunglasses who had been outside the front of my shop the day I had lunch with Lilou. Inwardly I groaned. I'd thought he was a handsome holidaymaker, but he was obviously a dealer too, and hot on my tail. You couldn't trust anyone! This industry was with rife with chameleons and I thanked my lucky stars I hadn't entered into conversation with him that day, encouraged by the white wine racing through my bloodstream. Another competitor in an already suffocating industry.

He ran a hand through his blond hair, and gave me an ostentatious smile. "Is this Andre's place?" An American! My mind shrieked a warning; stay well away. I could already tell he'd be a problem with his playboy good looks, and that swagger that came with money, and ambition and the desire to win at any cost. I'd seen it one too many times to miss those markers now.

I pursed my lips, and pressed the button for my window. Slowly the glass blocked him from sight but not before I caught his wink. Really, how did winking help the situation? Did he think I'd dissolve into a hot mess, and tell him everything? Amateur. "It doesn't take long for them to sniff out a deal," I said to Dion.

"Forget him. He doesn't know the back-story."

I leaned back into the leather seat, and closed my eyes. "Oui. You're right. Andre will send him on his way."

Chapter Five

Antiques missing as suspected smuggler ring hits Paris

Paris gendarmerie are investigating a robbery that took place over-night at the prestigious Vuitton Auction House on Rue St Honoré in Paris. They believe the theft is linked to the recent spate in the town of Sorrento, Italy, but won't release any further details. The Vuitton Auction House released a statement today saying that their security cameras had been interfered with and the thief overrode the high-tech alarm systems, including the state of the art infra-red sensors. It's suspected that the rare collection of jewelry stolen would fetch up to two hundred thousand Euros on the black market in America, where it's believed the antiques are being shipped to, after police raided a southern Californian home and found some earrings believed to be the ones stolen from Sorrento. Anyone with any information is asked to visit their local gendarmerie or call the hotline direct.

My stomach lurched. A smuggler ring? Had they multiplied? It wasn't just a rogue cat burglar like in the movies? I whipped open the newspaper once more, scanning the next page in case there was any more detail but found nothing. It appeared that the thief was interested in jewelry, and France had a wealth of it under lock and key, especially in Paris, where so many exclusive auction houses were situated.

The jewels would be lost forever, and with it their story. It was migraine-inducing, picturing those precious keepsakes being lifted in the dark of night, hastily wrapped, badly treated, and gone for good.

Blood drained from my face right down to the tip of my slipper-clad toes but it was auction day, and I had no time to make any calls or hunt out any leads. I had to win the cello to secure the scroll.

Once dressed and ready, I hurried down the Boulevard Saint Germaine, making my way toward the 8th arrondissement. The perk of living in Paris meant I didn't own a car; I walked everywhere. If it was too far I used the Metro. Driving was such a nuisance in this bustling city and I was glad to avoid it.

With sunshine on my back I was almost certain I could feel the presence of the illustrious François Mollier, the famous cellist who'd died over half a century ago. I'd found out that the reason his descendants were selling some select pieces from his musical collection was to fund a theme park set on the grounds of his estate. The idea had me crying into my soup bowl, but there was little I could do, except secure the cello knowing it would go to Andre who would worship it. Mollier's château and expansive grounds should have been a museum, a place for the people to visit, and celebrate his achievements in a world that still hadn't forgotten him, and never would, not a place for bumper cars, and mechanical bull rides.

Pausing, I imagined the cello with its soon-to-be new owner, red-headed Andre, alone on his balcony at night-time with his own château silent. His eyes slowly closing as he clamped the cello tight, drawing the mother of pearl bow back and forth across its taut strings, relaxing into the sound, and letting go of bad memories, like a vapor.

Mellifluous notes drifting above, stars shrieking in the inky sky. Beautiful music would invigorate the antique instrument and summon the ghost of François Mollier, who'd visit standing off in the distance in the realm of here or there, a faint smile playing at his lips . . .

Whimsical, but totally possible.

Time was stealing away, so I picked up the pace, finally arriving at the Rue du Faubourg Saint-Honoré in the 8th arrondissement where the Cloutier Auction House was situated. It was a grand old building with a French baroque façade that stood out among the less imposing neighboring structures. A burnished gold sign announcing the house hung perpendicular, and creaked softly as it swayed. Nerves fluttered but more from anticipation than anything.

A doorman wearing an immaculate, sharply pressed suit, and top hat nodded as I rushed past. "Bonjour, mademoiselle."

"Bonjour, monsieur." I flashed him a smile as he opened the heavy black door and ushered me in. "Merci."

With quick steps, I headed down the entrance hall and into the bar area.

Exclusive auctions held around France were filled with collectors and dealers from all around the world who were backed up by old money, families with recognizable names, or lots of available cash. It was a sacred circle, and you had to pass some invisible test to be accepted by them. It'd taken me an aeon to be invited in, and I was still looked at as the new girl, but they weren't threatened by someone who often bid on items that were perplexingly valueless in their eyes and were only sold at some auctions as part of a deceased estate.

But sentimental or not, I had a varied range of customers who, like me, held antiques with rich histories in high esteem. It could be something as small as a tin of buttons rescued from a Dior 1940s' collection. The men would frown over their spectacles at me and mutter, "Buttons . . .?" their confusion apparent. But I'd have a customer who collected vintage buttons, and I knew they'd adore such a bounty. Who wouldn't? Some amazing seamstresses had probably thumbed those little plastic discs – what had the buttons overheard? Talk about hemlines, waistlines, the progression of fashion . . .

Auctions were jovial affairs. Champagne flowed freely because punters paid more when they were relaxed after a few glasses of bubbles, though no auction houses admitted that's why they supplied copious bottles of Moët & Chandon – it was the way it had always been done, a tradition that had always made the numbered paddles raise that little bit easier.

The antique trade was still a bit of a men's club despite half-hearted protests that it wasn't. But it suited me just fine to be one of the token women. My presence was largely ignored. They didn't see me as a threat, and I could go by unnoticed and savor the lots alone.

Today, while they clinked glasses, and told tall tales about their latest conquests in the world of antiques, I casually flounced out of view and into the auction room, ready to take my seat at the front.

I spotted Gustave, the security guard.

"Bonjour," I said, holding my handbag to the side while we air-kissed each cheek.

"Bonjour, Anouk," Gustave replied, his brown face crinkling into a smile. He was a robust man, about late fifties, with a big heart. He'd been working here as long as I could remember, and often saved me a seat if I was running late.

Laughter rang out from the bar area. "They're in fine form today," Gustave said, raising an eyebrow.

"Half sozzled already?"

"Oui." Gustave tutted. "Monsieur left the front door unlocked last week! Can you imagine? Had the gall to blame me."

43

I inhaled sharply. "He left it unlocked?" Anyone could have walked in and scurried away with something valuable. Monsieur Cloutier in his old age was getting business mixed with pleasure, a mistake I vowed not to replicate. Hence the rule: no champagne when working. I had to keep a clear head and focus.

Life was all about appreciating the steamy *pah* of escaped air as you broke into a twice-cooked soufflé deflating its cheesy goodness, and pairing it with a wine and lingering over lunch with friends. But *not* during work time.

"Not fair on you, Gustave. Let's hope he doesn't make that mistake again."

Gustave rocked on his heels, and smiled. "He won't. I'm barreling him out when my shift finishes each day, and locking it myself, but I'm not here all the time. There's a lull between security staff; the place is empty for an hour, so I've asked him to rectify that. Just in case."

"You heard about the robberies, then?"

His eyes clouded. Gustave loved the auction house like it was his own, so he followed industry news. Monsieur Cloutier was lucky to have such a loyal employee, especially as age crept up on him, and made him forgetful. Age or champagne, that is.

"Terrible." He nodded. "And we don't need to make it any easier by being lax with security."

"Oui." I felt a shiver, as if I was being watched. I turned, surprised to see the American standing behind me. He'd been out the front of my shop, at Andre's estate, and now here. I didn't like it – it meant he was on my trail and that usually implied he was after my contacts. I hadn't heard him approach on the noisy wooden floors. Had he eavesdropped on our conversation? I'd hate for anyone to know about the door being accidentally left unlocked, especially a stranger. He must've had ties with someone to be here, though, and that meant trouble.

"It's you," he said, appraising me coolly.

"Excusez-moi?" I said in faux surprise as if I didn't recognize him. His azure blue eyes twinkled, and he thrust his hands in his pockets and took a step closer. In response, I folded my arms and stuck out my chin. Who did he think he was?

"It's you. The girl who everyone talks about. You're famous, you know."

"Me?" I stumbled slightly on my heels, put on the spot by such a thing. I wondered if the 'everyone' he was referring to were talking about the Joshua disaster. It'd taken months for the speculation to die down, but it cropped up now and again. I remained poised, adopting a haughty expression as if his presence bored me. "I hardly think so."

He grinned, Cheshire cat-like. "Humble, too, I see."

"Is that all, Monsieur . . .?"

"Black."

His smile slid into a smirk, showing his even, white teeth. He had a strong jawline, and was classically handsome in that all-star American way. He ran a hand through the neat blond of his hair.

"Well if that's all, Monsieur Black, I'll be taking my seat . . ." I said over my shoulder, as I walked across the shiny wooden floor to the front row seat I favored. It gave me the perfect view of the antiques on offer, as well as good visibility to the auctioneer. The American followed me and stood just in front of the stage.

I surveyed him as I sat. His clothes fit like they were tailor-made, his shoes shone like they'd never been worn before – even his nails were manicured. Rich playboy with too much time on his hands. A rich *American* playboy at that, which meant goodbye antiques. He'd probably ship them to somewhere where there was too much humidity for their moderate French wood, letting them buckle and bow, and another masterpiece would be scarred for its lifetime.

"Mind if I join you?" he said, indicating the empty chair beside me.

I clenched my jaw. "It's a free country." I didn't like anyone to see how I bid, or what I was interested in. It was better to remain incognito if possible, but sitting right next to me he'd be able to ascertain what I wanted.

"Great." He let my jibe sail past, as if he hadn't heard, and sat. There was something about him I didn't trust. He'd obviously been following my tracks too closely for comfort. And I didn't buy the innocent act: *oh it's you.* Please.

"I've got my heart set on something magnificent," he said. I gathered the swell of my skirt, and tucked it, facing away from him.

"Wonderful," I said, my voice heavy with sarcasm. Better he know I was disinterested by his presence.

"The cello," he said. "Have you seen it? It's magnificent." I turned back to him, my heart sinking. He gave me such a penetrating stare it took all my might not to react. Surely Andre wouldn't have asked him to secure it for the scroll too? Instinctively I knew this stranger was trying to unsettle me. I toyed with telling him to back off, but maybe playing it down would be better with a man like him. They thrived on competition, and it would only encourage him if I acted irritated. He didn't say the Mollier cello though. I quickly scanned the lots in front, recognizing a German cello . . . Fingers crossed he meant that one.

I changed tack. "This is an exclusive auction house, Monsieur Black. Were you invited here?" I gave him a chilly stare, but he didn't cower. His smile widened, flashing those too-white teeth of his.

"Of course I was invited." He winked. I stifled a groan. They were all the same these young, handsome Americans. They thought a wink here, a slow saucy smile there would be enough to weave their way into a woman's embrace . . . Well this *belle fille* wouldn't be so silly ever again.

"I see what you're doing, you know," I said. "And it's not working." His attempt to ruffle me was transparent. But my main concern was the cello. I'd promised Andre I'd secure it, and now this imposter was in my way. "This is a very select circle, so watch your step. It wouldn't take much to have you . . . barred."

His lips twitched but he was saved from answering as the crowd wandered in, their chatter accompanying heavy footsteps. I hadn't seen Monsieur Black on the circuit before. And he was American so there was less chance he was related to someone here, maybe my bluff would make him think twice.

I made a show of saying, "Bonjour, it's a lovely day for an auction." A collector I knew took a seat beside me. Raphe shot me a puzzled look, knowing I kept silent when an auction was about to begin and usually ignored everyone so I could watch them behind my sunglasses, Audrey Hepburn style.

"Everything OK, Anouk?" Raphe frowned, perplexed over my effusive greeting. I hadn't uttered a single word to him before, usually nodding a greeting, or giving a small wave. My striking up a conversation in an auction room had him surveying me as if I'd partaken of too many glasses of champagne.

A smile crept across my face. I could still feel the American's gaze like a laser on me. To Raphe, I said, "Très bien." *Very good.* I opened the program and pretended to study the lots, though I had them memorized from my earlier visits, and knew the story behind each one.

The auctioneer stepped up to the podium, and grappled with the microphone before introducing himself. I zoned out, fanning myself with the program, unable to switch off my worry that Monsieur Black was going to bid against me. The scroll and the profit I'd make on selling it would help me immensely, and I wouldn't let some stranger take it from me.

The first lot was called, and the bidding commenced for an Asian xylophone. It was exquisite, bowed like a boat, its wood intricately carved with roaring dragons breathing fire. It wasn't my specialty so I subtly studied the people to the left of me, studiously avoiding the American who sat on my right. I watched them tense when someone bid them up, or feign disinterest as they gave the auctioneer the tiniest, almost imperceptible, finger raise.

We were all given numbered paddles to bid with, but most of us used them only once we'd won, so they could record our number to process our payment. They were too obvious, bright white, and showed the competition who was bidding. If you had a reputation for quality buys then there was a chance attendees would bid against you, without having to do their own research on a piece. It was better to be as invisible as possible when you bid.

Thirty minutes later the French cello was introduced. The auctioneer gave a short spiel about its origins. He rhapsodized Mollier, and the maestro's many accomplishments, drawing sighs of longing around the room.

The bidding commenced slowly at first. I was surprised to feel a rush of cool air, as Monsieur Black left his seat for another elsewhere. Good.

From the corner of my eye I could see the gnarly hand of a painter known only as Ombre raise up. My heart lifted. Ombre's modus operandi was a few early bids before bowing out to resume drinking the free champagne, and chat to anyone lingering by the bar in the hopes of selling his surrealist artwork. So far the stranger hadn't bid. Was he toying with me?

A few collectors joined in, heartily bidding, until one of them pulled out with a shake of the head.

I made an effort to act disinterested while waiting for the auctioneer to call it, and on the third count caught his eye and raised an eyebrow in my signature move. A subtle way to bid without anyone knowing it was me. I took the bid up to ten thousand Euros – it was affordable, a downright bargain for such a piece, and what I'd envisaged spending.

"Last bid at ten thousand Euros? Going once, going twice . . . Eleven thousand next bid."

I stiffened in response, but raised an eyebrow. There was

no need to ponder who was bidding against me; it must have been the American! Typically here to splash his cash and draw attention.

"Twelve," the auctioneer said taking my next bid. "Thirteen, away from you."

To the auctioneer, I mouthed, "Fifteen." If I had to bid him up, I would, and hope he'd stop.

"Twenty, against you."

Twenty! I'd expected to buy it for ten thousand! Though it was worth every cent of twenty thousand Euros, sadly my funds were limited and I had to be cautious. I couldn't let Andre down, and I'd all but secured a buyer for the scroll. Time to let him know I meant business!

"Twenty-one," I called high and loud, drawing the attention from the crowd. What was he doing to me? My emotions were usually kept under wraps, but with him goading me, my rules vanished.

"Twenty-two, away from you," the auctioneer called. I wanted to spin on my seat and face my opponent, but I wouldn't give him the pleasure of seeing my face fall when I had to bow out.

I did some quick calculations and knew it was well beyond my savings. *But he was American!* Another beloved piece of French history would be freighted to some fancy summer home on a coast far from here to collect dust.

And poor Andre would wander those cavernous halls, a shadow of bad memories in his wake.

My face reddened. "Twenty-three!" Anxiety gnawed at me – my stomach roiled. I'd send myself bankrupt being caught in a bidding war. It was his flippancy that galled me. Just because he could afford the cello didn't mean he deserved it.

"Twenty-four, away from you."

Damn him to hell! Anger coursed through me, my hands shook, so I planted them under my legs. The auctioneer called it, and looked past me, and then back, waiting in case I bid once more. I worried my bottom lip, clamping down hard, as conflicted emotions tore through me. I hated letting people down, really despised it, especially in business, but going higher than twenty-four would be making a bad choice. It was a little more than I had in the coffers in case I got stuck with the scroll for a while. I slowly shook my head no.

He picked up his gavel. "Last call, for the Mollier cello, a magnificent instrument played by the maestro himself . . ."

A sob rose in my throat but I swallowed it down.

"Une fois, deux fois, trois fois," *Once, twice, three times*, the auctioneer closed the bidding. With a bang of the gavel the cello was lost to me. And I would have to explain to Andre that the deal was off. This wasn't my year, that was for sure. It went to show you could never be complacent in business.

Time slowed, as the other lots were called. I stayed riveted to my seat, until *finally*, it was over. With as much poise as I could muster I made my way out of the auction room, tugging my skirt straight, wondering who my new nemesis really was, and how I'd go about finding out. The melancholy notes of the cello would drift up under a different sky, *if* it ever got played again. Of course, he couldn't let his win go unnoticed. With his hands deep in his suit pockets he sauntered over to me.

"Who were you going to sell it to?" he asked.

I scoffed. "As if I'd tell a stranger my business."

"But I'm not a stranger, I'm a friend, a fellow antique aficionado." He was goading me, and I just couldn't understand why. For fun? His way of flirting? A way to ease his boredom? Whatever it was, it rankled. This was my lifeblood, and he had bid against me on purpose.

"You *are* a stranger, Monsieur Black—"

"Tristan," he said.

I sighed and continued: "Monsieur Black—"

"Just call me Tristan; we don't need to be so formal, do we?"

Now he was telling me the rules? "Do you make a habit of interrupting every time a person tries to speak?"

He reared back, and laughed. "Are you angry with me for some reason, mademoiselle?"

"Are you dense? You knew I wanted that cello. You don't need it. America has some fine *objets d'art* . . . Why don't you hop back on your private jet and go hunt in your own country."

His lips curved into a wide smile. "My private jet?"

For years, I'd heard men identical to him harp on about custom leather seats, and dinner degustation menus aboard their private planes. Memory-foam pillows, and round beds, and any number of things they boasted about to one-up each other with their vast wealth. Why couldn't they fly on a domestic plane like everyone else? Their carbon footprints were yeti-sized. "Yes, fly it to America or somewhere else, and leave France alone."

"I've just been to Italy," he said. "And nothing there compares to what I've seen here today . . . The quality is breathtaking." He flicked me a loaded stare. Was he flirting with me? Did he think I was a fool?

Women veering past did a double take when they saw him. I wrinkled my nose in disgust. If they'd spent two minutes talking to him they'd know he had no substance. He was an empty shell with a few dollars to his stupid name. *Mr. Black?* Honestly, it sounded like a pseudonym to me.

"You should pull your bid on the cello," I said, giving it one last try. "You don't really want it."

"I only bid on it at the very end, because I knew *you* wanted it, and I couldn't let the weasel win it from you. If I didn't know better I'd say he was bidding for it just to upset you. Something about his smarmy face made my blood boil."

"Wait, you weren't bidding against me the entire time?"

He frowned. "Of course not! Not until you stopped, and he was set to win it. I couldn't let him have the satisfaction."

"But you said you were interested in the cello when we first sat down!" I narrowed my eyes.

"In the *German* cello, not the French one."

Could I trust this Tristan Black? "Which guy was bidding against me?"

He turned and surveyed the people milling in the bar area, some drinking champagne to celebrate, some to commiserate. "That guy." He pointed to a guy wearing almost identical clothes to himself. Goddamn it! It was Joshua.

I softened slightly toward Tristan; he'd picked up on Joshua's vindictiveness and tried to protect me against it. Why Joshua continued to torment me was beyond me. But Tristan had stepped in unwittingly, and no matter what his motivations were, I was grateful for it.

Tristan leaned forward, standing inches from my face. Up close, his eyes were mesmerizing ocean blue. I shuffled backward, not wanting to be hypnotized by his cosmetic qualities. I could see how a girl would fall for his kind. "So I guess we can make a deal, now? The cello is all yours, if you want it."

"For how much?" *Don't drop your guard. Nothing is ever what it seems.*

"For the price I paid," he said, shrugging. "I know you have a buyer for it."

"Because you were hot on my heels that day?" The red sports coupé driving spy!

He lifted a palm. "Isn't everyone around here guilty of that?"

Touché. "And that's it? I pay for the cello, and nothing else?" Usually a deal like this they'd tack on ten percent at least.

He smiled, and this time it reached his eyes. The aquamarine of them sparkled. "I wouldn't rule out a dinner date, but yes, that's all."

A smile played at my lips. "A dinner date? I don't think so." Tristan Black would have to learn things didn't just fall in his lap no matter how generous he might seem to any unsuspecting person. There was always an agenda with men like him. Always. And he was choosing the wrong girl if he thought I'd be silly enough to go along with his whims.

"Why not?" He laughed. "I won't eat you."

"Very funny." I wondered what would be a fair compromise. Ah! "Perhaps we can share a drink at the May Gala, if you're invited that is . . .?" If he was invited to the gala, then he was connected with someone influential in Paris. It would be a good way to find out just who he really was.

"The gala . . ." A blank look crossed his features. "Oh the *gala*! Yes, I'll be there and I'll hold you to that drink, Anouk."

Before he could add any more addendums to our deal I said, "Let's go to the office and sort out the paperwork for the cello."

We explained to the clerk and she switched our details for the piece. Gustave the security guard called me over, waving frantically, as I was waiting for the invoice to be printed.

"Excusez-moi, Tristan. I'll be right back."

I rushed to Gustave, my heels click-clacking. His face was pinched, and he motioned for me to join him behind the curtain in the antechamber just near the office.

"What is it?" I whispered.

"Shhh," he said and pointed. Joshua wore a mutinous expression and was making his way straight to Tristan.

"Oh no! We have to stop him!" I went to push the curtain back but Gustave grabbed my arm to stop me. Tristan Black didn't deserve to cop a mouthful from Joshua. As much as I distrusted the newcomer, I couldn't stand by and watch him get berated on account of me.

"Wait, Anouk. I have a feeling your Monsieur Black can look after himself just fine."

"He doesn't know the story, Gustave. He has no idea what he's dealing with! I have to warn him . . ."

"Wait. I think you underestimate the new guy." Gustave pulled the curtain aside an infinitesimal amount so we could peek out.

Joshua tapped Tristan on the back with an index finger, pointed like a gun.

I held my breath, wishing for the hundredth time Joshua would just walk off and disappear out of Paris for good.

Tristan took his sweet time, chatting to the office clerk, and totally ignoring the finger in the back.

Joshua tried again, this time using the palm of his hand.

Tristan turned, annoyance clouding his face. "What can I do for you?" he said, his voice clipped.

"Any reason you snuck in a bid like that? Or was it just to win her over?" Joshua pulled a sour face like he'd been sucking lemons, angry that someone had got the better of him. "She's not worth it, you know."

I gasped. That lowlife! Gustave shot me a look that said, *see?*

I clung on to the curtain that separated us from them. Through the gap I could see Tristan pull himself up to full height. "*She* has a name if it's the person I think you're referring to, and I don't like your accusations, or your tone."

Shivers raced down my spine. "Yeah?" Joshua snarled like a beast. "Watch your step, I'm warning you now. *She*," he spat the word, "isn't who you think she is."

I reeled back. "What does that mean?" I mouthed to a shocked Gustave who shrugged. It was bizarre to hear myself discussed, and it was especially odd when it made no sense.

"Well who is she then?" Tristan asked, an edge of menace in his tone.

I inched closer again, intrigued too.

"Who knows? It's all an act with her." Joshua's lip curled. "What you see isn't what you get. *Comprendre?*"

An act with *me*? With him more like it! The hide of that guy. I wanted to storm outside and berate Joshua for making trouble. Again. But Gustave held my arm firmly, shaking his head.

"The only thing I understand," Tristan said, leaning right into Joshua's face. "Is that you're a man with no principles, and if I see you bid her up again for no reason, there's gonna be trouble. *Comprendre?*"

I bit back on a laugh at the way Tristan mimicked him.

Joshua narrowed his eyes, and said, "You were warned. Next time I won't be so nice."

"Duly noted. Now go away." Tristan shooed him like he was a fly and turned his back, leaving Joshua standing there like a fool.

He finally stalked off, with an angry glint in his eye. I'd never seen anyone upset Joshua before. I had a new level of respect for Tristan knowing instinctively how to act around that rat of a man.

When we could finally talk properly without fear of being caught behind the curtain I said quietly to Gustave, "Why did he say it was all an act with me?"

Gustave pursed his lips and then said, "To make trouble. You know he manipulates the situation in his favor."

I nodded, not convinced it was that simple. "Every day I wonder if I was under some kind of spell to have ever thought I loved that man."

Gustave gave me a paternal pat on the back. "Don't beat yourself up about it, Anouk. None of us knew what he was like."

"I was so awful to Tristan a few minutes ago and then he goes and does that." I gave Gustave a thin smile. "So, we walk out and pretend we saw nothing?"

"You're just protecting yourself with new faces on the circuit, and rightfully so." Gustave smiled. "We walk making small talk, and you don't mention what you just saw."

"Oui. Thanks."

We wandered back out, chatting in French, pretending we were mid conversation about classical music. "Ah, there you are," I said to Tristan. I waited for him to tell me about the altercation but he just put his hands together and said, "Paperwork is all done."

"Merci." In light of what I'd just witnessed I said, "That was very nice of you, Monsieur Black. I do appreciate it. That cello is very special to a customer of mine."

"My pleasure." He raised his eyebrows. "Perhaps we can have a dance or two at the May Gala?"

His expression was so genuine, so sweet that I surprised myself by saying, "Oui, of course."

Would the usual gala glitterati make a beeline for the stylish Monsieur Black? Perhaps a little digging would unearth his secrets, and I'd have some tidbits to share when my colleagues enquired after him. He was sure to make an impression with his powerful saunter, and strong jawline. It was his eyes that caught me off guard; they were so blue, hypnotic, and I reminded myself to be careful. Business and pleasure did not mix.

Chapter Six

Safely ensconced in my shop with the door bolted for privacy I made some calls about Tristan Black.

Rachelle from the little flower shop near the Notre Dame was usually a hive of information. An unassuming Parisian with russet curls, and wide brown eyes. I'm sure the flower shop was a front for something because she knew too much about everything, but I never asked her directly. Often she tipped me off about antiques that were making their way to Paris from outer regions of France. "Non, Anouk," she purred. "I haven't heard of such a man. What did he do? Rob you? Because if so, I know a man who can sort him out!"

My eyes widened. "Non, non, he hasn't. I don't need a man to . . . sort him out, I just wondered if you'd heard anything on the usual channels."

"Nothing. But if I do, I'll let you know. And, if he does step out of line, you let *me* know . . ." Her voice was as hard as steel, and I smiled. Joshua's betrayal had made my colleagues protective of me, and it was sweet even if I was a little alarmed at exactly what 'sort him out' might've entailed.

"And Anouk, tomorrow, if you go the flea markets on Rue des Rosiers, find a man with a carnation in his pocket, wearing a pink bow tie. He has something for you. Tell him I sent you, and he will know."

"Merci. I'm intrigued."

"My maman was very happy with the gift you sent. It was so sweet, Anouk. Every morning I hear the music as she warms up; the dedication she has to her ballet is astounding." Rachelle's maman had always wanted to be a ballerina, and now finally had the time to try. People thought it was preposterous. *At sixty?* they'd cried, *how silly*. But why couldn't a woman learn to dance at sixty? She wasn't expecting to grace the stage at Opéra National de Paris!

I'd found some vintage ballet shoes that had never been worn and a leotard and sent them with a note saying *Dance your way to happiness*. I liked the idea that passion didn't fade away no matter what age a person was, and if she wanted to plié her way around her living room where was the harm in that?

"Your maman is a wonderful woman," I said, meaning it.

We gossiped about a few things before saying au revoir.

Next, I phoned Madame Dupont to see what she'd make of the newcomer and what had happened earlier. I fell into a walnut leather wingback chair that I'd rescued from an estate sale. The executor of the estate had wanted to clear the belongings out fast, and had ignored my pleas to save the chair, and other valuables littered on the verge like lost souls. *Take it*, he'd cried, *take it all!* And I did. The leather was crazed, and dimpled, and it sighed wearily when I took my place on it. It was like an old friend, and I'd never get it rejuvenated. I loved it, scars and all.

"Anouk, my darling, did you get the cello?" Madame said huskily.

"Oui, not without a little drama." I filled Madame Dupont in on the morning.

"Ooh la la, I adore him already! Joshua must have been seeing red! What a delight! What does he look like this devilish Monsieur Black?"

I shook my head. I could have bet money Madame Dupont would ask such a thing. "Like a man with too much money."

"Parfait!"

"Parfait for what?"

"For you, Anouk! Lilou and I are in agreeance on this matter. It really is time to throw yourself to the wolves and see what happens . . ."

"I'll get eaten alive!" I laughed. Honestly, they had this idea that I was missing something in my life, but they just couldn't see I wasn't made like them. Love did not come first for me.

Madame's loud drawing of a cigarette filtered down the line. "Is he a collector, or a dealer?"

"I don't know, he spoke like a collector, but he was out the front of my shop the other day and then he turned up at Andre's estate as I was leaving, so I suppose he could dabble in both. A way to alleviate the *ennui* I suppose."

"He's a dashing American. A knight in shining armor! I can't wait to run into him." In the background the ticking and chiming of various clocks rang out. I wondered how Madame Dupont could stand the disharmonious symphony.

"Oui, and he has that same innate charm, exudes confidence. Eyes the color of the ocean," I sighed. Why couldn't men like him be French, staid and solid? That kind of man I could go for.

Madame Dupont let out a sensual sigh. "If I was your age, Anouk, there'd be no stopping me. In fact, even at my age, there'd be no stopping me, because who dares wins. Why don't you dare, just this once?"

A customer knocked on the door, and I motioned for him to come in. It was Elliot from the wine bar, who often browsed the shelves for décor, and stopped for a chat about business. "Won't be long," I said to him.

"No rush." He moved about with his hands in his pockets, peering at a selection of mirrors hung from gold hooks along the walls.

I lowered my voice. "Madame, aside from your many *petit* affairs, I'm just like you. I don't want to be tied down, to follow any particular set of rules, or form. I've never really dreamed of walking down the aisle, maybe I never will, and is that so bad? You haven't, and you're the happiest person I know." They were just words, though. I wasn't sure how I felt about marriage. I envied the idea of it. But I couldn't see it happening for me.

She tutted. "We're *not* the same, Anouk. I could never be as sweet of heart as you! I chose to remain single because I couldn't commit to one person. But it isn't easy. There are plenty of times when I wonder if I made a huge mistake with some of the men I've loved and let go. Maybe I would have enjoyed love, after the dizzying novelty of that first rapture faded and was replaced with something more fulsome? Truer, deeper? But I never gave it a chance. And that might have been a huge mistake . . ."

Madame Dupont had never spoken this openly with me about her love life. "Do you really regret it, Madame, or do you just think it's what I need to hear?" I couldn't see Madame Dupont as lonely, even now, men flocked to her, but maybe she did crave that more solid love, one that had longevity.

She took some time to answer. "Regret is such a miserable word. But there have been plenty of times alone, where I wished I took the risk and gave someone my heart, and not just a sliver of it. After one stumble *you've* pulled the shutters down. Closed up shop. I'm just saying, don't waste your life protecting your heart, or you'll get to the end of it, and realize it wasn't worth it." Her words poured out with so much melancholy, it was hard to know what to say, and whether she truly meant me, or if something had happened to make her so forlorn.

Speaking gently, I said, "I see, Madame, I really do. But I'm not 'closed for business' I'm just not interested, and there's a big difference."

A laugh escaped her. "Listen to me, having an elderly moment. Forget it, Anouk, I don't know what came over me. Some days, my life flashes before me in the blink of an eye, until I get to the scenes I wish I could change, and they play over again and again, until I can't see straight. Promise me though, you'll stop pouring every ounce of yourself into work. Save a part of your life for something else."

"I promise, Madame Dupont."

I hoped to ease her anxiety, but really, without work, what else was there? I was grateful work kept me moored to this place.

"And you owe it to that man to go to the gala and have some fun with him. He earned it after dealing with that pig Joshua."

I smiled at the memory. "Oui, I will, Madame. It's not often someone reads Joshua so well. It was like he had heard about him already, or he knew what to watch for. Joshua backed down pretty quickly. I think he was intimidated by Tristan . . ." And that was a first.

When we wrapped up our chat Elliot from the wine bar had found a selection of goods and had them lined up along the front counter. "What can you tell me about these?" he asked, settling on a stool.

"For that we'll need coffee!" I smiled and went to brew a pot, returning with everything on a tray.

Most of my customers spent hours in the shop, carefully selecting pieces and then making their choice after hearing their stories. It was the highlight of my day when I could impart the histories of each antique and watch the customer's eyes widen when something resonated with them and the decision was made, as if by someone else.

"So this one –" I pointed to a golden French gilded mirror with cherubs "– is a Louis Phillipe, circa 1890, and once hung in the boudoir of . . ."

Chapter Seven

The four seasons in Paris each had their own charm – I was hard pressed to choose a favorite. The elemental cycles seemed to change at a time I most needed them, as if the planet regenerated itself, which was cue for me to do the same. Layers were peeled back – literally, and figuratively – coats were vanquished, flowers bloomed, fashion became bolder, smiles wider, strides sashayed into saunters, as spring cast its magnificence over the city. A rejuvenation for earth, body, and soul.

The gentle warmth and smudged blue skies were so provocative, they urged even the most sedate to wander the uneven boulevards of Paris with a basket loose over an arm, freeing a person to sniff and select plump, fat tomatoes, ripe fragrant peaches, rounds of creamy camembert, and baguettes so fresh and wholesome you wanted to hug them to your chest like a baby as you dawdled home, stopping only to add a bouquet of lively carnations with egg-yolk yellow buds that screamed sunshine, and the promise of warmer months to come.

I made a mental note to go the markets later and find some fresh ingredients for dinner. I wandered to my balcony to see what was on offer in my own pots. My herbs seemed to double in size overnight, their stems reaching upward in supplication for the sun. It was the season for simple dishes: poached salmon with beurre blanc sauce and a handful of fresh parsley. Newly plucked asparagus with a buttery tarragon topping. Today, in an ode to my maman, who was an incredible cook and had taken many years to teach me the French basics, I made vichyssoise for lunch, which sat cooling on the stove. I snipped a handful of chives to add to the pot of potato and leek soup, her favorite spring recipe, best served cold.

Time in the kitchen was one of life's greatest pleasures, and aside from when Lilou graced me with her presence, I cooked for one, which did cast a gray cloud over the meal. You could only chat to a soup bowl for so long before your voice echoed dismally back reminding you of your extremely solitary life. Still, I enjoyed the comfort of cooking, and making delicious French meals, slowly, carefully following my maman's old recipes. And work always called, so really I was lucky to have no ties to pull me every which way.

After rinsing the chives and roughly chopping them I garnished the vichyssoise, and the peppery scent of the herb added a little élégance to the meal.

Even though it was just me and the bowl of soup, I still set the table with the silver vintage cutlery, a crystal wineglass, and a sharply ironed napkin, which I set on my lap. After dusting my hands on the tea towel, I poured myself a glass of crisp sauvignon blanc.

I ate my soup slowly, and tried very hard not to mumble to inanimate objects just to make conversation. Silence was golden, and I had the birds outside chirping away for company so it wasn't like I was completely and utterly alone. *Chirp, chirp, chirp.*

Really, if I wanted someone to dine with, I could invite any of my neighbors over, and that would prove less problematic than a relationship with a man. Though, I shied away from getting to know my neighbors, as they rotated so often, what would be the point? Lilou knew them all though and they often asked about her in passing. Then a new group would move in, and they'd ask after her too, even though up until now, she wasn't actually living here. She had an ease with people, and made friendships quickly.

Lunch consumed, I moved to the balcony with my wine and the newspaper. Once again the front-page headline screamed for attention.

The Postcard Bandit hits Paris again!

A brazen robbery was committed overnight at the exclusive Arles Auction House on the Boulevard Pereire in Paris. The suspect has been dubbed the Postcard Bandit by the press because of his trademark calling card: vintage postcards with famous love poems typed on the back, with the original verses changed to taunt police.

Gendarmes were quick to snuff out the press romanticizing such a criminal act, and warned people about aggrandizing the person responsible. The gendarmes released a photograph of the Audrey Étoile collection stolen, in the hopes it will be recognized by collectors around Europe. If you have any information regarding the robbery please contact your local gendarmerie.

My stomach sank. The collection of jewelry pictured was exquisite. We'd been ogling photos online of the upcoming Parisian auction so I recognized them, including a diamond-encrusted timepiece Madame Dupont had her heart set on. The collection was elegant, and timeless, subtly simple, the diamonds set in each the pièce de résistance.

Madame Dupont had joked she'd get that fob watch no matter what she had to do! When I laughed, she'd fallen silent, and reiterated her point. I groped for the memory of exactly what she'd uttered . . .

Anouk, that watch was once Zelda's. I must have it for myself . . .

Madame Dupont was obsessed with the roaring twenties of Paris – the jazz age – and adored Zelda Fitzgerald, heralding her as an icon and a woman who was gifted and creative, but often cast as just a flapper and wife, rather than the talented artist she was in her own right. Madame Dupont had been downright *fervent* about that fob watch.

I frowned. Was that what her heart-wrenching spiel on the phone had really been about? That she hadn't given in to love because she wanted her independence and now regretted it? As much as she loved the idea of Zelda, she believed staying single she could accomplish so much more without a man holding her back. But even so, Madame Dupont wouldn't resort to . . . I blushed at my treacherous thought – of course she wouldn't; she *couldn't*. She wasn't a thief!

Once or twice she may have manipulated the truth in the past for reasons known to only her, but she wouldn't be so shameless or immoral to actually steal! Money mattered little to Madame Dupont because she had plenty of it. She only continued working because she claimed her business kept her young. But committing a brazen robbery? Madame Dupont could easily have bought the entire collection ten times over if she had wanted to!

Shame spread through me. How could I have dreamed up such a thing?

I read the article once more. *The Postcard Bandit.* Stealing was one thing, mocking the investigators was another. Whoever it was didn't like authority. Another long afternoon at the shop would give me ample time to think. I thanked the universe I hadn't been sitting in front of Madame Dupont when I read the newspaper, lest she suspect my mind went straight to her. It was the heady rush of daytime *vin blanc*, and the angst of missing antiques. That's all it was. Madame Dupont was as innocent as a newborn baby . . .

I finished the last of my wine and headed back to the shop, hoping the walk would invigorate me, and clear the detritus in my mind. Madame, the thief! *Really.*

The late afternoon was quiet. Everyone was soaking up fine

weather, and the cloudless sky, so I found my rolodex, *oui*, I still used a rolodex because I liked the musty smell, and the eggshell-colored cards. I flicked through, scanning the details of my clients, searching for one in particular. I always jotted notes about their purchases, their style, what they desired, so I could help them better. Some cards had only one line, *1920s' Lalique vases, present for aunt*. Others had minuscule scribbles over a handful of cards, my longest and most loyal customers.

I found the card I was looking for. Eva, a woman who collected crystals and other spiritual paraphernalia. She said they had magical powers, and healed any ailment. The different color crystals worked on various emotions: turquoise for balance, amethyst for creativity, and scarlet to conquer fear. The reason I remembered those colors and what they represented was that Eva told me time and again. They were traits I needed to work on.

I dialed her number.

"Anouk, darling! What have you got for me? Yellow, perhaps for enlightenment, because I've been seeing the world so clearly lately!"

"Yellow, perhaps . . . I have some pictures to send you. Next week, there's an auction, full of crystals from an astrology shop that closed down. All sorts of colors, and sizes being sold in bundles. As far as I can see, there's been very little interest in it. I thought I might bid for you – what do you think?" A group of women huddled outside, their faces pressed against the window as they pointed to various curios while slurping milkshakes through striped straws.

She shrieked, "You are too good to me, Anouk! Oui, send me the pictures, and I'll tell you which bundle I need most."

"I think they'll each go for perhaps a hundred Euros per lot, maybe less."

An audible gasp rang out. "It amazes me people just don't see the value! But it's great for me. Let me flip your tarot, and see what's in your future because I know it must only be good things."

"Merci," I laughed. There wasn't a dealer in Paris who'd bother with a sale like this, especially an auction they'd have to attend in person. But for me it was all part of the business. I had customers who spent the equivalent of a small house, and others the cost of a dinner out. They were all important to me. I could see the relevance in everything, from collecting postcards, to candelabras, or pianos. We each desired different things, driven either by budget or simply love.

Eva always read my tarot, and I played along, never really believing but not disbelieving either.

"Oh," she said. "Oh. Ah."

"What is it, Eva?" I asked, staring out the window of the shop, watching the peach roses sway in the breeze.

She gasped. "Anouk, you have to tread very carefully. Your life . . . it's about to take a strange turn."

"How so?"

She took a long time to answer. "The cards are showing me some kind of altercation and you're in the middle of it. All I know is, you're about to become embroiled in something that you can't extract yourself from. Be careful, Anouk." Her voice dropped to a whisper, provoking shivers up my spine.

The door opened suddenly, sending a gust of spring air into the shop, and in he walked. Tristan. I nodded hello, and gripped the phone a touch tighter.

"Anouk," she said. "Are you there? I haven't scared you have I?"

Eva's readings were usually lighthearted. A joke about soup for one, and some lucky guesses about antiques I'd win, and road trips I'd take, but this was new. Perhaps she could see the quarrel from the day before.

"No, you haven't scared me. I'm sure I'll be fine, Eva. But thank you for the warning."

Her voice was a whisper. "*Anouk, don't trust him.*"

"What? Who?" I tried very hard to keep my voice level. Did she mean Joshua? Because that advice had come far too late!

Or someone new? I gazed at Tristan, trying to sense if it was him she meant.

She collected herself. "I don't know who, exactly." She laughed embarrassed. "But be careful of those who try and befriend you."

Turning slightly, I whispered, "OK, I'll be very careful." I surveyed Tristan out of the corner of my eye as he wandered around picking things up, and placing them down, like he'd been here before.

In a brighter voice Eva said, "Well, let's talk soon."

We said our goodbyes and I promised to send the pictures of the crystals.

Tristan approached the counter. "What have you got to be so careful about?"

"You're an eavesdropper too?" I folded my arms, and watched the light in his eyes change at the challenge in my voice. I had a feeling women probably threw themselves at him, and he never had to work hard for anyone's attentions.

"Yes. It's one of my many talents." He rocked on his feet, a smug smile firmly in place.

"I see." I tried to keep cool, but there was something so indescribably alluring about Tristan and it caught me off guard. It wasn't just his looks, or the way he held himself, it was something I couldn't pinpoint. Maybe it was just that he'd called Joshua out on his behavior. Whatever it was, I didn't like the flutter it provoked, and tried to stamp it down. "Can I help you with something?"

"I thought we could take a walk. It's a beautiful afternoon." His tone implied an assumption I'd say yes.

I gave him a thin smile. "It's a lovely day, but as you can see, I'm working."

"I can see that, but I also see the sign on the door that says 'Open by appointment'. Can't they call if they're desperate? Besides, it's nearly closing time, and I've been here long enough to know that on a sunny day it means don't expect all the shops to be open when the owners could be heading for a sumptuous dinner on a terrace."

He was right, sadly. I was usually one of those types to take off and enjoy the evening somewhere other than in the confines of my musty shop – normally my own home. But I didn't need to let him know that. "How typically American, thinking you can strut in and order me around."

He threw his palms in the air, a smile playing at his lips. "That's rich coming from you. I think you're the bossy one in this relationship. American has nothing to do with it. The French, on the other hand, you know what the world says about them . . ."

"Oui," I said smiling despite myself, "*They sure know how to make those soufflés rise.*"

He let out a barrel of laughter. "Yes, it has nothing at all to do with arrogance."

I affected a look of surprise. "Arrogance? You won't find an arrogant French person unless you've stepped on their toes."

"I promise I'll tread carefully. Shall we?"

What harm was there in going with him to soak up some fresh air? Really, it *was* stuffy in the shop . . . I wanted to know who he was and why he was here, so this was a good opportunity to find out.

"Fine," I said. "I have to go to a flea market. You can accompany me, but don't even think of buying anything I have my eye on."

With a dazzling smile he said, "I wouldn't dream of it. I know you have friends everywhere looking out for you. Who knows who's behind seemingly innocuous curtains?"

I pulled a face. "You knew we were watching you that day!"

"Not until after when you and Gustave, was it, were chatting. The conversation was as clunky as wood."

I swatted his arm. "You see too much, Monsieur Black."

In the filmy light of afternoon we wandered side by side. I was intrigued by him, but wary too. What did he want with me? It was something more than just friendship and I was watching for it, not as naïve as I'd once been.

69

"Mademoiselle Tour Guide, which flea market are we attending?" He thrust his hands into the pockets of his jeans, and turned his face to me just as a splinter of sunlight peeped through the leaves above. It landed on his blond hair like a spotlight, making him almost ethereal.

"We're going to Marché Dauphine on Rue des Rosiers. I have to see a man with a pink bow tie, with a red carnation."

Tristan raised his eyebrows. "Very *Alice in Wonderland*. I'm surprised you're taking me. I thought you kept your antique sources a secret."

I hailed a taxi; the flea market was in the Saint-Ouen and too far to walk. "Ah, there's the thing, you don't know the code word, so without that, you won't get very far." I winked, enjoying myself for some inexplicable reason. He could hunt around Marché Dauphine all day long and not be shown the special antiques. There was a strict system in place, and unless you knew the right source, you'd never find the gold.

A taxi pulled up with a screech of brakes.

"Perhaps I should blindfold you just in case." I hunted in my handbag. "Except I don't have any ribbon. It's your lucky day."

The taxi dropped us on the Rue des Rosiers. The street was bustling with daytime shoppers. Bistros were busy with waiters scurrying outside, trays topped with wineglasses held aloft, as people sat on cane chairs facing the street. It was a hectic quarter and I liked the feeling you could be swept away in it all, and carried along, stopping to shop, or to eat and drink.

"Do you find many valuables here?" he asked, taking in the expansive arcade that was home to hundreds of bric-a-brac shops upstairs and downstairs, and along one big uneven cobblestoned alley.

"Sometimes. You have to know someone usually, who knows someone, you know."

He laughed. "I do know."

"But there's a wealth of glorious cherishables here, whether they're worth money or not. Beauty abounds."

"Cherishables?"

"Cherishables," I agreed. "Lovely little finds that have tiny value but lots of heart. Tea tins, picture frames, old perfume bottles. Half the fun is finding them, and the other half imagining where they came from."

"That's why you don't mind me tagging along . . . The chances I'd find anything *you* want would be impossible in a place this size. And I don't know someone who knows someone, at least I don't think I do."

I gave him a cheery smile. "Exactly."

Inside the market a strong smell of another era permeated the air. The wonderful aroma of antiques. "Don't you love that scent?" I asked.

He made a show of breathing in deeply. "I could live on that and that alone."

"Very amusing. Can you see anyone wearing a pink bow tie?" We wandered along, surveying each vendor for a pink bow tie, and checking out laden tables full of odd and ends. Mismatched antique linens, embroidered with someone's initials. Cutlery sets with crazed ivory handles.

"No, but look at this," Tristan said, taking a brooch from a stack of costume jewelry. "I think it's a genuine opal."

It would be highly unusual for a vendor not to know the worth of something. There was always someone to show it to, opinions to be gathered. But the opal had sat discarded in a pile of cheap beaded necklaces and plastic earrings.

Tristan inspected it closer. "It's transparent; there's no layering on the side. From what I can tell, it's real. And for something so large, it would be valuable." He handed me the brooch.

"You're right, it does look genuine." Synthetic opals were hard to spot, but there were a few markers that set them apart from the real thing, and this opal didn't have any of those. "A bargain at one Euro." I pointed to the price on the box. "I didn't know you were an expert on jewelry." I rubbed the smoothness of the opal between my fingers. The blue rivulets in the gem were the color of Tristan's eyes. It was magnetic, such a find, and felt cool to the touch, like something that had been taken from the depths of the earth.

"I dabble in this and that so it pays to know a little bit."

"Hmm," I said, not quite believing him. His line sounded rehearsed. Although maybe he was another Dion, hands in pies all over the place, to garner a living. Tristan's was more fruitful by the look of things.

Tristan told the vendor the brooch was real. I found it surprising he'd be so honest. I expected he'd keep the opal's authenticity a secret and grab himself a bargain. Wonders would never cease. The vendor frowned. "Not possible, I check myself." He snatched it back and scrutinized it up close. "Not for sale!" he said, making us laugh.

"Well, there you go," I said. "Maybe it's easy to find treasure here if you know what you're doing."

We continued on, checking out stacks of vinyl records, crystal glassware, tiger-head ceramic sugar pots, faded pink ballet shoes. But I had an important customer arriving later, so I couldn't dilly-dally as long as I hoped. She was a loyal friend of the little antique shop, who was driving from Toulouse especially to find a gift for her daughter's wedding trousseau. Trousseaus were out of fashion these days, so it was a thrill to be able to help furnish one again. She was looking for linen, and bedding and the other things that would help her daughter make a home with her new husband.

Someone whistled for attention, and I followed the piercing sound. Upstairs stood a man with a pink bow tie and a red carnation in his pocket. His wild black curls stood out at every angle. He gestured to me to meet him in his shop.

"That's our man," I said making my way to the stairs.

"Is this really how Parisians source their antiques? It's a very unusual way of doing business." Tristan's footfalls were light on the steel steps.

72

"Ah," I said, "you don't understand. These are sentimental pieces. No one would bother about them, except me or someone who owns one of the little bric-a-brac shops. It's what makes it fun."

The pink bow tie man greeted me in French. I told him Rachelle sent me, and he fussed about searching for my prize. Finally he unearthed it and passed it to me, triumphant. I gasped. It was a 1950s' Hermès Kelly bag. They were still wildly popular, and vintage ones especially. "Where did you get it?" I asked him, checking for imperfections. The black leather was in good condition, the padlock and key fob still worked – only the gilded metal had tarnished. The inside lining still held the faint trace of perfume, something spicy, oriental.

"I got it from a young man who bought it for his future fiancé as an engagement present. He was going to propose to her in Monaco."

I frowned. "And yet . . ."

The man lifted his palms. "She left him before he could. But –" the man held up a finger "– the very next day he met the love of his life, a more . . . practical girl. So he swapped the Kelly bag for a TV, and that's how it came to me."

I swallowed back laughter. "He swapped it for a TV?"

He nodded. "A plasma TV, secondhand but still in very good condition."

Men and technology. I didn't want Tristan to see how I went about business negotiations, and just as I went to tell him to leave me be he said, "I'm going downstairs." He took his cell phone from his pocket. "I have to return a call."

"Great," I said. When he'd retreated I started my spiel. "So, what do you want for it?"

Pink bow tie man crossed his arms, and gazed heavenward as if he didn't already have a figure in mind. "It's so rare, and in immaculate condition—"

"I think the handle has been replaced." I pointed to the leather handle, which was suspiciously darker than the rest of the bag. If

73

anything it should have been lighter from the previous owner's touch. "And the lining has smudges of lipstick on it, and maybe nail polish. I'd have to get it professionally cleaned."

He continued: "It's not often the padlock and key fob still work for a 1950s' edition."

"I'll give you a hundred for it."

His mouth fell open. "Three hundred!" He made a show of being offended, and I returned with a casual shrug as if I couldn't care less what happened to the bag. It was a farce by both of us and we knew it.

"Two hundred and that's my final offer." I studied my finger-nails intently.

With a few grunts and groans about going out of business he said, "Deal."

We shook and I passed over the money. It was a fantastic buy and I'd sell the Kelly bag in a matter of hours once it was cleaned and made beautiful again, just as it deserved. I thanked him once more, and waved goodbye, clattering back down the steps in my high heels.

Tristan was standing near the exit deep in conversation and didn't hear me approach. I overheard one-sided snippets of his conversation, but he spoke low and fast like he was giving directions. "It's too *late* now. You told me it was the only way we'd get . . ."

I tapped him on the shoulder and he blanched and ended the phone call.

"Problem?" I asked, pointing to the phone he'd hung up so abruptly.

"No." He double blinked. "Sorry. A call from America about some . . . investments."

"Right."

"Shall we?"

Whoever called had ruined the mood. Tristan's expression was dark as he strode purposefully ahead, leaving me no choice but to take huge strides to keep up with him.

"I have to get back to the shop," I said, glancing at my watch, thankful I had a reason to slip away.

His shoulders relaxed, and he donned a smile. "Sorry, I was a million miles away after that phone call. Can't you stay?"

"No, sorry, I have a client coming. But another day, maybe. Are you OK to get back to the 7th?"

"I think I'll manage." With one step forward, he kissed the apple of my cheek, taking me by surprise. It was customary to kiss cheeks with friends and even acquaintances but it sent shivers down the length of me. I mumbled something and walked off, hoping I wouldn't stumble in my heels. Minutes later I realized that I hadn't used my opportunity to the fullest. What had I found out about him? Absolutely nothing, except that he could spot a genuine opal. I'd been too starry-eyed by the wares and his take on them to question him.

Chapter Eight

The laptop screen blurred. I'd been at it since 4 a.m. because sleep had eluded me. I was scrolling through various popular online auction sites. If you spent enough time searching you'd be rewarded with some beauties. Antiques being sold that needed rejuvenation, or unique items I knew I had buyers for. People online wanted quick sales, and the 'junk' cleared out. I'd found countless treasures bidding at online auctions over the last couple of years, but it took time to sift through so many pages.

I got up to replenish the coffee pot when front door handle wiggled and Lilou burst in. "Ma chérie!" She rushed to me, dropping her bags to the floor, and squeezed me tight. "It's so good to see you."

Trying to breathe through the tresses of her silky hair, I pulled myself back, attempting to recover from such a surprise. "You too."

A scraggly stranger stood behind her and I hurriedly gathered my robe tighter.

"This is Henry!"

I gave him a polite nod. "Bonjour." I guessed Claude had lost his shine.

She gave Henry a quick smooch. "Don't be shy. Make yourself at home."

Henry yawned and stretched in reply. His hair stuck up at odd angles, and his clothes were creased. Perhaps they had been sleeping under the stars, a necessity if their money had run out.

"Lilou, it's nice to meet your new friend . . ." I laughed nervously as he threw himself and his dirty boots on my Louis XVI French chaise longue. "That chaise, the distressed pink velvet you see . . ." I spun back to Lilou. "Perhaps take Henry to the bistro downstairs until he finds his way to wherever it is he's going." I coughed into my hand while discreetly surveying him sprawled happily as though he was settling in for the duration.

She grinned, and tossed her long mane of hair. "Oh, he's not going anywhere." They exchanged a glance, the sweet early love goggle-eyes. "He's a couch surfer!"

My mouth fell open. "A what?" Apprehensive, I pictured him standing on the chaise, arms out wide, while he rode a metaphorical wave. The idea sent shivers down my spine.

"A couch surfer, Anouk," she said with a tut. "A person who goes from couch to couch as they travel the world. It's a way to travel stress free, even if you're almost penniless! I told Henry he could stay here. It's the least I could do after couch surfing my way around Normandy with him. Don't worry, we'll cover the chaise with a bed sheet. You won't even know he's here."

I covered my face with my hands. Lilou was crashing her way into my life, and now so were her boyfriends. My solitude would be lost for good. And my sanity. "Lilou, this is too much."

She rolled her eyes dramatically. "Don't be such a killjoy. Henry *saved my life!*"

I glanced at him, with his lazy smile, and ruffled appearance. What was she thinking? Allowing some vagabond in here? He could be a serial killer, a thief, a Trump supporter . . .

"And how did he manage that?" I asked.

"Well, remember Claude?"

"He didn't last long," I said. Claude, the boyfriend who'd replaced Rainier. And I could guess had been sent on his merry way as my fickle sister moved on, like clockwork when his spell was over.

She inhaled dramatically, as though she needed a huge breath to get the story told. "We had a fight because he wanted me to visit his parents and I said no, because really, that's way too serious after a few weeks, and I want to concentrate on my career as a jewelry designer." She was off on a quickly spoken monologue and it took all my concentration to keep up. "And my money invariably ran out . . . Luckily that's when I ran into Henry, who showed me how to travel with virtually no money. It's been incredible! Why should seeing the world be reserved for those with excess cash? This way we can all be pilgrims!"

It took me a good thirty seconds to work through her monstrously long explanation and make sense of it. "Pilgrims?" Flashes of Lilou in strangers' houses raced through my mind, scaring me silly. Perhaps it was much better if she lived with me so I could keep her safe. She was young and naïve about the world.

"Pilgrims! All of us! So Henry can stay and I can make jewelry and when we have the urge to travel, we'll couch surf!"

"It's a very nice idea," I said, choosing my words carefully but ending up sounding stern like my maman. "And . . ." Henry had taken his boots off and left a trail of sand on the chaise. "However, I work from home at nights, and that peace and quiet is crucial, especially if I'm on the phone to clients . . ." Henry let out a yawn so loud it would've woken the dead. "When you informed me you were moving in a few weeks ago, before you flitted off following a music festival, I thought you meant just *you*. Couch surfing is a great idea in theory, but my apartment, it's not really made for so many . . . people." I had time to get used to the idea of suddenly living with my sister, but another person, a couch surfer at that? I didn't think I could cope.

She flashed a cheesy grin ignoring my singular use of *you*.

"You'll get used to it, Anouk. During the day I'll be at Madame's. She offered me the use of the room above her shop as a studio, and Henry will be searching for work, so you'll hardly even see us."

"Lilou, I meant . . ."

She gave me a hard stare. "Anouk, come on, give it a few weeks' trial and if it's not working he can leave. I really thought you'd be happy I'm going to pour all my energy into my business."

She had me on an emotional tightrope and she knew it. "I'll give you one week. And if one thing is damaged –" I gave the chaise a pointed stare for emphasis "– I'll be livid."

"Great!" She beamed.

"And call Papa."

"Papa?" she said. "Why?"

"Be honest about the course you're supposed to be doing. Tell him you've quit. He's paying for it, Lilou."

She grappled with a retort. "But he'll do something crazy, like take away my allowance, or race here and demand I go home, and I can't. That town, it's stifling."

I tilted my head. We'd had this same argument so many times and I was tired. "You know he *means* well. He only wants the best for you. For some direction in your life. The jewelry business is a great idea – *if* you stick with it. Last month it was designing vintage-look postcards, the month before it was dream catchers. You tend to get carried away, Lilou. You don't stick at anything."

"Little do you know! I've been making jewelry for months!" She put her hands on her hips, ready for battle. "Shall I bring up the past? You haven't always been so together either, you know."

I pinched the bridge of my nose as a headache loomed. I'd always been together. Disallowing the love mess I'd stumbled into recently my life had run smoothly, steadily. With grim determination I'd plotted my future like an author would their next novel and continually plugged away at it, hoping to get it right.

I'd always been an organized type. From my early teens I had a clear plan for my life, and had worked hard to achieve it.

Sometimes I wished I was more relaxed, and not so driven, but it wasn't in my nature. It was exasperating being the responsible older sibling when Lilou was so flighty but I did admire her for her gumption and her utter lack of giving a damn. But I could never tell her though, give an inch and she'd set sail hundreds of miles away. "I think you're mistaken, Lilou."

"Well . . . remember that time Marguerite chopped your braids off? Who was there for you when you thought your whole world was ending? Hmm?"

I gave her a wide-eyed stare. "I was eight years-old. And there's no way you'd remember that because you were a toddler then!"

She clucked her tongue. "OK, well what about that time you thought you were pregnant to that surfer guy from Australia and I comforted you all night long until we could head to the doctor the next day? Hmm? How quickly you forget!"

I stifled a laugh at the incredulity on her face. "That was *you* who had the pregnancy scare and he wasn't Australian, he was from New Zealand, and *supposedly* the love of your young life! One of many, dare I mention!" Poor Henry looked crestfallen at the mention of another guy.

Her eyes narrowed as she tried to remember. "Anyway –" she pointed a finger at me "– I've always been there for you. And it would be nice if you would do the same."

There was no chance I would get her to admit her folly. "You beggar belief, Lilou. If I come back from work and one thing is damaged or out of place, you're both out no matter how much you try to sweet-talk me. And . . ." I paused for effect ". . . I'll ring Papa and tell him *everything*."

She gasped and shook her head. "You wouldn't."

"I would." I pulled my shoulders back and did the big sister act. I'd never rat her out to our parents but she didn't need to know that. "Get some sheets on my chaises if you're going to spend the day watching TV and sprawling on them like that." I gave Henry a pointed look. "And make up the spare bedroom while you're at it; you can both sleep in there. We'll discuss all of this properly when I get home tonight, including Papa and the course he's paying for."

"Merci, Anouk."

We kissed cheeks and I left, knowing that as soon as I was out of sight music would be pumping, and the apartment would no longer be a single woman's sanctuary. The noise I could deal with, for a week or two, but the hard part would be making Lilou see reason about her future, or lack thereof.

* * *

When I arrived at the shop after breakfast with Madame Dupont, Tristan was there, leaning against the façade like some kind of movie star. My breath caught at the sight of him. It wasn't just the way his muscled physique was evident under his clothing, it was the way he held himself, almost like he was ready to pounce. There was something primal about him, and it unnerved me, because I couldn't look away.

"Another visit so soon?" I said.

"Well, you see, I had an interesting night. There's a painting I'm interested in. It's rumored to be in Paris, but do you think I can find it?" He smiled and ran a hand through his hair, before continuing on quietly. "When I make enquiries all roads seem to lead back to you, but when I press people for details everyone clamps their mouths closed. It would seem that you have some great friends in Paris, Anouk. We should all be so lucky. And I know if you have the painting, then for my own safety I should leave it alone." He grinned, making a joke about how ruffled I was when I thought he was stealing the cello from under me.

But I was genuinely shocked to hear he was asking about a painting, because I knew which one he was after. The one Joshua stole from me. It wasn't worth bucket-loads of cash when I bought it, but I had thought it would be a good investment for

81

the future, and when the painter sadly died the value shot up. It was one of the largest portraits he'd done, and it was all red, every single brush stroke, completely unique to his other work. No one had been able to find it, including me. I'd made a ton of enquiries after Joshua took it, but to no avail.

Whoever Tristan had spoken to had kept my secrets, and for that, I was grateful, and a little fuzzy with the thought they cared enough to keep quiet about the catastrophe that had landed me in such an embarrassing mess. Still, how he knew about the painting in the first place was a concern. The quicker he forgot about it the better, but I could tell from the set of his shoulders he wouldn't be appeased with a vague answer. How could I say Joshua had stolen it from me without looking like a fool? It had taken me years to build up my reputation as a trader of quality antiques, so the fewer people who knew about my stupidity the better. I certainly didn't want to tell a stranger.

"Well?" he asked, his gaze trained on me.

"Well what?" I folded my arms.

"Why are they so protective of you?" That I could answer in the vaguest possible way.

"Let's walk," I said.

We crossed the Pont d'Léna and came to the entrance of the Trocadéro Gardens where water from the fountains streamed into the air like champagne. "The antique circuit is tight-knit and we look out for one another, that's all." I said, hoping this would help him understand just what kind of community he had walked into. And, despite the intense competition between us, we Parisians did stick together and kept mute on personal matters. I could have hugged them all in thanks, and I wasn't the hugging type.

He cocked his head. "Do newcomers ever get into the inner circle?"

"The French are . . . distrustful of newcomers. It's inbuilt in us, to preserve our heritage. I'm French, and when I moved to

Paris, it took aeons for me to find my niche. Aren't you more the fly-by-night kind?"

"Is that what I seem like?" A fleeting look of hurt crossed his features.

"A little," I said, truthfully. "We've seen your kind so many times." If he wanted to be part of the French antique world, really part of it, privy to the most selective auctions and gossip, it would take years for him to build up their trust and be included. Somehow he'd wangled an invitation to the gala already, so he must have had some connections somewhere. "Tristan, it's nothing personal, it's just the way it's always been done. It's traditional, and sort of like a test that takes years to pass."

I was met with silence, so continued: "Like any industry there's always something to upset the balance, a person or entity who isn't as honest as they first seem." Tristan seemed earnest enough to understand there were rules in these situations and they applied to everyone differently. "So it's reasonable to suspect you'd be the same. The painting you want . . . is gone. No one knows where, but it will be suspicious to everyone you even asking about it, because of the drama involved."

"What drama?"

I swallowed hard. Why couldn't he just take the hint and leave it be? "It's a long story, and one best left forgotten."

We walked, curving around clusters of people out for an early morning stroll.

Something had been bugging me, so I asked, "Why did you go to Andre's estate that day?" If he really didn't want to step on people's toes, following my every move was a bad way to start. Was he following the others too? We were well trained in the art of stealth, and they'd know if he was sniffing out their clients, and their deals.

He had the grace to color. "For the scroll. I heard about it from a friend who knew Andre's grandfather. But when I got to the door, he denied even owning such a thing. I realized you'd already made some kind of deal with him. The fire in your eyes when you saw me was a good indicator." He laughed. "I can see why you were angry. After meeting that dubious guy at the auction, I imagine he's stolen quite a number of things from under you. I'm not like that, Anouk. You have my word."

Except I knew that words were just words sometimes. It would take a lot more than an empty promise for me to believe Tristan. It was ingrained in me to be careful, and the one time I wasn't I stumbled. "Look," I said turning to point into the distance at the structure tourists and Parisians loved. "This is one of the best places in Paris to view the Eiffel Tower from."

He followed my gaze, but I knew he wasn't taking in the view. He was deep in thought, his eyes glazed over. I couldn't help thinking Tristan was a carbon copy of Joshua, with the 'I just want to be accepted' act. If I wasn't so suspicious, I would have enjoyed the walk more. At face value, Tristan was charming, and sweet, with eyes so blue you could get lost inside them. Instead, I held myself stiffly and like some kind of tour-guide pointed out the other sights to see from this vantage point. "Behind us is the Palais de Chaillot, and that's the Fountain of Warsaw . . ." My voice petered away. Even to me it sounded forced, and I understood I was trying to veer the conversation away from the antique circuit, because I was already saying too much.

"Forgive me," he said, his face softening as though he'd shrugged off the earlier conversation. "I hadn't intended to make this all about me. I wanted to get to know you better, and if that takes time, as is your way, that's fine by me."

Did he mean romantically? My heart sped up a little at the thought, but I knew I would never understand the vagaries of a different language's subtle nuances to trust his words. "I'm really busy, Tristan, with work, and . . ." My brain scrambled for more examples. "Family, and life, so . . ."

He threw his head back and laughed. "So no friendships?"

I was caught off guard, and wished I knew what exactly he was after. "No, no time for much else."

"You have to eat though, right?"

"I eat at home." Stop talking, Anouk! I sounded like some kind of flat-lining hermit. "Usually late, in front of the computer while I work."

I eat at home. I chat with my soup bowl. I lie to myself about love.

The realization my heart was a turncoat gave me an urge to flee. My carefully constructed fort was wobbling and that's exactly what happened when you didn't protect yourself. It happened with Joshua because I believed in love at first sight. And that proved to be the biggest mistake I'd ever made. If only you could take a man on his word, his actions, but I knew I couldn't. Mesmerizing eyes or not, Tristan sent alarms bells ringing. He was too similar, almost like the universe was testing me to see if I'd mess up again.

And for a brief moment of time, I wanted to say yes, let's date, let's have dinner, because why shouldn't a girl be able to act impulsively? But my job, and the amount of money invested in my work, made me hesitate. I had to. Tristan wanted that painting, so maybe getting to know me was simply for information about something worth a lot of money.

"Great," he said. "I'm a night owl too. And there's nothing like a home-cooked meal. I'll bring the wine." And with that he pecked me on the cheek and sauntered off, giving me zero time to respond.

I stood there opening and closing my mouth like a fish out of water until I collected myself. Why was I attracted to men who were a mystery? I snapped my mouth closed. Who said I was attracted to him? I stumbled from the park, realizing there was no point lying to myself. There was something about Tristan, an energy, an intensity to his gaze, and if I was truthful part of me wanted to explore those feelings. Sadly, it could never happen.

Chapter Nine

Night fell across the sky like spilt ink, the moon a yellow orb illuminating the evening as I chatted with my last customer. I'd already flipped the sign to Closed and locked the door so we could chat in private. Gilles was an elderly widower who lived on Rue de l'Odéon – a famous street in the 6th where Sylvia Beach had moved her bookshop Shakespeare and Co in 1922, and published James Joyce's *Ulysses* from. Gilles would tell me stories of how busy the street was still with people wandering up and down, trying to get a sense of what took place there, perhaps looking for the ghosts of those great people. I'd walked down there often enough myself, imagining I could see them leaning against the brickwork of their shops and chatting about books.

Gilles visited me once a week, and spent the other evenings strolling the boulevards of Paris with his little dog Casper. He had been coming to my shop for years but he had never once bought a thing, and never would. It wasn't antiques he craved, it was people and a way to assuage the loneliness for a while. While I usually required an introduction for someone to enter my shop, the haunted look Gilles had worn made him an exception to the rule.

When he stumbled upon my shop all those summers ago, his

grief was so apparent it was like a shadow cast behind him. These days his visits were happier affairs. I'd make us tea, and we'd talk into the night, pretending he was looking for a piece of jewelry, or a music box, something his wife would have adored.

Tonight, our conversation had come to an end as Casper pulled on his lead, a sign he was ready for home, and his dinner. Gilles finished his tea and reached for his cane.

"*Désolé*, Anouk. These music boxes are *charmant*, but they're not quite what I was looking for."

The music boxes were among the best I'd ever found, in pristine condition and played 'Clair De Lune' with such clarity, I hoped they'd one day go to a little girl who'd listen to them over and over again, face rapt, heart aflutter. "I understand." I patted his hand and gave him an apologetic smile. "These things cannot be rushed. Maybe next week I'll have some different ones?" I said gently, keeping up our charade.

"Well, in that case, I'll be back next week," he said, just like he always did.

"I'll look forward to it." I moved from around the counter, and chucked Casper under his furry chin, and gave Gilles a hug. Under his jacket he was all bones, and I worried about him between our visits.

"Au revoir."

I waved goodbye and watched them retreat along the promenade, their shadows lengthening behind them and eventually disappearing. My heart tugged for Gilles as I imagined him in his tiny apartment all alone in the pitch black of night, eating soup for one. At least he had Casper. Gilles's wife had died fifteen years before, and still he couldn't quite believe she was gone. He spoke of her as if she had just stepped out and was coming back any moment. Her death left a gaping hole in his world that could never be filled, so he walked. Pounded the cobblestones of Paris, and chatted to his fluffy white dog, until the day drew to a close. It wasn't as if he wore his grief on his face anymore, but it was there, just off in the distance, hovering near. Still after all this time, it was there. There was something poignant, touching about it.

I wondered what that would feel like, to love someone so completely that without them everything in the world paled, faded to gray scale. That never-ending ache for a person gone. At least they'd had that eclipsing once-in-a-lifetime love that was so hard to find.

I cleared our tea things away, and left the shop to sit in darkness, save for a small lamp that glowed dull yellow in one corner. Outside was eerily silent. It was a rare snatch of time when the city stilled like it was taking a deep breath, ready for the frivolity the night would bring. Dinner, dancing, laughter. A lull in the long day, for me to walk alone, and reflect on the inexplicable business of living.

Along Rue De Babylone I stopped to sniff a bouquet of flowers. They were as pretty as any I'd seen, pale pink, as delicate as tissue paper. Peonies. One of the most beautiful flowers on this earth with petals folded inward protecting the heart of the bloom.

The shopkeeper was packing up for the night, and gave me a nod. I shook my head no. As much as I loved them, I bought my flowers from Rachelle from the little flower shop near the Notre Dame, and I'd feel guilty spending my money elsewhere.

I continued down some other avenues eventually passing Église Saint-Sulpice, a Catholic church with an ornate façade and a paved square with a fountain.

Turning the corner, I came to the little boulangerie where I bought my baguettes and whatever other delicious morsels they had on offer. Tonight I had my heart set on decadent simple trois quiche au fromage, a three-cheese quiche. Comfort food French style.

I went to the counter and ordered, and tried my best to keep my eyes from the mouthwatering palmiers on display, the rolled sugar-dusted puff pastry biscuits were hard to resist late at night with a cup of café noir. But I reasoned, I'd be on a caffeinated sugar high, and that wasn't the best idea.

With my quiche in hand, I headed to my apartment, surprised to see the balcony in darkness and no music blaring. Lilou and Henry must have gone out in Paris together, and once again, I wondered how Lilou managed to live such a lifestyle on her meager budget. She had said that she was focusing on her jewelry business but it didn't look like much work was going on. I hoped she would persevere and really push herself, because she was good at it, her creativity was spellbinding, and I wanted her to believe in herself and stick with something.

But living with her was another thing entirely. Bracing myself for the worst, I opened the front door but I was surprised to find the living room orderly. Aside from an empty plate or two on the coffee table it wasn't as ravaged as I'd expected it to be. Perhaps she was growing up, finally. Taking the quiche into the kitchen I choked on my former happiness. Mon Dieu! Every cupboard must've been bare, dirty saucepans, pots, plates, mugs, and wine-glasses littered every available surface. What had she attempted to cook today to use every single piece of crockery? And why? She hated cooking.

Dinner would have to wait. I was the type of person who couldn't relax with a mess like this greeting me. My maman had taught me to be tidy, organized, and clean. Somehow Lilou had missed out on that lesson growing up. I filled the sink, and rolled up my sleeves, muttering and cursing under my breath, when the doorbell buzzed.

I hurried to answer it. There was my sister, bright-eyed, leaning against the doorjamb. "Lilou . . ."

"I forgot my key," she said, with her megawatt smile in place. "This must be for you." She handed me an envelope with my name written across the front and flounced past me.

I tucked it away into my pocket. "Lilou, what happened in the kitchen? You've completely burned my cast-iron pot. How is that even possible?"

With a shake of her head as if I was complaining about the

weather she said, "Aren't you going to read it?" She pointed to my pocket where the envelope was buried.

"Aren't *you* going to answer me?" I crossed my arms, feeling like the petulant older sister once more.

Henry walked in sheepishly, running a hand through his hair. "Sorry about the kitchen; that was my fault. I'll tidy it up now."

I raised a brow but remained silent as Henry walked past me. Would I have to stow away my best bakeware? I had dishes that my maman had given me that were passed down from her mother. My kitchen and its stock were special to me. Just then the phone buzzed, and I gave Lilou one last glare before retreating to answer it.

"Bonsoir?"

"Bonsoir, Anouk. Where have you girls been? It's impossible to get hold of you!" My papa's voice thundered down the line.

Even though I was twenty-eight, an adult, and responsible for my own life, I still gulped. "Papa, *désolée.*" I threw a dark look at Lilou, who'd gone lily-white on hearing Papa's name. "I've been busy with work. I didn't get any messages from you."

He scoffed. "I'm not talking to a machine. That's ridiculous! I refuse to leave a message like a blathering fool. Now where is Lilou? I had a letter from the school saying she's missed the examinations, and I told the woman that's simply not possible. Absolutely not! Not with you making sure she attends."

I scowled at Lilou who was acting out a charade, with her palms together and head cocked to one side. She mouthed, 'Tell him I'm asleep!'

"That's odd," I said, my mind spinning with what I could say. I wanted to tell the truth, but I knew that would be the end of Lilou's freedom in Paris. She'd have no choice but to go home, and as much trouble as she was, I didn't want that. But how to get out of this conundrum?

"Why don't I phone the college tomorrow, Papa, and see what's going on? I'm sure she's been attending . . ." I scrunched my eyes closed at the lie, and hoped he'd believe me. "And I know she's been doing *very* well with her jewelry-making business, so well in fact, she's thinking of it as a possible career choice." In the background Lilou jumped and clapped, doing a happy dance across the living room floor.

"What! She's thinking what?" he roared. Oh dear. Too soon.

"Oh you know, it's just an idea at this stage. She's *very* good at it."

"Very this, very that. No, Anouk, and don't you encourage her. Making jewelry won't pay her rent, and next week it'll be something else, and her life will be wasted. She needs a good job to attract the right sort of man to make her husband."

I rolled my eyes so far I almost fell over backward. "Papa, please, that kind of talk is archaic."

He huffed and puffed like a disgruntled bear. "Anouk, please, at twenty-eight you should be married and have children by now. See what this independence does? It makes women into spinsters."

"Papa! You can't say things like that; it's not nice!" I closed my eyes and tried hard to keep my breathing even. Poor Papa hadn't so much moved with the times, as stayed rooted in another era. He didn't mean to be insulting, but someone had to tell him off, and it usually fell to me.

"What? It's true – admit it. If you'd listened to me, you'd have married that boy down the road and I'd have a hundred grand-babies by now, but instead you strutted off and opened a shop in Paris, and fell into the trap of the 'modern woman'. I won't have both my daughters make the same mistake."

"Oh, Papa, be realistic! The boy down the road wasn't inter-ested in me, nor I in him. I'm actually pretty sure he preferred the company of men . . . It was only you who was determined he'd do and that was only because he lived so close by."

"The company of men? Every man needs some time with friends. What does that matter? I'm sure he wouldn't have begrudged you some time with your lady friends."

I bit my bottom lip against laughter. "That wasn't what I meant."

"Well what did you mean?"

There was no point telling Papa the boy down the road was gay – he'd just protest otherwise. "What I mean is, you can't map out our lives, Papa. We know you care, but sometimes you just have to let nature take its course."

"I can so, and I will! Where is she?" he asked. "I want to get to the bottom of this examination debacle so I can call the college back and let them know, in no uncertain terms, that I expect her certificate sent to me once she's done. I've got a feeling they just want more money out of me."

At that moment I wished I'd been honest with him from the start. Never again, I vowed, would I get myself embroiled in Lilou's mess. I'd gone too far with the white lies now to change my story. "Ah, she's . . ." Lilou's eyes grew wide. "Asleep. She had a big day at . . . study club." Study club! That'd be the day.

"Well tell her to call me. No more of this dodging me or I'll make a trip to Paris myself, you hear?" In the background the TV burbled. As usual Papa had the volume too high.

"Oui, Papa. I'll tell her."

"Good," he said.

"How's Maman?"

"She's making dessert."

"But how is she?"

He grumbled to himself. "She's as she always is. What is this? The Spanish Inquisition?"

I sighed. He was a man of few words once his steam ran out. "OK, Papa, send Maman my love and we'll talk soon."

Before I could put the phone down Lilou threw herself at me, and hugged me tight, squeezing the breath from my lungs. "Oh my God, thank you, Anouk! You were very convincing! Did he go on about the spinster thing again?"

I nodded, a giggle escaping me. He was like a father from

a historical romance. "See what independence does? It makes women into spinsters!" I mimicked his gruff tone.

She bent double with laughter. "He's a throwback from the 1900s!"

We spent the next ten minutes dissecting Papa's foibles, before gathering ourselves. I said more solemnly, "What are you going to do about the classes? They've called him about you missing the exams. And we've both lied about it. It can't end well, that's for sure."

In typical Lilou style she flung herself on the chaise and shrugged breezily. "I never told Papa I'd do it. He just *assumed* I'd follow orders, and I won't, Anouk! I'm not a baby anymore, even though everyone thinks I am. I know I can make this jewelry business work, and I also know no one believes me and that's fine because I'll prove you all wrong." Her eyes were full of determination, but they were every time she had her heart set on something new.

Gently, I suggested, "Maybe you should work at it, as hard as you can, and then you can tell Papa to keep the allowance he's giving you. Then you *will* truly be free."

She laughed. "Well, let's not rush into it. Free money is free money and I am the baby of the family."

I shook my head, even though I couldn't stop a small smile breaking out. "You're unbelievable."

It wasn't until I was in bed that I remembered the envelope. I went to my jacket to find it and ripped it open.

Dear Anouk,

I'd hate to see you waste away with work consuming you like it does. I've been practicing my technique for fromage soufflé (see what I did there? I even say it with a French accent) and I think you'll be impressed.

Tristan.

I smiled at the words, trying to picture Tristan in the kitchen baking . . . His French needed a little work though. It was soufflé au fromage, not fromage soufflé. How had Lilou come into possession of the letter? My letterbox was in the foyer but only I had a key to it. I made a mental note to ask her in the morning. Still, what was the point of dinner? A tingle raced down my body at the thought of those eyes of his, and I wanted to scold myself. *This is how it started last time, and look what happened.* But what was the harm in sharing dinner? A girl had to eat.

Chapter Ten

In abject horror, I switched off the morning news program, and hurriedly dressed for work, my mind a jumble of worry. Another theft. And this time one of our most cherished jewelry collections. A set of sapphires so deep blue they made you think you were in the depths of the ocean. They'd been on display at Avant – one of the busiest Paris museums – and were snatched in broad daylight without triggering any alarms. It was almost like the thief was invisible. If they could steal something so boldly, when would this end? When there was nothing left? There was no more time to ruminate.

I had to walk to work, and try not to let the thefts darken the sunlit day. My thoughts kept drifting to Tristan and the letter he'd left. Lilou told me it had been propped against the front door, and I wondered how he knew where I lived. A man who cooked was a real man in my eyes. When I imagined my romantic life, whether it was fantasy or not, I always envisioned bumping and jostling with my partner in the kitchen, laughing and baking together. My diary was the only thing privy to those secret desires: the things I wanted in a man.

Outside, breathing in a deep lungful of rose-scented air, I couldn't help but smile. Paris was glorious any time of year, but more so when the flowers blossomed and exposed their colorful buds, shimmying seductively like burlesque dancers in the breeze.

Visiting Paris was like falling in love. It swept you up, and transported you to another time; history was everywhere – and I could never tire of it. There was always something to admire. From the gothic architecture of the Notre Dame with its gargoyles perched atop, surveying the city, to the grand structure of Les Invalides with its golden dome – the final resting place for Napoléon Bonaparte inside. But if you spent enough time you'd find places so extraordinary, you'd never want to leave.

The Promenade Plantée was one such place, a five-kilometer verdant walk built on the tracks of the abandoned Vincennes railway line. People said they could still feel the vibration as they strolled along the tracks, as if a ghost train was still making its daily journey. If you took the long walk you'd be rewarded with the elevated vista hidden deep in a secret garden, where lovers kissed, and people proposed, surrounded by rose-trellised arbors, and murmurs of the past. It was a favorite haunt of mine. I'd take a book, and pretend I was waiting for my Mr. Right . . .

Not today though. Work beckoned. The wind blew gently, carrying with it the chatter of crowds, a world of accents. I stopped briefly and watched people mill at the foot of the Eiffel Tower, their heads craned backward as they took in the spectacle, wide smiles threatening to swallow them up. It never failed to make my heart swell that such a monument could produce an overawed reaction from people from all walks of life. It was gargantuan up close, and photos never did it justice. *La Tour Eiffel* was a feat.

As I turned the corner, I walked into a plume of smoke and perfume. Madame Dupont leaned against the limestone wall of her Time Emporium and waved. I smiled, and went to greet her. "Bonjour, Madame . . . are you OK?" She sucked hard on her cigarette and her hands shook. If I hadn't known better, I'd say she looked guilty, like she'd done something she regretted.

Hadn't Madame Dupont mentioned she was visiting the Avant

museum yesterday? To discuss lending them a variety of antique timepieces for an exhibit of which if I recalled correctly she said they'd offered to pay her handsomely. Could she . . . No. Lack of caffeine was addling my brain. She would never . . . I'd already been through this in my mind and decided she was innocent. Right?

Her face was pinched and her pallor gray despite her usual heavy makeup, and she fluttered her hands like she was nervous. "Chérie, it's not you is it?"

"Pardon?" I tried to pay attention and tamp down the worry Madame Dupont was somehow involved in the thefts. She was wealthy; she had no reasonable motive to steal. Unless she was in on it with a paramour . . .

After the inexorable draw on her cigarette, Madame Dupont repeated herself with more detail, whispering, "It's not *you*, is it? The thief." She darted a glance this way and that to make sure no one was close by to overhear. "I won't tell anyone if it is!" she whispered frantically.

Clarity dawned and I couldn't help but laugh, relieved. "Me?" My voice pitched incredulously. "For one very brief moment, I thought it might be *you*, Madame! You were the one who wanted to go to Sorrento after all! And I couldn't find you for those few hours before we left, remember! And didn't you go the Avant museum yesterday? I take it you've heard this morning's news?"

She laughed too in that husky way of hers, relief flooding her eyes and bringing the color back to her face. "Yes, and it struck me that *you* collect postcards, and you were also in Sorrento . . . and well one thing led to another, and I thought it was better if we were honest with each other." Madame Dupont was shrewd, but you'd never know it by her outward effervescence and the way she put people at ease, because underneath that façade she was still questioning every little thing – Madame Dupont was nobody's fool. For her to suspect me though, well, if I hadn't also suspected her, I'd probably be a touch hurt. Really, it was crazy, but I suppose we both held our antiques in such high esteem that the thought they were getting stolen from under our noses had us both on high alert.

"Well, I can assure you, Madame Dupont, it most certainly wasn't me."

"Nor me. Perhaps we better think on it, though, as it is a probability that we've seen the thief, and he's masquerading as one of our own."

I nodded, wondering if anyone we regularly saw at auctions and events could possibly be the Postcard Bandit. "Oui, Madame. You're right. Perhaps we'll need to pay closer attention to the guest lists, and see if anyone stands out."

"Let's discuss it at the gala next week – I'm going to Monaco tomorrow, a last minute thing . . . I have a date and must dash, so many things to organize." Madame Dupont smiled a goodbye, before catching my eye, hesitating. She said quietly, "For the record, I wouldn't have told the gendarmes if it *was* you."

I gave a nervous little laugh. "I am sure I would have been torn too and . . ." My voice trailed off. I wasn't sure I'd be as forgiving, much as I loved Madame, stealing was stealing, and without a clear motive that wasn't greed I couldn't imagine why a person would even think of such a thing. But if greed was a motivating factor, then no matter who the person was I'd have the most epic internal battle on my hands. Thank God, it didn't seem that was the case.

"Enjoy your date, Madame . . . Who's the lucky guy?"

She gave me a cat-who-got-the-cream smile. "Someone fabulous of course. A . . . Monsieur Neeson, and that's all I'm saying."

"The actor?"

She blanked her features. "Now that would be telling."

With a shake of my head, I held my breath and leaned through the fug of cigarette smoke to kiss her goodbye.

* * *

After a particularly busy day, I locked the shop and headed out into the blue-black night much later than normal. Overhead stars twinkled, like they were showing me the way home. My mind was on dinner, what ingredients I had in the fridge if my new lodgers hadn't eaten the kitchen bare. I had some paperwork to catch up on so a simple niçoise salad would suffice. Lost in reverie, I turned a corner, and found the avenue deserted. A cat's plaintive meow echoed.

I was reaching into my memory, mentally scanning the shelves of my fridge when I had the oddest sensation. Goose bumps broke out over my skin though there was not a soul anywhere near me, which was very unusual for Paris in springtime even this late. I quickened my pace and hoped no one was following me. There were certain streets in Paris that should be avoided late at night, places where the shadows were too deep for a woman to wander alone. Fear clouded my vision as footsteps other than my own sounded close behind me.

I stepped up my pace, darting a glance both sides of the road, wondering which way to go. To the left I knew there was a bistro around the corner, to the right a few hundred meters further, there was a house lit up and music floating out. What if they didn't hear my frantic knock at the door?

My breath came out ragged as I broke into a run, but was stopped when someone grabbed the strap of my handbag. "Give it to me!"

My heart raced. Damn it, why did I walk this way! "No!" I should have let it go, but I had the day's takings inside, and my finances were critical still. Squaring myself for a tousle, I turned coming face to face with the mugger and gave an almighty tug on my handbag strap. His face was shrouded under the cover of darkness, and a cap that he wore pulled down low. The pungent stench of alcohol filled the air. "There's no money in it; let it go!"

He let out an icy laugh that sent shivers up my spine and took a step closer, pressing his chest against mine. Suddenly the bag and the money seemed insignificant. I lunged backward and tripped, hitting my head on something cold. With two quick steps he was over me, his mouth like an open scar over mine. I let out a blood-curdling scream and hoped the person in the house with the music would hear.

"Well aren't you pretty?" he said.

I could taste terror, bitter and acidic. "Don't you dare touch me!" I screamed.

Within seconds the man was wrenched from me and I took great big gulps of fresh air, before scrambling to my feet to run, but not before I locked eyes with Tristan who held the mugger by the scruff of his dirty sweater. My legs went rubbery with relief.

"Go," he said, indicating the lit part of the street. "I'll catch up with you." He had a murderous glint in his eyes, but I didn't argue.

"Should we call the gendarmes?" My first thought was that the despicable excuse for a man would attack another girl in the darkness.

"I'll do it," Tristan said, eyes blazing. "Go now."

I hurried away, into the warmth of the streetlights, where everything seemed safer. My heartbeat eventually returned to normal, but my hands wouldn't stop shaking. I touched the spot on my head where I'd hit something, and my fingers came away red with blood. What would've happened if Tristan hadn't arrived? It didn't bear thinking about. I'd never sleep again if I let those kinds of thoughts swirl around my head. I should have carried my pepper spray in my hand so late at night. I should have stuck to brightly illuminated avenues. I should have . . .

I heard footsteps behind me and for a moment my heart stopped in terror, but it was Tristan, his face dark with anger. "Are you OK?" he said, looking me over. He took my hands, which were scratched from the tarmac; a few nails were broken. "You're shaking. It's the shock. Let's get you home."

Tristan wrapped an arm around me and I burst into tears, scaring myself with the intensity of my sobbing, as if it was another girl, not me who stood there. He wrapped his arms around me tight, murmuring to me. In the warmth of his embrace I felt safe. As if nothing could hurt me there.

"I've got you," he said. "I've got you now, Anouk."

* * *

Tristan escorted me home, the night air cold against my cheeks.

Inside, he took a rug from my bed and bundled me in it, motioning for me to sit on the chaise. Minutes later, he returned from the kitchen with a half glass of red wine.

"Drink it all," he said. "It'll warm you up. It's the shock; it's making you shiver like that." Robotically, I did as told, feeling a calm descend over me. I was at home; the door was locked. Tristan was here.

"Will you be all right?" he said.

I deflated a little, enjoying his proximity, not only because of the attempted mugging, but because he really cared. Or so it seemed.

I pasted on a smile. "Totally fine, thanks for your help."

"You're not getting rid of me that easily," he said. "I'm going to get some things. I'll be back as quickly as possible."

He returned thirty minutes later with two paper bags in hand, but shooed me away from peering in. He'd topped up my wineglass, ran me a bubble bath, and led me into the steamy room, indicating that I should spend as long as I wanted in the scented water. I wasn't used to someone thinking of my needs above theirs. Door closed I plunged into the bath water, the heat stealing the breath from my lungs, in that deliciously comforting way.

I soaped myself down, wanting to get any trace of the mugger and the street grime off of my body. My head throbbed, but the cut must've been minor, as it had stopped bleeding. I was thankful I wouldn't need to ring for a doctor.

It was easier to pretend this was any other night, lest the fear collect me again. I smiled when I heard Tristan singing, his sultry voice accompanied by the sounds of drawers opening and closing, cupboards clicking shut, as he tried to familiarize himself in my apartment. What was he doing? Cooking?

I made a pact to be gentle with myself tonight, to ease my way into conversation with Tristan without following my usual rules of etiquette. I wouldn't second-guess everything. I'd just be grateful for his company. The safety of him.

With the bath water draining noisily, I dressed for comfort – a pair of cotton pajamas that I'd never ever wear in front of a guest usually, but felt like a warm hug tonight.

Wandering from the cocoon of my bedroom, I went to find Tristan and assure him I was OK and he didn't need to babysit me in fear the shock would send me into some catatonic state or something.

As I leaned on the doorjamb I studied the scene before me. There was a man cooking in my kitchen, tea towel slung over one shoulder. He looked for all the world like he'd been here a million times before.

"Feel better?" he asked.

I nodded, suddenly shy. "Much. Thanks for everything; I really appreciate it. You don't have to . . ." I waved a hand at the bench.

"I want to," he said. "Sit down, and talk to me while I cook. A full belly is essential for a great night's sleep, and that's what you need most of all tonight. And the wine will take the edge off."

I moved to the small dining room table and watched him work. He had big strong hands. I'd never noticed that before. With the dim overhead light shining on his blond hair, and the ease with which he moved around he was almost ethereal. Like I was lost in a dream. Maybe I'd bumped my head harder than I first thought.

The knots in my shoulders eased with each sip of the burgundy he'd uncorked. "You look at home in the kitchen," I said. I wouldn't have pegged him for a homebody, but that's what he seemed like, humming while he caramelized onions, diced garlic, stirred pots.

He flashed me a grin. "Let me guess, you thought I had a private chef aboard my yacht catering to my every whim?"

So maybe he wasn't the playboy he resembled? That could only be a good thing. "Something like that," I said, a touch contrite. "I guessed you'd have talents, but wouldn't have thought they'd be so domestic." I could tell by the smells, and the way he controlled various pots and pans that he knew what he was doing.

"I'll try not to take offense." He laughed. "I don't often get to cook in a kitchen so well supplied. Moving around from hotel to hotel doesn't allow much opportunity for that."

The bench was covered in flour, and he had a fingerprint dusting his cheek. Under the crook of his arm, he hugged the glass bowl tight, as he whisked soufflé mixture with fierce determination.

It was almost as if we'd been here before, in another life, it felt so familiar. I took a sip of wine to swallow down that ridiculous thought, and finally said, "It must be hard moving around all the time, not being able to set down roots."

He shrugged. "You get used to it. I take a few weeks off a year and head home to my little log cabin in the middle of nowhere. Hike up mountains, take the boat out, which is smaller than a Peugeot I might add, and have my fill of all of those domesticated things, enough that I can head back into the fray, anyway."

I searched his features, trying to place him in that setting. I imagined his toasty warm log cabin in the woods somewhere, with the river a startling backdrop to a simple life. I wondered if he lived there alone, and spent those weeks in silence, or if he had a barrage of women who wanted to make home sweet for him.

As if he was reading my mind he said, "It gets lonely sometimes, with only a mournful wolf howl for company, but mostly I relish it. I take enough supplies to last me, and the day is my own. Time slows; it's the most miraculous thing. Like I can just be . . ."

I folded my arms to keep warm, as the sting of cold still reached some visceral part of me, even though I was inside on a spring night. "It sounds to me like you need more of that. If that's the place that rights your wrongs, then you should seek it out more."

"Rights my wrongs?"

"You know, put the world to rights, or whatever the saying is in America." While my understanding of the English language was more than adequate sometimes things were skewed in translation.

"Yes," he agreed, and turned away, abruptly as though he didn't want to pursue that line of conversation. Perhaps he missed home. There were times when I missed the simplicity of the small town my parents lived in where I was raised. That instinctive pull to a place, a feeling, a time where things were easier.

"I don't know what possessed me to walk that way home tonight. I guess I was distracted, and not thinking. If you weren't there . . ." My voice petered off. Why was he always close by?

Wiping his hands on a tea towel, he could read the question in my gaze. "I was hoping to catch you before you locked your shop for the evening. I've been invited to the estate sale in Saint-Tropez and wanted to ask your advice on a few pieces. In my haste to get to you before you closed, I somehow got lost. Those laneways are like a rabbit warren at night-time. Before I turned the corner, I heard a scuffle nearby, and a woman's terrified voice. It wasn't until I pulled him away that I realized it was you. I've never been so grateful to get lost before."

I shuddered at the memory. "Thank God you were. It's like it was fate – one minute earlier and you would have turned that corner. It all happened so fast." I tried to remember where the mugger walked from, which side of the road he was hiding, but couldn't quite remember. "Do you think he was following me?" What if the man was waiting for me? Did he know who I was, and that there was a chance I'd have a stack of cash from the shop? I didn't want to live in fear each time I locked up late at night.

Tristan shook his head. "No, not at all. I think he was a drunk who thought he'd try his luck. You just happened to wander down a badly lit road and he saw an opportunity."

That reminded me. "Will the gendarmes want a statement?"

He clenched his jaw, and averted his eyes. "I gave them my details and they said they'd call if they needed more information."

"He won't get away with it, will he? I mean I'm fine, thankfully it didn't go any further, but I'd hate to think he's there lying in wait for the next girl."

Tristan stood so quickly the table and its contents shimmied. "Trust me, he won't ever touch another girl again." A muscle along his jawline pulsed. "Now," he said brightly, changing the subject along with his demeanor, "French onion soup, that should warm your soul and keep you from worrying."

He took soup bowls from the overhead cupboards, spoons from the cutlery drawer, and napkins from the bureau. "If I didn't know better, Tristan, I'd think you'd snooped around . . ." I laughed as he set the table.

"Of course I did. I'm American. It's what we do. I didn't expect to find every single kitchen accoutrement a person could want."

Laughing, I lifted a palm. "I'm French. It's what we do."

We stared at each other over steaming bowls of aromatic French onion soup, and it struck me this was something I yearned for but didn't admit it even to myself. Someone to break bread with, to sip soup with, in the heat of the kitchen. Someone you could trust, and feel safe with. Someone to laugh and love with. *Someone to laugh and love with?* The poor man had stumbled upon me in the shadows, and stopped to help, that's all. I couldn't shake the feeling that tonight and what might have been was a lesson in learning to really live again. I'd been so desperately heartsick over Joshua that I'd taken pains to protect myself by hiding away, but I couldn't protect myself from everything without living in a bubble. Tonight proved that.

When Tristan relaxed his whole face lit up. He took our bowls to the sink, and continued with the next course. "Trust me, this is going to be the best cheese soufflé you've ever tasted," he said. "You're lucky I'm even letting you watch me make it. It's a secret recipe passed down from generation to generation."

I raised a brow. "Is that so? Tell me about your maman and her secret recipes." I leaned against the counter, eager to hear about his family.

His eyes clouded and the smile disappeared from his face. "OK," he said, "I've fallen at the first hurdle. It's not really a secret recipe, it's stolen from the internet, and claimed as my own with a tweak or two." His voice lifted, becoming too jocular, forced, and I wondered what'd provoked the change. Asking about his maman? From the tense set of his shoulders it was obvious my question had bothered him.

For me, cooking was filled with memories: family celebrations, maman teaching me from a young age how to slice carrots, which herbs matched which dish, as I got older how to perfect the balance of flavors. Each moment in her kitchen had been a part of my education and I treasured them. She'd be cooking dinner for Papa right now, fussing over the wine choice, checking on her bubbling pots. Perhaps he wasn't close to his maman? Maybe family memories conjured up hurt for some reason. While my family weren't all living the same little town anymore, we were still so close, and I felt sorry for people who weren't the same. Family meant everything to me. I didn't press Tristan for any more details in case I cast the evening in a dark cloud, though I was curious.

Forgoing my rules and regulations for one night, and deciding to live in the moment, I turned up the music, and refilled his wineglass. "You have some flour . . ." I touched the spot on his cheek that was dusted white, my finger lingering longer than necessary. What was I doing? I had never been the one to initiate contact with Tristan; it had always been him leaning in for a kiss in greeting or goodbye. I didn't even know this man at all, yet here we were in this domestic scene as if we'd been friends forever.

It was a friendship, I reasoned, and that was OK, wasn't it?

"You just wanted to touch me," he joked.

I rolled my eyes, happy to diffuse the swirling emotions with humor. "It's true. There was no flour there; I made the whole thing up."

Tristan added the cheese to his egg mixture, and folded it through before pouring it slowly into ramekins.

"You'll make someone a good husband one day," I said, watching him. He was paying close attention to each step. That fierce concentration was back. I wondered if that's what he was like in business. Focused, driven, ambitious. But what exactly was his business? Why couldn't he be more upfront? I was the reserved one, yet had shared a number of things with him.

"Are you offering to marry me?" he said arching his brow, which I hastily rewarded with a scoff.

"I haven't tasted it yet." I indicated the soufflés, which I knew would puff up and rise to perfection because he'd followed each step precisely, after I saved him from beating the eggs to death.

"Hold your marriage proposal until then . . ."

He put the ramekins in the oven and moved to sit at the dining room table. "Do you see yourself getting married?" I asked, realizing we'd jumped from light and breezy to the nuts and bolts of real life. After the scare in the laneway, it felt normal to discuss our private lives, as if we'd bonded quicker than usual because of it. Even though Tristan clearly loved cooking, I couldn't see his type settling down, kids clutching his ankles as he baked soufflés, and I was keen to know what he'd say to such a question. I was certain the novelty of a domestic life would wear off if it was routine. I knew men like him. They chased rainbows, not realizing they weren't tangible. Just pretty colors, and hot air. For some reason, Tristan seemed like the type of man who would thrive on excitement, the thrill of the chase, spontaneity.

"Yes." He stretched out his legs and leaned back in the chair, cradling his wineglass in his hand. "I'd like to settle down and have kids, go to their football games or ballet classes . . . the whole shebang. But with my job, it's not that easy. I travel, and haven't really been able to stay in one place for any length of time."

I cocked my head. "Can't you change the way your job works? Set up a base somewhere, employ others to travel? You're in charge aren't you? It's your business. I'm still a little muddled as to what it is you actually *do* for work . . ." I'd thought he was a collector, and then a dealer, and now I wasn't sure he was even *in* the antique trade. Maybe he just liked acquiring beautiful things. Somehow he wangled getting invited to all of the auctions, and that only happened if a person was well known by the establishment. Tristan spoke in riddles, and I never quite got the full story about any aspect of his life. Was it an American quirk? Something I was missing in the language?

"It is a muddling sort of existence, truth be told." He played with the stem of his wineglass. "I answer to a lot of people, so while I'm in charge, I'm only a puppet, really. And the strings get pulled every which way, and I bounce from place to place, fixing things."

"What does that even mean?" I laughed, shaking my head. "That's not an answer."

He nodded, his eyes sparkling with amusement as if he liked toying with me. "I'm a consultant for businesses, which basically means flying around the world and reading their data, finding solutions to problems and moving on again. Truthfully it's not the most exciting job going around. The travel side sounds glam, but aside from that, it's a harried lifestyle, with no routine. Collecting antiques is a way to alleviate the monotony of reading spreadsheets and crunching numbers. They're a memory of each place I've been, and I like beautiful things . . ."

Blushing, I brightened a little. If he wasn't in the antique trade, perhaps his interest in me was genuine. Maybe he was a lonely traveler who just wanted to stop, and take a breath, and buy some treasures to remember his time in the city of love. It *could* happen.

"What about your social life?" I asked. "Do you make friends in each place? It seems a lonely nomadic existence if you don't." Flying around the world had its merits, but not if you were constantly alone with no one to touch base with. Even the most solitary person needed a friend, though Tristan didn't strike me as the solitary type. Maybe he had a girlfriend in each city – who knew?

"My close friends are all in America. I've got a house that's hardly lived in, a car that doesn't get driven, and fish that someone else feeds while I'm away. It's only recently I've realized I want more out of my life. And I don't know how I can fix it." He blushed. "It's hard to explain." A sadness filled his eyes.

"You should do what makes you happy. It's a cliché but life is so short. That's why we French sleep in, have a leisurely breakfast, a longer lunch, wine with most meals – day-to-day life shouldn't be hurried or endured, it should be relished, each and every minute, in case tomorrow never comes."

He sipped his wine, gazing at me over the rim of the glass. "Your life is heaven compared to mine. After this job, things just might change with me."

The room filled with the delicious scent of the soufflé, making my stomach rumble. I cleared my throat hoping to mask the sound.

"Looks like your body is betraying you." He laughed. "There's nothing wrong with focusing on work if it's what you enjoy. You don't have to conform to anyone's idea of what life should be. I know I certainly don't conform, but the difference is, sometimes I wish I did."

"And lose the playboy persona? Never!"

"Yeah, I'd miss my private jet, not to mention my yacht." He smirked at me from over the rim of his wineglass.

I threw my napkin at him. "Yes, of course you would. My swaggering American friend."

He let out a volley of laughter. "If only you knew. Let me seduce you . . . with my cheese soufflé."

"All right, Romeo. Let's see what skills you've got . . . in the kitchen, of course."

Our flirtatious words tumbled out. Instead of blushing, or fumbling, I rolled my eyes and made a joke of it. Innocent fun between two adults.

After he left, I went straight to bed, bone weary from the long day. But the past wouldn't let me forget how a heart can be broken. While Tristan was double-take gorgeous, muscular, with a knee-trembling presence, it wasn't *that* I admired, it was the quiet times, when he wasn't aware I was observing him. The light in his eyes changed color, his features softened, and I could see him as he'd age, and what kind of man he'd be, the type who dreamed of real love, and having a family, lingering over the little things in life – or maybe that was just wishful thinking on my part. Lilou came home, banging the door nosily, and laughing with Henry. I'd completely forgotten about them, and was now grateful they hadn't been home to gatecrash our dinner. I scrunched up the pillow, and closed my eyes with a sigh, as shards of moonlight filtered through the curtains.

Chapter Eleven

After finishing breakfast – framboise pâtisserie and a scalding café noir – I cleared the dishes away, and gave the table a wipe down. I couldn't help smiling as I hummed my way around the apartment. Tristan had made such a mess in the kitchen last night, but not a speck of flour nor a dirty dish remained. A man who cooks *and* cleans . . . *Good with his hands*, Madame Dupont would tease me, waggling her eyebrows suggestively.

Despite worrying I'd be chased around my pillow with nightmares about the attempted mugging, I had slept soundly. A full belly, a night of laughter, and feeling safe with Tristan was the tonic I'd needed. I wasn't sure what I felt, but there was a spark there, and I needed time to think about what it meant.

Wandering to my bedroom, I threw open the cupboard doors and debated what to pack for my overnight visit to an estate sale in Saint-Tropez. Noting the time, I blanched. I had to hurry; my train was scheduled to depart in two hours.

What'd happened to the girl who was always on schedule? I'd dawdled over breakfast earlier this morning enjoying the quiet, lost inside a daydream. Lilou was out at her 'office' working on a new jewelry collection and Henry had raced out the door before I had left my bedroom.

It was nice to have the peace and quiet of my apartment, with only the scent of their half-drunk coffee for company.

I had such a languid morning and didn't keep to my timetable. I caught myself grinning once or twice, remembering the night before with Tristan. Time to snap out of such a girlish reverie and get myself back on track.

Saint-Tropez waited for no one, me included. The salty scent of the Mediterranean never failed to perk me up. I longed to feel the sand under my feet, the breeze in my hair. But first to finishing packing, and quickly. I pulled some fitted dresses from the cupboard, both with wide belts that cinched at the waist. Added some scarves, and gloves in case the occasion called for it. A pair of wedged heels, and some ballet flats, just in case.

My maman said I was an old soul, caught up in a past life, which I'd never been able to shake, from the way I dressed, to my shop, and my dreamy obsession with the past. Maybe she was right. Perhaps that's why I found the loosening of traditions so heartbreaking. It felt like Parisians were racing to become more and more modern, and with it we were closing a door on our history. Memories would be lost for good as generations left this world, if we didn't cherish their possessions and their stories that connected past to present. Sentimental thinking maybe, but that was why I worshipped antiques. Lived and breathed them.

Checking my watch, I sighed, and quickly grabbed a book – Paris Fashion in the 1920s – and stuffed it into my handbag, hurrying from my little apartment.

Excitement coursed through me as I rushed to the station. Waiting for me in Saint-Tropez was a writing hutch formerly owned by Anaïs Nin. If I closed my eyes I could see her as a young woman with her brown wavy hair dusting the tops of her shoulders, as she stared outside, waiting for inspiration to strike. She'd been ahead of her time, and an icon to so many.

Anaïs wrote novels in Paris in the thirties. Since then the hutch had moved from place to place, long after the erotic writer left France for the United States. Luckily it had remained on French soil and had been passed down to other writers who had tenuous links with Anaïs. I had a buyer lined up for it who wrote romance novels, in keeping with the theme that it be used for creative types. Marie, the writer who wanted it, was giddy with the thought, and had sent me photos of her disorderly office with a spot the perfect size for the hutch.

The most rewarding part of my job was seeing a customer's eyes light up when they took delivery, their hands finding their face, mouths hanging open, and the still of the moment, as if time stopped as two worlds collided.

Past and present. Then and now.

Using the hutch, I knew that Marie would have an epiphany, an idea that hauled her from the well of writer's block; was it her subconscious, or was it Anaïs, giving her a ghostly hand up when the words wouldn't flow?

You would have been surprised how many customers called me with shy voices and told me stories about their antique, and how they were visited by ghosts – the former owners checking in. As if every now and then, they traveled back from their fluffy perch in heaven to check their beloved antique was still being cared for.

It was especially true for antiques used by artistic people. They found it that much harder to let go and move to the next place. A violin from the early 1800s was heard during the night, the soft lament of the strings ringing out as the new owner was roused from sleep and followed the sound, catching the curtain shiver once or twice, even though the windows were locked tight, and the door bolted.

Or a typewriter, once used by some robust, whisky-fueled writer, would suddenly come to life, its keys clacking in the dark of midnight. It was just a brief visit to touch base with the precious medium that made their art immortal. The clink of a glass to whisky bottle heard, a goodbye, before silence enveloped the room once more.

Even I'd had a visit. I had an old clock, once owned by a fifties' French actress who was notorious for arriving late on set, and then staying up all hours with whatever beau took her fancy. When I first took the grandfather clock home, it would tick-tock louder at the witching hour, as if it was greeting her, and I wondered if I sprinted to the living room if I'd catch her curvaceous shadow caught in moonlight as she revisited the one thing that always beat her in her life – time. She died tragically, young and beautiful, and in the afterlife chased the thing that had evaded her.

Ghosts visiting their prized possessions? It was all sorts of crazy, and I'd be dubious myself, if I hadn't seen it firsthand. I wondered if Anaïs would be there in spirit today, whispering to me through the ages . . .

Outside, I ticked off a mental list of who'd be there. Tristan. Ombre. Louis from the art preservation society and maybe . . . the thief! It was highly probable the robber would be circling around with us none the wiser. I'd subtly note attendees, and see if I could narrow down any new faces and suspects.

Once boarded, I settled in for the long journey on the TGV, which would take me to Saint Raphael where a car would be waiting to drive me further on to Saint-Tropez. I pressed my face against the glass as the view whipped past. No matter my age, I never quite got over the thrill of a long train ride, my journey to somewhere different an energy boost. As we made our way out of Paris the vista changed to open fields with lush green grass, houses dotting the expanse. The rhythmic rocking of the train lulling me into a daydream. I must have fallen asleep, as when I woke there was a posy of pale pink peonies in my lap. Their perfume wafted up to greet me, so deliciously potent I was sure the whole carriage must have inhaled their sensual scent. With a smile, I opened the note attached.

You're beautiful when you sleep, like something exquisite out of a Pre-Raphaelite painting. I couldn't disturb you . . . Perhaps we can meet again in Saint-Tropez?
Tristan

I darted a glance around the carriage looking for him. He must have boarded without my seeing him, and a flutter of nerves swarmed – and something new, a tingle of anticipation.

After dinner last night, things had changed between us. Nothing was openly admitted, but it was almost tangible, the energy shift. A touch here, a glance there was suddenly loaded with meaning, but neither of us had made a move. I still didn't feel like I knew him well enough, but like Madame Dupont would say, *well enough for what?* It's not like I was going to sign my business over to him. I wasn't going to accept a marriage proposal and try for children. I was simply *entertaining* the idea that maybe, just maybe, I might like to date him in the future.

As the train slowed, I gathered my things ready to depart, hoping to catch sight of him. I dilly-dallied as long as I could on the platform but my car and driver were waiting so I made my way over, suddenly eager as I'd ever been to get to a place.

* * *

The salty Saint-Tropez wind whipped about. I made my way past the marina where boats docked, waves lapped gently against their hulls, the sound like a *shush*, as if even the ocean was saying 'relax'.

The tightness in my shoulders sprang loose, leaving me so relaxed I was almost floppy. The natural beauty of the elements disarmed me. With the wide-open expanses, the varying hues of blue sky and never-ending ocean, it was easy to just be.

I checked into a hotel with a balcony that overlooked the brilliant cobalt water, the ripples glittering bright like diamonds. The room was small and sparse because nothing could compete with the view outside. The only noise came from a cluster of children on the shore, and their happy squeals punctuating the day.

Slipping into wedged heels, I wandered into the bright afternoon, ready to tackle the hilly walk to the estate sale.

Chapter Twelve

Homes were clustered around the bay, their windows reflecting lapping waves. I took a hastily hand-drawn map from my purse, and tried to place where I was. Not far, by the directions.

I trudged upward, the view distracting me from the steep climb.

On the peak of a hill a centuries-old château stood regally; even the battering from the squally sea winds could do nothing to it except tint its walls dusty with salt.

I continued toward it. While it was my business to buy from places like this, sadness always engulfed me that such fine objects had to be sold for whatever reason: death, debt, or just clearing out. For example surely no one wanted to part with the Anaïs Nin hutch, but for some reason this estate was shedding its treasures . . . So while I bought and sold, I did so gently, knowing sometimes the reason was a sad one.

Out of breath from the ascent I reached the top and had a full view of the château. Wrought-iron gates swung wide open, exposing lush green grass. Garden beds were a riot of color with azaleas spilling out in shades of plummy pink. The château itself loomed large, its vastness stealing a chunk of cerulean sky. Bougainvillea climbed up stone walls, shrieking in vibrant fuchsia, their tissue-paper-like petals fluttering as they clung on in the forgiving breeze.

I imagined the interior of the château: the burble of laughter reverberating through cavernous hallways. The echo of voices bouncing off the vaulted ceilings. A grand old ballroom – did it stay silent, its parquetry floors no longer privy to the tap of high heels shoes? What memories must these old walls have absorbed over centuries? I prickled with curiosity, my mind spinning through the decades, picturing the fashion of the mademoiselles changing from generation to generation. Yet still this grand old tribute stood, weathering it all.

In the distance dogs barked, their *woofs* woeful as though they were locked away for the day to save a buyer getting nipped. I made my way along a seashell path, its edges layered with ranunculus. At the door a man wearing a suit gave me a nod. His sunburnt face crinkled into a smile. "Do you have your invitation?" he asked.

I took it from my purse. "Are there many people here?"

"Oui," he said, giving the invite a cursory glance. "Many. Go through. Follow the passageway to the right, and you'll come to a parlor. Drinks and canapés are being served there. If you want to see the lots, they're in the sunroom just beyond that. You have thirty minutes before it commences."

"Merci," I said, taking a program from him. My business instinct kicked in. I wanted that hutch and I only hoped no one would bid me up. You never knew who would turn up for estate sales. The thought made my stomach clench. Punters here were unpredictable; often the only prerequisite for an invite was wealth. It was the type of industry where people came to events like this just to be seen, to splash their cash, and then go on their way. I couldn't do much to protect the pieces, except try to win some and make sure they went to a home where they would be adored.

My wedge heels clacked nosily over the wooden floorboards, which were polished to a shine. When I found the parlor, a waiter approached holding a tray aloft. "Champagne?"

I shook my head. "Non, merci." I'd toast once the Anaïs Nin hutch belonged to me.

I waved to a few people I knew, not stopping to chat, and made my way to the sunroom. As always, my heart lifted when I was surrounded by exquisite antiques. So much history crowded into a space, their futures up in the air, as if they were holding their breath too, awaiting their fate.

It was late afternoon when filmy sunlight filtered in, landing on the furniture like a soft spotlight. Two security guards leaned up against a wall, their arms crossed loosely as they chatted, their voices reverberating in the high-ceilinged room. They nodded to me and resumed their conversation.

There was a huge collection of items: lamps, world globes, a regal four-poster bed with dramatic velvet drapes. Rare books – probably first editions – which were locked in a glass cabinet. I gave them a passing glance; if there was an Anaïs Nin edition it would pair well with the hutch. I ran a finger along the glass: *Stein. Hemingway. F Scott Fitzgerald.* A fine trio of American novelists who'd made Paris their home for at least a little while. If I got the hutch at a reasonable price I vowed to bid on those beauties for my own collection.

The air in the room hummed as I felt the presence of someone behind me, yet I hadn't heard their approach, as noisy as my own had been. I whirled and came face to face with *him*, my heartbeat increasing just a little.

"Thank you for the flowers. Peonies are my favorite." A blush crept up my cheeks, and I frowned at my body betraying me. Game face should've been on, no matter what may have changed between us.

He smiled. "Lucky guess then." Tristan was dressed immaculately, pleasure-seeker style, his blond wavy hair pushed back, the sparkly blue of his eyes a shade lighter than the Mediterranean outside.

"Yes, it was." He'd made a lot of lucky guesses when it came to me.

"Anything take your interest?" I arched a brow.

"Very much," he said, not looking away from me, and I felt a rush of heat flash through me. No matter how hard I tried to switch it off, I couldn't.

Summoning my best poker face I said, "Let me rephrase, anything in the *auction* take your fancy?"

He gave me a slow once-over as he pulled on the length of his tie, and then locked eyes with me again.

"The sketches – I'd like them very much."

The art work he was alluding to were some very rare black and white drawings believed to have been done by Matisse that were discovered recently between the pages of a book. They'd fetch a huge amount of money I was sure. They were achingly beautiful. "I hope you don't have too much competition."

We stood awkwardly, something I doubted happened to him very often. Electricity practically sizzled between us. In order to quash it, I fidgeted with the straps of my handbag, and gave him a jittery smile. "Well, I better find my seat," I eventually managed.

"Sure," he said. "And maybe we can catch up later?"

"Maybe." I had to push every thought out of my head or I couldn't concentrate on my job.

It was getting harder to act noncommittally in his presence. It was as though my body had a mind of its own, and every fiber of me leaned toward him. It had danger written all over it, and yet something in me desired him just the same. I didn't immediately take my seat; instead, I ambled around the lots once more, hoping to see the sketches he wanted, knowing I'd never see them again after today.

I found them in a cabinet under tight lock and key, right next to the security guards. Up close the drawings were even more exquisite than the photos online suggested. Matisse must've been an amazing man to conjure up such beauty with the flick of a pencil. No wonder the halls rang out with more footsteps than usual. Many, I knew, would covet these sketches. Under my lashes, I surveyed the punters, scanning their faces. Some I knew, a few

I didn't. My mind carried to the recent thefts, and in a way I was glad so far only jewelry had been stolen, because losing the Matisse drawings to the black market would be a crime against history.

What would a thief do? Blend in, or stand out? There was little to go on in the newspapers. No physical description, at any rate. All I could do really was secure the hutch for my customer and know it was safe from being shipped elsewhere, and that there was record of its origins . . .

With my head down, staring into the display case, I stood on the shoe of someone and stumbled. "I'm so sorry," I said, glancing at the man, and inhaling sharply. The snake. He always had to edge close to me for the upper hand.

What was he here for today? Unintentionally I glanced in the direction of the hutch, only for the briefest second, but that's all it would take if he was paying attention. I wanted to kick myself. May as well have held up a flashing sign saying BUY THE ANAÏS NIN HUTCH! *Merde!* Had he seen? I wanted to cup my head and weep.

Lesson one when attending an auction: never, ever give away what you're after. Joshua would circle like a shark, if he knew I was after that piece.

"Don't start with me." I gave him a hard stare, and fluttered my hand ushering him on. Then I looked determinedly at a vintage 1920s' Murano glass lamp, hoping he'd think it was that I yearned for and not the hutch. It was a stunning piece of *Italian* craftsmanship . . .

He stepped close. "Anouk, my lovely little Frenchie. How nice to see you here. Anything you want to gift to me today?"

I could have slapped the smarmy expression off his face and be damned by the consequences. "Your time will come, Joshua. Mark my words." But it probably wouldn't. People like him never seemed to get their comeuppance.

"So is that a no to dinner? It would be a shame to waste a night in paradise. My new girl isn't a patch on you in the sack."

My skin crawled with the thought. "You're a pig. Why don't you pack up and leave? Go ruin someone else's life." That he could stare at me like it was a game broke something deep inside me again. I dropped my voice. "You're lucky I don't tell everyone what you did to me. It's only embarrassment that stops me."

"Oh come on, Anouk! You made some bad business choices. There's no point harboring a grudge!" His boyish good looks, and faux affability fooled them all. There was little I could do to stop him without looking like an imbecile myself. Though I wanted to stamp my foot and scream to the world that he was a con man.

"Say one more word and I'll tell them everything, consequences be damned," I bluffed, hoping my steely voice was convincing.

"Try it, Anouk, and you'll look like the scorned woman." His face darkened and he stalked off straight in the direction of the precious hutch. *He saw me glance at it!* I spotted Tristan chatting to the security guards, and a wave of relief washed over me. He hadn't seen me chatting to Joshua. The last thing I wanted was for him to think I needed to be rescued.

Biting back fury, I retreated to the parlor and took a champagne flute from the waiter. I drank it down fast, knowing I was breaking my own cardinal rule, but needing something to stop the staccato beat of my heart. Damn Joshua for upsetting the balance yet again. As a waiter passed, I switched my empty flute for a full one, and knocked it back. The effect of the alcohol was almost instantaneous.

Flushed, and slightly calmer, I teetered back into the sunroom for the auction. My wedged heels clomped noisily, announcing my arrival.

All eyes were on me as I made my way to the seating area. Next time I'd wear ballet flats, and try to blend in. My carefully crafted rules were tumbling down like a house of cards around me as the two American men were each pervading my senses for different reasons. I always prided myself on my poker face, and acting a certain way in business – but the mask was harder to wear these days.

There were no vacant chairs at the front. I was forced to take one at the very back, which meant the auctioneer wouldn't see my eyebrow raise. I'd have to bid glaringly obviously with my numbered paddle, leaving me open to others bidding against me because they'd wonder at my interest in such a piece. Damn it all to hell. This is what I got for losing focus.

The sale began and I cursed myself for drinking champagne in the middle of the day. The drone of the auctioneer was making me sleepy, as sunlight crept in through the windows and landed in soft shards on my face bringing with it more heat.

When the Anaïs Nin hutch was announced, I put my game face on, paying zero attention to the auctioneer, and instead glancing heavenward, as if I was daydreaming, which was easy to do in my post-champagne haze. There were a steady stream of bids for the hutch, and it took all my strength not to wince. The woman beside me leaned over to her friend and said, "I heard Anaïs Nin wrote *Delta of Venus* on that very desk. Can you imagine?" And then she raised her paddle, and joined in. *Merde!*

The bids escalated quickly, the price already double what I had anticipated it would sell for. Eventually bidders dropped off until there was only one man left, Piers, a regular on the South France circuit. Piers had an antique shop in Monaco, where, it was rumored, Grace Kelly had once been a regular customer.

I saw my chance. Piers always stuck to his budget and didn't let emotion get in the way. He was entirely about numbers with no trace of sentimentality. The auctioneer called it, "Going once, going twice, third and final . . ." I raised my paddle, but so did Joshua who was smack bang in the front row. The auctioneer took his bid, and hadn't seen mine so I had to do the unthinkable and stand up to be seen. "New blood," the auctioneer said, unprofessionally, with a smirk. He was probably mentally spending his fatter commission.

Joshua turned and gave me a wolfish grin, before pivoting back and leaving his paddle up signaling he wasn't going to stop.

I kept going way beyond my budget, caught in the cross fire and wanting so badly to win that any rational thinking once again had escaped my mind. Then a cloud pitched the sunny space I'd been standing in into shadow, and that snapped me from my frenzied bidding. *What was I doing?* I'd send myself bankrupt if I kept this up! But it was a matter of principle – I couldn't let that man beat me.

The women beside me kept up their chatter, giggling and pointing. "Isn't he a feast for the eyes," one of them said, indicating Joshua. Her friend concurred. *Really?* My brain was about to explode. "He's actually a fraud," I hissed to their startled faces. They frowned at me, like I was insane. "He's a con man," I said with more force. They tutted and shrunk away from me in their seats, exchanging wide-eyed glances with one another.

Without intending to, my paddle went up once more only to be shot down again by Joshua. Frustration sizzled through me, and I fought hard to sit still in my chair. I wanted to pull the paddle from his hands, and break it in half.

The auction was becoming too tense. I was so far over budget I knew I had to stop. I had to let this go. When I glanced over to clear my sight of Joshua's smug face Tristan caught my eye and gave me a nod, as if asking if I wanted him to bid for me. But I shook my head. I couldn't owe another man, no matter what happened. I would never put myself in that position again.

As I made that heartbreaking vow the auctioneer gestured toward me, asking for one more bid. "Non," I said.

Joshua twisted in his chair, giving me a bawdy wink and I could hear the *ping* as my heart broke in two.

I knew Joshua only bid on the hutch because I wanted it. I'd thought I was almost free of him, but here he was always one step ahead, wanting to torment me for his own pleasure. If everything in life happened for a reason, I'd dearly have liked to know what it was that sent him into my life . . . What lesson could I learn except don't trust anyone ever again? It seemed a somber punishment for no crime except loving the wrong man. With as much grace as possible, I stood, and made my way out of the room, hands shaking with anger.

Outside, birds chirped from their vantage points in leafy trees. I stomped down the path, ruing the day I'd ever laid eyes on him.

I'd just about reached the gate when my arm was pulled back. "Wait," Tristan said.

With a deep breath, I stopped, shading my eyes to glance up at him.

"Let's go have a drink; you look like you could use one. And perhaps you can tell me why that guy is so hell-bent on hurting you." He was too close for comfort. I could smell his aftershave, his minty breath, the powdery scent of soap and even if I didn't need him fighting my battles the thought of opening myself up, admitting to Tristan what had happened in my past was appealing. I hadn't spoken to many people about what had happened with Joshua, and maybe Lilou was right – I should be honest with people who stepped into my life. Hiding behind a smokescreen clearly didn't help matters. The worst that could happen was that Tristan thought I was stupid, and if that was the case, better I find out early.

"Let's go," I said. "I've had enough of that guy to last me a lifetime."

Chapter Thirteen

We made our way through the garden and somehow I managed to walk down the steep hill without toppling forward on my wedged heels.

"I'm fighting the urge to pummel him, and I just want to know the full story," Tristan said, pulling me out of my own thoughts.

"Pummel him? Oh, Tristan, he'd probably love that, so he could sue you for everything you've got. He's one of those men who sees dollar signs in everything." Was Tristan a 'kiss and tell', and 'love them and leave them' type? Or worse, the 'steal from me, and throw it in my face at every opportunity' breed?

"I'm going to freshen up," I said, indicating the street my hotel was on. "There's a bar on the beach if you want to meet there in an hour or so?" I had to give Marie the bad news about the hutch before she heard it elsewhere. And after being so close to Joshua, I had the urge to wash his presence off my skin like he was toxic.

"See you soon," he said, giving me a sweet smile.

Showered, and dressed, business calls made, I left the hotel just as evening fell, and walked along the promenade in the balmy Saint-Tropez air. Moonlight shone through sapphire clouds as the sea reflected its blue to the heavens. The marina was lit up with colorful pink, and green lights, neon shining from the hull of boats, which were big enough to live aboard. Couples meandered along, holding hands, and whispering to each other. Saint-Tropez was the perfect setting for new love.

Perky jazz notes of a band drifted toward me and I followed the sound, coming to a bar by the water. The musicians were playing on a stage set atop the sand, their backdrop the waves rolling in, an accompaniment to their more robust melodies.

On the deck plump white lounges beckoned. As I sank into one a waiter dressed in light blue linen trousers and a white T-shirt materialized and handed me a drinks menu. Being in the French Riviera it would be gauche not to sip on a fruity cocktail and enjoy a few hours beneath the blanket of twinkling stars.

It was only a moment before Tristan joined me, taking the lounge opposite. He was as disarming as the coastline, with his intense blue eyes, and easy smile. The way he held himself so sure, so solidly as if to say: I belong here.

I ordered two Saint-Tropez cocktails, and realized I was doing what Lilou would. Taking charge with no thought to anyone else. "If we're here, I figured . . ."

"The perfect choice." He grinned, and relaxed further into the lounge.

His gaze ran slowly from the roll of my hair, parted to the side, and curled into soft waves, pompadour style, to the curve of my lips, painted scarlet red. "It's like you've stepped out of 1940s' Paris. Your hair, the way you dress. You're not like anyone I've met before."

I went to protest, but he lifted his palm.

"You don't see women who look like they're from a black and white film. You're utterly eye-catching. Even the way you move, it's like you're from another era. Dramatic, feisty, and spellbinding."

My mouth opened and closed, as my mind raced to catch up. In the end, I simply said, "Merci."

"It's true." The strength of his gaze, and the way he spoke about my style had me dumbstruck. Was there more to him than I had first thought? Or was it just a front in an attempt to make the evening livelier, by schmoozing me into bed? Somehow I wasn't so sure he was the love 'em and leave 'em type after last night. He hadn't made a move, instead, cared for me as if I was as fragile as glass. And I just wanted that, that surety, a man who'd make me forget that love was sometimes a battlefield.

Our cocktails arrived and we sipped in silence.

"So what's the deal with that guy?" The look in his eyes was so genuine I felt myself relax.

"Joshua . . . Well, he's a con man to put it bluntly, and I was completely fooled by him. I became quite the laughing stock in Paris, I'm sure." And whether it was the sea, the soft wind ruffling my hair or the fact that I was completely caught off guard by a man listening to me, really listening, I went into detail, leaving nothing out.

And then came to the hard part, the part that hurt the most: "We were going to open a museum, well, *I* thought we were. He even offered to put everything in writing, just in case anything happened between us. He was so fervent about it that I dismissed it. It would have held us up, and I trusted him with every part of me. His dream was my dream; it didn't occur to me not to believe him. Anyway, we needed capital to prove to the financiers that we could make the loan repayments for the stock we'd buy. Joshua told me he had money but it was tied up. Said there was a buyer for a piano I'd just bought that was once owned by French pianist and composer Fania Fénelon. And that it would easily be enough to get us started until he could free up some cash and pay me back. Then we'd just make our loan repayments and everything would work out in the end."

Tristan rubbed his temples, and groaned. "I can see how this ends . . ."

I bit down on my lip, overwhelmed at how gullible I had been. "It wasn't just the piano, he had buyers for all sorts of things, including the painting you were after, and I was so blindsided by him and the idea that my dream was so close to coming true, and we'd be able to share some really rare antiques with the world, and most importantly the stories behind them." I blew out a breath. "I sell antiques for a living, but there's a part of me that feels guilty not everyone can afford them, lay eyes on them, learn about them. This was a chance to fix that. I know there are museums all over Paris, and the world, but this was going to be *different*. Hands-on, classes for people on restoring antique work like paintings, old books. Real musicians playing the instruments and the music their maestros made. Something that would inspire the youth of today to invest their time, learning about history in a fun and interactive way."

The jazz band fell silent as they took a break, and the spell was broken, the confession weighty all of a sudden.

"How did you find out he was up to no good?"

"I found the piano being advertised online at an exclusive American auction house. That and most of the things he'd taken. He assured me it was a mistake but it didn't take long to follow the trail and it led back to him. There'd never been any customers. My world came crashing down. I confronted him once more, and then he vanished. I couldn't get the gendarmes to help; he'd already spoken to them. They showed me a slew of text messages from me, to him, saying he could take those things. They were gifts. I was bitter from the breakup, they said. I couldn't find one trace of any business deal, and that's because he made sure there was none.

"I cursed myself for not putting everything in writing like he'd offered, but I knew it would have been fake anyway. Soon enough the bills mounted up, including the one for the piano, which was missing, and I was in dire trouble. No piano, no loan, and no money back from him. It was a scramble to keep my shop, and I had to ask for a lot of favors in order to survive. I spent almost every waking hour trying to find buyers for what I had, selling some at a loss just to get some cash in. I put off my debtors as long as I could. My friend, Madame Dupont, offered to lend me enough to bail me out, but I couldn't accept. And even now I'm still trying to make my way back into the black. So there you have it."

I cautiously glanced at him, expecting to see him running for the water to get away from me. But he didn't. He just stared at me for an age, like he was trying to make sense of it all. "A dark time for you – it's amazing you managed to hold on."

"I broke all of my rules in order to do so, but I had no choice."

"That's usually the way rules are broken," he said. "Desperation. I still want to pummel him."

"I told you – life on the French antique circuit is never boring." I tried to laugh the seriousness off but Tristan remained silent, steepling his fingers. Waves rolled to shore with more force as the wind picked up.

"A man like that needs to learn a thing or two," he finally said. "Maybe someone needs to show him." His voice was low, almost a growl. It was there again, that fierceness in his eyes, like he had an instinct to save me, as if I couldn't do it myself.

"You don't need to protect me, if that's what you're implying." My thoughts drifted back to the shadowy laneway, the taste of fear on my tongue. "Well, not all the time, anyway."

He gave me a gentle smile. "I know, Anouk. I know you can look after yourself." A wistful expression crossed his face. "But it doesn't stop me wanting to settle scores for you. I can't help it."

I'd never had anyone offer to fight my battles before. In one way it was sweet, knowing someone was instantly on your side, no matter what; on the other, I didn't want to be thought of as someone so delicate they couldn't stand up for themselves. Tristan was the kind of man who righted wrongs, it seemed, and I was grateful he was on my side after my confession, at least.

It was the first time I had told anyone the whole story, every nuance, every bruise on my soul, every bad word uttered and the scars they'd left behind. I didn't see pity in his eyes. Instead there was compassion as he stared deeply, almost hypnotizing me.

I leaned toward him, pulled in by his quiet understanding when a man strolled too close to my lounge and bumped into it, causing me to spill my drink. The spell between us was broken as I searched in vain for a napkin. I looked up to see who was so clumsy, and deflated. He just couldn't let me go. The blood drained from my face and I made a show of waving to a waiter, hoping Tristan would be distracted by me and not recognize Joshua swaggering off with two drinks in hand.

But of course, I underestimated Joshua. It was no fun for him unless he could goad me and watch my crestfallen reaction. He sat at a table just near us, and managed to gloat to his date who'd just taken her seat, "You'll love the hutch I bought for you today, and if you don't we can use it as kindling, easy come, easy go." They both laughed. His eyes flicked to me to make sure I'd registered his ridiculous comment.

Tristan glanced from Joshua to me, and the look on his face was murderous. I shook my head, implying he wasn't worth it. That's exactly what Josh wanted. Attention.

If there's one thing I was certain of when it came to Joshua it was that he'd never burn something he could make money on. It was purely to rub my nose in it, but I refused to take the bait. Stoically, I blinked back tears, and thought of escape.

"So," I said. "Why don't we . . ." Before I could finish Tristan was down on his knees in front of me. Instinctively I knew he was only in that position because he'd seen Joshua and wanted to help me save face. He cupped my cheeks, and lifted a brow like he was asking for permission. Instead of talking I pressed my lips against his, and the world around us faded as I closed my eyes, and let the sensation of someone new pervade me. Tristan's lips were soft against mine.

The power of a first kiss that takes your breath away . . . My heart beat hard and fast with the thrill of him. But was it real? Or a way to make Joshua jealous. At that moment I didn't give a damn, just fell into the sensuousness of it all, breathless, as I kissed him with everything.

After eternity Tristan pulled his lips from mine but stayed close, and gave me a lazy smile. "You sure can kiss," he said, his eyes hooded.

"I'm French. We invented kissing." I laughed, electricity zapping through me, making my voice shaky. From the corner of my eye I could see shock register on Joshua's face. For good measure, I kissed Tristan once more, softly, my lips lingering over his.

Tristan slowly eased himself up. The second round of cocktails arrived, and I held the cool glass against my flushed cheek. Despite the sea breeze, I felt feverish.

"Let's have dinner," he said taking my hand in his. "And get to know each other better."

"That sounds perfect."

After a long, slow dinner of fresh seafood and crisp white wine Tristan walked me back to my hotel. I'd enjoyed sitting under the soft moonlight, finding it surprisingly easy to be with him and talk conspiratorially as I pushed our kisses firmly from my mind.

At my door, he took my hand. "I wish I could stay," he said, his eyes blazing with heat. "But I have some business to attend to in Paris early in the morning."

"I hope you get some sleep on the train." He must've been exhausted from consecutive late nights, and early mornings, both times, because of me.

"I will," he said with a laugh. "Perks of having a job in so many time zones, you learn to snatch sleep whenever you can."

"Well, you're missing out," I said, smiling. "Sunrise in Saint-Tropez is glorious."

"Sunrise in Saint-Tropez with you . . ." He broke off, and shrugged glumly. "I hope we can be friends, Anouk. After . . ."

Friends? Was that code? I blanked my features. "After tonight?"

A shadow crossed his face and for a brief moment he slumped slightly, losing that fluidity that set him apart from other men. "Yes, afterward."

Something had suddenly changed, but I wasn't sure what it

was. Maybe I was so used to second-guessing everything, and it was nothing. Did he regret his spontaneous kiss? "I'm sure we can." I said, brightly, trying to evade any meaningful chat in case he apologized and walked away for good.

He kissed my hand, his lips lingering on my heated skin, and I was glad he had to leave because right then I had the urge to pull him into my hotel room, let any rational thought disappear, and enjoy the moment for what it was. Saint-Tropez had the ability to make you feel like someone completely different, like the rules had been washed away by the waves and anything was possible. Real life seemed so very far away.

"I'll see you in Paris." He took me in his arms, and I closed my eyes. I pressed myself against the warmth of his body and breathed him in. Someone new, someone different. The scent of second chances. He'd passed some test of mine tonight, one that I hadn't even known I'd set, and I only hoped he was as genuine as I thought. "And thanks for a great night. You're beautiful, Anouk, and that makes life so much harder."

I laughed. "Why is that?"

"A beautiful French woman steps into my life, and suddenly Paris is even more appealing. A man can lose his heart in a place like that. Quickly, too."

Was he warning me? Whatever we had would no doubt abruptly end, when his time here was cut short, but should that stop me? If Madame Dupont was here, she'd say *absolutely not, take the risk*! So for once in my life I was going to. Damn it all to hell, if this failed because he was some heartbreaker, if that was the case, I'd never chance it again. But really, lightning didn't strike twice. There could never be another man like Joshua; fate wouldn't allow it.

"Paris is the place for . . . whatever it is. So let's see what happens."

Maybe it was the wine, or the magical night, but I felt brave, and brazen. When we returned to Paris things might seem different without Saint-Tropez's spell. But only time would tell.

He gave me a mournful look. "I really have to go . . . or I'll miss my train."

"I'll see you at the May Gala."

He smiled, and then kissed me once more. My legs went liquid and my pulse sped up. I could still feel his lips against mine as I watched him walk away under the moonlight.

Chapter Fourteen

After a peaceful morning strolling barefoot along the sand, soaking up the sunshine, gazing out into the vast blue of the sea, I headed home from Saint-Tropez refreshed and a little giddy with all that had happened.

By mid-afternoon, I was back in Paris and unpacked, ready to get some work done. The apartment was relatively tidy, and Lilou and her couch surfer were nowhere to be found. Papa's call had obviously worried Lilou enough to make her wary, and clean up after herself for a change. Ironically, I missed her chiming voice, but knew it wouldn't be long until she bounced back into the apartment.

The phone rang, and I dived for it. My heart sank a little when the screen announced the name Dion. And then I felt guilty. Dion was a great friend and colleague. I guess I was hoping it would be Tristan.

"Bonjour, Dion."

"Anouk," he said briskly. "Madame has asked me to call and tell you we'll pick you up for the May Gala."

I fumbled with a response. What if Tristan called and wanted to escort me? Still, I reasoned, I shouldn't drop my friends for a man. That was the first sign of lunacy.

"That would be great, Dion. Thank Madame for me."

"Sure," he said and rang off.

Falling softly onto my chaise, I touched my lips. They still buzzed at the memory of our kisses. Something about Tristan niggled me though. When I replayed our conversations, I thought there was an undercurrent of warning to them. I wanted to be free and breezy about it all, but I couldn't switch the worry off completely.

In the quiet of the apartment, I dozed off as diaphanous rays of sunlight hit my face, warming me from the outside in. When I awoke, Henry the couch surfer was there, bent over my desk, rifling through my paperwork. I held my breath, and watched him for a beat.

What was he doing?

Stacked by my computer were dozens of invoices yet to be paid, and confidential papers in relation to my shop. At first I thought he was just tidying, but he held some of them up, studying them.

"Excuse me," I said, sitting up. "What exactly are you doing?"

He jumped, and put a hand to his chest. "Anouk . . . you startled me."

"Why were you going through my desk?" I kept my voice neutral, but if felt like an invasion of privacy. I hardly knew the guy, and here he was going through my paperwork.

A blush rose up his cheeks. "I wasn't. I was tidying it. Lilou's a tough task master; she told me to dust everything properly, so that's what I'm doing."

I stood, and joined him at the desk, taking my paperwork from his hands, and flicking through it to make sure it was all still there. "You're dusting," I said, incredulous. "With no duster?"

"Well, I was about to grab one. I was just making a neat pile of the papers . . ."

The front door flew open and Lilou sauntered in with a box from the patisserie. "What?" she said glancing from me to Henry, sensing frost in the air. "What's going on?"

I held the paperwork against my chest. "Henry here was rifling through my desk, but claims he was dusting. I'm really not sure what's going on . . . This is what I meant, Lilou, when I told you I like my own space."

Henry shook his head. "I was about to dust, like Lilou told me to do. Like I just said, I was ordering the stacks, and was about to get the feather duster when you jumped to the wrong conclusion."

I narrowed my eyes.

Lilou flounced past and put the patisserie box on the coffee table. "Anouk! Don't be so stuffy. You're acting like Henry is some kind of spy, or something. Who'd want to go through your paperwork for God's sake? It'd be enough to send anyone to sleep. Coffee?" she said, changing the subject.

I breathed out trying to force my body to relax. Maybe I had been quick to assume he was doing the wrong thing. I was sensitive about anyone seeing my sales figures, and stock tables. "OK, I'm sorry, Henry. Just don't tidy my things in future," I said. "My desk, my bedroom, my bookshelves are fine to be left. I have a system. Just clean up after yourselves, that's all I ask."

Henry had his hands raised in surrender and had such a guileless expression on his face I wondered if I'd overreacted. But he hadn't been ordering the paperwork, I was sure he was flicking slowly through each invoice, reading them. Curious perhaps, and nothing sinister? Still, it struck me as odd . . .

"Sorry, Anouk. I was only trying to help."

I nodded and stalked off to my room, hiding the paperwork in a drawer. Amongst the invoices were letters from debt collection agencies, people who were still chasing me for unpaid bills, and on many of the invoices was red writing that shrieked *final warning*. I'd paid as many as I could, and I just needed another couple of windfalls to settle the rest. Some jewelry collections that were unique, and I could find a buyer for, someone I trusted. I didn't want anyone, especially a stranger, to know my business.

Evening fell and Lilou knocked on my door, peeking her head

inside my room. "You've been at it for ages." She motioned to my laptop, which sat open, the screen casting a white glow over me. "Come and have something to eat. I've got a box full of delicious morsels from Jean Claude's Patisserie."

My mouth watered at the thought of his little edible pieces of artwork.

"Come on," she wheedled. "There's a coffee and hazelnut dacquoise with your name all over it."

"Hazelnut – you're sure?" I asked. She knew my weaknesses all right.

She waggled her eyebrows. "I'm sure. There's two in fact. So let's make a pot of coffee to accompany our cake binge, yes? And you can tell me what's really bothering you today, because I'm sure it's not just Henry shuffling a pile of dusty paperwork . . ."

Shimmying from the bed, I closed my laptop and tucked it into a drawer. Lilou was a lot more prescient all of sudden, and the thought gave me pause. Perhaps my little sister wasn't the hapless girl about town I mistook her for these days. If only that would filter into her work life.

"I'm fine," I said, following her to the kitchen. The day had dissolved into night; outside streetlights glowed yellow against the inky backdrop of evening. I'd been so caught up in hunting auctions online, I hadn't stopped to have dinner, never mind lunch. Suddenly I was ravenous.

Boiling water for coffee, and getting our cups ready, Lilou said, "You aren't yourself today, Anouk. Is it the shop?"

I helped make coffee, and got some plates from the cupboard. Henry was nowhere to be found. I was glad for the sisterly privacy. Lilou didn't know too much about the financial debt I faced. Firstly, I hadn't wanted to burden her, and secondly, I didn't think she'd understand the magnitude of it anyway. At the time when she'd asked, I brushed it off, saying it was a bump in the road, and I'd just work harder and everything would be OK.

"It's not the shop, not really." We sat at the table with the box of petit fours between us. "I want to throw caution to the wind, live for the moment, be free of the things that hold me back, but I just don't know how to do it. I'm always thinking of what could go wrong, or if I'll be hurt again, and no matter what, I can't switch that off. It's exhausting."

She poured two steaming cups of strong coffee. "Is this with a guy, or business?"

"It's a bit of both." I expected her to grill me for intimate details but she didn't. Instead, she took her time stirring milk into her coffee.

"It's like anything, Anouk. It just takes practice. The longer you try something the more natural it will become. So you might find it hard to switch off all that angst now, but eventually it will come naturally if you keep at it. I know the whole Joshua saga from reading your diary don't forget, but letting him dictate the course of your life in this way means he wins, yet again."

I frowned. "He's not dictating my life at all . . ."

She sighed. "He is, because you're letting what he did stop you from living now. Whether you realize it, you've changed, in such a huge way. Every decision is now fretted over, because of money, trust, and every other niggle you can think of. I know he hurt you emotionally and I'm guessing financially, but he'll keep hurting you if you base your choices on what he did. Not everyone is like that. In fact, most people aren't."

Tears stung my eyes. I'd thought I'd hidden my innermost feelings well. To hear her say I'd changed so dramatically hurt a part of my soul, I really hadn't thought it was obvious to anyone. Instead of acting bereft I always shrugged it off to people as a lesson learned. Maybe I had tunnel vision . . .

"What if I let all my fears go, though, and it happens again? I don't think I can handle that."

"But what if it doesn't happen again? What if you find love and even cloudy days seem sunny? Can't you take a chance, and put it all down to experience?"

139

I sipped my coffee, amazed at the change in my sister. This was a girl who took off when the wind blew, who loved someone new every third week. "I suppose I could try," I said, feeling suddenly like a teenager in the throes of puppy love. "What's the worst that could happen?"

Chapter Fifteen

The evening of the May Gala arrived. It was being held at Hôtel d'Évreux, a private mansion by the Place Vendôme. In the daytime the salon was bathed in light from its domed glass ceiling, but tonight we'd be showered with the spectacle of the constellations in the night sky.

Nervously, I pulled at the ruching of my red satin gown to center it, and glanced at my reflection. The strapless dress with a love-heart bust exposed my décolletage, before draping around the middle, and cascading to the floor. I slipped on heels, and clipped on a pair of ruby raindrop earrings, deciding against the matching necklace; because the gown was formal enough it didn't need accessorizing.

There was a knock at the door. With one final look, I spritzed on some perfume and hurried to answer it.

"Bonsoir, Dion. You look handsome!" He gave me a meek smile and I grinned back.

"Madame Dupont is in the car. She insisted I wear the full tux, flower and all. I really do feel like a penguin. How are you supposed to walk casually all bundled up like this?" he lamented, but his eyes shone with happiness.

Dion was transformed with his newly shaved face, a haircut,

and brand new suit that looked like it had been tailored especially for him. Shiny black shoes and a pink peony finished off the outfit. "She was right, you look amazing, very suave."

He ducked his head, embarrassed to be the center of attention. "Shall we?" he asked.

"We shall." He took my elbow and we made our way slowly down the stairs.

In the balmy evening, he opened the door to the limousine, and gestured for me to hop in first. I gave Madame Dupont a cheery wave.

She practically shone in the dark of the limo, wearing a midnight blue satin dress complete with diamond earrings and tiara. "You're the picture of elegance, Anouk. Ravishing, if I do say so myself."

"Likewise, Madame. You're breathtaking in blue."

I sat down and took a proffered flute of champagne, and Dion went to the front of the car to drive.

She waggled her eyebrows. "I hear that Saint-Tropez was more about a certain man, than antiques. Does the grapevine lie?"

I blushed to the roots of my hair. Public displays of affection were usually reserved for teens. And there we'd been kissing by the bar on the beach when I knew full well half the circuit would've seen.

Damn the gorgeous man for making the world around me vanish.

"There may have been a few kisses stolen, and that is it. Oh, look, we're here." I flashed her a smile thanking the Parisian traffic for being smooth and easy for once. Madame Dupont couldn't grill me now, because we'd have to circulate with other guests and she would be rushed by starry-eyed people hoping to be in her spotlight.

"You little minx," she said, laughing. "I'll meet you in there. This no-smoking inside thing is so tedious. I'll get my nicotine fix and come find you."

I watched Dion lean over to light Madame's cigarette and smiled as I took the invitation from my red clutch to hand to the security guard at the door. Inside clusters of people stood chatting, their voices reverberating in the cavernous room.

A waiter approached with a tray of champagne and I took one, thanking him.

"A vision in red," a voice whispered, sending a thrill down my spine. "Care to dance?" Tristan said circling slowly around and stopping in front of me. With his blond hair, and bright blue eyes, he stood out from the other men in the room, who all blended into one in their black suits with their dark hair.

I usually held up a wall at these events, discussing the latest auctions and networking until it was an acceptable time to leave. But this dazzling man had other ideas, and with him staring deeply into my eyes, I thought the hell with it. "Let's dance." I drank my champagne in one mouthful, enjoying the effervescence as it flowed through me.

He grinned, and took my hand, leading me to the dance floor where couples swayed to the sounds of a piano. Tristan pulled my body tight against his, and wrapped an arm protectively around my back.

"I haven't been able to stop thinking about you," he said.

"Oh?" I said, enjoying the feeling of him pressed against me.

"Oh is right." He laughed. "I'd like to spend more time with you."

"Sure," I said, feeling as light as air. "But promise me one thing." I gazed up at him starry-eyed. "Promise me you're trust-worthy." I surveyed him closely for a tic that would give him away, a muscle tensing in his jaw, or his gaze flickering, but his expression stayed the same.

"That snake really did a number on you. I can see why you're hesitant," he murmured and leaned forward to capture my lips in a kiss.

"Let's not spoil the night talking about him."

The room and its inhabitants faded away as we waltzed our way through each song, murmuring and staring at each other. I wanted the night to go forever, a first for me at one of these events.

"Sometimes," Tristan said, "I want to gather you up and escape with you. Would you come?" he asked.

"And where would we go?"

"Somewhere far away where no one could find us."

I lifted a brow. "Your log cabin in the woods?"

"Yes. Why not? We could fish for our dinner. And eat by the fire . . ."

The image of such a place made me woozy. I was a homebody, there was no question about that, and I liked the vision of the secluded cabin in the woods, and the couple inside . . .

"Sure," I said, enjoying the flirtation. "I'd love to hide out with you for a little while." Even saying such a thing sent shivers of desire down the length of me. What could be nicer than getting to know someone in their world, with only nature for company?

"Great," he said, pulling me closer, and dropping his face close to mine. "We might just do that. Soon."

Were we pretending? Our lives were so very different and no matter what, his job would beckon soon, and he'd fly away. Was he alluding to a long-distance romance, where we met at his cabin, and stole some time? Or was it just a fairy tale? Whatever it was, for that moment, I imagined us in that place, with a roaring fire, as we lay entwined, satiated after a long day and being together. I was gone, I knew it then. I wanted the fairy tale to come true.

It was only much later, once I was home in bed, still dizzy from the music, champagne and his closeness that I realized he hadn't answered my question about being able to trust him. He'd deflected it to Joshua. Was that his protective instinct or something more?

Chapter Sixteen

The end of the week crept closer and with it the hold on my composure. Tristan had canceled our first official date the night before, begging off for work, which I understood. I'd been so busy sourcing stock for the shop, I hadn't had a moment to myself either and was looking forward to the empty morning stretching out in front of me. Until I wandered into the kitchen and found it in disarray once more. Even the threat about telling Papa didn't work on Lilou anymore. She was back to being a complete slob around the apartment, claiming she was working late, and needed to sleep in, so there wasn't time left to clean.

Padding through the kitchen, my patience was taut like a rubber band about to snap, as I picked up dirty plates and set them by the sink, tossed empty bottles into a bag, wiped down the wineglass-ringed bench. Grabbing a notepad, I scrawled a message, highlighting tasks for them to do with a threat about immediate eviction if they didn't. I felt like the wicked stepsister. The killjoy, as Lilou dubbed me. Guilt and Lilou went hand in hand, and I envied her the younger sister status, her ability to float through life without any responsibility.

With a sigh, I scrunched my eyes closed to walk past the rest of the mess, and took the newspaper and a coffee to the balcony.

Golden rays of sun beat down in the tranquil light of dawn. Paris was silent bar the faint echoes of birds, somewhere off in the distance as they chirped to one another about the coming day. Soon, the boulevards would come alive: car doors slamming shut, shutters banging open, children ambling to school, as the town woke together as if timed. But for now, it was just me and the birds and I relished the peace.

After a sip of café noisette, a rich espresso with a splash of milk, I flicked open the paper. More bad news.

The Postcard Bandit Strikes Again!

Overnight the Dopellier Auction House was robbed, the Postcard Bandit claiming responsibility once more. Gendarmes say the bandit is getting more brazen. The postcard inscription taunted gendarmes about their lack of evidence, and was signed with a letter T. A first they say, as previous postcards have had no hint of the author. Investigators say the thefts are likely to escalate as he gains notoriety. Anyone with information is urged to contact their local station.

I went on to read the rest of the article, a heavy sensation settling in my belly.

It couldn't be? It just couldn't. I'd already jumped to conclusions with Madame Dupont before, it was silly to even think of it again. But gulping back sudden anxiety I had to admit it was possible. And with my track record for dating bad guys, it was more than plausible.

Signed with the letter T?

Tristan Black?

It couldn't be him. But he'd canceled our date the night before simply because of . . . work. Not to go and rob an auction house! It's not like he'd been in Sorrento for the first spate of thefts. He would have caught my eye for sure. And then I remembered, our first chance meeting . . .

I closed my eyes and tried to recall the conversation. *I've just been to Italy and nothing there compares to what I've seen here today . . . It's been a revelation.* Color flooded my cheeks. I'd thought he been flirting with me, but what if he was comparing the jewelry from both countries? He had been to Italy! Had he been playing me like a song this entire time, and I'd hummed along, just as he'd expected? It did seem suspicious he'd arrived in Paris just as a robbery happened.

But wouldn't it be obvious it was him? Thieves would be more thief-like . . . Cagey, narrow-eyed, with a pencil mustache and a bag of loot on their shoulder even.

I tried to calm my erratic heartbeat and focus. Was Tristan capable of such a thing? I didn't know him well enough but this kind of thievery would have to be meticulously planned, and executed. Was he a cunning cat burglar? Or was I making excuses, because deep down I felt something for him already, and I was scared to get hurt? Was that what all the talk was at the gala? Escaping with me somewhere secluded . . .? Somewhere no one would find us? I gulped back worry.

What were the facts and what did I know about him? For one thing, he was new to the Paris antique world. No one on the circuit knew him, yet he'd been invited to prestigious events including the May Gala. He had been in Italy when the first thefts occurred. Then he canceled our date on the very night a museum was robbed . . .

My mind whirled. It was almost too farfetched, like something out of a Hollywood blockbuster movie, and yet, he'd waltzed in with his story set, winning me over with the saving bid on the cello . . . Did he have me lined up from the very get-go? Why would he bid or even attend auctions? Surely the criminal would prefer to stay in the shadows?

I laughed at my stupidity.

He was hiding in plain sight!

Of course he'd bid on things so they didn't suspect it was him, the overconfident newcomer. And that's why he flirted with me. *No,* they'd say, *he's very friendly with eccentric Anouk.* All done to blend in and to make it seem like he was one of us, when in fact he was doing reconnaissance! Was I the most gullible person around? He went straight for the only woman at the auction, and I played right into his hands . . .

I blew out my cheeks, cradling my head to stop the throbbing. I'd go to the gendarmes! Tell them everything. But what exactly was that? They'd laugh me out the door – *he's been to Italy!* Half the circuit traveled to Italy to attend auctions. The Parisian gendarmes knew me well and would fob me off just like before.

Sipping my coffee, I mulled over the possibilities. There had to be a way to get him to talk. It would only be a matter of time before he slipped up, especially if I asked the right questions, in an innocent, guileless way. He wouldn't have a clue I suspected him. But then what? Get him locked up? When I thought of him cooking in my kitchen, the way he pervaded my senses, could I do that? He saved me from a mugger, throwing himself into the fray without a second thought!

But.

Justice should prevail. For the sake of our prized antiques I'd catch him out. A perverse thrill ran through me. Espionage – who would have thought I'd be caught up in something like this? It wouldn't hurt to grill him softly by the playing the ingénue. A slow smirk settled across my face. No longer would men make a mockery of me! Leaning back in my chair, I played out the scene in my mind, only to be interrupted by the loud yawns of Lilou who walked out to meet me on the balcony with Henry's arms wrapped around her middle, squid-like. "Bonjour," she said sleepily.

"You're up early." Of all the mornings for her to be awake!

"Henry's going for a job interview."

The headline screamed from the page, catching Henry's attention, so I snapped it closed.

Lilou pulled the paper from my hands. "Actually, he'll need this."

I snatched it back. "There's a shop downstairs that sells newspapers." Annoyance flashed through me. My peace had been interrupted, first with the mess in my beloved apartment and now with my vow to catch a thief. There was a lot to consider this sunny morning.

"Anouk." Lilou put her hands on her hips and tried to stare me down. "It's only a newspaper."

"Exactly, and for a Euro you can be the proud owner of your very own."

She gave me a cheeky grin and stole my coffee, raising it in the air as if she was toasting, before taking a deep drink. "Delicious."

I crossed my arms and glared at her. "It's time we had that talk. You know the one where you start doing as I say or I *will* call Papa and tell him everything . . ." The words had no sooner left my lips when the front door swung open and the sound of my maman's raised voice carried out to the balcony. Maman? She usually avoided Paris like so many in her little village did. The constant motion in the city made her dizzy.

I stood at the balcony threshold, as Maman stormed through the living room.

"Anouk! Lilou!" She threw her handbag on the chaise. "ANOUK! LILOU!" she shrieked, gazing wildly around the room.

"Out here, Maman!" I said. Huffing, she followed my voice, oblivious to the fact we had all watched her spectacular entrance.

"Oh God, they must've found out about the course," Lilou hissed. "Lie, lie, lie and I'll make it up to you."

But how? Papa would be furious. "I'll try but this is your last chance *and* you have to clean up!" I whispered back. Henry shuffled his feet and shoved his hands deep in his pockets, giving me an innocuous smile.

Wide-eyed Lilou nodded. "Anything, yes."

Maman joined us outside, her face rosy red with exertion.

"Maman," I said, suddenly fearful when Papa wasn't following a few steps behind like normal. "What is it? Where's Papa? Is he OK?"

She snatched the coffee cup from Lilou, which gave me an enormous amount of pleasure, and drank it in one gulp, smacking her lips, and saying belligerently, "*Your papa?* Your papa is fine! Just like always." Lilou visibly relaxed, enjoying the reprieve.

She sat heavily, resting her hands on her belly.

"OK-K-K. So where is he?" I asked. Maman didn't travel alone. And she didn't drive. She relied on Papa for transport and on the odd occasion when they deigned to visit Paris they caught the train. They lived in a small village by the coast, and preferred the routine of their quiet, orderly lives. We usually visited them and not the other way around.

My maman pursed her lips, and breathed heavily like she was trying to stop herself from exploding. "He's at home! Feet up, TV blaring, with a big plate of croissants in front of him." She wrinkled her nose, disgusted by the thought, but the picture she painted sounded just like Papa. There was nothing new with that scenario.

"What's wrong with that?" I asked, as I busied myself pouring more coffee. "You never travel without each other. What's going on?

She huffed. "I'll tell you what's going on . . . I've left the fool, that's what!"

My jaw fell open. "You've . . . left him? As in left him at home, or *left left him.*"

With a tut she threw her hands in the air. "Where do you get these phrases from, Anouk? I didn't scrimp and save for school for you to speak like a simpleton! 'Left left him', if that's the only vocabulary you have!"

I blanched. My maman was usually poised, reserved, the quiet one in our family. This screeching woman was a million miles away from that. I struggled to comprehend what had angered her enough to walk out. I'd always looked up to my parents, put their love on a pedestal, because it had lasted so long, and was strong, or so I'd thought.

"You've obviously had a shock, Maman. We're here to listen . . ." Lilou said, her voice syrupy, earning herself an arm rub from Maman. I shot Lilou a glare. She volleyed back a smirk. Even as adults we sometimes fell into habits from childhood.

"Get me a vin rouge," she said to Lilou. "And then I can tell you."

"Maman! It's not even nine yet!" I said, scandalized.

"Excusez-moi?" She threw me a challenging glare. "Who is the parent here?"

I bit my tongue. "Well . . . you don't normally drink alcohol."

She snorted. "I don't normally do anything, and *that* my belle fille is going to change."

I tugged Lilou's arm and dragged her into the kitchen. We hissed back and forth finally coming up with a plan.

"Make sure she hasn't had some kind of nervous breakdown," Lilou whispered.

Could she have? "Oui, now go, so I can talk quietly to her and make her see it's not the time to drink red wine!"

"If she wants wine, give her wine. It's her life." She shrugged as if it was perfectly acceptable to drink wine at breakfast time.

I shook my head. "Go!"

She shepherded Henry to the bistro downstairs but came back a minute later, with her hand out. Sighing, I threw some crumpled Euros at her. "Just go, and let me speak to Maman!"

Lilou laughed. "OK, OK. But don't try and fix everything for her. Just listen."

I held in a sigh. "What would you know?"

Maman bellowed for me, so I hastily shut the door on Lilou's smug face.

I raced back outside to Maman who'd kept up a one-way conversation, muttering and cursing even though no one was listening. Where had my diminutive mother gone? She wasn't one to use bad language – the only thing I'd ever heard her mutter under her breath was a song.

"Forty years! Forty long years I've given that man and for what? Make lunch, make dinner, make the midnight snack! My soup is too hot, my soup is too cold! My soup isn't salty enough!"

I sat quickly and picked up the coffee cup, and handed it over to her again, hoping the caffeine would calm her down, not hype her up anymore. And prayed she'd forget about drinking wine! My maman was usually so staid, alcohol didn't figure into her life, unless it was one glass with dinner.

"He does love his food just so. But he's always been that way, Maman," I said softly. My papa was finicky when it came to meals. Everything had to be laid out on a blindingly white tablecloth, the cutlery shined, his plate warmed, and Maman would serve it up to him like a waitress, asking if it was the right temperature, whether it needed more pepper, if he'd like vin rouge, or vin blanc. I could totally understand if she felt unappreciated but I'd always thought she enjoyed the process.

Maman was always found with her nose pressed in a recipe book, hunting for new ideas. When I phoned home every Sunday, she peppered me with questions about the latest spring menus in bistros around Paris, or would ask me to hunt for hard-to-source ingredients and post them to her.

"I shouldn't have wasted my life with him." Her eyes pooled – she was sincerely hurt. I could count on one hand the amount of times I'd seen my maman cry, and I'd never have guessed it would be over my papa.

She'd never uttered a bad word about him, even on those occasions when he deserved it. So fiercely loyal, often telling us to listen to his wisdom, when we thought he was anything but wise. I waited for her to continue, noting the worry lines between her eyes, the gray pallor of her skin.

"Start from the beginning, Maman, and tell me what's made you so unhappy. It's not just the soup, is it?"

"The soup, the cutlery, the washing up! It's all of it!" She leaned back sending an exaggerated sigh to the heavens. "I won't be a doormat any longer for that selfish excuse for a man!" If their love was built on wobbly foundations, what hope did the rest of us have? A part of me deflated. I hadn't seen this coming, and I felt like the most self-absorbed daughter.

My papa was traditional, and believed women should settle down, have babies, keep house. It was like talking to a rock when we tried to explain things had changed, and no one thought like that anymore. He didn't leave his little village often, and had no real idea how much the world had progressed, because he didn't listen to any opinion other than his own. He was set in his ways, which is why I let Lilou have some freedom here. It had been stifling living under his rule as a teenager; as an adult it would be much worse.

Maman had always backed up Papa, and said he knew best. Had she just been going through the motions every day, desperately unhappy this whole time? The thought was enough to make me doubt their love, and I hoped it wasn't so.

"Maman . . ." For the first time in my life, I was at a loss for words.

She shrugged at my confusion and looked past me. "The only thing that man loves me for is the dish of food I place in front of him." She mimicked placing a plate down, and then acting Papa's part, rubbing his voluminous belly and slapping his suspenders. "I'm a servant." Her voice was so full of regret, it brought a tear to my eye. "My life consists of menial tasks and not once does he help or ask me what *I* want."

Outwardly Maman seemed to relish doing her home tasks from sewing curtains to baking citron tarts or pottering around their little vegetable patch. I wondered if Papa was just as shocked at her outburst as I was, if she actually told him how she was feeling. I wouldn't have put it past her just to pick up a bag and waltz out the door in an effort to show him she was indeed invisible to him. "But he does love you, Maman. You know that surely?"

She harrumphed. "He loves me, oh yes he does, he loves me on macaron Mondays and even more on boeuf bourguignon Thursdays! But wait . . . he's even more passionate about chicken fricassee Fridays!" Her palm came down hard on the table, making the cups jump and clink together. My arm shot out for a favorite crystal vase, which teetered over, water spilling out and drowning my newspaper. I righted the vase and tried my best to flick the remaining droplets off the print, but it was no use, the ink blurred.

"Did you speak to Papa about how you feel?" I broached gently. He was a man of few words but he *loved* her, I was sure of that, and no matter what, would hate to see her upset.

"Why do you think I'm here?" She narrowed her eyes, and gave me that same steely glare. "I said to him: I'm not a doormat! I won't be swept under the carpet, non, non, non! And do you know what he said?" She put her hands on her hips. "He said, what's for lunch! See? Do you *see*, belle fille? He only hears me when I'm talking about food!"

What a mess. Food ruled for my hardworking papa. He was a tall, broad man with a penchant for locally made wine, and lots of hearty French dishes. His life was spent outdoors as a stone-mason, a physical job that left him weary come home time, and it's how he justified such a huge appetite, though these days he mainly supervised his employees. "Maybe he didn't hear you? I can't imagine Papa ignoring . . ."

"Oh he heard me. He heard me when I took his lunch and threw it outside for the birds. *Then* he understood just fine." She took a deep, steadying breath. "So, I'm here now, and my new life will begin in earnest. I won't have my hands and feet chained to the kitchen anymore, unless I choose to cook."

I admired her for taking a stand if things had gotten so bad. "OK, a mini break, just what the doctor ordered." Maybe some time apart to cool their heels would be the thing that would help glue them back together. "What will you do?"

"I'm going to find my youth, belle. I'll wander the streets of Paris. I'll have lunch at some fancy bistro. Every minute of the day will be mine to do as I please."

I stood, giving her a kiss on the cheek. My once silent apartment was full to bursting and I wondered how I'd cope. At least with Maman here I could hopefully convince Lilou to be honest with Papa or attend the course he was paying for. She'd be on her best behavior with Maman loitering and that would free me up from worrying about her for a while.

"I have to go to work. Will you be all right on your own?"

She put her feet up on my seat, and angled her face to the sun. "Parfait," she said. "Today is the first day of the rest of my life."

I thought of Papa sitting in the lonely little house by himself. He'd be lost without Maman, and probably not able to do any simple tasks like cook meals for himself, because she'd always handled it all. Then I smiled sadly. Perhaps it would do him good to see how much work Maman did around the house. If she wasn't there it would mount up, and he'd appreciate her more. Still, I had to check he was OK. Once I was up the road a way, I pulled out my cell phone and called him.

"Bonjour, Anouk," he said, without his usual boom.

"Papa, what's going on?"

"Is she there?"

"Oui, she's upset."

"Did she tell you?" He grumbled something inaudible. "She threw my lunch outside! For the birds!"

I swallowed a smile. Perhaps Maman was right, he only listened when it came to food. "I know, Papa, but she feels invisible. She tried to talk to you, but you didn't pay any attention."

He sighed. I could picture him sitting by the kitchen window, where the phone hung on the wall like it had done for decades. "I was half-listening," he said, as if that was enough. "She talks to herself all the time! I didn't know she was upset with me. I still don't know what I've done. We sit together breakfast, lunch, and dinner, how can that make her invisible – *she's right across the table from me!* When's she coming home?"

"I don't think she is, Papa," I said softly. "Maybe you should ring her at my apartment? Say sorry?"

"Sorry for what?" He was truly puzzled by her absence and expected her to return home without any discussion.

"Papa! She feels like a slave. Like you don't care about her unless she's holding a plate of food. Can you try to understand?"

He tutted. "Anouk, your maman's job is inside the home! I make the money and she makes dinner! It's the way it's always been. Why should I apologize? Now I'll have to work and come home and cook. And clean! I suppose I'll have to go to the market for food! Tend the vegetable patch." He let out an incredulous grunt.

Poor Papa, he was stuck in another era where men ruled the roost. He had no idea how much he was living in the dark ages. Someone, *me* most likely, was going to have to drag him into the future. "So? Most people go to work and then come home and do all of that and more. I think you should ring her and say sorry. And then I think you should try to woo her back with a little romance."

He scoffed. "I'm sixty, Anouk, not sixteen! We've always lived this way; I don't see why anything should change."

Obstinate as expected! "Can you just think about it? Like would it kill you to stand side by side and help Maman cook at nights? Dry the odd dish or two? You could talk and *listen* to one another."

"The world has gone mad," he said sadly. "She'll see sense, eventually. I'm not saying sorry, because I've done nothing to warrant this."

"You're a stubborn fool, Papa!" My patience was stretched once more. Why couldn't he at least *try*?

"You'll see, Anouk. She'll get bored and come home asking for forgiveness. In the meantime, I'll cook, clean, iron, I'll show her how easy her life is by doing it all."

"You do that, Papa. I have to go. Keep well, and I'll call you soon." With his high domestic standards, there was no way he'd be able to cook and keep house like Maman did. She worked non-stop each day, cleaning the house from top to bottom, tended the vegetable patch, and the fruit trees, and cooked three proper meals a day.

A week without Maman and he'd be more malleable to the idea of helping out more. While he still worked as a stonemason, young laborers did the heavy lifting for him these days, and Papa spent a fair chunk of the day at home, getting under Maman's feet.

While he wasn't into romance per se, thinking it was a young person's game, he could still do something simple like prepare a candlelit dinner, or even just join her to pull weeds in the soft sun. He would still grumble and mutter to save his pride, but I was certain I could convince him, even if it took a week worth of phone calls. While it had been a shock seeing Maman rant and rave, I was sympathetic to her cause. With this drama unfolding at least he hadn't asked after Lilou, a small mercy.

Chapter Seventeen

Sometimes when I arrived in the morning I would pause and stare at the front of my little antique shop, likening it to something out of a vintage poster; the façade faded pastel pink, with a warped wooden planter box full of fruity-scented peach roses.

I fumbled with my keys as Oceane from *Once Upon A Time* strode briskly over from the direction of the little bookshop where she worked. Her cropped blonde hair stood up, windblown from the walk. As always her classic features drew the eye. She had high cheekbones and full lips, with intense icy blue eyes. She caught the attention of men and women alike, but had no notion of it, which made her even more beguiling.

When she caught sight of me her face split into a grin. "Bonjour!"

"Bonjour," I replied. "You look like you're in a hurry." Oceane never walked when she could march. She was the kind of person who'd make you dizzy if you tried to keep up with her. She was a powerhouse of energy, and with her long legs it was impossible to match her pace unless you jogged, which of course, I just didn't do.

She shook her head, her blonde hair catching in the bright sunlight. "Non, non. I'm just wasting time before I start work."

I unlocked the door. The shadowy shop always had the ability to loosen tension in my body, as if being surrounded by tokens from the past grounded me. The same smell greeted me, like it did every day, a mix of old and new, as antiques fought the fresh flowers for space in the dusty, musty, floral-scented air. Oceane was the perfect customer to wander in: someone newly in love, flushed and hopeful with the future . . . someone who reminded me it was possible. After my traitorous thoughts about Tristan and my maman's sudden appearance and shocking declarations, my ideals were up in the air.

Oceane surveyed a display case by the cash register. Above her hung a variety of vintage parasols. A soft breeze blew in from the open door, catching them. They swung lazily back and forth. Dust motes danced from the gaggle, raining down on Oceane, making her sneeze. She craned her neck upward and laughed, touching the point of a pale ginger parasol made from fine cotton. "They don't make them like that anymore," she said.

"No, they don't." Above, they swayed like they wanted attention, a moment of adoration for their ruffled former loveliness, one an ivory antique lace discolored over the years to eggshell leaving it swollen as if it'd absorbed memories like pollen floating through the air. Another ruby satin, whisper thin, like parchment, so delicate I wondered if it would disintegrate if it was ever opened again.

"We should bring them back in fashion," she said with a gleam in her eye. If Oceane paraded around town with something unique, it wouldn't be long until her posse of friends followed suit. "I'll take the green one." The parasol in question was made from thick brocade, its green like the flesh of an avocado. Emerald beads dangled from the edges. If anyone could make that work as a fashion statement, Oceane could.

"Why don't you come for dinner one night next week?" Oceane asked. "Bring that new man of yours." Her eyes twinkled mischievously.

"How do you know about him?" Paris was a big city, but sometimes too small for its own good.

"The May Gala – everyone's talking about it. You wrapped in the arms of some delectable stranger for the entire evening . . ."

I hadn't much thought about the gossip. Foolish of me. "It's really nothing. I'm happily and *totally* single." Imagine if he was the thief, and my Parisian counterparts knew I was dating him. I would never live it down.

She tilted her head. "I don't believe you."

I pasted on a smile. "It's true. We're acquaintances nothing more." My heart dropped saying the words, but perhaps I had to get used to it being so.

"I detect there's more you're not telling me."

Because my worries were of such a criminal nature how could I say? *Oh, it's nothing, the guy I've half fallen for might be a jewel thief, no big deal . . .*

"It's . . ." I weighed up an answer that would be believable. "It's just, he's leaving soon, I'm sure, so I've decided that it's not worth pursuing. Long-distance love is too complicated."

She frowned. "But it's doable. You travel for work. And how romantic would the reunions be?"

I thought of the log cabin, and how much I'd liked the idea. Little did I know it had been make-believe. I hadn't been wrong when I thought it was fairy tale-esque. "Yeah, for the lovey-dovey type. Nope. I have my business to think about. I couldn't get away, even if he was the one. Which he isn't." There. I almost convinced myself with my no-nonsense tone.

But Oceane gave me a sideways stare. "Well if you say so. In that case, what about dinner soon? A girls' night out?"

I smiled, touched. I'd expected Oceane to try and match me up with someone else, or throw some clichés at me about fish in the sea. "A girls' night out would be fabulous," I said, and meant it. I couldn't think of the last time I'd socialized with a group of women that wasn't linked to work.

"Consider it done. I'll text you when and where. And thanks for the gorgeous antique."

We kissed cheeks and Oceane stepped out with her parasol, which she opened and strolled along like she was back in twenties' Paris, catching the attention of passersby before giving me a backwards wave.

And finally I had a moment to myself to focus on the matter at hand. This morning, and reading about the Postcard Bandit seemed like a lifetime ago. I booted up the laptop and searched for more information on the stolen jewels, seeing if I could read between the lines, and find something that linked Tristan.

Scrolling through various new bulletins, the content was almost identical. Their hypothesis was the thief was highly trained in security, knew how to override complex alarm systems and blank CCTV footage in the blink of an eye. They knew the thief got in and out within sixty seconds, and reset the alarms so no one was any the wiser until it was too late, the jewels gone, and not a sniff of the perpetrator.

Sixty seconds.

It took me longer than that to apply my lipstick. Not to mention my false eyelashes . . .

He'd have to move like lightning. The auction houses were heavily alarmed, from infrared monitors to detect motion, and ultrasonic detectors inaudible to the human ear, to photoelectric beams, which were exactly like you'd see in the movies. Gustave from Cloutier's had explained all the technicalities to me a year or so ago when the auction closed for the day for various installations. There were also security guards on site, usually in a stuffy office somewhere watching the CCTV live.

How did he get past them all in sixty seconds? There was usually a delay in the footage arriving on screen for the guards, but only by a few seconds – not enough to get in and out without being seen. Unless the guards slept their shifts away, but then how would the thief know when to strike?

Did he drug their café au laits? Float down from the ceiling like Tom Cruise in *Mission Impossible*? Or worse, pay them off to simply look the other way for sixty measly seconds?

I searched for news about the robberies in Italy. The stories were much the same. All it had taken was sixty seconds and collections of rare jewels were missing. He'd ignored a painting by Picasso, a collection of coins from ancient Egypt, and many fine things that were almost priceless. A painting would be too conspicuous to carry down the street. Coins would be hard to sell on. Jewels he could drop into his pocket and stride away, knowing there'd be many a buyer on the black market.

Anyway, it wasn't my job to work out the logistics of the robberies, I only had to help catch the thief and that was by getting a confession. If Tristan was innocent then no harm done, but otherwise, it was best I know. The gendarmes could investigate the technical aspect once I had him recorded, bragging about his ability . . .

With a quick glance at the front door to make sure I was still alone, I hunched over the laptop and typed in Tristan Black into a search engine. My eyebrows shot up when a page rose to greet me.

Black Enterprises.

I'd searched for his name before and had found nothing. And now suddenly he had a website? Suspicious. I clicked the link, reading hastily. Maybe it was lost in translation, but for the life of me, I couldn't see what Black Enterprises actually did. There were tabs about consulting, but consulting what? It was like it was code for something.

Frowning, I clicked the About tab, and there was his face: his sexy, white-toothed smile, the flirty gaze, and swept-back blond hair.

"Must be fascinating reading."

I gasped, and banged the laptop closed. "It's not actually. A whole bunch of gobbledygook." My heart hammered, and I forced a smile. Tristan stood on the other side of the counter. He couldn't possibly have known what I was looking at, but the twinkle in his eye suggested he did.

He lifted an eyebrow and gave me a loaded stare. "So you weren't drooling over a picture of some buff playboy?"

"Of course not," I snapped, flustered by being caught unawares.

"You should shine that mirror; there's a few fingerprints smudging it."

My face flushed scarlet. He'd seen the laptop screen in the reflection of the mirror behind me! Well why wouldn't I search for him online? Every woman searched the internet first up when they were interested in a guy didn't they? Checked his Facebook, his photos – it wasn't stalking, it was living in modern times.

"You're pale," he said, running a finger along my cheek. "Like you've had a shock."

If I wanted to catch him I had to act completely normal. "Oui, I got the end of month statements through; that's enough to shock anyone."

He laughed. "I'm sorry I had to cancel our date before, but what about dinner later to make it up to you? I'd love to smuggle you outside now, but work calls . . ."

I gulped. "Sure, sure," I said, my mind scattered.

"Great." He kissed the tip of my nose, provoking a blush. It was only after he'd left that my heartbeat returned to normal and the entirety of the situation hit me. What if Tristan really was the thief? Would I warn him to run, or would I tell the gendarmes? Worry sat heavy in my belly. I wasn't cut out for this. Gilles walked in with his dog Casper, stopping me short. I couldn't rush him – it was his one social interaction for the day. Forcing a bright smile, I welcomed him in. I'd visit Madame Dupont as soon as he was gone and see what she made of it all.

Chapter Eighteen

After Gilles and Casper ambled from the shop, I locked the front door and careened around the corner to the Time Emporium. Madame Dupont waved, scattering the smoke in all directions.

"Madame! Thank God!"

"You heard about The Bellamy Auction House in the Latin Quarter?"

I gasped – another auction house in under twenty-four hours! "No, I hadn't! When did this happen?"

"The thief stole a collection of antique watches earlier. The gendarmes have only just released a statement."

"What time were the robberies?"

She checked her watch. "Oh, about an hour ago . . ."

Gilles and Casper had visited my shop just after Tristan left . . . and that was just over two hours ago. Could he really casually wander in and see me, and then go and commit a crime? The time frames fit. And he'd said, *I'd love to smuggle you outside now, but work calls.* I blinked back alarm. It really was him; I could feel it.

"I suppose they were very valuable?" I asked, trying to tamp down the panic.

She gave me a grave nod. "Very. From the family Capulet." Her eyes clouded. A collection of timepieces owned by nobility now lost just like the precious jewelry collections. It was a travesty. "I was hoping to secure the collection. They were exquisite. And now, *poof*, they're gone," she said, her voice gravelly.

She shook her head sadly, and ditched the burnt-out butt of her cigarette into an ashtray by the door before lighting up a fresh Gauloises. "Whoever it is, is clever. They can override complex alarms and get in and out in sixty seconds. No mean feat when some of these auction houses are cavernous. It takes longer than sixty seconds to get through the entrance halls. I suspect by the time the gendarmes have formulated a catch-him-if-you-can plan, he'll be long gone and with him, everything we hold dear."

She rattled on and on, and I waited for a break to butt in but finding none grabbed her arms. "Madame, I have bad news. I think the thief is Tristan! I'm sure of it."

Madame Dupont laughed raucously. "Oh my dear, you're doing it again."

"Doing what?" I asked, lowering my voice. I could feel one of Madame's talks coming on. She was so good at reading people and situations that I usually listened to her advice, but I don't think she heard the seriousness in my tone. I wasn't talking about the weather, I was talking about dating a jewel thief!

"You're purposely sabotaging your love life. Because of the stumble with Joshua you've sworn off men, and Tristan managed to creep into your heart and just like that you panic. You're going to have to trust a man at some point, so don't ruin it with him. If he's a thief, I'm Madame Bovary." She arched a brow.

"Madame, I know what you're saying but I really do think it's him! I'm not sabotaging anything. I'm telling you we should be very careful. If you think back, so many things point to him."

The look she gave me was full of pity. Was I sabotaging myself? I admit, there wasn't a lot to go on, but when you know, *you know*.

"Darling, please. Blaming an innocent man isn't a good idea. Rumors can ruin reputations so tread carefully."

I pulled a face. "I'm only telling *you*, Madame. You know I wouldn't blame someone for no good reason. Maybe we can sit down and talk about it at some point?"

"For you, anything. But unless there's any proof, which I don't think there will be, promise me you'll keep your heart open?"

Grudgingly I nodded.

Was Tristan really capable of visiting me at the shop, and an hour later pulling off a heist? Was I his alibi? I needed some time alone to ponder it all.

After saying my goodbyes to Madame Dupont, I locked the shop and went home much earlier than normal.

I nodded hello to the waiters at the bistro below my apartment, as they rushed around serving. Ignoring the delicious scents wafting from the bistro, I headed up to my apartment, taking the stairs, rather than the lift. Laughter echoed down the narrow staircase, and I smiled. Maman's laughter? Maybe she'd made up with Papa?

Inside the apartment the unmistakable smell of Maman's cooking floated through the space. I unwound my scarf and followed the smell into the kitchen. Maman was wearing an apron, and patiently explaining to a young man in chef whites the basics of making the perfect bouillabaisse.

I paused waiting for some explanation and found none forthcoming. The young man with a boyish face was writing down everything Maman said like it was gospel.

"You see, the base is the most important step in any recipe. Get that right and you're halfway there. Think of it like you would when you're in the early stages of love. That base has to be respected, croon to it, stir gently *gently*, use only the best and freshest ingredients. Anything else is cheating, and we cannot have that."

The chef continued to scribble in his book.

"Ah, Maman?" I said.

Two surprised gazes flicked to me. They'd been so absorbed they were oblivious to my presence. "Oh, Anouk, this is Luc."

"Luc," I said nodding to him. "Luc's here because . . .?"

Maman ignored me and handed Luc the spoon. "Come, Luc,

try mine and then try yours, and taste the difference." It was then I noticed the array of pots and pans in the sink. She was teaching him to cook? I was certain he was the sous chef at the bistro downstairs. Surely he knew how to make bouillabaisse?

Luc did as told and murmured to himself in delight. "I recognize my mistakes – I can taste them! It leaves a bitter mouth feel as if I'd poured poison in there. Merci, merci!" he said, expansively. "Can I take yours with me? So the others can taste?"

Maman nodded. "Of course, and come back tomorrow and I'll show you the right technique for your roux. You're not quite cooking off the flour when you add it to the butter, but that's easily fixed."

"Oui, oui." Luc lifted the hot pot with a tea towel and kissed Maman's cheek. He was flushed and hopeful, clearly inspired by whatever had taken place.

I waited until the front door clicked closed before facing Maman. "What was that all about?"

She padded around the kitchen, running a sink full of sudsy water, and soaking the silver pots before answering. "I tried Luc's bouillabaisse for lunch and it was no good, tasted bitter. I called him over and explained."

I folded my arms and leaned against the kitchen bench. "And next minute he's up here having a cooking lesson?"

Steam rose from the sink, fogging up the little window. "Oui. He was missing so many elements, and instead of orange zest and fennel he used lemon and cabbage. He seemed eager to learn; he hasn't been taught properly. Downstairs caters for the tourist crowd so it's more about quantity than quality, and that's just not acceptable. If you cook you do it properly or you don't do it at all."

I smiled, struck that Maman was willing to help, not knowing if the young man would be amenable to it, or would take offense at her advice. If you'd asked me what my maman was like I would have tossed around words like reserved, quiet, private. Today had been full of surprises. "It was a lovely gesture, Maman."

She slipped on rubber gloves and moved to the sink. "It was fun. I can't remember the last time someone listened to me like that. Like what I said was important."

I rubbed her arms as she scrubbed the pots, gazing out the fug of the steamy window. "Well, I think Luc is very lucky to have a teacher like you. And even luckier you're sharing secret family recipes." Taking a clean tea towel from the drawer, I dried the dishes Maman had washed. It was a scene out of so many of my memories with her, us chatting away in a hot kitchen, getting chores done.

Maman chuckled. "Well, I held a few ingredients back – can't have the young man knowing all our secrets, can we?"

There was a calmness about Maman whenever she cooked and she poured all her heart into it, making sure each element, each stage, was lovingly executed. She claimed rushing, or cooking under duress made the meal taste like stress. Apparently you could tell how a person was feeling by the way they chopped their *mise en plus*. And if you didn't get the preparation right, then you were on the back foot from the get-go.

"I had a lovely day," she said. "And I'm going to wander around the 7th arrondissement later. I haven't seen the Eiffel Tower sparkle at night-time. What kind of French person am I that I haven't seen that?"

"I'll come with you."

"Non, non, I'm not here to be babysat, Anouk. I'm a grown woman; I can handle myself. I want to breathe in the air, take my time, and see what I stumble on. What a freedom to do exactly as I please."

"As long as you stay out of the shadows. Keep to the well-lit avenues."

Life was so complicated at times. But Maman's peaceful expression showed me that it was never too late to try something new. I only wished Papa could see her now.

* * *

Henry the couch surfer was getting on my last nerve. Once again, I'd caught him sniffing around my things and this time I was certain he wasn't tidying. Today it was the armoire in the hallway, nestled between the bedroom doors.

Sneaking up behind him, I tapped his shoulder, causing him to jump in fright. "What exactly are you snooping around for? Money?"

I didn't trust him one little bit. Lilou saw the best in everyone, but I did not.

Startled, with hand on heart, he said, "I was looking for clean sheets for the chaise longues, God forbid my skin come in contact with the velvet."

"You put clean sheets on yesterday."

"Did I? I must have forgotten."

We faced off against each other, eyes burning, when there was a knock at the door.

I froze. I didn't want anyone to witness my apartment and the shambles it had become. Bed sheets on furniture, jackets and shoes strewn about. Discarded newspapers on the floor, where Henry had given up job hunting and left them where they lay.

Maman wandered from the kitchen with a tea towel over her shoulder. "Are you going to answer that?" She indicated the door.

Before I could answer Henry wrenched it open, revealing a smiling Tristan. Oh God, I hadn't had a moment to even think about him and where he might be.

"What can I do for you, Tristan?" *Oh, the dinner date!* His visit to the shop seemed like a lifetime ago. What an interminable day.

Mortification colored me scarlet, as I pictured the mess behind me. A girl still had her pride, and I didn't want to be thought of living shambolically, no matter who it was. If I closed my eyes would this all disappear? When he'd arrived the last time, the apartment had been tidy, and now it was anything but.

He wandered in, nodding to Henry, and Maman.

"You're early," I said. I tried to don a serene expression but was feeling as tense as a coiled snake. Had he even mentioned a time? My mind was scattered like marbles, and I had no time to collect myself.

Maman popped on her spectacles, and leaned forward taking a good, hard look at him. I could see the cogs whirling inside her brain. Her glance flicked to me, and then back to him as a slow smile settled across her face. "Ma chérie! You have a beau? *Finally!*" She had attempted to whisper but the words carried around the room. She was most likely planning grand-babies already.

I cringed. Now he'd know I was living in squalor *and* I was desperately single. "He's not a beau . . ."

He cleared his throat. "No? Aren't we going on a date?" His eyes were shiny with mirth as though he was thoroughly enjoying the spectacle that was my life.

"We're going out for dinner." But I caught myself before saying anymore. If I wanted to get him to talk I had to act natural.

With a silky smile he moved to Maman, taking her hand and giving it a quick kiss as though he was some kind of gentleman. Which he wasn't. He was a thief. And a crafty one at that. I held in a groan as Maman's cheeks flushed. He had that same magnetism over everyone.

She nodded in my direction. "I'm glad she has a beau. All she does is work, work, work, and lives like a hermit. No real friends to speak of. Well, there's Madame, but even she has a busier social life than Anouk. For a while I thought maybe she'd end up alone . . ."

"That's enough, Maman." For a woman who was usually reserved she sure was speaking a lot.

"What?" she said, perplexed. "It's true. You can't make love to a piece of jewelry, can you?"

"Maman!" My skin went puce from my toes right up to my forehead. "Excuse my maman," I said. "She's not herself at the moment." Who was this woman?

He laughed. "Can I take you out for a drink before dinner?"

"No. I'm busy, I have things that need to be sorted out—"

I had to phone Papa and start putting the idea of romance into his mind. Get rid of Henry, explain to Lilou he was creeping around in a suspect way, and figure out how I was going to catch Tristan . . . And now, have a serious word to Maman about appropriate things to say to strangers. Whew.

"She's not busy at all. A girl can only read the marriage announcements so many times before she dies of a broken heart!" Maman gave me a pointed look.

I wanted to dissolve into the carpet. So, I liked reading the marriage announcements? Was that a crime? It was nice to know there were couples who'd found their happy-ever-after. It wasn't as though I cried reading them, well once or twice, maybe, but not every single time.

Maman hurried on. "Take her. Put that sparkle back in her eyes!" I had an awful feeling Maman had indulged in the cooking wine . . .

Lilou walked in through, arms full of boxes. "Well hello, gorgeous," she said. "It's Prince Charming, come to rescue me from the wicked sister!" She dumped her things on the dining room table.

"Lilou! Please!" What must he think? I risked a peek at him from under my lashes, and was surprised to find he seemed bemused rather than offended by my suddenly crazy family.

"What?" my sister said, confusion lining her face. "Oh! You cunning little fox! You *do* have a new boyfriend." She clapped her hands. "You've kept that very quiet."

Her face was flushed with happiness for me as if I'd just announced I was getting married or something equally amazing. "Some secrets are worth keeping, aren't they, Anouk?" She grinned.

"Yes," I said, hoping she'd leave it at that.

"We all have secrets." A small smile played at the corners of Tristan's mouth and he took the liberty of drifting around the living room picking knickknacks up, and scrutinizing them before moving on. "It's human nature."

The air in the room hummed as though too much had been said. I didn't like being spoken about as if I wasn't there. Maybe I just wasn't ready to hear what they thought of my situation in case I agreed with them.

When Tristan came to my bookshelves he dropped to his knees and bent his head sideways to read the spines. "Crime novels? I wouldn't have pegged you for that."

I didn't want to give him the satisfaction of knowing they were Joshua's. Let him think that I'd done plenty of research when it came to catching a thief. "Yes," I said, huffily. "There's nothing better than reading about criminals, *especially* when they get caught."

He ignored me and went back the books. "*The Jewel Heist*"? He pointed to a book. No doubt it would read more like nonfiction to him.

"Read it have you?" I asked pointedly.

"What's for dinner?" Henry said blithely.

Before my head exploded I said, "Let's get that drink, Tristan."

Chapter Nineteen

In the twilight, I could think rationally, as Tristan and I walked sharing a silence. What my family said had touched a nerve. Did they really worry I'd end up all alone? That my lack of friends was because I felt I couldn't trust anyone?

Friendships had been a struggle as my shop took over my life. But I was happy, wasn't I? Subsisting on the thrill of securing treasures from the past was enough. I had Madame Dupont – we shared breakfast and gossiped. Oceane was also a friend. We sometimes sat by the bank of the Seine and drank wine. Now we were going to have a girls' night out sometime. That was a full and rich life.

It wasn't as though I hadn't tried with men. The idea of love wasn't repellant. I was just a little bruised after my last brush and now I was potentially semi-dating a jewel thief.

At the ripe old age of twenty-eight I still had plenty of time. Love chose us, not the other way around, so while I waited, I'd kept busy, just like always. I'd set goals, and achieved them. The man next to me was a perfect example of why I had to protect myself. A girl could easily fall for his wily charms, but it was a smokescreen. It dawned on me I was walking next to my enemy, someone who wanted to rob France of its glory, yet, it didn't feel quite that way. He was good at his role, damn him. To stave off a month of crying into my pillow, if he *was* a big, fat liar, I had to step carefully.

Tristan took his jacket off and slung it over his shoulder.

Our footsteps echoed on the cobblestones as we strode side by side. "Your family is great. Lots of fun," he said with a chuckle, shaking his head.

I gawped openly at him to make sure he wasn't being sarcastic. "I think they're suffering heat stroke."

He threw his head back and laughed. "Possibly, summer *is* just around the corner. They're looking out for you; it's sweet."

My shoulders relaxed a little. "It's usually only me and my soup bowl." May as well admit I talk to inanimate things. "So I'm finding it a little suffocating having so many people staying. My life is usually . . . sedate, quieter. I'm not used to so much noise, and mess. Chaos."

"You're good to those around you. Not just your family, but others too. Everyone talks about you and your little shop."

He stopped and lifted my chin with a finger. My heart pumped so loud I thought he'd hear it. Slivers of moonlight shone between us as I tried desperately to remember he could be the bad guy. He wouldn't think I was such a sweet person if he knew I was considering him a criminal, and debating what I'd do if he was. I was mute, lost in the blue of his eyes.

He gave me a penetrating look, as though he was debating what to say. "Why do you do it?"

"Do what? Work?" Did he not understand most of us had to work in order to live? He'd obviously become so enmeshed in the glitzy glamor of his high-flying life, he'd forgotten how real people survived – by hard work.

His hand dropped to his side. The cleft of my chin still buzzed from his touch.

"Nothing." The mask slipped back on. "Nothing. Let's get that drink."

Flummoxed, I followed him into a softly lit book-themed wine bar. Benches were made from stacks of old hardbacks with a length of polished wood across the top to sit on. Walls were scribbled with passages from books written about Paris. Writers who'd fallen in love with the city and gone on to write fiction about it. Paris had burrowed under their skin and they never really recovered from it. My favorite was a quote from Hemingway's *A Moveable Feast*.

Even though the late, great Hemingway had loved this place, life went on without him, or perhaps *with* the shadow of him, as we still lived vicariously through his economical prose, getting lost in his musings about Paris in the twenties, a time I wished I could transport myself back to.

Tristan found a table in a dimly lit corner, and hung his jacket over the back of the seat.

"This place is amazing," he said. His American accent rang out in the small space. "Makes me want to read their books again." Smiling, he pointed to a quote by F Scott Fitzgerald.

"American literati have always loved Paris."

"Americans in general love Paris, especially this one." We sat, and stared at one another for too long to be comfortable. With candlelight throwing shadows, it was almost possible to forget that I was sitting across from a thief, and instead I pretended for one lonely minute that he was a man with a good heart, and a romantic soul. Someone to love and be loved by. Until reality struck . . . Perhaps I was under too much stress: *to love and be loved by?* More likely my subconscious was reeling because everyone I held dear thought I was going to end up living an empty life and had only just thought to mention it to me. In front of Tristan.

"What's wrong?" he asked. "You look so sad of all a sudden."

I blinked the worry away. "It's nice to . . ." I stiffened. *Don't say to be out with a man!* "It's nice to re-read books you love," I finished lamely. It was difficult being spy-like around him. It was

175

as though any reasonable thought vanished from my mind, and my mouth moved of its own accord. It was the intensity in his gaze, and the curve of his lips, like he was always on the cusp of smiling that special smile, the non-rehearsed one.

"Champagne?" he asked.

"Oui."

Tristan motioned for the waiter and ordered a rare vintage. Reality came crashing into my subconscious. The champagne he'd ordered was expensive. No doubt funded by the money he'd made from selling the stolen antiques. Stolen *French* antiques. And here I was about to sip from the fruits of theft. Did that make me an accomplice? Would the champagne taste like betrayal? The thought was enough to make me switch on, and remember my mission. Get him to talk. Refill his glass until he was a step away from inebriated. Not my usual style, but needs must.

The waiter carried the bottle over, held aloft on a silver serving tray. He uncorked it with a flourish and poured slowly, allowing the froth to settle as bubbles raced up the flutes.

"Cheers," I said, holding my glass up. We clinked, and he gave me one of those winks. Honestly. He was so American.

"To new friends," I said.

He ran a hand through his hair, which shone under the lights making him seem almost angelic. Innocent, even. "To new friends."

I took a deep gulp, and urged him with my eyes to do the same. How much would he have to drink before his tongue loosened and he fessed up? His eyes locked with mine, recognizing the challenge and he took a long sip, smacking his lips exaggeratedly. "Thirsty?"

"Very," I said.

"Bottoms up."

Bottoms up? Was he propositioning me?

He must've seen my jaw clench because he said, "It's an expression, the bottom of the glass, not your actual . . . derrière."

"Oh," I managed, hoping the blush creeping up my neck wasn't visible under the moody lighting. "Bottoms up." We clinked again, and drank the remnants of champagne in our flutes.

Hastily, I refilled his, pouring clumsily, foam rising up and threatening to spill over. While I waited for it to subside, I filled mine more slowly. We sculled again, drawing worried glances from the waiter who was no doubt bamboozled as to why we were quaffing a three-hundred Euro bottle of champagne like it was water.

My stomach rumbled, reminding me I hadn't yet eaten dinner. It was almost a sin for a Parisian to drink alcohol without a meal. If it wasn't a formal sit-down dinner, if wine was served so were canapés. Wine and food were painstakingly paired up, and enjoyed. But if we ate it would slow the conversation down. Just this once, I'd have to forgo my French values.

"I haven't met anyone like you before," he said, giving me a slow once-over that made me squirm. "There's so many layers to you."

"You make me sound like a cake."

"A very sweet one," he said, laughing. "I thought I knew what your life consisted of, but there's a lot more to it. I suppose we never really know everything about a person, do we?"

He meant my family, and their genuine worry I was one step away from a cat-lady, obviously. "OK, you're right. I mean, there's things no one knows about me." I tried my best to appear beguiling, channeling every French actress I could think of. A quick glance over my shoulder to make sure no one was eavesdropping. That's what guilty people did, didn't they? If I acted a touch shady, perhaps he'd share his underworld dealings. "But you'd probably run out of here if you knew."

He sat up straighter. "What kind of things?"

I topped up his champagne flute. He returned the favor, refilling mine, the bubbles bursting on my tongue, as I took a sip. Perhaps this is why people crossed to the dark side, to be able to afford champagne that tasted like stars.

"Oh, I couldn't possibly tell you," I said with a breathless giggle.

"Then I'd have to kill you, and blood is so messy." I flashed a smile, and had another guzzle of champagne.

Tristan leaned back on his chair, and clasped his hands over his lower belly. I couldn't help but picture the tanned, lithe body under his clothes. The champagne made me flush, or maybe the room was hot – I felt a little intoxicated by my role as temptress.

"You can trust me, though, can't you?" he drawled. I topped up his glass again, bringing us to the end of the bottle. I signaled to the waiter for another one, and hoped Tristan would pick up the bill, otherwise I'd have to leave my antique onyx bracelet as collateral.

"Trust you, Tristan? I don't know a thing about you. Not really." Through the glassiness of my own eyes, I tried to determine if he was feeling merry from so much champagne but he was hard to read with only the flicker of candlelight in our darkened corner of the wine bar.

"Sure you do," he said, flicking me a saucy eyebrow raise. "You know I'm American. You know my name. You've –" he held up his fingers and made quote marks "– researched my company online."

That was enough to make me choke on a mouthful of champagne. "Your company?" I said incredulously. "An obvious front for something more sinister, trust *me*," I said. "I know exactly what it's like to have to hide who you really are."

I hoped my musings were making sense to him; they weren't making a lot of sense to me. *I should have had dinner!* The champagne had a way of relaxing me to the point I was almost floppy.

Tristan gave me a half grin, and leaned across the table. "So you're saying outwardly you act like this Marilyn-esque ingénue but really you're a calculating manipulator . . ."

"Moi? Non!" I laughed, my voice too high, too manic, but I suddenly found the situation hilarious, because he was describing himself. And I guess he hoped that underneath all my bluster I could be molded into a criminal like him. Little did he know, I was sharper than he gave me credit for, and my act was just that an act . . .

"You've got me," I said. "Cunning, and more clever than most people think. If only they paid attention to . . ." I lowered my voice and leaned across the table ". . . what was right in front of them."

"You've got away with it for so long, haven't you? No one's suspected the young glamour puss right under their noses."

I nodded. "Years," I said, thinking fast, but foggily.

He shook his head as if he were awed by it.

"I've seen a lot of crooked people in my life, but never one like you."

A gasp caught in my throat. My role-playing was working! "Thanks," I said. "I suppose it's easier to fly under the radar when you know what you're doing."

He drank his glass down in one gulp. "Have you ever wondered what you'd do if you were caught?"

Caught? Caught for what? He was the thief. Not me! I racked my brains. I had never so much as stolen a piece of candy, but then I thought of the debtors I still owed, the pressure that was waiting for me back at the house and I steeled myself. Better to play along than give up the role now, so I flashed him my most coquettish grin and said, "I'd lie my pants off."

"Now there's a vision . . ." His shoulders dropped forward ever so slightly as the alcohol worked its magic around his bloodstream.

"Focus, Monsieur Black." I winked, American-like. I hadn't had this much fun in ages, completely uninhibited, and undaunted by anything. I liked the feeling. Although I knew none of it was real, it was fun to play a part, and pretend to be that vavoom type of girl for a change.

"It's hard to do anything around you, Anouk. I get so easily distracted and that's not good."

I was fuzzy-brained. Thoughts were slipping just out of reach. It felt like we were having two very different conversations. "It's not ideal, is it? Soon you'll be leaving, right? Off to the next place, following the sun . . ."

"My life isn't as exciting as you seem to think it is." That same pained expression returned, as if his criminal life took a toll. Maybe guilt caught up with him on brief occasions? But he could easily choose to stop, and do the right thing.

"I don't believe you," I said. "Otherwise why would you continue to do it? Searching for a Bonnie, are you, Clyde?"

He laughed, a low deep sound. "Are you available for the position?"

I folded my arms. This was as close as a confession as I'd gotten tonight. My belly flipped, at the realization. And I just hoped my expression didn't betray me. "More champagne?" I said, buying time.

He nodded, clasping his fingers together, as if he was waiting for an answer like he was interviewing me for a job. "I do wish I could stay once in a while," he said. "But I can't, sadly."

Yeah, because then they'd catch you.

"It's a real shame."

He gave me a wan smile. "Sometimes it is."

I weighed up what to say next. My brain was screaming to tell him to stop stealing to fund an empty lifestyle but would he listen? I didn't know if he stole because it was a thrill for him, or if he needed the money to pretend to be someone else. Misty-eyed, I toyed with other reasons . . . What if he funded an orphanage with the money? Could I forgive him that? Or maybe he was building a hospital for women in a third world country?

I gazed at him, my head spinning at the thought, with his bright blue eyes, and shock of blond hair, those shiny white teeth, and aquiline nose, maybe that perfection was all a front for a soft and squishy heart – he was a modern-day Robin Hood! Robbing from the rich to give to the poor. Wouldn't that be the most romantic thing?

"I've lost you," he said, catching me mid-daydream.

I waved him away, stuck in my mind about what might be. "No, I think you've found me." The room spun on its axis.

"I think we'd better have dinner."

Chapter Twenty

Filmy sunlight filtered through the gap in the lace curtains, bringing with it the mind-numbing bang of sledgehammers. I cupped my head, realizing the crashing was coming from inside my brain. The night before coming flooding back.

Oh no!

Groaning, I pulled a pillow over my face as the memories came thick and fast. *He was a modern-day Robin Hood.* What was I thinking! The champagne headache hit me anew. I'd failed at my first mission in the worst possible way. In my fog, I couldn't remember getting any information out of him. All I could recall was the things *I'd* said, and even worse, the assumptions I'd made after too many glasses of bubbly. He funded an orphanage? What had my desperate heart conjured up? Built a hospital for women? Urgh.

Vaguely, I recalled we had walked home, stumbling and laughing, both pretending to be someone other than who we were. I could have kicked myself for wasting an opportunity to catch him out. In my attempt to get him to talk, I'd quaffed as much champagne as he did, which I bitterly regretted today.

The clock beside my bed shrieked ten a.m. in neon green. I wrenched back the covers and stopped dead. Beside the bed was a note:

Anouk,

When I close my eyes, I can still taste the champagne on your lips. We're doomed to wander alone, or that's what you said anyway. Who knew you were such a poet? Hope your head isn't too sore. You sure can put it away.

Until we meet again,

Tristan

WHAT! We kissed again? I closed my eyes and tried to summon the memory of it, and came up blank. Surely, I'd remember kissing him? The kisses in Saint-Tropez had pervaded my dreams. I ran my hand across my traitorous lips as if I could feel him there but nothing.

In snapshots, the arrival home played out in my mind . . . Maman had just returned from seeing the Eiffel Tower alight again, while Lilou danced around the apartment, Henry strumming a guitar and crooning out folk songs.

Tristan was lying! I'd walked past everyone, and taken a glass of water from the kitchen and then flopped into bed and fallen into a dead sleep. I narrowed my eyes. Nice try, Mr. Black, but you're going to have to do better than that. Next time I'd stick to sparkly water, and I'd be better prepared.

How did his letter get here though? He could have given it to Lilou or Maman . . . I'd have remembered if he crept into my room.

I'd have to ramp up my investigations.

But right now, I was woefully late for work. On the bedside table was a glass of water and a sheet of painkillers. A groan of relief escaped me.

"Are you awake?" Lilou edged into the room, giving me a maternal smile. "You need to rehydrate. Get that water into you, and take the pills. I've made you a smoothie for breakfast, full of hangover-busting vitamins."

"Since when did you become the responsible one?" I asked groggily, realizing with a dull throb of pain that our roles had been reversed. Lilou was playing nursemaid to me – there was one for the books.

She shrugged. "Just being a good sister. I could envisage the wake up wasn't going to be pretty."

"Oh, God, don't tell me. I don't want to know what I said or did."

"You were fine," she giggled. "Sometimes it's good to let loose. You can't be staid all of your life!"

"If today is an indication of what cutting loose entails, I am more than happy to be staid. Want to walk to work with me?" Lilou was still hanging out at Madame's under the guise of making jewelry.

"Non, I can't," she said. "I have an appointment with a buyer from Charbonneau's. I have to leave soon."

I gasped. Charbonneau's were a group of designer retail shops that were known all over France. They were very exclusive and reputedly impossible to sell to. I had Parisian fashion designer acquaintances who had tried and failed multiple times to get appointments with their buyers. And now Lilou had one, for what, her handmade jewelry?

"A Charbonneau's buyer?" I noted she was wearing a smart gray pantsuit, her hair was tied into an elegant chignon, and she wore barely there makeup. She looked . . . grown up. In charge.

"Yes, for my jewelry sets. I sent some samples to their team and they called for a meeting. I was up late last night finishing a range of designs for winter in the hopes they'll put an order in. They're keen, so I figured I may as well put my all into it."

I sat up too quickly; the room spun. "Wow, Lilou, that's amazing. I didn't realize you were planning that far ahead."

She gave me a businesslike smile. "You're not the only one who loves what they do."

* * *

An hour later, I was clip-clopping my way around the corner to my shop, catching a glimpse of the Eiffel Tower, standing regally on show, when Madame Dupont wandered out from her Time Emporium.

"Ooh la la," she said giving me a slow appraisal. "Looks like someone spent the morning in bed. You missed our breakfast, but I can see why . . . You got a better offer?" She gave me a youthful grin, and I cringed. I'd totally forgotten about our tête-à-tête to discuss Tristan!

"Sorry, Madame. I slept in."

"Don't be sorry." She lit a cigarette and took a long pull, blowing out smoke rings. "You're all flushed and hopeful looking." She gave me a knowing smirk.

"Oh that," I said. "Non, non, Madame. What you're seeing is the result of far too much alcohol on an empty stomach."

"With him?" She narrowed her eyes, and leaned right up close to my face. "I know you, and your hands never flutter, your gaze never darts, you're normally demure, straight-faced, even under all that makeup, and yet this morning, you're fidgety, rosy-cheeked, downright scattered."

"It's just because I'm running late."

She grinned. "And you have two different shoes on."

I sent a fervent prayer up that I'd dissolve into the pavement but no such luck. What kind of Parisian was I? In my haste I'd thrown on any old thing, and had grabbed at the shoes in my closet without any thought.

"Oh the shoes," I said with a quick cough as plumes of smoke drifted between us. "I thought I'd try something new . . . One white one black, change things up a bit."

Madame's gravelly laugh rang out. "You think you can lie to me?" She clucked her tongue. "Tell me every last detail!"

With a tight smile, which I'm sure resembled a grimace, I said, "I can't remember many of them, actually. It's all a bit of a blur. I better go, Madame. But if I do remember anything, I'll phone you. If you don't see me later, send hangover food."

She laughed like she was proud of me so I kissed her cheeks, holding my breath so smoke didn't overcome me, and strode off.

"Darling, there is one thing." Her voice wavered, and she hesitated. I motioned for her to continue. With a glum expression she said, "He came into my shop, and asked if I'd be interested in the Audrey watch."

I turned so fast I almost tripped over, and pounding head and all I raced back to her. "What? What did you say?"

"Your handsome American came into my shop. It could have been a sting to see if I'd buy stolen goods. I'm so sorry, Anouk, but maybe you're right about him."

"He was trying sell you the stolen timepieces?" Would he be that obvious?

"Well, he enquired about selling me some pieces, wanted to know the worth of certain things, but he didn't actually have any on hand. But when you've been around as long as I have you pick up those nuances. He was cagey, distracted, like he was on a time limit, and was pumping me for information. I hate to say it, but I think you're right, he could be the thief . . ."

My poor heart could barely take it all in. "I've kissed a criminal. A number of times! Including last night!" And I didn't want him to be the smooth criminal. I wanted him to be the fishing, cooking, resident of the log cabin, by the lake in America, as he so described.

"*Merde*," she said, her eyes wide. "I think it's best if we don't panic."

I shook my head. "I was trying to make him talk. And my grand plan was getting him tipsy . . ."

She scrunched up her nose. "But let me guess, you got tipsy instead? Anouk, you need some lessons in how to deal with men."

I harrumphed. "That may be, but what about him? What if he's the one?"

"Then you buy a small island off Brazil and go make a million babies."

I clucked my tongue. "Not *The One*, but the one who is the thief!"

"I know that," she said. "Hence the need to hide out! It could be so romantic! On the run from authorities, living life for every sunrise in case it's all snatched away." Her expression softened, as she no doubt pictured me hiding out in some jungle with a half-naked Tristan.

"Oh my God, Madame! Non! The fact he's stealing from France doesn't bother you?"

"Well of course I'm loyal to my country. But with a body like that, and that powerful saunter of his, imagine what he'd be like, that stamina . . ." She had a faraway look in her eyes.

"Madame! Honestly!" If sex kept you young, it had definitely worked for Madame, but I wasn't so sure how it had affected her morals. Imagine running off to Brazil with Tristan! Hide out with the bad guy? It was absurd.

"You'll see, ma chérie. Sometimes, it's the liars and thieves who make your pulse race, and what's a girl to do?"

I cut her off, and held up a hand. "Madame! Did he say anything at all that you think we could tell the gendarmes? I know he was in Italy before he came here. But that's not enough."

"Really? You want to get him arrested? Can't you do that *after* a little fling?"

In the sunny day, with my body aching from lack of sleep and adequate hydration I could easily do it. Get him convicted and out of my life. I was peeved he wasn't the person I needed him to be. He was trouble. And so what if he oozed sex appeal? I wasn't so shallow to only admire a man who was outwardly appealing. After two bottles of champagne things might have got hazy, but I wouldn't be so careless again.

I stared her down and she eventually capitulated. "OK, OK. All he said was he had to go away, but he'd be back."

"Go where?"

"America."

And when was he going to tell me? I pursed my lips. "He's going sell the antiques he stole!" What a mess I'd made. "He was probably trying to gauge what price you'd pay, and then use that as a guide for his black market buyers!"

"Or maybe not. He *is* American after all; maybe he's going to visit his parents? Why are you so sure it's him anyway? I do think we need to be careful about this . . . delicate situation."

I huffed and puffed. "He just arrives one day, and no one has ever heard of him? He comes from Italy where a jewel thief has just been? His website advertises a big fat nothing, and he didn't even have a website when I first met him. It was made after. He can tell a real opal on sight, which the vendor couldn't even tell. He cancels dates coincidentally the night another robbery takes place. The postcard bandit signed off with the letter T – *Tristan Black*?"

She narrowed her eyes. "That's it?" Laughter barreled out of her. "That's all you've got to go on? Anouk, please! There could be a number of reasons to explain all of that."

I steeled myself. How could I tell her about all the little signs? I just *knew*; I could feel it, read it in his body language. He was involved. "You'll see, Madame. Until then, promise me you won't tell anyone."

"I won't," she said fervently. "But let's not be too hasty to lay blame. Perhaps we should just leave it to the investigators. And let the gendarmes do their thing. I'm sure they know who it is and they're tracking them."

"I promise," I lied. I didn't trust the gendarmes one little bit after their lack of help with Joshua.

"Though . . ." she tapped her chin ". . . we do have an insight they don't, being part of the inner circle in the antiquarian world. Let me muse, my dear. Maybe we could compile a list of pros and cons, pardon the pun."

187

I gave her a grateful hug, glad she was finally listening to me. "Oui."

We kissed goodbye and I headed into the sanctuary of my shop.

I flipped the sign to appointment only. I wasn't at my best with two different shoes on, and a tsunami of a headache, but I was here at least. The air inside was thick with age, musty, as if overnight the treasures leaked memories from their pores, filling the space with that particular times-gone-by scent. Sometimes I wanted to capture it, in case it ever evaporated for good. The phone buzzed behind the counter so I dashed to answer it, praying it wasn't Tristan.

"The Little Antique Shop," I said.

"Bonjour, Anouk. I'm Vivienne and I was hoping for some help, some . . . advice. My papa passed away a few weeks ago and we're going through his apartment. Would you consider giving us an estimate on some of his antiques?"

Her voice was raspy, as if she'd been crying. "Oui, of course. My condolences about the passing of your papa." I had these types of requests all the time, and I tried to be as gentle as possible.

"Merci, merci. It's just we're not sure about . . ."

I interrupted, knowing instinctively what was coming next. "I'll give you an estimate, and that price will stand, but there is no rush. You'll know when the time is right, or not. And it may never be right, and that's OK."

We finished up our call, and I promised to visit her at the end of my workday, glad the visit would be a distraction from the bedlam in my mind.

Chapter Twenty-One

As the sky darkened I made my way to the address Vivienne gave me. Tourists with cameras slung around their necks sauntered past, slowly, as if they'd walked enough steps for one day. My headache had abated after copious amounts of water.

The apartment was the 8th arrondissement, just near the Arc De Triomphe. I introduced myself to the doorman and he buzzed the apartment, sending me up in the lift.

Vivienne answered the door dressed immaculately in a chic pantsuit, her shiny brown hair was bobbed and her face made up, yet you could still see hollows beneath her eyes from her grief. "Come in," she said, kissing me quickly. "Thank you for visiting so soon. My father owned Leclére Parfumerie, so apologies if the scent is overwhelming."

A wave of sadness washed over me. Vincent was a lovely old alchemist of a man. "I've been buying jasmine perfume from your papa for years," I said quietly. I hadn't heard of his passing. To think he was gone from that little shop just off the Champs-Élysées. What a gap his death would leave. He was unassuming, and doddery, always lost somewhere between his lab, and his reverie. He lived and breathed his concoctions. "Paris won't be quite the same without him."

"Thank you," she said. "It happened so suddenly, we're still in shock. My brother will run the parfumerie now, after a period of mourning."

Her brother was similar to Vincent – dreamers, lost inside their minds with their creations. The reason the parfumerie had been so successful was because Vincent kept his compounds a closely guarded secret, and tried new things.

"I'm glad your brother will continue his legacy." At least their magical perfumes would live on.

"My maman, too," she said. "Even though they separated a lifetime ago. She'll move back from Provence to help my brother." I recalled Vincent's ex-wife. She was a lovely bubbly woman, but Vincent's affair with his work came at a cost.

Perhaps, she would find comfort in the little shop after all these years, and a level of understanding. Vincent's passion resonated with me; it was how I felt about my shop too.

The apartment smelled like the parfumerie, a mixture of heady scents, all fighting for space. The old man still played with his concoctions at home, too. The thought made me smile.

The living room was a reflection of the man himself. Cluttered with disorderly stacks of books whose covers were gray with dust. An old leather couch, wrinkled, dipped on the left, the seat he must have favored.

"As you can see," Vivienne said, "it's all a bit of a jumble. He liked collecting, whether it was old perfume bottles, or paintings, he loved it all."

Suddenly, I wished I'd taken more time to know Vincent. Walking into his apartment was like finding gold. I knew from the trinkets that took up every nook and cranny that Vincent had prized every little find. Like me, I bet he sat there most nights, and gazed at them. They were wondrous. The abstract painting on the wall, daubs of red so scarlet they were like a cry for attention. The perfume bottles, lined up in size order on a mirrored shelf, so their bottles reflected upward, double the beauty, each wafting a faded, barely there scent, one last trick of osmosis, which sweetened the air.

"He had eclectic taste," I said with a smile. On a side table a cluster of seashells perched, leaving a faint trace of the sea.

"He loved the ocean," she said, following my gaze. "His last perfume, the one he vowed to perfect, was a re-creation of the beach. He wanted to capture the Mediterranean in a bottle, not just the sea air, the waves, and sand, but the feeling you had when you stood there, staring into Mother Nature's most glorious creation. Peace, relaxation, and above all hope. That's what he was like – it was a quest for him, and he was lost to it."

The thought of Vincent trying to bottle that, not just a perfume but a *feeling*, was so incredible goose bumps broke out over my skin. Tristan flashed briefly into my mind. He always smelled rugged and sea swept. But I pushed the vision of his face firmly from my mind, and instead thought of poor Vincent not achieving his dream. I wondered how close he got to perfecting the idea.

"Perhaps your brother can continue his dream, and finish that scent?" I know I'd buy something that conjured up those nostalgic moments in life.

She smiled, and it changed her features dramatically. All at once she appeared younger, more vibrant. "I hope so. He's as good as Papa, but is crippled with self-doubt sometimes. We'll see, anyway. Shall I make some coffee while you look around?"

I nodded my thanks, not sure where to start in the jumbled apartment. Vivienne left the room but I knew I wasn't alone. The edges blurred, like her father was here, standing off to the side, watching me with that same lackadaisical smile of his. Vivienne wasn't ready; I could feel it instinctively. The apartment with myriad pieces had to stay complete.

"Your things are beautiful," I whispered into the ether, hoping Vincent could hear. A breeze blew in from the balcony, ruffling the curtains like a sign he was pleased.

Vincent had an armoire in the corner of the room that drew

my eye. I opened the cupboards, and inside where stacks of notebooks. I flicked them open, curious as to what he'd written. Smiling, I quickly closed them, and shut the doors. They were full of chemical equations, complex diagrams, and colorful sketches, the secrets to his perfumes, and that was not for me to see. Even in death, I respected his privacy. I'd have to tell Vivienne to put them somewhere safe.

Leaving the room, I inched down the passage, stopping to admire black and white photographs hanging on the whitewashed wall.

When I came to his bedroom, I hovered on the threshold, unsure if I should enter the chamber. Shadows played here, dancing along the walls, like children were playing in the next realm, half here, half there, and I knew this was where he died. It came to me, him clutching his heart, staggering down the passage, seeing the photos for the last time. Or maybe I was imagining things. With a steadying breath, I entered the room. Moonlight shone through thick drapes that were left open. What was in here that he wanted me to see? Just then Vivienne's brisk footsteps sounded.

"This was his favorite room," she said, leaning her head against the doorframe. "It was the view he loved."

I followed her gaze, and through the mottled windows you could just make out the top half of the Eiffel Tower. The lights flashed, like tiny fireworks. "I would sit here every night too, and soak up that spectacle," I said.

"I can still feel him here."

I gave her arm a soft pat. I could too, but it wasn't my place to say. "The high-back chair, it was where he sat every morning, fresh, ready to tackle another day?"

She smiled, and lifted her head from the doorjamb. "Yes," she said, surprise shining in her eyes. "He used to sit there, and pull on his boots, exclaiming, 'Today will be a good day. Today will be the day I make a perfume so immortal, it will outlive us all.'

And we always believed him. He was like a nutty professor, but so fervent that it seemed like anything was possible, if only you put your heart and soul into it."

This was why antiques, and a person's belongings were more than just 'things'. A person's lifetime seeped into the medium and made it ripe with possibility, with passion. With love, and loss and hope.

"He was writing a memoir, you know." Her voice was barely audible, as if she was overtaken by picturing her papa sitting in his chair, face shining with enthusiasm that he got to follow his passion every single day.

"But he didn't finish it?" I asked.

She shrugged. "From the stack of pages, I think he expounded maybe too much. His gift was perfume, not words, but I'll read it, one day, when the time is right. His greatest regret was letting our mother go. But it was too late. She fell in love with another man. And Papa was too polite to step in, and confess his mistake." Lost in her recollections, her voice came out a whisper. "He was too gentle for this world. Life only made sense to him when he was lost among fragrance charts."

I mulled his story over, as a feeling of recognition hit me. I too, chose work over almost everything else. Sure, I had other responsibilities, but my little shop was my refuge, my best friend, the place I hid in times of crisis. Would I have the same fate as Vincent? Choosing antiques over love, and not realizing until it was too late? The thought made me shiver.

"Did your maman ever hint that she still loved him?" I asked gently. Hoping at least there was some kind of happy ever after for the old man, no matter how tenuous. Perhaps if he knew she loved him, but had promised herself to another man that might have been enough to get him through the long, lonely nights in the dark of winter.

Vivienne lifted a shoulder. "She never confided in me, out of respect for her second husband. But when Papa died, she was the first person to say his legacy needed to continue, and that someone would have to help my brother Sébastien. Her second husband recently died too. So she's moving back to Paris after all these years . . ."

The mood sobered, as we thought about love, and its sometimes crushing defeat. Did they let their love go too early and regret it always? I would never know. These pieces of furniture – his favorite high-back chair, the ottoman at the foot of his bed, the roll-top desk where he wrote his memoirs – would know. Over decades his tears would have salted the wood, his laughter thickened the fabric – they'd have absorbed part of him, and that's what made them so special.

"I think you need more time with your papa's belongings," I said. Vivienne and her brother needed space to sit in the apartment and reminisce, and perhaps when their maman arrived, she might wander through the rooms, a scent, a photo, misty moonlight filtering in would bring her closer to accepting his death, and knowing he lived a good life in spite of it all.

She gave me a grateful smile. "I think you're right." She gazed around the room, as if she was looking for her papa. "I was thinking pragmatically, but being here, surrounded by my papa's memories, it's much harder than simply clearing the space. It feels almost like a betrayal moving so quickly. I'm sorry I made you rush over so soon."

I shook my head. "Don't apologize. It's so hard to know what to do in circumstances like this. All practicality goes out the window, and you just have to be kind to yourself."

"Thanks for understanding. No wonder everyone speaks very highly of you."

I blushed. "You know where I am if you need a friend." It wasn't like me to offer friendship but I felt like Vivienne needed someone to talk to. Someone outside of her family who would just listen.

She hugged me tight and said her thanks.

I left her gazing out the bedroom window, the ghost of a smile on her face, as the Eiffel Tower flashed in the distance.

I trudged down the stairs, hands in pockets, musing about it all. Life moved so quickly, and when it came to death, rushing forward to expel grief didn't work. But people in the midst of that pain did what they thought best, what they were told to do, when really it was better to do it at your own pace, and understand there was no quick fix for grief.

Footsteps sounded from below, and I moved to the side of the staircase to make room, only to blow out a sharp breath seeing his face. How could those innocent eyes hide so much cunning? His boyish good looks, and floppy brown hair led a person to believe he was the boy next door who'd grown into a sweet, funny guy. In actuality, he was the opposite.

"Well, hello, Anouk. You're as lovely as ever."

I scowled. "You leave her alone!" I demanded.

"Excuse me?" He donned a look of surprise. "I'm only here to price some antiques of course. Terrible loss. Such a great man," he said. His voice was heavy with sarcasm. How I hated him!

"How did you find out?"

"A call from the family. Why, are you suggesting I'm being underhanded?"

I narrowed my eyes, knowing he'd been unscrupulous in order to get Vincent's address. Vivienne wouldn't have called him. Joshua's so-called business didn't even have a name. It was all done on the sly. "Don't lie; it makes you even uglier," I said.

His smile disappeared and was replaced by a stony glare. "Come on now, Anouk. This is business. You can't expect me to walk away every time we see the same client."

If it was purely business, I'd have to accept I'd lose to him every now and then, but it wasn't just business. It was a cat and mouse game and I didn't want to play. "No one in the family called you. So back off. They're not ready to sell."

He smirked. "Oh, no? A few suggestions about the stages of grief, and a little hug here and there, and I think she'll be more than ready. Her husband just left her you know. Her father died, her stepfather died, poor woman's bereft. *Vulnerable*. And I can help with that too. All part of the service."

I shivered at the coldness in him. He'd take advantage of anyone if it furthered his cause. "You're a vile excuse for a man." I lowered my voice to a hiss. "Leave her alone. She doesn't need you stealing her papa's things."

He laughed, nonplussed at my vitriol. "But it's OK for you to play your game?" He pitched his voice to mimic me, '*Take some time, sit, reflect with your father's things.*' What a load of sentimental crap! Life is about living, and he's dead, and his furniture will only gather dust. So maybe it's best if I handle things from here?"

There were so many charlatans in the business and Joshua was at the pointy end of the pile. His lack of compassion and empathy disgusted me, and I only hoped Vivienne was no fool. I knew from experience how charming he could be when he switched that personality on. I fought the urge to run back upstairs and warn her, but it would come across as tacky, like two school kids fighting over a toy. Instead, I pushed past him, my heart heavy.

"Oh, Anouk?" he said his voice silky smooth.

I didn't bother to turn.

"Anouk?" He said more forcefully.

Grudgingly, I spun to face him. "What?"

His eyes twinkled and I knew he had a trump card. I stiffened in response. "Your boyfriend . . ." He paused for effect, and I willed myself not to cringe. "Quite the enigma, isn't he? I wonder if you know him at all?"

I knew it would come up after he'd seen us in Saint-Tropez. I clenched my teeth at the retorts flashing through my mind, and eventually said, "You were good practice for me, a lesson in liars. Perhaps he's going to rob me just like you did." I wouldn't give him the satisfaction of knowing the damage he'd done to my heart at the time.

His eyes widened. "Rob you? I have no idea what you're talking about, Anouk! Perhaps you should be more careful when it comes to gift giving. Only a child would ask for her things back when the affair was over . . ."

Tears prickled but I fought them back. "I hope someone treats you the way you treated me. Then you'll know. You almost bankrupted me, Joshua. I don't know how you can live with yourself."

He let out a chuckle, and I turned away unable to hold the sobs that threatened to spill. How could I have been so blind? Even Lilou had warned me, saying she thought he was duplicitous.

I sent up a silent prayer that Vivienne would see straight through Joshua. I had a feeling, vulnerable or not, that she'd see a predator like him a mile away.

My shoulders slumped south thinking of people like Vivienne who were trying to wade through their grief with Joshua types waiting in the wings with faux platitudes, and seemingly genuine concern.

There was no question I could have priced the contents of Vincent's apartment, and made the deal simple and fast, like ripping off a Band-Aid, but it wouldn't have been the right thing to do. It was so far wrong, it was headache-inducing, thinking that Joshua was up there, schmoozing, flirting if he thought he read her right, and doing whatever he could to tamp down anything I'd said. I shook the negative emotions away, and focused on walking home in the cool, dark evening, my steps heavier than before.

Chapter Twenty-Two

Summer swept in and days grew longer, the sunlight brighter, which lengthened time, making sleeping in a waste of such fine weather.

As I dressed for work, the apartment came alive with morning noise. Lilou was chatting into her phone about jewelry design and Maman was humming in the kitchen. I went to join her, and make coffee. Much as I hated to admit it, sometimes it was nice to wake to the sound of laughter, and know it wasn't just me in the apartment.

As my parents' rift dragged on, I expected Papa to turn up, to make amends, but he never did.

"You sound happy," I said to Maman, noting her hair was done, she wore lipstick, and a new fitted dress covered in red roses.

"I have the chefs coming over for a cooking demonstration," she said, taking ingredients from the cupboards and lining them up along the bench.

"Chefs? Plural?"

"Oui. They want to know my recipe for sorrel and asparagus vichyssoise. The scent wafted down when I made it last week, and it piqued their interest. Their taste buds are screaming for it, so I said I'd teach them. They've been serving pumpkin soup all year – can you believe that?"

I smiled. Maman's soup recipes changed with the season. To make the same recipe over and over again was almost sacrilegious to her. All her food changed with the seasons, and she scoured the markets for the freshest ingredients.

"That sounds like fun, Maman." The change in her was evident for all to see. She was back to humming, and baking, but still sadly not speaking to Papa.

"It *will* be fun. I've been honest and told them I've only cooked in a home-style Provencal kitchen for your papa, but they said they can't learn everything from a book, and would I mind? Of course I don't mind. If they're not inspired at their age, they will never be, so it's back to the traditional way for them."

I kissed her head, happy that they'd made her feel important. "What about Papa? Have you spoken to him?" I knew full well she hadn't, but how else to get her to open up about it?

She ducked her head. "*Non*, and I will not. This . . ." she gestured to the bench laid with ingredients ". . . is exactly my point. To the chefs, I'm not invisible. They're interested in what I have to say. Today, they'll get their hands dirty right beside me. Once we've made a mess, they'll help clean it up. And then, when they go, they'll thank me profusely. And those men are practically strangers. Do you see, Anouk? It wouldn't take much for your papa, who is supposed to know me better than anyone, to do the same." Her words poured out measured, calmly. Her anger had evaporated as the days marched on and had been replaced with resignation.

"I totally understand, Maman. And I'm glad you've found some happiness here, but I do worry about Papa, all alone, too stubborn to apologize."

She stopped, and rested her hands on a mixing bowl, gazing out the window like she was weighing up what to say. "Anouk, this once I won't give in. If he loves me, then he will apologize and change his attitude. To talk and your words to float through the air not being heard eventually cuts you like the blade of a knife. Was what I had to say so unimportant to him? I felt like a slave, working so hard, and so unappreciated. Enough is enough. Here when I talk, people listen, *really* listen. And it's a beautiful thing. Does Papa miss me? I don't know, because it's not like he ever heard me when I was there. All he'll miss is his cook, his cleaner, and his gardener."

What could I say? There'd been no hint Maman had been so unfulfilled until the day she arrived in Paris and my heart tore in two for both of them. "OK, Maman. Hopefully he'll come to his senses soon. Enjoy your day with the chefs."

She kissed my cheeks, her hands squeezing mine, the same that had squished my face as a child, that held me when I cried.

"I will, and say hello to Tristan for me." She arched a brow.

I gave her a long look. "I haven't seen him, Maman."

"You will," she trilled.

I shook my head. "He's not my boyfriend, nothing like it." He'd disappeared, just like that. Off to America, if what he told Madame was true, and I often wondered if I'd ever see him again. It wouldn't have hurt him to let me know. Did he owe me that? I wasn't sure. Maybe he knew I suspected him as the thief, and vanished. Nothing was clear anymore, except I was back to living my life the same, monotonous way.

Back to singing under her breath, Maman simply shrugged, as though she didn't believe me. I couldn't confide in her about my suspicions – she had enough to worry about with Papa. "He's a nice boy."

I made a face. "Au revoir, Maman."

* * *

Warm weather bit my skin as I walked along the boulevards. Paris was pulsing with tourists. The endless queues to climb the Eiffel Tower were thick, and snaked backward, people mostly patient waiting their turn to trudge up seven hundred and four stairs to be rewarded with a spectacular 360-degree view of the bustling city.

Alone, I admitted I was confused about my feelings for Tristan. The night at the book bar played on my mind. In my attempts at prying information, I'd been bold, hadn't overthought anything, and I had enjoyed it. And then shame washed over me. How could I enjoy spending time with someone like him? Did I have no moral compass? Why would I be a magnet for men like him, and Joshua? I should have just dated Lilou's magician friend and be done with it. I shuddered at the thought.

Opening up the shop, I stowed my bag, and filled a watering can. I went outside and gave the peach roses in the planter box a gentle drink.

I emptied the watering can, feeling the sun on my back, and wanted to lounge like a cat in the warmth, but I had things to do and went back inside. It was the height of summer. The promenade was filled with people clutching melting ice creams.

The door of the shop flew open and Madame Dupont rushed in. She was decked out in a shimmery silver dress, as if she was off to the opera – not just another day in her Time Emporium.

"Madame Dupont, are you OK?" Her hands fluttered nervously as she stopped to catch her breath.

"Anouk." She nodded. "It's happened again," she said, her chest heaving from exertion.

I gasped. "Another robbery?"

"Oui! Last night. This time it was The Louis in the 7th arrondissement."

My hands flew to my mouth. The Louis was the most exclusive auction house in all of France, and their security was top notch. "The Cartier jewelry?" I asked, despondency making my eyes cloud. I'd been counting down the minutes until I could bid on a piece of Cartier history.

"And this time he was more brazen; he stole almost half of the lots."

This was a huge loss for all of us. There'd been lots of buzz about the upcoming auction because it was to feature Cartier jewelry that dated right back to the 1900s. The entire collection had belonged to Catherine Lacroix, a French actress who was famous in the fifties. She'd passed away a day after her ninetieth birthday and had stipulated her entire collection be auctioned and the money go to PETA, a charity she put her name and fame to, to further their cause, and help save animals everywhere.

The Cartier range was exquisite from simple solitaire studs, to magnificent necklaces, thick with diamonds. Madame Dupont had wanted to buy one of their famous designs, aptly named the mystery clock.

"This is terrible," I said. "Do the gendarmes have any idea yet? Surely there's footage or something this time."

"I heard through a source," she said gravely, "that the gendarmes are investigating, but won't leak any of the evidence in case the robber flees. This is such a tragic loss. And a huge mark of disrespect for Catherine Lacroix who trusted her beauties would find the right homes and the money to go to those animals she loved so well."

There'd been no sign of Tristan in France; maybe he was just in the wrong place at the wrong time with the other robberies. Was he innocent? The idea gave me hope.

"She'd be horrified," I said. "Her legacy gone."

"Insurance will pay it out," Madame Dupont said, sadly. "But it's not the point. The point is, half of it's gone and into the hands of someone who doesn't deserve it. Anouk, do you think it's your beau? That beautiful man?" Her face fell as she considered Tristan as a heartless criminal for the first time without romancing his part in it.

I shrugged. "Maybe it's not him. I haven't seen him for weeks." My voice was hopeful; no matter how I tried to mask it, it still spilled out.

Her face brightened. "It's his eyes," she said. "Those eyes make a woman melt. I just get the feeling the robber would be . . . sharp-featured, somehow. You know the type, black heart, no soul, eyes that make your blood run cold . . ."

"So we're basing Tristan's innocence on his looks?" We'd never make it as spies, as I'd done the very same thing myself.

She shook her head, disagreeing with me. "All good investigators trust their gut feelings. I'm trusting mine."

"I don't know, Madame. It's suspect that the robberies began just after he arrived. I think we have to be realistic. Our mold for the typical thief – black eyes, black soul – might be wrong," I said. "Short of catching him out what else can we do?" I wrinkled my brow. "I suppose we could write a list of all the auction houses in France, but what good will that do? They all sell jewelry. There's no way to tell which place will be targeted next."

"Are you suggesting we take matters into our own hands? Like a good old-fashioned stake-out?" Her heavily made-up face shone with the idea and I couldn't help but laugh. This was the sort of thing Madame Dupont lived for – some high-stakes adventure.

Before the idea took hold I said, "Well no. I wasn't suggesting a stake-out. I was . . ."

She held up a hand adorned with so many gold rings I wondered how she had the strength to keep it aloft. "It's the only way! The gendarmes are probably taking bribes! Surely it can't take this long to solve the thefts? We'll do it ourselves." She surveyed the shop. "We'll need a camera. Have you got anything other than that box thing over there?" She gestured to an old Le Phoebus box camera, a relic from the 1870s.

I laughed. "All my cameras are antique. They're perfect for arty, moody pictures but not for zooming in or sharp detail." I caught myself. What was I considering? Hiding in a car in the middle of the night! It was something only an unhinged person would do. "But, Madame, what are the chances we'd be at the right place at the right time? There's been no routine to these robberies. It might take months and even then we could be at the wrong place – or worse, see nothing because he gets in through the roof or something!"

Madame Dupont went to light a cigarette but thought better of it when I stared her down. "Darling, you've got to believe, otherwise what else do we have? It'll be fun! We'll take my old Bugatti . . ."

I shook my head, but it was lost on Madame Dupont who was gazing through me, plotting silently. "We can't take that car! It's not exactly inconspicuous." Madame's vintage Bugatti was rumored to have been a gift from movie star Olivetti who she'd had a brief affair with in the seventies. It was eye-catching, too recognizable.

"Okay, I suppose you're right, so we'll hire a car? Something plain: a Peugeot or a Renault. What about that?"

"But we could spend months sitting in a car all night long for no reason! It's ludicrous, Madame Dupont, it really is. It's not as though he's got a key and will waltz in the front entrance."

"You never know." Madame Dupont smirked and went to the door, standing on the threshold, with her arm outside so she could smoke a cigarette. "Darling, what else have you got to do at night-time? Lilou says you're back to those long lonely evenings playing Solitaire on the computer! Did I not tell you to stop that? What kind of life is that? If you want to play cards at least go to the casino! Flutter those eyelashes . . ."

She shook her head as if she was disappointed in me, and I could see why Madame Dupont and Lilou got along so well. Age was just an insignificant number for Madame Dupont and she was still as flighty and spontaneous as Lilou. Madame Dupont told me constantly I was wasting my youth, and my curves. I could only laugh.

But still, I said, "I don't play Solitaire. I play Sim City. I like building villages. Those people depend on me."

"Those people? On a computer game?" Her mouth fell open.

"They've suffered enough. There was an earthquake, and it's

taken a long time to rebuild. Morale is down, it's tense . . ."

Her face drained of color. "It's much worse than I thought."

Guilt tapped me on the shoulder. "I'm only joking, Madame. I don't play Sim City. I occasionally play Solitaire, but my life isn't as empty as Lilou would lead you to believe."

She threw her head back and laughed. "*Merde!* I was so worried! I was planning to kidnap you, and force you to holiday in Saint Barth's or somewhere you couldn't escape. Back to Operation: Aquamarine—"

"Aquamarine?"

"The color of his eyes," she said dreamily. "He won't suspect we're talking about him, if he stumbles on us. So make sure you use that code word whenever you want to discuss it. OK?"

"One minute ago you thought he was innocent!" I couldn't keep up. What insanity had I gotten mixed up in? "I'm sure the gendarmes have investigators staking out the auction houses, and they'll have night-vision cameras, and . . ." I struggled to think of modern-day spy accoutrements. "And . . . guns. And what will we have? An old box camera!" Not exactly cops and robbers' M.O.

"I'll buy a camera! I'll buy two! Binoculars . . ." She wrinkled her nose in contemplation, and then snapped her fingers. "Got it! We'll also need newspapers to hide behind in case someone walks past. We can cut out eye holes so we can still see what's going on right in front of us! It's genius."

We were going to get arrested for disturbing the peace, I was sure of it. "Eye holes? Madame, who'd read the newspaper in a dark car at night-time? Don't you think that'd be a dead giveaway?"

"OK, OK, well it doesn't have to be a newspaper. We just need to blend into our surroundings. I'll get us some overalls, khaki-colored. Wait!" She held up a hand. "Dion! He will know what we need. I'll call him now."

I hid a smile. "OK." As crazy as the idea was it was growing on me. It was hard to resist Madame's enthusiasm. It would be good to know if I was in love with a criminal mastermind. "But I'm not committing to months of this, just so you know."

She blew out a plume of smoke. "Give it a couple of weeks and if we get any proof it's him, then we can discuss the next step. Who knows, it could be a team of women, it could be Lilou's boyfriend, it could be anyone!"

"OK. I guess we've got to help. France can't keep losing its precious jewels. And you're right, Lilou's boyfriend is suspect now I come to think of it. He turned up at the same time as the robberies began too, Madame . . . Don't you think that's weird?"

She sighed. "I think you're grasping at straws to save your man . . ."

I colored. Was I? "Well, he's also been snooping around my apartment, studying my paperwork."

"He's innocent. Probably looking for money, that's all. He's a couch surfer with limited funds. I don't blame him," she said to my appalled face. "Let's make that list. Every auction house and their upcoming auctions. See which jewels he's most likely to target."

An hour later we'd made a long list of potential targets. Madame Dupont left with instructions she'd pick me up the following night once she'd hired a car, and asked Dion to source an abundance of spy paraphernalia.

I hid the list inside my handbag. Could we really catch a thief?

The phone buzzed, halting any thoughts of trying to back out of our plan.

"The Little Antique—"

"Anouk! *Je l'ai mis la maison en feu!*"

"What? Slow down, Papa! You set what on fire?" I stood, galvanized, until I remembered I was too far away to help him.

"The house is on fire! Well, the kitchen more specifically."

In the background the whining of fire engines sounded. "Oh my God, Papa, get out of the house!"

"I can't because I don't have a cell phone, and then how would I tell you?"

206

I held in a sigh. "Papa! Mon Dieu! Just leave, and go to a phone box!"

"OK, OK. Tell Maman to come back, I'm sorry!"

"Just leave, Papa, and let the firemen put it out!"

My pulse thrummed with fright. The line went dead.

I snatched up the phone again and called my apartment. Maman answered, "Bonjour?"

"Maman there's been a fire. Papa set the kitchen alight somehow."

"OK, well thanks for letting me know."

"Maman!"

"What? It's a cry for attention. I bet he was trying to get the creases out of that great big heavy tablecloth he insists on using, and set it on fire with that antiquated iron."

Shock rendered me mute. It was like she didn't care at all. "But, Maman, the house is on fire! The house is ON FIRE." Maybe she'd misheard?

"Sorry that he can't cope, but now he might realize how silly his expectations are. You'll see, ma chérie. It's not time yet."

"Time for what? What if your entire house burns down to the ground?"

"The house won't burn down. He'll be exaggerating like he always does. Anouk, if you really paid attention you'd know he's too egotistical to apologize so he's hoping this will work instead."

Who was this woman? She adored her house, and all the homemade decorating she'd done over the years. How could she be so certain it would be OK?

"I hope he hasn't inhaled too much smoke . . ."

"He hasn't."

"Maman, why are you being so callous?"

She let out a long, weary sigh. "Matteau, my neighbor, called. He saw smoke and went to check Papa was OK. They dumped a heap of water on the tablecloth and the curtains next to it, and it went out. The fire truck was already on its way. Perhaps

207

he should have called them to cancel, and not you, in the hopes you'd tell me, non?"

"So he wasn't in danger?"

"He might have been for a few minutes, but they got it under control. This kind of trickery won't work."

I shook my head, dazed over it all. Papa would rather Maman come home because of a fire, than because he smoothed things over, and capitulated to her compromises. Love was impossible sometimes.

"Wait until I speak to him!"

Chapter Twenty-Three

The following afternoon, I was tidying the shop. With a feather duster I tickled the armoire that housed spools of antique lace ribbons, arranged in color order from pastel pinks, down to golden browns, in various textures and sizes. The day had been deathly quiet because of the glorious sunshine, and for once, I was glad for the peace. It gave me time to ponder the stake-out, and what we'd do if we actually saw Tristan break in to an auction house. Cuff him? I couldn't see me or Madame Dupont running across the cobblestoned street and lunging at him, taking him down. Did we even have handcuffs? Take photos and show the gendarmes? But what if Madame Dupont was right and he was bribing them?

What if it was someone else? It could be anyone. The narrow-eyed milliner who was always draped in layers of expensive jewelry. The man from the hobby shop who had ties with politicians – he was always talking about high-tech gadgets. Henry . . .

As the sun began its slow descent amber rays shimmered through the lace curtains, like fairy dust. Nerves fluttered in my belly like the tips of butterfly wings. One night, I promised myself, and then I'd tell Madame Dupont we were being silly.

Bundling up the takings, I stuffed them into my bag, and locked up the shop.

Instead of walking home, I went to the Metro. I had to see a client in de Ménilmontant, the 20th arrondissement. Marianna often called on me to visit, and price antiques she'd found at vintage fairs, and flea markets.

The train station was full of bustling bodies in the race to secure a spot. Peak hour, and the glum faces of weary travelers, sapped after an unusually hot day. Elbowing my way on like a seasoned Parisian does, I held the strap above to keep from falling over, as the train shimmied and rocked its way forward.

At the first stop, a wave of commuters exited, and another throng barreled their way on. I was being bumped and jostled, and rued the fact I'd left work so early. In my haste to get back in time for Madame's arrival, I'd hit the busy hour.

The hair on the back of my neck stood up. Someone was encroaching into my personal space, a common misdemeanor on the Metro. I was about to turn to tell them off when he spoke.

"I like your hat."

It was him. The thief. The robber. The bad guy.

I turned to face him. Tristan. "I didn't think the likes of you would use public transport," I countered, while my mind spun furiously. Had he been in Paris the whole time? Or had he come back just to steal the Cartier jewelry? My heart sank.

He stood out on the Metro with the bright blond of his hair, and dazzlingly white teeth as he flashed a smile. The rest of us wore muted expressions, vacant eyes. But not him. He had challenge written all over him in big, fat capital letters.

"Sometimes I get bored of fast cars, and private planes."

I felt wobbly, startled to see him on the Metro and confused by the pulsating need to reach out and touch him that had flowed through me. Shaking my head I reminded myself he was probably trying out a new escape route. I shouldn't trust a word that fell from his silky lips. "You're only adding to the chaos being here. There's not enough room for commuters as it is," I snapped.

He cocked his head, and tried to gauge my mood. A surliness

settled over me, but I had to hide it. This moment was too good to pass up. I needed information. I needed to know if he was the robber, the Postcard Bandit everyone was talking about.

The train trembled along, shuffling us together. "Did you miss me?"

I choked out, "More than I can say."

A grin split his face. "Good."

I found myself soften, only to shake myself again to figure out how I could gather intelligence without being obvious. "What are your plans for this evening?" I asked. Hoping he'd say something I could use in an effort to find him later that evening from my hidden vantage point in the car Madame Dupont hired.

"Busy, I'm sorry. But I'm free tomorrow night if you are? Dinner first, though." He coughed into his hand. "If you prefer?"

I blushed to the roots of my hair. Drowning myself in champagne had been a mistake. "I have quite a few auctions to attend, and lots to peruse tomorrow."

"At night-time?" He frowned.

"Oui, I go through the pictures online and make my selections. What about you? Have you seen anything you like lately?" All I needed was a name!

"There's one thing I want."

I bumped hard against him as the train took a turn. "And that is?"

"A secret."

This wasn't going well at all. I was only digging myself deeper into his web of deceit. Should I tell him to run? I swallowed back genuine fear that he'd get caught, and spend a lifetime in jail. *Why did he have to be this way?*

"So when can I expect the pleasure of your company?" he asked, his voice saccharine.

It was now or never. My mind rushed with so many emotions, but I thought of Joshua and the drama that had ensued, and knew

I couldn't go through that again. It'd have to be a clean break. "I'm not interested in you in that way, I'm sorry."

"That way? What exactly is *that* way? Do you mean sexually?" His voice boomed around the small space, drawing wide-eyed stares.

"Shush, don't do that brash American thing!" I hissed.

"Answer the question. Do you mean you're *not* sexually attracted to me?" He was goading me, trying to get a rise, and he'd succeeded.

I raised my voice to match his. "No, Tristan Black, I am not sexually attracted to you at all. Not even a little bit." Heat rushed to my face.

He threw his head back and laughed. "You're a liar. You've always been a liar. And you know how I can tell? The way . . ." He paused, and gave me a smirk. I tensed for what he'd say next. "You kissed me back. You can't fake that kind of passion."

"Did you kiss him back?" a round, brown-skinned woman beside me asked.

I pursed my lips, as I noticed all eyes were on us. This was like being a performer in some kind of street theater. "I did but only because . . ."

She stopped me with a look. "How many times did you kiss him?"

I gulped. "Twice, or maybe three times, five at the most, but it's not what it sounds like."

The woman exchanged a knowing glance with Tristan and said, "Sounds like someone doesn't want to admit how they feel. Tread gently, because you might scare her off. Probably one of those types with all the *issues*, you know, you read about it in those magazines—"

"Excuse me, I'm standing right here!"

She shrugged. "You kissed him back. I know I'm old but that sounds like you're attracted to the boy. I mean, look at him." It was like a tennis match; people were turning their heads from me to him, and back again.

"So he's got a nice face, big deal."

She guffawed, and a few commuters joined in tittering.

"What?" I asked her. "What's so funny about that? I happen to prefer men who are . . . a little uglier." *Way to go, Anouk. You prefer men who are . . . uglier?*

"He's got more than a nice face, and I can tell he's got feelings for you. What's stopping you from giving him a chance? You're a pretty girl. You two match, you know that? With your blond-haired blue-eyed loveliness."

Tristan stood there like he was the King of England, smirking, while his loyal followers made goo-goo faces at him. "I don't date Americans." I stuck my chin out.

She rolled her eyes. "That's the craziest thing I've ever heard. I bet you dream about him, don't you? That's how you know – if they steal into your subconscious like that."

"He certainly does *steal* . . . into my, er, subconscious." The crowd nodded and continued staring at me. It was very unlike Parisians to get involved in other people's conversations on a busy train. Tristan had that way about him, like he'd hypnotized them into being his cheer squad. How did he do it? Maybe he'd hired a rent-a-crowd to do his bidding?

"Excuse me." I pushed past them all, relieved the train was screeching to a standstill just in time. "This is my stop."

Once the train pulled away, I halted, and leaned against the tiled wall on the platform. It was so mind-bendingly obvious he was the culprit. He could manipulate a carriage full of Parisians into believing him. It was all down to practice. It's probably how he managed so many heists. Used that intense gaze of his to brainwash innocent people.

I hurried out of the Metro, rushing to my meeting with Marianna feeling frazzled. Madame Dupont would be at my home soon, and I had to shower and try to dress inconspicuously, so I would need to make this fast. I was more determined than ever to catch him out. After my extremely hasty appointment with Marianna I headed home, mind spinning.

When I got to my apartment, I froze. My handbag! It was gone. That didn't stop me from manically patting myself down. Did I leave it at work? No, I'd taken my ticket from my purse to get into the station.

It was him again! Mournfully I added sleight of hand to his capabilities. Of course he'd be a master at pickpocketing – he could break into auction houses protected by FBI-quality security systems without being caught. I raced back downstairs, desultory, all my fire gone.

Madame Dupont arrived, beeping the horn happily, her face animated. I rushed to the car, and threw myself in the front seat. "Don't you want to change first?" she asked handing me a pair of overalls that resembled the jungle. "They're camouflaged."

"He stole my handbag!" I said.

"Who did?"

"Tristan! He just so happened to be on the same train as me."

Her mouth fell open. "Where is the list we made of suspect places? Don't tell me it was in your bag? He'll know we're onto him!"

I gasped, and cradled my head. "Oui, it was in there. But it's in a hidden pocket. Maybe he won't see it?"

She rested her hands on the steering wheel and gazed out the windscreen. "Why would he steal your bag?"

I lifted a shoulder. "Money? I had today's takings. But it would be small change to him."

Madame's mouth twisted. "The keys to your shop? Do you think he'd rob you?"

"The secret room!" My pulse quickened. Maybe the lore about the secret room had intrigued him? But the contents seemed minor compared to what he could steal. I mentally assessed what was in my purse. Apartment and shop keys, including those for the secret room, whose alarm he'd easily be able to override. The list of suspected targets. Various lipsticks, a compact. My cell phone. Was there anything incriminating on it?

"Oh, Madame!" I cried out. "My cell phone has our text messages! What if he reads them?"

She drummed her fingers on the steering wheel, as she pondered. "We spoke in code, remember? He can't know that Gargoyle by the river means the Bell Tower Auction House. He won't know what we're on about. Using the word Aquamarine was a brilliant touch. He won't know we're referring to him!"

"Oui, but what about the message about the stake-out?"

"All we said is we were going to meet." She took her phone from a velvet clutch and scrolled through our messages. "Hang on, can he even read French?"

We stilled. "No! He can't!" The air hummed with hope. "When we were in Saint-Tropez, he asked the waiter to translate the dinner menu!" I sagged, as relief flooded me.

Madame's cackle rang out in the small space. "OK, OK, so he can't read our messages, he might not find the list, and at the very worst he's got the keys to your shop and apartment. Something tells me if he wanted to sneak into your secret room, he would have done so by now. Maybe he stole your handbag so he can simply return it to you? It's the oldest trick in the book when Cupid comes knocking."

I blew out my cheeks, considering it all. "Do you really think he'd do that?" A weight lifted.

"Of course. He's not sure where he stands. It's a reason to visit you."

She was right. He didn't need my keys. If he'd wanted to break into my shop, he would have done so already. "OK, let's focus on the matter at hand. We don't have the list, but we don't need it. We know our first guess was the Trésor Auction House. Let's head there, and wait across the road. I'm sure nothing will happen until it's dark, but better if we're there before him."

She twisted the key in the ignition and the car burbled to life. "Oui," she said. "Grab the camera from the backseat and hold on!" Her hands whitened around the steering wheel as she stared straight ahead.

I didn't know whether I was terrified or electrified. Nervous laughter barreled out of me as I reached for the so-called spy gear behind me. The backseat was piled high with cameras, binoculars, and some strangely shaped goggles. "How much did you buy?"

"All of it," she said, grinning. "There's heat-reflecting cameras and a GoPro for our heads. I don't want to miss anything. We can set them all up, and watch the footage later."

I shook my head. "What are these?" I held up the goggles that resembled something the little yellow Minions would wear.

"Oh, they're night-vision goggles. If we have to chase him we'll be able to see him a mile away."

"Let's hope we don't have to chase him," I said, picturing us wearing night-vision goggles, and GoPros, and scampering down the street in our high heels. Even though Madame Dupont was dressed in her camouflage gear, she'd still worn sky-high stilettos. We were Parisian. We could do a marathon in them if we had to.

She tutted. "Where's the fun in that? I personally would love to chase him." We sped off down the street, Madame Dupont cornering like she was on the Monaco Formula One track. I gripped the armrest, and tensed as the momentum sent me sideways.

Finally she zoomed into a parking space, skidding to a stop. Burnt rubber permeated the air. "Way to blend in," I said, giving her a hard stare.

"Come on, I drive like any other Parisian. Like I've got somewhere to be."

"You were one step away from pulling the handbrake and going in backward!"

She smirked. "I was too! You know me so well. I watched some stunt-driving footage for pointers . . . I'm sure I could have slid in backward."

"Madame, you'll give the game away." I shook my head as we got our gear ready. We put the cameras in the foot well, and reclined our seats so we were at eye line with the dashboard.

216

"I feel ridiculous wearing these." I pointed to my face, which was adorned with the heavy night-vision goggles, and the GoPro strapped to my head like I was some kind of intrepid adventurer.

"Darling, relax. You look as beautiful as ever. Would a glass of wine help? You're coiled up tight like a snake."

Who knew spy gear was so weighty? I truly felt like I was going into battle. "We shouldn't drink on the job, surely?"

She waved me away, making a face. "It's purely medicinal." She leaned over into the backseat and brandished a bottle of vin rouge, and two glasses. I had to hand it to her: she came prepared.

We nursed our glasses of wine and waited. Moody gray shadows darkened the sky and the air cooled, the earlier heat dissipating for another day. I checked my watch. We'd been exactly an hour, but it felt more like five.

Madame Dupont crossed her arms. "I expected a little more action, I must admit."

A knock on the window had us jump in fright. Lilou's pretty face peered in. "What are you doing?" she muffled through the glass.

Madame Dupont unlocked the car and Lilou bent herself to fit in the small backseat.

"How did you know where we were?" I asked.

She frowned. "I didn't. I was on my way home from an appointment. I got a huge order from the shop on Quai Voltaire. They commissioned me to make key rings."

"Lilou, that is incredible!" I said, pride making my voice hitch.

She waved me away. "What's going on here?"

"We can't tell you, Lilou," Madame Dupont said gravely. "It's top secret."

"You're trying to catch the jewel thief, aren't you?"

There were no secrets in my life, despite my efforts to keep them, damn it! "Have you been going through my room again?" I'd cut out newspaper articles about the thefts and had hidden them in my closet.

"I needed business attire," she said with a shrug.

"Lilou!"

"What?" Her faux innocent expression was fixed firmly in place.

"Why can't you buy some with the allowance Papa gives you?" Money ran through her fingers like water.

"Anouk, no one could live off that paltry amount! It wouldn't even keep you in lipstick!"

There was no point fighting with her. We had a job to do. "If you stay, you have to promise not to say a word to anyone. Deal?"

"Deal. Pass me your wine."

Another hour crept past, even slower than the last. Lilou leaned through the small gap between the front seats. "So who exactly are we looking for? Who do we suspect?"

I exchanged a glance with Madame Dupont and gave her an almost imperceptible headshake. "No suspects. We might not even be in the right place."

"OK," she said. "Oh look there's your boyfriend! Call him over; I can switch seats with you."

Madame Dupont and I snapped to attention. "Shush, Lilou," I hissed. "Get down, don't let him see you!"

Lilou dropped down and whispered. "Lover's tiff?"

I wanted to shake her. "He's the robber!"

"What!" Her voice came out like a shriek.

"Be quiet! You're going to get us caught!"

With nimble fingers, Madame Dupont reached for the binoculars without taking her eyes off the suspect. Against the goggles, with the GoPro crowding her head I wondered how much she'd actually see. I was certain we were doing it all wrong.

"He's jiggling the front door locks of the auction house," she said barely audible.

"That's his method? Check if the door is open? Doesn't seem very clever to me," I said, squinting to make him out through the haze of my night-vision goggles. All I could see were splodges of green, almost fluid smudges like spilled liquid. Did they need to be switched on or something?

"OK, he's on the move," she said. I wrenched my goggles off, and dislodged the GoPro at the same time. Rubbing my face, I leaned forward, peering over the dash.

"What's he doing now?" Lilou snaked her way into the front seat, squashing me further into the foot well.

"*Merde!* Can't you be quiet? We're trying to watch!"

"Shush," she said. "I'm trying to see too. I've got better eyes than you. Younger."

I shoved her with my elbow for good measure.

"He's making a phone call," Madame Dupont said. "Duck down, quick! He's coming this way."

I scrambled lower, which was virtually impossible with Lilou on top of me, her limbs akimbo. She was a tall girl, and didn't fit well when there was another body vying for space.

"What if he sees us?" Panic rose up; my stomach flipped with angst.

Madame Dupont sat deathly still. I couldn't even make out the rise of her chest. "Madame?" I whispered, snatching a hand from under Lilou's leg to reach out to Madame. It would be just my luck she perished on our mission. I'd never forgive myself. Perhaps her ox-strong heart wasn't cut out for these types of things. "Madame?" I asked querulously.

I was inches away from touching her arm when she sat bolt upright, and flicked the key in the ignition. "He's crossing the road. Stay down!" she screeched.

My heart pumped so loud I could feel it in my ears. She was alive! And he was about to catch us!

"Mon Dieu, he's looking straight at me. Hold on, belle filles. Un, deux, trois!" She gripped the steering wheel tight and with a screech of the clutch she pumped the gas and the car shot forward with a scream of burnt rubber.

I was thrown forward into the underside of the dash, as she

careened, zigzagging across the road like a madwoman. When we were far enough away, she slowed. I managed to clutch my heart and ask, "Did he get close enough to see in?"

Catching her breath, Madame Dupont took a moment before she responded. "No, I don't think he did. That was the most fun I've had in ages!"

What was I mixed up with here? A woman who thought this was an adventure! I opened the door just as Lilou gave me a shunt with her foot – I promptly fell onto the pavement in a messy heap. It had been claustrophobic being squished by my sister, and I welcomed the fresh air and space to think. Lilou sprang out behind me and hoisted me to my feet.

"Madame Dupont, are you coming in?" I asked. "Shall we debrief?"

"No thank you, I've got a date," she said. "Make notes." Her brown eyes twinkled mischievously. Honestly, she was a never-ending well of energy. "I'll watch the footage later and see if I can spot anything else."

Before I could respond, she roared off down the street, taking the left turn at an alarming speed.

Chapter Twenty-Four

Coughing through the plume of exhaust fumes that Madame left in her wake, I turned to go inside, exhausted after the stake-out.

Lilou grabbed my arm and wrenched me back to the curb. "You want to tell me what's going on?"

Could I trust her? She wasn't likely to take it seriously and then where would I be? "No, I don't, really. And don't mention anything to Maman. I don't want her to worry."

She folded her arms. "Tell me or I'll find your diary and read about it for myself."

I glared at her, but she stood firm. "I don't *know* what's going on. But I think we've just proved Tristan is the jewel thief. And that's all I can say right now. Don't breathe a word of it to anyone, especially Henry."

She scoffed. "Why's he the thief? Because he rattled a few door handles? That hardly means he's a criminal. And what if nothing goes missing from there?"

I stifled a sigh. This is why I didn't want her involved. "Those are all good points. But there's more to it than that."

She gave me a benign smile. "You love him, and you're trying to find an excuse to walk away."

What *was* it with everyone lately? "I hardly know the guy, and I most certainly don't love him!"

"Then why do you blush every time someone mentions him?"

"I'm blushing because my life was in Madame's hands zooming up those roads like a rally driver. My blood pressure is sky high. I feel *faint*!"

"Yeah, right. You always do this, Anouk. Try and find a way out so they don't break your heart first. So you risked it with Joshua and it didn't work out. That doesn't mean you have to give up entirely. Tristan might be the best thing that ever happened to you, but you'll never know because you're looking for a way to distance yourself."

"I didn't know you were a psychologist." Honestly, it was like no one thought I had a brain in my head.

She shrugged. "Calling it as I see it."

The breeze blew past, bringing with it the scent of Maman's bouillabaisse from the bistro. I would recognize that scent anywhere; it reminded me of home. "Merci, Lilou. When I'm ready for advice from someone who changes boyfriends like they change shoes, I'll be sure and ask you."

She put her hands on my shoulders and stared into my eyes. "Anouk, don't you see? I'm *not* going to settle for second best. When I find the right guy, I'll know. And I've been with Henry for months. He's got potential, but I doubt he's the one. Still, I wouldn't have found him by hiding. One setback, and you've given up. Now you've hatched some plan to catch Tristan out. You didn't see the way he looked at you, like you were a prized piece of art . . ."

With an eye roll, I said, "Yeah, probably wondering if he could sell me on the black market."

"No, he was probably wondering why he has to try so hard to get your attention. And now, what, he's a wanted man, a jewel thief? I don't think so somehow." She shook her head like I was crazy.

It wasn't like Lilou to speak like an adult. I hadn't pegged her for someone who noticed anything other than herself. Had she been paying attention this entire time?

Still, I was the big sister who'd seen a lot more of the real world and its orchestrations than she ever would. "You wouldn't understand. Life is easy for you – you're given an allowance, and you work when it suits. You follow the breeze, and any man that comes your way. One of us has to be responsible, and that falls to me. Do I need to remind you Maman is still here, refusing all Papa's phone calls? He's falling to pieces without her." I gave her a hard stare. "Have you called him since the fire? Do you even *know* about the fire?"

She kept me pinned to the spot. "Do you ever think maybe you should leave well enough alone? Maman and Papa are *adults*. Why should you step in and fix things? I know you mean well, but you spend all your time worrying about us, when you should be worrying about yourself. We'll be OK. And if we make a few mistakes along the way we'll learn from those." She shrugged like it was nothing. But really, she just didn't understand.

I blew out a breath. "That sounds great in theory, Lilou. But if I don't help things will spiral out of control. Papa is falling into a depression because he thinks his family doesn't need him. He set the house on fire, on purpose if what Maman believes is true! You're treating my apartment like it's a hostel. If you want me to stop worrying, then start behaving like an adult. Make your own money; pay a few bills. Call Papa and tell him you love him. You know?" It was hard to hear Lilou say I was interfering in their lives, when they were taking over mine. Who'd help them if I didn't?

"Fine." She dropped her arms to her side. "But just listen to me about Tristan, OK?"

Why did everyone think they knew that man? He was as fake as a spray-on tan, but disguised himself well enough everyone had something good to say about him.

"I can't promise that. But if he's innocent then I'll give it my all and see what happens."

After a tumultuous night's sleep, I woke with a clear plan. Nab the thief, and worry about my love life, or lack thereof, later. It was just before seven so I crept to the kitchen phone and dialed Madame. Sleep eluded her as she'd aged, and I knew she'd be up, reading the papers, and drinking coffee, in her front parlor.

"Bonjour, Anouk! I've been waiting for your call."

"Bonjour, Madame. Any word?" With her network, I knew she'd have put the feelers and would know before any reporter did whether the auction house had been robbed overnight.

"Oui." Her voice was bright, and high, like the mission had given her yet another lease on life. "I've heard from a source, no robbery overnight, not there, not anywhere. He must have been doing some kind of reconnaissance. I think we should go back tonight. The GoPro footage showed nothing, just his lovely little saunter down the street."

I chortled at her typical Madame Dupont response. "OK," I said. "I was so sure he was going to break in." I bit my lip, contemplating it all. Something niggled. "Don't you think it's strange he'd be so obvious?"

"What do you mean?" she asked. "He didn't actually *do* anything."

"Tristan didn't rob the place, but he did case it out, and his face wasn't covered, he was easily recognizable on the multitude of CCTV cameras around the building. Isn't that weird?"

"That is odd, unless that's his ploy. If they questioned him, he could counter with he wouldn't be so silly to be in the vicinity, if he was the thief. It's quite brilliant really."

"Mhmm," I mumbled, unconvinced. "Risky, though. It would be easier not to be in the vicinity and save being questioned at all."

"I have to go, ma chérie." Peals of sultry laughter rang out behind her. She was incorrigible. "Let's chat tonight."

I hung up the phone, and made a pot of coffee, my mind full of Tristan.

*　*　*

A week later I was in the shop zombie-like and bone-numbingly exhausted after spending most nights on the lookout. I wanted to curl up in bed and sleep for a month. But Madame Dupont refused to stop, even though I could see it was costing her too. I felt as though she was keener to prove Tristan's innocence than nab the thief. But hope was fading for me. My handbag hadn't materialized, so the locks had been changed, and alarm codes reset. Not that it'd matter to the likes of him, the criminal mastermind. The cash was gone, but at least it hadn't been much, on that slow summery day.

They'd been no robberies, but Tristan had kept a low profile too. Thankfully I had customers aplenty to keep my mind occupied.

With my eye pressed tight against my loupe, I inspected a lapis lazuli gemstone. It was taken from an old brooch whose coupling had disintegrated over time. As gems went, it wasn't worth much money, but it should have been because it was so stunningly beautiful. It was polished to a shine – bright cobalt blue with gold flecks that shimmered like the sky.

"I know it's probably not worth anything," the woman said. She was wearing a polka dotted dress, and smelled like summer, a hint of coconut, and sunshine. She fluffed her ginger curls and gave me a smile. "I have the whole set." She tapped her handbag. "A ring, earrings, and a necklace, as well as the brooch. They're all in the same condition, a little rough around the edges but not without charm."

"What's the history behind them?" I asked.

"They were my aunt's. She left them to me, but they're not my style." She motioned to herself. She was draped in white pearls. "It seemed a waste to hide them away in a jewelry box."

"Tell me about your aunt." I nursed the gemstone in my hand. It was weighty, the stone too large for the brooch that had housed it.

The woman leaned her elbows on the counter. "She was a marine biologist. Hence the lapis lazuli. She always wore blue. She didn't really like people." The woman let out a laugh. "Much preferred mammals. The last time we spoke was the happiest I'd ever heard her. I had to tell her to slow down so I could catch what she was trying to say; her words were tumbling together in her excitement."

"Why was she so excited?"

"Aunt Molly was sailing to the Southern Ocean to help save whales. She was one of a select group chosen for their various abilities, and she was certain they'd achieve their goal. Her skill obviously was being a marine biologist, but they had all sorts on the voyage."

"Sounds like she was passionate about it," I said. The gem winked under the lighting, and I knew the previous owner was standing off to the side somewhere listening to her story be told through her niece.

The woman's lip wobbled, and I sat on a stool behind the counter, giving her time to compose herself.

"They saved the whales. Aunt Molly and a few of the crew jumped aboard the whaling ship, and managed to cut the lines to the harpoons. But after, as she went to board her own ship, she fell into the water. They searched for her into the night, and again at first light. But she was gone, vanished without a trace."

"I'm so sorry. They never found her?" Goose bumps broke out over my skin. There was more to the story, I was sure of it.

She shook her head. "I found out later she had stage four cancer. I don't think she wanted to be found. I think she saved the whales and then joined them one last time. It would have been her worst nightmare being surrounded by people as her condition deteriorated. Getting pounded with platitudes, and false smiles would have driven her mad. Instead, she died on her terms."

It became hard to breathe, like the air had been sucked out of the shop. And I knew I was feeling her last moments, in the gentlest possible way. With a hand on my throat, I said, "You have to keep these gems; they represent so much." I was in awe of Aunt Molly, living her last minute the way she wanted to. Throwing herself into the vast blue of the ocean, after rescuing a pod of whales for one more day.

"I thought so too. But it's like I can hear her, see her sometimes, just a brief flash, and I think she's telling me to pass them on. There's someone who needs them more, someone they will inspire to do great things."

I realized Aunt Molly was right. The gems just had to wait for their next owner to find them.

"If you're sure, I can give you . . ."

She put her hand over mine, and closed my palm against the gem. "No, I don't want anything for them. Just that they go to someone you think is worthy. The word around Paris is that's what you do best."

Heat pooled in my palm where the gem flashed. "That's quite a compliment. I'd love to find the collection its perfect partner. But you can always ask for them back. It takes time to find someone who'll understand your aunt's story, because it will also be theirs, so there'll be no rush."

The woman tilted her head and surveyed me. "You'll tell her story?"

I nodded. "That's the most important part."

After she'd retreated into the summery day, I took a cloth and polished the lapis lazuli set, thrilled the captivating jewelry wouldn't be kept in a musty drawer anymore. They deserved to be on display, shining brilliantly until they caught the eye of someone special. I already knew it would be someone who loved animals, someone who helped protect them.

Key in hand, I unlocked the glass display cabinet and shuffled some jewelry around to make room. Lost in thought, I imagined Aunt Molly, exuberant that she'd completed her mission to save the whales – but was she scared in the end? I liked to think she just closed her eyes, and heard the music of the whales as they spoke to her under water, a symphony of thanks. I was a little teary thinking of such a thing.

Perched over the glass to check the positioning of Aunt Molly's treasures, I didn't hear the door, and jumped, and clutched my heart when a voice said, "I believe this belongs to you."

How did he always creep up like that? My gaze dropped to the floor, to check he wasn't wearing some kind of special spy shoes, but they looked like regular summer loafers. I snatched my handbag from him. "The old steal the bag so you can return it trick?" I raised an eyebrow and sauntered back behind the counter.

He grinned, his blue eyes flashing. "You dropped it," he said. "You're just lucky I was there and saw it fall from your shoulder as you leapt out of the train like you were being chased."

I unzipped my bag. "Oh, I'm sure that's exactly how it happened." With a glare at him, I rifled through it, checking my cell phone, which was switched off. Maybe he didn't have time to decipher the French messages if it had run out of battery.

I wanted to clap a hand to my forehead. I had to remember Tristan wasn't an ordinary man, no matter what Lilou said. If the phone had run out, he could have easily charged it. There was a pin code security on, but again, he could override that if he wanted to. It just depended on the real reason he took the bag. The roll of Euros was still held tight with a rubber band. I couldn't check the secret pocket with him there, in case he hadn't seen our list of suspected auction houses.

"Now you've thanked me and we're all caught up . . ." he said.

"I didn't thank you." I glowered. "It's caused me quite a bit of grief actually."

"I can see it in your eyes, how truly happy you are to be reunited with that red lipstick of yours."

So he *had* gone through my bag! But why?

"What?" He widened his eyes acting the innocent. "It wasn't zipped up. A few things spilled out."

I folded my arms, and pursed my lips.

"As I was saying, I came to invite you to a little party I'm hosting. You and your family . . ."

"Why?" How did this figure into his plan? My first instinct was to say no, but maybe this was a better way to keep tabs on him. I wouldn't take my eyes off him all night, even if I had to follow him to the bathroom and hide behind a ficus or something.

"The grand reopening of the Ritz Paris is worth celebrating, no?"

"Of course." There was much excitement about the grand reopening, after major restorations had seen the Ritz Paris closed for the last few years, and a further few months after a fire had broken out, delaying it.

It was every girl's dream to spend a night at the Ritz in one of their sumptuous suites, or visit one of the many bars and restaurants, each steeped in history. As a worshipper of antiques, I could only imagine how much beauty I'd find there. And I bet he knew it; he *knew* I couldn't say no to such an invitation.

Tristan's gaze was playful. "I told them to watch out for you – you drink champagne like water and then kiss strange men."

"Let's hope there are canapés to soak up the alcohol this time, non?"

"Touché. I'm a bad date."

"It wasn't a date."

"OK, it was a drink, followed by some French kissing . . . And a promise from you, that you'd love me forever if I was a Robin Hood in disguise."

What a faux pas. That night would haunt me for the rest of my life. "Robin Hood? That doesn't make any sense." I blanked my face, hoping a blush wouldn't give me away. Had I told him I was spying on him? I clearly wasn't cut out for this type of lifestyle.

"You were full of mysterious quips," he said. "If you didn't speak English so well I'd blame it on translation, but there's more going on in there, more than you let on." He stepped forward and ran the pad of his finger along my temple. My mind raced, and my heartbeat matched its pace. It was hard to know how to react because I wasn't sure what he knew. *And* he was touching me again. It irked that some secret part of me liked it. *Remember, he is a mirage; he isn't real.* "If that's all, I have to get back to work."

Why couldn't he just be an antique collector? Why did he have to steal?

Thief! Robber! Criminal! While I couldn't yell the words, I felt better thinking them.

Outside, a busker set up his music stand, and blew on a trumpet. The tinny sound drifted in. People sauntered slowly past, eating ice creams or drinking chocolaty milkshakes. Paris in summer was almost carnival-like. Music, food, gaiety. Just outside those doors was a city full of frivolity.

He followed my gaze to the musician, and then said, "You're right. Some people dedicate their life to work no matter what it costs them." His eyes were full of melancholy.

"Are you referring to me?" My family had harped on to him about my obsession with the shop, and the fact I didn't have many friends, and no love interest. Anyone would pity the person they'd described.

His gaze darkened. "Why do you stiffen like that? I wasn't referring to you."

"Well who were you referring to?" I wasn't going to take anyone's pity.

I couldn't read his expression. He distanced himself, like he'd done so many times before. It was almost like he was angry, not at me, but at something inexplicable. I surveyed him for the longest time, wondering if guilt was nudging up against him. "Forget it," he said. "So I'll see you at the Ritz? Nine o'clock tonight?"

"Sure, we'll all be there. You won't miss us." I'd be his shadow, and this time, I'd keep hold of all my faculties. I had a premonition the catch-up was a ruse, and I'd find out why. And *this* time I'd be prepared.

Chapter Twenty-Five

Maman stumbled along the uneven cobblestones. I grabbed her elbow to stop her falling into the street. "I told you not to wear those heels!" I said.

She laughed, and hitched her skirt up so she could see her feet, as if she could make them cooperate on the pencil-thin heels just by watching them. "Ma chérie, I've never been to the Ritz, but I've always wanted to. I can't wear my peasant shoes, can I?"

I tutted. "You should've worn whatever was comfortable. We don't need to try and be anyone other than ourselves!" The sentiment came out more like a command than I'd meant. But my family, including ring-in Henry, had jumped and yodeled like they'd just won the lottery when I told them they've been invited to Tristan's party. I had tried to tamp down their excitement, but they wouldn't hear a word of it.

"Anouk!" Maman scolded me. "It's *the Ritz*. I may be a simple village dweller but even I know you don't sashay in there in any old thing! You of all people should know that."

"Oui, she's right," Lilou concurred. She was practically skipping ahead in her excitement.

"See?" Maman beamed at me. Her features shone with happiness, and she looked beautiful, as if she'd found the fountain of

232

youth. Lilou had taken pains to fix Maman's hair into a high stack of cascading curls. Back home, she usually wore a house coat, and simple shoes, and her hair was always tied in a tight bun; here she was flourishing, shedding layers to reveal a different woman, maybe the one she'd always wanted to be.

"You need to relax, Anouk," Lilou said. "Is it because you're nervous about dating again? It's like riding a bike. You just get back on after a fall . . ." I narrowed my eyes at her. She knew exactly why I was nervous. At least she had kept the secret so far.

I replied, "I'm not dating him! And you're all animated like he's some kind of celebrity, and he just isn't."

She went to counter, but I held up a hand. "Now's not the time, Lilou."

Maman groaned as she wobbled along. "Honestly, Anouk, sometimes I worry you've spent too long among inanimate objects and it's warped your mind. Tristan is a lovely man. He wants to get to know you better. *All* of us better. And what's wrong with that?"

"Wait, what? How do you know he wants to get to know us?"

She bit her lip and had the grace to blush. "He told me."

I cocked my head. "When did he tell you? He only invited us this afternoon . . ." She hadn't seen him since that awkward night when he arrived at the apartment and squirreled me away to drink too much champagne, right?

With a squirm, she said, "He dropped over this afternoon after he saw you. I guess he wanted to make sure we *got* the invite . . ." Her voice faded away. "I wasn't supposed to tell you."

That man! "See what I mean? Why the pretense, hmmm?" He managed to dash around Paris like it was a small village. Was there no end to his manipulations? "And what else did he have to say?"

She shrugged noncommittally. "I got the impression he's lonely. You might think he leads an exotic lifestyle, and maybe he does, but I detected a real emptiness in him. He's drawn to you, sees something he likes in the way you live, and us too. I don't see

233

why you can't offer friendship? It would be churlish not to. I didn't raise you to be so judgmental."

How could she understand? I hadn't told her my suspicions about Tristan, so she thought I was being petulant for no good reason. "Fine." I gave in. It was not the time to explain, and if I did, they'd act out of character and he'd know we were on to him.

Maman grabbed my hand and pulled me along. "Smile." She smoothed her fingers along my forehead. "Stop frowning."

The change in my maman was incredible. Here she was doling out advice, calm and relaxed as could be, wearing a sky-high pair of heels, and one of my vintage wrap dresses, so vividly yellow it was like sunshine. I felt a pang for my papa home alone with charred curtains, waiting for Maman to come back. If he could see her now, in her element, he'd fall in love with her all over again. I wondered what they each needed in order to be happy.

No one wants to see their parents split up, but Maman was like a bird free of her cage, and it made me wonder how much she had settled for in her life, when perhaps she always yearned to flutter her wings elsewhere. Would I suffer the same fate – by holing myself up at work, talking to customers and claiming they were my friends, not realizing my life had flown by, and end my days with only a collection of beautiful, meaningful things and no one to share them with?

Before I knew it, we were outside of the Ritz Paris; its awnings were concertinaed, like the half-lidded eyes of someone in love.

We were greeted by a doorman who welcomed us with a flourish, tipping his hat. A frisson of delight washed over me at the honor, even if it was at the hand of the ruthless Monsieur Black.

Inside we stopped, bumping into one another as our mouths fell open at the view before us. Hotel Ritz Paris was sumptuous from the glittering chandeliers above, to the ornamental walls, and plush carpet beneath. Gilded golden mirrors clung to walls, and an ambient glow followed us as we inched our way forward.

"I've never seen anything so beautiful." Maman's voice was hushed.

A handful of men in sharp black tuxedos smiled and welcomed us further in. "Welcome. Monsieur Black is waiting for you in Bar Hemingway."

Being surrounded by such opulence stole the words from our lips. It was like being in a dream, golden hues, and shimmering crystal. I had never laid eyes on so much glamour all at once. It was hard to move, let alone speak.

Maman composed herself first. "Thank you very much; we're honored to be here."

We were shown into Bar Hemingway, and my breath hitched. Black and white pictures of Hemingway lined the walls. In some he was on the verge of laughter, his hair silver; in others he was much younger, and his expression studious like he was lost inside his mind with his characters. Once upon a time, he sat here, and told stories to an eager audience. Would I feel his presence still? Did he hover under the slivers of moonlight, waiting for someone to tell a tale, a long story with twists and turns made better by a cocktail, or two?

Leather couches were angled along one side, with high-back chairs around mahogany tables that were littered with his books. The bar was sleek, bottles lined up on mirrored shelves, bright lighting shining down catching the amber liquids and turning them gold. Manly stools lined the bar and that's where Tristan sat, in Hemingway's spot, nursing a tumbler of whisky on the rocks. He gave us a huge grin and stood to hug Maman.

"I'm so glad you could make it." He kissed the rouge of her cheeks, and pulled out a stool for her. His words were so silky smooth, and genuine, I did a double take.

"This place is magnificent," Lilou said, shaking his hand in her excitement.

"Ah," he said, taking my hand and staring deeply into my eyes. "You're spellbound. I knew you'd like this place."

"I want to live here," I said. "It's breathtaking."

"And so are you." His smile reached his eyes, and I wondered what had changed. In his relaxed state, he was the epitome of the perfect host, making us feel special in such a grand place.

"What will you have to drink?"

I gulped, my head pounding. I couldn't turn this man in to the gendarmes! What would jail do to a man like Tristan? I'd have to reconsider my position. Tonight was the night; I could feel it in my heart. If I proved it was him, I'd tell him to run, and be done with it, as long as he promised to return what he'd stolen.

"Anouk?" He touched my arm. The drink, right.

"Sparkling water to start." I flashed a grin, hoping to appear relaxed, unsuspecting.

A barman appeared and took everyone's drink orders. Tristan settled next to me. "Where are your friends?" I asked. It seemed a bit over the top to have Bar Hemingway to ourselves with scant attendees.

"They'll be along soon," he said, his eyes clouding. "They had a few things to do en route. Besides, the most important people are here." He gave me a long, penetrating stare that had me fumble with my clutch to break the moment.

From it I took out a small gift. It was wrapped in ruby tissue paper and tied with a gold ribbon. Maman had insisted I bring Tristan a gift to say thank you. I knew just the thing, and consulted with Dion and Madame Dupont to make it happen so quickly.

"For you," I said and gave him the box.

My family gathered around, keen to see what I'd chosen too. He unwrapped it gingerly, and held it aloft. "A pen! How handy!" Laughter rumbled out of him, and we all stopped to see if he was impressed or thought it gauche.

"A pen?" Maman mouthed to me. "It's very . . . practical."

I nodded. "It's not just any pen, it's a *fountain* pen."

"I'll treasure it always," he said, still a touch of laughter in his voice.

I took it from his hands. "It's a fashion statement in Paris, you see," I lied, and hooked the pen in his breast pocket so the blue glass bead of the top was showing. It had a mini camera hidden under the glass, which was now trained on Tristan's face, and we'd catch whatever lies fell from those smooth lips of his after he left the party. The footage was being played live back to Madame. Whatever he said or did for the length of time the battery ran, we'd catch it on camera and have undeniable proof. Whether we chose to use that proof remained to be seen.

We took our drinks and thanked the barman.

"What?" I asked, as Tristan stared at me with a goofy grin, which was so unlike him.

"I didn't think you'd turn up tonight, that's all."

I raised my eyebrows. "Well, you didn't leave me much choice by visiting my family . . ."

A waiter wandered over with a tray of canapés. I made a show of deciding what to eat, my gut roiling.

"Ah, here are my friends." He gestured to the door.

Two older men wandered in, their faces lined with fatigue. It struck me as odd they were his friends. They weren't at all what I pictured them to be, which was an offshoot of Tristan with those fun-loving good looks and a sharp, tailored wardrobe. These men were downright dour, with little sense of style. One wore an ill-fitting suit and tugged at his collar as though it was strangling him; another wore a polo shirt and linen trousers crinkled like he'd slept in them. These were his high-flying friends? Their expressions were grave. What kind of friends come to the Ritz with faces like that? You'd have been forgiven for thinking they'd just attended a funeral.

My hackles rose. Something was up. They were part of his team.

The backbone of his operation? Of course it would take more than one person to break into an auction house, and nab the jewels and get out so fast. I'd watched enough movies to know specialists were needed to override the various aspects of security while one devious thief made their way in for the hit.

We'd been so naïve!

Before I could think Tristan motioned for the men to join us, and made a round of introductions. The newcomers were Ben and Jerry. Their gazes lingered on me far longer than necessary, and I wondered what they were cooking up in their criminal minds. I wished Madame Dupont was here to guide me, but with only Lilou who knew the truth, I had to use the time with this gang of unlikely looking thugs to my advantage. Only in movies did the criminals have that swagger and smart way of dressing. It was a brilliant guise to hide behind cheap clothing and bad haircuts. Tristan stood out among them for being so suave.

"So," I ventured, gazing at the newcomers, "been in Paris long?"

They shook their heads.

"Italy is lovely. Have you been there?"

Jerry, the ill-fitting suit guy said, "We have. Gorgeous place. You've been also?"

"Oui," I said.

Jerry nodded. "Where did you stay?"

Dare I tell the truth? What harm could it do? "Sorrento. And you?" I stilled to watch their reaction but they remained stony-faced, like rocks.

"Sorrento too."

"A lovely place for jewelry."

Ben nodded. "A fine place."

It was like talking to grass. Even my soup bowl had more personality.

"The jewelry in Paris is exquisite too," I said.

Ben and Jerry confirmed it with a nod.

"Especially Cartier – have you heard of it?" They didn't flinch; in fact they were like statues with zero movement.

"We have."

My family were chatting happily to Tristan who kept shooting glances at me. Every now and then their laughter rang out as though whatever Tristan was saying was hilarious. They were rapt, following his every word.

"Drink?" I said, not waiting for a response. I topped up their glasses with a bottle of red wine that had materialized.

"So," Ben said. "Quite a party."

I frowned. I wouldn't exactly call it a party with my family, Tristan, and these two guys. "Oui. The Ritz is magnificent."

Tristan stood and made his way to the bar, whispering something to the barman, who threw a quick glance at me. I had the distinct impression they were sizing me up for something. The barman polished glasses and kept his eyes trained on me, while Tristan ducked behind a chambray curtain. How could I follow him when they all were studying me? I hoped Madame Dupont was watching the pen footage, but still, I didn't want Tristan to steal away unnoticed.

"Excuse me," I said to Ben and Jerry. "I think I left my oven on. I'm just going to call my neighbor." I exited hastily, stumbling on the thick carpet. The barman's gaze followed me and then he exchanged glances with Ben and Jerry.

I pushed the thick drapes aside and tumbled into Tristan's arms. "My neighbor," I said. "She's left her oven on." *Merde!* "I mean, I've left mine on. I must call my neighbor to check."

He held me by the arms, a smile curving at his lips. "I don't think your oven is on."

I squinted up at him. "I'd better check." I wanted to phone Madame Dupont and ask what she'd seen on the pen footage, but I couldn't have him listening in.

"Did you cook something before coming here?"

"No, I mean, yes, it was the *kettle* you see. I was going to make a pot of coffee. It could be boiling dry as we speak!"

"I wish for once you'd be honest. I can help you." He held me in his arms, and it was all I could do to stop the truth tumbling from my lips. *Run, run! If I can work it out, anyone can!*

I gave him a tight smile. "I don't need help. I'll just call my neighbor to go and check."

He let out a groan. Why was my dried-out kettle upsetting him so?

"Anouk, you've got a great family. Have you ever thought about them? What it'll all mean?"

"I can always buy another kettle, Tristan. It's really not that big of a deal."

He shook his head, and dropped his hands. "OK, if that's how you want to play it."

A shadow of pain lined his features, and I wanted to shake him to confess. "Excuse me? I'm not the one with two expressionless goons as sidekicks. Playing what exactly, because I might ask you the very same question."

"They're good guys, and they have a place in my life."

Yeah, as his tech support. Code breakers. "I bet they do. It must be nice to have friends you trust."

"Trust? Well that's a two-way street."

How dare he? The man was irredeemable. "I better go make this phone call before my apartment burns to the ground. I won't be long."

"Take your time."

I bustled into a sitting room and pulled out my second cell phone, the one Madame Dupont called the ghost phone. She said it couldn't be traced back to either of us.

"Anouk!" Madame Dupont cried. "I have so much to tell you! Are you alone?"

"Oui," I whispered. "But I can speak for long. What's going on?"

"The barman is one of them! Tristan told him to keep an eye on you."

"I knew it! But why?"

"They said something about you being in the right place at the right time. I don't know what that means, but I think perhaps they're going to try and pin the robberies on you!"

My stomach heaved. "That selfish, unworthy . . ."

"Try to remain calm. We need to think."

"He's got two goons with him: Ben and Jerry. They give me the creeps. How can we find out who they are?"

"Dion," she said. "Let me ring him and get him up to speed."

"OK, OK. What do I do in the meantime?"

She cackled high and loud. "You flirt. You pretend to drink a lot of champagne, talk too loud, act as though nothing is amiss and you're having the time of your life."

"They're all watching me. It's going to be difficult."

"You can do it. Keep an eye on him. And I'll see what Dion can find out."

We said our goodbyes, and I hung up, determined to put an end to this.

Game face on, I sauntered back into Bar Hemingway wondering what Ernest would make of this scene playing out in one of his favorite watering holes.

Tristan was dancing with Maman, swinging her around, and doing a double step. Her face lit with joy. My heart tugged watching them. I hadn't ever seen Maman take to someone like she had to him. It would tear her in two when she found out he was trouble.

"Here's Anouk!" she cried. "Time for the old woman to stand aside." She offered Tristan's hand to me, and I took it grudgingly but made my face bright.

He pulled me tight against his body, and slowed his dance steps.

"She really likes you, you know." *And when you wind up in jail, she'll be bereft.*

"I think she's great too. I hope she and your father can work things out. I'd love to meet him." I stood back and gazed into his face. What was he thinking? As if he could breezily meet my papa, and then move on, leaving me the fool, when my family found out who he really was. I was damn tired of men leaving casualties in their wake like it was nothing.

"Don't make a bigger mess of things, Tristan. Leave my maman be." She'd obviously taken him into her confidence, which was so rare for her and I hated to think of the fallout.

"I know," he said. "I've tried to stay out of things but it's proven impossible."

241

"Try harder." We were both inching around the truth. Why was life so complicated?

For the sake of my maman, who was ogling us like we were young love personified, I leaned my head against his chest so I didn't have to gaze into his lying eyes. The steady thrum of his heart beat against my face, and I listened to the sound knowing it would be the last time I'd hear it.

"Where are your parents, Tristan?" After the night in my kitchen when he'd closed his features and turned his back, I'd wondered what the story was with them. Would they be disappointed their son was a thief? Were they estranged?

His eyes shadowed, like he was pained. "They're not around anymore."

"Not around?"

"They died. A long time ago." His words were clipped as though he wanted to shut that line of conversation down. It obviously hurt him, but I pressed on, wondering if their deaths made him the way he was. Able to steal without conscience.

"How?"

"I'd rather not discuss it."

I frowned. "Do you have siblings?"

"I don't have any. What's with the interrogation?" His voice was light, but I sensed he was trying very hard to make it that way. He really was adrift without anyone to anchor him down. What a lonely existence that must be. It didn't make anything OK but it went some way to explaining why he had no compunction stealing – it was because he had no one to be disappointed in him.

I shrugged. "You know me, and my family, and all their confessions. I was just hoping I could understand you better. Your motivations, so to speak."

We stepped along to the music, but limply, so focused were we on each other. "I've enjoyed meeting your mom and Lilou. I miss it, you know. Miss calling on my parents for no reason, and having them gather round like I'm the only star in their universe."

242

"Would they be proud of you, do you think?" I asked, hoping I could appeal to some part of him that was still connected with them. I felt his sadness – it was almost tangible – through his hands, which cupped mine. No parent would want their son to be locked away forever. And even if I didn't tell the gendarmes, eventually he would get caught. Watching his face soften at the memory of his loss made him so much more real, and I ached for him, for what he must have been through.

"It's hard to say. They were . . ." His gaze moved upward as he grappled for a description. "Homebodies, the type of people who preferred to be still with one another, rather than live hectic lives. They worried about me, endlessly. But I can't change who I am or what I do . . . not yet anyway."

His eyes sparkled. I wasn't sure if it was unshed tears, or just the glassiness of memory. I hadn't heard Tristan speak so honestly before and I knew he was being sincere because it rippled off him in waves. "I'm so sorry. They're still around you know. It's not like they don't visit from time to time. You could still save them the worry by . . . changing."

He cocked his head, and his lips twitched like he found my sentiment amusing. "They're still around? They're not, you know. They're as far away as can possibly be."

"You wouldn't even think of being a better man, even in their memory?"

"And how do you recommend I become a better man? I wasn't aware I was lacking."

"I think you know."

He sighed. "And this is where I tell you that you're the worst kind of hypocrite there is. No don't stop me," he said as I went to interrupt. "You have a family who adore you, you're the center of their lives, and you don't give a damn. I'd swap lives with you in a heartbeat to have that kind of love in my life again. That unconditional embrace that only a family can give, and yet, it means nothing to you."

243

My eyebrows shot up. "And where are you getting that information from? I don't see how I'm the hypocrite! It's about time you were honest . . ."

Maman teetered over, and cut in on our dance, because our clipped tones rang out as the conversation soured. "Anouk, Lilou wants you. Allow me another dance before I turn into a pumpkin."

The midnight hour had been and gone and the exchange had left me confused. In one way I felt heartbroken for Tristan as he'd opened up, but then in the next instant he'd accused me of taking my family for granted. How dare he! He was the one who would hurt them, not me.

*   *   *

An hour later, we stumbled from a limousine that Tristan had insisted we take.

As we spilled from its luxurious seats, the driver dashed around and helped lead us to the safety of the curb. Maman and Lilou were singing Tristan's praises, and declaring it the best night ever. I wanted to be able to join in on their merriment, but a somber cloud hovered over me. It would have been a brilliant night if it had been real. It was pure fantasy, and I wouldn't forget that. Learning about the death of Tristan's parents cast a pall of sadness over me, and I was torn still.

We stumbled up the stairs, everyone chatting about their favorite part: *when Tristan said this, when Tristan did that.*

I unlocked the apartment and threw the keys in the bowl on the bureau.

"Wait," I said, flinging my arms out wide to stop them stepping clumsily inside.

"What is it?" Lilou asked sleepily. Everyone was itching for bed.

"Something's changed." I scanned the apartment, tingles racing up my spine. Nothing was out of place on first glance. The chaise longues still had sheets draped over. Cushions in each corner.

Balcony door closed tight against the bracing winds of pre-dawn. But something made the fine hairs on my neck stand to attention.

"Come on, Anouk," Lilou wheedled. "We're tired."

"Someone has been here," I said. The goons. Ben and Jerry. I was certain of it. But why? Why me?

"That's ridiculous," Lilou said. "Everything is still here. The paintings, the Laliques." She pushed past me and beckoned Henry to do the same. Maman followed shortly after, struggling with the stairs after a night on high heels.

"Wait," I said again. "Just let me look around before you touch anything."

There was a clue on the edge of my subconscious but it was just out of reach. *Think!* I'd known the party was a ruse. I'd thought my role was keeping a close eye on Tristan but that was before his friends turned up and had my senses taut with unease.

It hit me like a brick. He'd gathered us all at the Ritz so Ben and Jerry could break in here without any threat of being caught by one of the many who now called the apartment home.

Tristan had wanted to be certain that we'd all go to his party. That was why he'd hosted it at the Ritz, knowing no one could resist such an invitation. He'd visited Maman, turning on the charm to make sure she'd come in case I didn't tell them.

Had he made Ben and Jerry bug my apartment? They must've known I was onto them. Now I wondered what they would do to silence me.

Tristan knew we'd found him out; he just needed proof. All his double-talk was an effort to get me to confess. Well, two could play at that game, Monsieur Black.

"Actually," I said. "You're right, Lilou. Nothing is missing. It's been a long day, that's all." If he was listening I had to play it cool.

Everyone heaved a sigh of relief and made their way to bathroom and bed. I tiptoed around, looking for bugs. Did they really look like they did in the movies? I smiled when I saw the small black square no bigger than a thumbnail, stuck underneath the dining room table. I left it there, careful not to touch it, and kept hunting.

In the morning, I'd see what Madame Dupont had captured on the pen footage. A heavy feeling of unease settled in my belly. I'd have to go on as if life was the same, attending fairs, flea markets, and auctions while I compiled evidence. I'd confront him myself, and let him explain. There was a part of me that needed to know if he really had ever cared about me, see the truth in his eyes when I caught him out. It was the only way I would be able to move on.

Hours later I found myself having intense dreams about him, us holding hands by the sea, smiling, absorbing sunlight like a panacea, and I wondered what my subconscious was doing to me.

Chapter Twenty-Six

It was the first time I'd seen Madame Dupont appear anything other than poised and elegant. My early morning visit had caught her by surprise. Her long hair was unwound and tumbled down her back in knotty silvery waves. Makeup-less, she was even prettier, her face soft with sleep, and her eyes bright without the thick layer of kohl she usually wore.

"He ditched the pen," she said woefully. "I don't know how, but he knew what it was. It ended up in a bin in the bathroom at the Ritz."

My mouth hung open. "He knew?"

Madame Dupont nodded. "Must have and that means we don't have any footage of him with the clowns Ben and Jerry, after you left the party."

"Damn it! He's always one step ahead of us."

She wound her hair into a chignon and secured it with pins, and a silver sequin hair clip that sparkled in the soft light of dawn. "I suspect they always will be, since they're career criminals. Though we do have one trick up our sleeves." Her eyes twinkled.

"The bugs?"

She nodded. "You have to act normal. Don't change the way

you behave at home or they'll know. Keep asking your maman to call your papa . . . Berate Lilou for reading your diary."

"Have you bugged my apartment too?"

She laughed. "No Lilou tells me every day over coffee. Anyway so it's business as usual, but . . . you drop hints about a certain auction, let's say, The Cloutier Auction House. Because they've got a diamond arriving that will rival the Hope Diamond . . ."

I gasped. "And then we know he'll go for that auction!"

She nodded sagely. "Drip feed them information. We don't want to make it obvious, so pretend to lower your voice, and whisper, even though you'll be right above the bug so they'll hear."

"OK, good idea."

"Say it's arriving under the cover of darkness on Friday, and we'll be there waiting. It's crucial you still do everything as normal at home."

"Of course," I said loftily.

She stared me down. "I mean it, Anouk, keep singing to the soup bowl and howling over those marriage announcements."

Mon Dieu. "Lilou again?"

"It's sweet, you're a sensitive soul, that's all. Keep working, and don't think of him as anything other than a guy who's trying to woo you, so you don't make any mistakes."

I fiddled with the clasp on my handbag, my mind working fast. "I think it's obvious to him that I know. He skirted around it last night, and even through our double talk it was clear."

"Maybe so. But we have to try," Madame Dupont said, giving my arm a reassuring pat. "What is it? You look like you just got caught in the rain all of sudden."

I lifted my gaze to hers. "Why do I fall for the wrong men all the time? I guess I never really thought he was the bad guy. Deep down, I presumed it would amount to nothing. And now we know, and I . . ."

"You do feel something for him." She searched my face.

"It's crazy because really I don't know him. But it's visceral, and real, and I hate not being able to admit it. And he held my family enraptured last night. Like they mattered. Every single word that fell from their lips, he was really listening, but for what? Clues? Imagine if he pins the robberies on me? How stupid would I feel then? And my poor family will be mortified. They loved him too."

Madame Dupont smiled, and plucked a tissue from a box, and gave it to me, before sitting back at her ornate dressing table, and applying layers of heavy makeup.

"It's a challenge, all right. Why don't we see what happens? When we catch him at The Cloutier auction, we can give him an ultimatum. He can flee, with the promise to turn legitimate. Return the jewels. You could still love a man like that, who did the right thing in the end, couldn't you?"

"I don't know, Madame."

She reached over and patted my hand. "Let's see what the week brings."

I sat hunched, as Madame Dupont rouged her cheeks, and spritzed on perfume. I'd throw myself into work just like I always did.

* * *

"Is she coming home? What does she say?" My papa's voice was hollow, as if he was tired of waiting. With the phone against my ear, I opened the lace curtains in the window of the shop. Outside, people dotted the promenade, up early for a full day of sightseeing. Paris was on display with its clear azure sky, and bright bobbing sun, which glinted off the metal of the Eiffel Tower, making me squint.

"I don't think so, Papa." I sighed. It was hard to tell him just how much she'd bloomed here without hurting his feelings. She'd become a different person, and we couldn't rob her of that. "Why don't you visit? I think it's the only way. And you can see how much she's changed. Perhaps you'll have to meet her in the middle to make things work."

He grunted and grumbled. "So then I'm admitting I'm wrong?"

"No, Papa. It's not about who's right or wrong, it's about rekindling your relationship. Can't you try? If you could see Maman, you'd know she's happy. Perhaps she needed something different, just for once in her life, to make things about *her* for a change, to put herself first. Why shouldn't she chase her own dreams at least for a little while?"

"Her dreams? Running off to Paris and teaching some chefs how to cook? That's her dream?" His voice was heavy with sarcasm, but I knew he was hiding bruised feelings, as he grappled with his emotions, that Maman chose something other than him for the first time in her life. "Shouldn't they know how to cook already, if they're chefs?"

"Papa, you're missing the point. Maman feels like she matters to them. She's teaching them the real art of cooking, not the fancy Michelin-starred way, but the old way, like her maman used to cook. It's like she's preserving an art form and they love her for it."

"An art form? It's only bouillabaisse!"

I tutted. "Papa, it's so much more than that, and you know it."

He let out a long, weary breath. "Maybe," he admitted. "I don't see why she couldn't have done that here. We have bistros too. It's not like she couldn't have made friends here."

"Could she though, Papa? Not with the exhausting list of chores she had, each day blending in with the next."

"Fine, fine. You've made your point. I haven't been feeling well; sometimes I get this pain . . ."

"It's probably loneliness, Papa."

"Non, non, it's not that. I'm working too hard – your maman has left me without a backward glance. It's not fair or right. I get this ache, this numbness up my arm . . ."

I interrupted him, not wanting to let him wallow: "Really, Papa, what do you need to do every day? Eat, work, and sleep.

You don't need such exacting standards at home. The tablecloth can last a week without being laundered and ironed if you're careful. Why do you make things so much harder?"

"I just like things ordered."

I sighed. "Perhaps you need to think about how exhausted you feel, and then think of Maman doing that every day her whole life, and raising two girls as well."

He muttered to himself. "She took her vows, and I took mine, and look . . . she's nowhere to be found. Do you think she's with another man?"

"No! Papa, don't you *listen*?"

"I was simply asking, Anouk. This is very strange behavior for her. She loved those curtains. I thought she'd come back."

He was referring to the fire. "Papa, in this case actions speak louder than words. You have to *show* her how you're feeling. Come to Paris, show her you love her. Ask her what *she* wants."

"I better go," he said, brusquely. "Someone has to cook the coq au vin, and since there is only me here, I guess it's my job."

"Be well, Papa." Shaking my head, I hung up, conflicted. It was ego stopping him from visiting Paris, and agreeing on a compromise with Maman. He wanted her back but his pride wouldn't allow him to admit it to her. Instead, he'd wait, and hope Paris lost its sparkle, and she'd return to the village. He hadn't even asked about Lilou and the damned course, so I knew he was really missing Maman.

If only he could see her here, he'd know that something long dormant inside had sprung to life, and she wasn't going to settle anymore. Could they grow apart at this stage of their marriage? I thought about Agnes, who bought the ruby pendant for her parents' fortieth wedding anniversary – had they suffered through times of crisis? Perhaps they worked out their frustrations on the bread dough, side by side in their boulangerie, knowing it was only a tiff, and could be fixed. Like any great recipe, all it needed was some tweaking to keep it fresh. Maybe that's all my papa needed – someone to drag him by the heels, and into the twenty-first century, so he'd stop harping on about a woman's place being in the home.

My phone buzzed again, and I hesitated. What if it was Tristan? Could I act the same knowing he'd bugged my apartment? Hesitantly, I answered, "Bonjour?"

"Ma chérie." Madame Dupont's voice was high-pitched. "A source has just called. The flea market by the Seine, you must go now. They say Henry Miller's typewriter is there. The old man with the red beret, he has it."

"Oui, merci, Madame. I'll go now!"

If it truly was Henry Miller's typewriter, I had to have it. Another American who'd fallen in love with Paris, and written here in the thirties. If it was the typewriter he wrote *Tropic of Cancer* with, then it would be a real find, and I mentally started assessing ways I could find out. Miller had been friendly with Anaïs Nin, so securing the typewriter would ease some of the pain of losing her hutch.

I locked up and with quick steps made my way down to the Seine.

Stalls were set up along the side of the right bank where gentle waves lapped in the slipstream of boats chugging by.

Flea markets in Paris were serious business. While the laden tables might appear to be full of worthless knickknacks, they often hid valuable antiques. You just had to spend the time hunting for them or have reliable sources who'd tip you off first.

I spotted the old man with the red beret. His face was weathered, wrinkled from time outside: the salty winds in winter, and the sizzle of sunshine in summer. A cigarette hung from the side of his mouth, as he jabbered in French to someone. I scanned the tables looking for the typewriter, but could only see old books, swollen fat from the Seine air. There was no time for niceties. I tapped him on the shoulder, and he spun to face me. In his hands was the typewriter. But worse, standing behind him was Tristan.

And they had been speaking French! He knew the language all along? Did he replay all my phone messages when he stole my bag? My cheeks were aflame. There was no time to think.

I spoke in rapid-fire French to the stall owner hoping to bamboozle Tristan with the speed of my sentences. "I want this typewriter! This man you cannot trust him! I will make sure it goes to the right person!" I was exclaiming so hard I drew the attention of passersby.

The man in the red beret frowned. "That may be, but he was here first. I have already made the deal."

"Non! You can't!" I hissed, while trying to throw an *it's-all-under-control* smile to Tristan so he wouldn't guess what was happening. He had the jewels. What did he need with this? "He's American!" I tried another tack.

Red beret man's forehead wrinkled. "So was Henry Miller."

I huffed. He had me there. "Please, you're making a mistake." I took the typewriter from his hands.

Tristan's face dropped. "Anouk, please. Just listen to me. I *need* this, and I can't explain why right now." His eyes searched mine. Why did he seem so sad? I knew him well enough to know a typewriter wouldn't have provoked such a reaction – he looked positively stricken.

I stared at him, mind ticking. "Why do you want it? You don't have a shop, Tristan. You don't have customers. Can't you let me have it?" I appealed to his caring side. Truth was, there wasn't a whole lot of profit tied up in the machine, it was more sentimental, and I had customers who'd love it. And I just didn't want him to have it because he didn't deserve it.

The red beret man threw his hands in the air, and shook his head. "When someone wants to pay, let me know," he said and went back to smoking.

Tristan nodded his thanks and turned back to me. "Why do you want it? Henry Miller was American. I thought you only wanted to protect French heritage?"

"Henry Miller wrote in Paris! He was one of us!" We were going in circles, and I knew whatever it was, it was about much more than the typewriter.

Tristan shook his head. "He only wrote here because his work was banned in America for being too promiscuous." He raised an eyebrow.

"That may well be, but he fit here in Paris. The place shaped him as a writer."

He sighed, a long weary sound. "Anouk, give me the typewriter. You can have it back later, I promise."

"No." Why would he need something so minor compared to what he was stealing? Maybe he took black market orders and tried to fulfill them no matter how small. But it didn't make much sense.

"Anouk. Give me the typewriter and I promise I won't ever butt in on another of your deals."

"No . . ." I couldn't trust him. I knew I'd never see it again. As foolish as I was making it, it felt damn good to stand up for myself, and say he couldn't steal *or* buy things from under me. I wouldn't have it.

"I'll give you whatever you want, but I need *this*, and I'm not kidding around," he said, his voice apprehensive.

"Why?" I was thrown off by the change in his demeanor. He sounded as though he'd lost his last friend in the world. His shoulders slumped wearily.

"I can't discuss it with you. But trust me, I need this typewriter, and only this one." He glanced this way and that, a worried expression on his face. If I didn't know better I'd say he looked hunted. I had a feeling things were about to blow up in Tristan's world. "You putting your fingerprints all over it isn't helping," he said, an edge to his voice.

Ah! The taunting postcards typed by the Postcard Bandit. Was this the one he typed them on? And if so how had it come into Red Beret's hands?

I grimaced. "Evidence, is it?"

His face pained. "It's not my fault."

"What, Tristan? Whose fault is it then?"

We stood inches apart, like a Mexican standoff. He ran his hands through his hair, frustrated. "I don't like this any more than you do!" His tone was plaintive; maybe it was an addiction for him, like a gambler. He loved the thrill of the robbery, getting away with it, getting in and out so fast like some kind of superhuman.

"Then why do it?" I hissed back.

"I have to do it. Why do *you* do it?"

"It's my job!"

He scoffed. "I could say the same thing."

I raised my eyebrows. "Some job."

He scrunched his eyes closed. "I don't normally get emotionally invested. You've made this very hard."

"Emotionally invested? Well, sorry for making you care about something other than greed." I choked on the end of my sentence. I'd thought there'd been something real between us. In his kisses there had been something, something he couldn't have faked . . . could he? My mind snapped back to the times he'd been there for me, the things he'd said to comfort me. If that was all pretend then he was a damn fine actor.

"Greed?" He reared back as if I'd slapped him. "You don't know how much I've suffered because of you! It's impossible to do my *job* –" he made air quotes "– knowing what's going to happen! And you don't give a damn! You're fighting me all the way."

"Because your *job* –" I mimicked his air quotes with one hand "– is all built on a lie! And I will fight you to the death because it's my *job*!" Our conversation escalated as frustration got the better of us.

"Sometimes I want to shake you until you see sense!" He gripped my arms and stared into my eyes, the typewriter marooned between us.

"Yeah? Sometimes I want to trip you over so I can watch you fall! Why can't you just be who you pretend to be?"

He rubbed his palms wearily over his face. "Because it's my goddamn job, Anouk! Why can't you just sell antiques and leave it at that?"

"What nerve you have! Why can't I? Because you keep stealing them from me!"

He scoffed. "You are the most infuriating woman I've ever met!"

I shook my head. "You are unbelievable, Monsieur Black."

"When all this blows up, I just want you to know . . ." His voice was a whisper. "To know . . ."

"To know what? It wasn't your fault?" Tears pricked my eyes and I wanted to berate myself for caring so much. I hastily blinked them away.

"Damn it. To know *I didn't want to do it.* I wanted to run the opposite way, and let you go . . ."

"Oh, thanks, Tristan. I'm that repulsive to you?"

"What aren't you understanding, Anouk?" He cupped my face, and stared into my eyes, searching for an answer that wasn't there. After shaking his head at my confusion he pressed his lips against mine, kissing me like it was the last time he'd see me. In the heat of the moment I kissed him back hard, as all sorts of emotions coursed through me, but mostly that he'd go to jail and I'd never see him again. It felt like a goodbye kiss and I rued Cupid for making me feel anything for someone like Tristan.

The stall owner took the typewriter from my hands, shaking his head at us.

I felt as though we stood at a crossroads, facing off at each other. On tiptoes, I laced my hands behind his neck, and closed my eyes, kissing him with all I had, because curse fate, and wrong choices, and untrustworthy men, to hell with all of it. I'd give him one long passionate goodbye kiss on my terms.

Breathless, we parted, and stood stock-still. I grappled with what to say, how to warn him, but he knew, and he didn't care. That was the most galling part.

"Au revoir, Tristan. Remember you brought this on yourself."

Pain flashed across his features. "Don't do it, Anouk."

He thought I'd tell the gendarmes. "Go get your typewriter." A sob escaped as I trudged away.

Later that night, I spoke to the empty apartment about the huge diamond arriving at the Cloutier auction house. It took all my might to be animated, as if I was on the phone to Madame, excited by the prospect of bidding on such a stunning jewel. Was he listening?

Chapter Twenty-Seven

"You kissed him, *again*?" Madame Dupont asked, her voice incredulous.

"It was the last kiss. It was goodbye. Au revoir." I fluttered my hands uselessly.

She surveyed me. "We don't have to catch him . . ."

"Madame. Yes, we do! I gave him the chance to back away, and he chose not to." I wanted to see it for myself, see him rob a place. I could still walk away and not say a word, but I had to see it first.

She fussed with the newspaper on her lap, the one with eye holes cut out. I would have laughed at her folly, but I wasn't in the mood.

"OK," she said. "Then let's get him."

My hands shook. "He shouldn't have stolen the Cartier jewels."

"Oui."

My stomach knotted. "Or the pink diamonds."

"Oui."

"But mostly the Cartier. That was going too far."

"I understand."

"There's stealing and then there's being greedy and the Cartier was one step too far. One giant leap into all sorts of wrong."

"You don't have to justify it to me. I know."

"He never said he was supporting an orphanage, or building a hospital, did he?"

She patted my hand. "Anouk . . ."

"I know, I know, sometimes people are just made wrong. And despite his charm, his beautiful face, his soft lips, his saunter, his laugh, you know that really loud obnoxious one that is really quite cute after a while . . ."

She nodded solemnly.

"Well, aside from all that, he's rotten to the core. Because of the Cartier."

She didn't speak, but her lips twitched like she was about to laugh.

"What?" I asked.

"Nothing, nothing. Are we going to catch him or just sit here all night?"

I took a deep, steadying breath. "Let's catch him."

Madame Dupont gunned the engine and we zoomed through the boulevards, coming to an abrupt stop near the auction house.

Facing me, she said, "If you want out of this whole charade, just let me know. No one knows the things we do aside from Dion and Lilou. We don't have to tell the gendarmes . . . That's all I'm going to say."

I didn't trust myself to speak so I just nodded. We waited in silence until darkness fell. I was stiff from holding myself tight in the small space of the cramped rental car.

"I'll be glad when these stake-outs are over," Madame Dupont lamented. "My old bones suffer."

I patted her knee. "You've done a great job, Madame. You've been the brains. And we'll have to thank Dion – he sure is resourceful."

She laughed. "I'll miss spending the nights with you, though."

"Back to reading the marriage announcements for me."

An hour passed, and still nothing. The streets grew quiet as people hurried home, and locked themselves away as midnight approached. "Maybe he got the hint?" I asked hopefully.

"He's biding his time."

"You're probably right."

Madame Dupont fiddled with her night-vision goggles. "What if he's getting in through the side door? Should we go and check it out?"

"It's not likely he'd go through the front door, I suppose." What if I caught him mid break-in?

"I'll go," Madame Dupont said.

"Non, non. I'll go. I got us into this mess."

"Be quick," she said. "And take the ghost phone in case you need me."

I nodded and snuck out of the car, running behind trees, and stopping to sneak a look around before running to the next. I crossed the street, and hid behind a lamp pole, which was insufficient in girth to hide my curves. Tiptoeing around the side entrance, I found the laneway silent. Even the shadows didn't move.

With a glance up, I saw CCTV cameras hooked to the building. There was no way he could get in without being seen this way. I ran to the back of the auction house, my heart hammering at my audacity, knowing full well I'd be seen on the very same CCTV. I just hoped our instincts were correct and he'd have heard my bluster about the huge diamond arriving. Then I could at least explain to the gendarmes why I was sneaking around.

At the back I tried the big oval door, and found it unlocked. My hand froze on the door handle. Was this a setup? Why would it be unlocked with so many valuables inside? I remembered back to Gustave saying Monsieur Cloutier was getting more doddery and forgetting to lock up, but it seemed too coincidental. My mind screamed be careful, but I shoved the thought away, and walked inside. Imagine if they caught me? What would I say? *Oh, it was unlocked, I was hoping to catch the thief red-handed . . .* I was going to get myself arrested but something told me to keep going.

In the pitch black, I kept close to the wall, arms wide, feeling my way along in the dark. Why weren't the lights on? Usually the auction houses were lit up like it was daytime, in order for the security guards to make their rounds. Something wasn't right . . .

Somewhere in the distance a buzz rang out, like the muted sound of some kind of power tool. I froze. Was he making his way in? My heart seized, but I had to confront him.

Think of the antiques! Vive La France!

Edging steadily along the cool wall, my fingertips touched on something in my path. As gently as I could, I made out the shape, a display case, and inched around it without knocking whatever artifacts it housed. My breathing was shallow with concentration. I took a deep steadying gulp of air before dropping to my knees, and crawling toward the sound. Couldn't the guards hear it? Why hadn't they come for me yet?

On all fours, I could orient myself better. The noise grew more insistent. Obviously no alarms had been tripped or they'd already been overridden because my presence hadn't sounded any. Unless they were silent alarms? So did the sixty seconds start from when he was inside? Really, this could all be over in one quick minute if the newspapers had got their facts right. I gulped; it would be just my luck to be caught in the crossfire . . . My blood ran cold. Had he been setting me up all along? Maybe I'd played right into his hands thinking I was catching him when he was really entrapping me.

Should I jump up and make my way out? I had no choice; I was in too deep. Surely, I could explain my way out of it, if the gendarmes burst in.

The buzzing noise increased. I could feel the vibration in my body, as I grew closer to it. The air behind me moved. I froze.

Before I could think, I was hoisted up roughly, a hand clamped across my mouth, smothering any cries. I kicked and squirmed trying to get loose but he was too powerful. A seasickness sensation washed over me as I lost my balance, being swung over his shoulder.

I bounced along feeling sick as he broke into a run, but jiggled and writhed trying to free myself.

"Will you stop fighting me?" he hissed. *Tristan!* But the power tool still screamed out in the distance. Ben and Jerry? I couldn't see them as the hands-dirty type, but what did I know?

There was a creak as a door yawned open and Tristan plonked me unceremoniously onto the carpet, flicking on a light, blinding me momentarily. I shaded my eyes, and glared up at him.

"You are the thief!" I yelled.

He sat beside me, holding an earpiece, listening intently to whatever was being relayed. He didn't look at me, just raised a finger to his lips, and mouthed, "Shhh."

"I will not shush," I yelled. "I'm not going to be an accomplice to your crime!"

He shot me a dark look that made me squirm but I wasn't giving in. I'd come this far. "I'm going to scream so loud Madame Dupont will come running and with her the gendarmes!"

He clamped a hand over my mouth, and spoke quickly into a mouthpiece. "I have her, but she's going to scream the place down. Grab him as soon as he gets through the aqueduct."

The aqueduct! *Of course!* Paris was built on a bustling range of stone pipes that weren't in use anymore. Where water once flowed stale air now stood. A complex maze underground that was perfect for a thief to use as an invisible entryway, and even better as an escape route. Tristan's hand was still firm against my mouth, so I bit into the flesh of his palm, and tried to break loose. There was no way I was going to be caught sitting with the thief as though I was one of them.

"Ouch!" He pulled his hand back from the sting of the bite. "What did you do that for?"

"Fun!" I said. "Let me out of here!"

"Can you be quiet for one goddamn minute!" he hissed.

My ghost phone rang, startling me.

"Give it to me," he said.

It was hidden in the bust of my dress. He looked from me, to my décolletage, and thought better of it. I grabbed it, and held it away from him, managing to press the speaker button.

"Help," I muffled as Tristan lunged. His body landed on mine, stealing the breath from my lungs. With my free arm, I held the phone above me, and yelled as loud as I could hoping Madame Dupont would understand.

"It's Dion. Are you there, Anouk?"

I broke away for a second. "OUI! Tristan . . ." But his hand came firmly back down silencing me once more.

"Yes, Tristan! I found his paper trail. He's an undercover detective, working for the major crime squad in relation to the jewelry thefts!"

Tristan's body lost the fight. I felt him go limp above me. He dropped his hand from my mouth. I took a lungful of precious air, and said, "WHAT! He's what?"

"He's a detective! He's not the bad guy." Dion enunciated slowly like I was a child.

Shock sent me rigid. I watched Tristan's face twist angrily. "He's not the bad guy?" I said, mind spiraling.

Tristan pulled himself up, and offered me his hand. I shook my head no and held the phone in front of me.

"Well then who's the bad guy?" I asked Dion. There was so much to process, and with all the pummeling and grappling I found it hard to control my ragged breaths.

Dion's laugh reverberated around the room. "They thought it was you!"

I gasped and sent a viperous look to Tristan who had the grace to blush. "Me? Why me?"

"You'll have to ask him that."

"Merci, Dion."

I hung up the phone and got unsteadily to my feet. My ponytail had come undone in the scuffle. I tried in vain to pat it down, as I unscrambled my thoughts. They thought I was the jewel thief?

A flood of anger coursed through me. Tristan was wooing me in order to catch me out? The irony floored me, and I boiled inside.

Eventually, I managed to compose myself and asked, "Is that true, Tristan? Did you think it was me?"

He ducked his head, just as there was a commotion outside. Yelling could be heard, as a scuffle broke out. The real thief was being hauled up, and handcuffed. The zip of the cuffs brought a smile to Tristan's face. That goddamn phony.

Curiosity got the better of me. I peeked around the door, and saw them lead a man away with his hands firmly tied behind his back. Mon Dieu! I would have recognized that swagger anywhere. Still yelling at the gendarmes he managed to turn and shoot me a look full of hatred.

"Joshua? Why?"

He ignored me, but the look he gave me chilled me to the core. The gendarmes pushed him forward. "Walk, or we'll make you walk."

Not once did it ever cross my mind Joshua was capable of such a thing. I knew he was devious, with no morals, but I simply didn't think he'd have the brains to pull off heists this big. I couldn't trust any of them!

Tristan joined me by the door. "I'm sorry, Anouk, I really am. We thought it was you at first. But then I thought perhaps you were his accomplice. There were so many clues that pointed to you both. It was thought the breakup story and stolen piano was a farce and that you were still secretly working together."

"It was thought by whom?" My bottom lip wobbled, and I took great pains to clamp my teeth on it so he didn't see. How could he do this to me? Actively seek me out in order to put me in jail? Kiss me, and tell me lies, when he wasn't who he said he was.

"We knew your business was in financial trouble. You had a motive. You were in Sorrento." He rubbed his face, like he was exhausted. "Your bookshelves are filled with crime novels. The crimes were carried out exactly like the one described in *The Jewel*

Heist – exactly. You tried to film me with a pen! We moved fast after that, guessing you'd figured us out."

"*You* bugged my apartment the night of your party at the Ritz!"

He shook his head "No, it was bugged a long time before that. We got you all there that night so Ben and Jerry could search your house without anyone stumbling on them. They thought the typewriter was hidden there, because of something Lilou had said in passing. It was a long shot, but we figured we'd finally get the opportunity to search without a soul there."

"How did you manage to bug it months ago then if someone was always there?" As soon as the words left my mouth it dawned on me. "Henry is one of you!" That dodgy couch surfer! I knew he'd been rifling through my things searching for something. Evidence!

"He is."

"You violated every facet of my life! My maman and my sister will be hurt!" My voice rose, and shamefully cracked. Everything was a lie. "Does Lilou know?"

"She doesn't know for sure, but I think she's had her suspicions from what we've heard on her phone calls."

"This is too much, Tristan." What would my poor sister think? It was a betrayal, no two ways about it. What kind of people pretend to date someone in a ruthless calculating way just to infiltrate their lives?

"Why did you steal my handbag on the Metro?"

"Didn't you ever wonder how Joshua always knew where you'd be and what you were doing?"

God, this was like the plot of a spy movie . . . except it was real, and my feelings were beyond hurt. Both of the men I'd given my heart over to were manipulators. "So my handbag was bugged?"

"Yes, by him and then after the Metro ride by us. And then we figured with your big talk about a diamond to rival the Hope Diamond – that was clever by the way – that he'd take the bait. And he did. You actually helped us, you know."

"And yet all along you wanted to put me in jail?"

"I could say the same for you, Anouk. You thought it was me the whole time too."

My mouth fell open. "Well all the signs pointed to you. And you didn't dissuade me, did you? I would have warned you! That's the difference! You were ready to lock me up!"

"I wanted you to talk. Even when we knew it wasn't you committing the robberies we thought you might have been a party to it. We knew he wasn't doing them alone, and you kept saying all those dumb things. It was like you wanted to be caught!"

"Dumb things? I was trying to get *you* to talk!"

"I know, I know. I almost botched the entire case because of how I felt about you. My superior sent me back to America to cool down, with strict instructions not to kiss you ever again. They saw it all, and knew I'd gone too far. I wanted to tell you to run, but I was being watched too."

I searched his face. His eyes filled with unease.

People had been spying on us the entire time? "But . . . you didn't tell me to run."

"It's my job to catch criminals. And we have him now. I thought you'd be happy, Anouk. Now your antiques will stay in France, just like you wanted. We have the Cartier jewels. It looks as though they were too hot to sell, too well-known. We have faith we'll get the other items back too."

"Am I free to go?" I said, hating myself for the break in my voice. I was overwhelmed and wanted to flee. Maybe I should have been happy Tristan wasn't the bad guy, but I felt violated: my apartment bugged and searched, my sister was also caught up in a faux romance. Not to mention me. I had feelings for Tristan and once again it was all an act. While he might have been masquerading as the good guy, he was breaking a heart too. Had these people no decency? They'd swarm in, set traps, and leave, never mind the destruction they caused.

"You can go, but I thought we could . . ."

266

"No, Tristan, I just want to go home. Though home isn't the sanctuary it once was, is it?"

In my heart I knew Tristan was only doing his job, but I couldn't shake the feeling my entire life had been on show for a roomful of investigators. It felt like the worst kind of treachery.

Before I left, I turned to him. "I want the bugs, and whatever else you've put in my home removed."

He nodded, his face a mask of professionalism once more, like he'd flicked the switch and was wrapping up this job, and ready to move on to the next. "Sure. I'll have them do it right now."

Numbly, I got into the car, and stared straight ahead. Madame didn't say a word, sensing my need for silence. At my apartment, she patted my knee. "Dion told me," she finally said. "It's quite a shock, Anouk. But in time I think you'll see sense. He *was* doing the right thing."

I swallowed a lump in my throat. "But, Madame, it was all a lie, just like it was with Joshua. Once again I was a pawn, used by a man to get ahead. Now it makes sense why he was always right there when trouble found me. He was following me the whole time. To get enough evidence to arrest me!"

"For what it's worth, I think he must have real feelings for you. Dion told me Tristan was sent to America as punishment for almost ruining the investigation because he got too close to you."

"Yeah, he probably wasn't supposed to kiss the main suspect," I said bitterly. Rage flowed through me, as I remembered that our private conversations, which had never been private, were listened to by a roomful of gendarmes.

"You need to have a long, hard think about it all, Anouk. Things will look brighter in the morning; they always do."

Holding myself together stiffly, I nodded, unable to find the energy to disagree.

Chapter Twenty-Eight

It might have been deemed macabre, but when I wanted time alone I visited Père-Lachaise cemetery. As far as resting places go, it was verdant and lush, with well-maintained gardens, and immaculate lawns and walkways. I couldn't resist being in a place where I might stumble upon the ghosts of times gone by.

On a bench seat, looking down the hilly vista, I pondered the last few weeks. As Madame predicted, things didn't seem as bad, but I was still hurt by Tristan's duplicity, and my trust, whatever little shell there'd been left, was completely shattered.

So many questions buzzed through me, but I wasn't answering his phone calls to ask them. Was his entire background a fabrication? It must've been. And there I'd been starry-eyed soaking up every word. The confrontation he had with Joshua at our first meeting must have been planned. The Saint-Tropez kiss – planned. Were they all laughing behind their hands at me? *Look at her fall for the bait, and as easily as that!*

Lilou had accepted the fact she was dating an undercover investigator gracefully. They'd stayed friends, and there were no hard feelings on her part. Instead, she was endlessly fascinated and grilled Henry on his technique, how he found her and what ensued. I was privy to their conversation as he packed his belongings and left my apartment, Lilou waving him cheerily off. When I asked her later if she felt used, she reeled back in surprise and said, "No, I feel important! Without me, they wouldn't have caught Joshua as quickly. And I'll always have a soft spot for Henry. We'll still see each other when he's in Paris. It's not the end, but we're both busy with other things to settle right now."

My jaw had practically hit the floor with surprise. She'd been so *calm* about it all. The man chose her because she was my sister and it was a way into my apartment to spy on me! But Lilou didn't seem to mind, spouting the old adage, "All's fair in love and war," and flounced away, humming.

Maybe I was the odd one out. Even Maman tried to make me see reason. Harped on about how Tristan was categorically saving the world one antique at a time. But I had refused to listen. Hence my many forays to Père-Lachaise in the sticky heat of the day to be alone, except for whichever ghost chose to sit next to me.

The days were endless as summer moved in for the duration. I was considering an extended holiday, maybe to hide my face for a while, but I'd been told by investigators not to leave France, as there'd be a trial for Joshua, and I'd be part of it. I'd have to see them all again – I had no choice in the matter, and that irked me. Once again, other men deciding my fate. At least this time Joshua would be punished accordingly.

My phone buzzed, startling my reverie.

"Maman?" I answered quietly, respectful of the dead and where they rested.

Sobs met me, and then a high-pitched keening. "Maman, what is it?"

"Your papa, he . . . he's . . ." She gulped back tears. "The hospital called. He's had a heart attack! You must come quickly."

I could feel blood drain from my face. "Is he . . . OK?" Guilt rushed at me. I'd been so caught up in myself, I hadn't spared a thought for my papa in weeks.

"They say he's critical."

My chest tightened. Critical. My big, strong papa?

"Don't worry, Maman. I'm coming now. We'll go to him immediately."

Twenty minutes later a taxi dropped me at my apartment. I took the stairs two at a time, and practically fell through the front door, into Maman's waiting arms.

"Where's Lilou?" I asked.

Maman wrung her hands together. "She's gone by train. I wanted to find you first, she left, so at least one of us was on the way. Please, we must hurry." Maman pulled on a coat, and hitched her handbag over her shoulder. "Don't be mad, but I phoned Tristan, and explained. He's organized a private plane for us. We'll get there faster."

I blanched. She'd called him and told him? I didn't want any of them involved in our private lives. They couldn't be trusted not to use anything for their own gain.

"Maman!"

She steeled herself. "Anouk, be reasonable. It will take us most of the day to get there by train; this will take an hour and a bit. Come," she commanded. "There's a car waiting downstairs to take us to the airfield."

I wanted to rant and rave, but how could I? It was a godsend, really.

"Please let's just get to Papa," she said. "Nothing else matters."

Ben and Jerry whose real names were Detective Dean and Detective Morris were waiting in the car. They took us to an airfield just outside of Paris, and helped us board a small plane. Maman was effusive in her thanks, but I stayed silent. I was grateful we'd be reunited with Papa, but wanted to put the rest of the mess behind me.

Maman and I clutched hands as the plane taxied down the

runway, and closed our eyes, each lost in thought, and unable to voice our worry. What kind of daughter was I? Papa had said he wasn't feeling well, and I'd put it down to a cry for attention. If only I'd listened. Remorse plagued me, as the plane took off.

The small village hospital was running on skeleton staff when we arrived, racing in and desperately searching for assistance. A nurse approached us. "Anouk?"

"Oui," I said, wondering how she knew my name. She must have read the confusion on my face and said, "A Monsieur Riley called and told us to expect you."

"Riley . . .? Oh, Tristan." Of course Tristan Black wasn't his real name. I pushed the thought away. "Where is Papa? How is he doing?" Maman gripped my hand tight, and nodded to the nurse, still unable to speak.

"He's stabilized," she said. "The specialist has just been back and given him some more medication. It's best not to excite him, keep your voices low, and let him sleep. He's improved in the last few hours, but the next twenty-four hours are critical."

We nodded somberly and followed her into a small room, where my papa's supine body lay. Asleep, with wires protruding from under the blanket, he seemed diminished, smaller than the robust man I knew. His face was gray, a shade darker than the silver stubble of his beard.

I swallowed back tears, not wanting to break down in front of Maman, knowing that we needed to be strong.

We stood by his bedside, with the ticking of machines and rattle of Papa's labored breathing. The only thing that was the same were his hands: big, solid peasant hands, scarred from hard work, which lay splayed in front of him. I took one, and Maman took the other. Tears spilled down her cheeks, and my own eyes welled. We didn't speak, only listened to the beeps, and moans of the machines that kept Papa alive.

My mind fell to Lilou, and hoped she'd get here soon. I could only imagine how she felt, bumping and jostling on the train, the journey interminable in an emergency.

I sat gently on the edge of the bed and waited.

* * *

Dawn peeped through the curtains, hues of soft amber, and the promise of blue skies as the night slipped away once more. The nurse had kept up an hourly examination, checking his vital signs, administering medication while our silent vigil continued.

Every now and then Papa would groan, startling us, but then he'd quieten. Was he still in pain? It hurt to think of him lost inside a dream, his heart struggling to beat.

Quick footsteps echoed down the hall, and a doctor who looked too young to be qualified entered the room. "Bonjour," he said. We mumbled hello, and I moved to make room for him.

The air grew thick as we waited for news.

The doctor checked Papa's file, narrowing his eyes as he read. My heart beat staccato as I tried to decipher what his expression meant. "Will he be OK?" I asked, my voice coming out like a squeak.

With the file flicked closed, the doctor smiled. "He's over the worst of it, stable for now. There'll be more testing done over the next few days, and we'll keep him on the medication that makes him drowsy so his heart can recover. But overall, I think he's doing as well as can be expected in such circumstances."

I let out an audible sigh of relief, and Maman sobbed into her hands. The doctor smiled, and I took that as a very good sign. "We need a cardiologist, to run extensive tests. When he's able to travel we will organize his transfer. They'll chat with you about the long-term care plan. I would say though, he needs to make a number of lifestyle changes in order to prevent this happening again."

"Like what?" I asked.

"Simple foods, less butter, less cream. He has to exercise, lose some weight, so his heart can cope better."

Maman's eyes widened. "Perhaps you should tell him that when he wakes up?" Her face broke into a smile. "He loves his food."

The doctor laughed. "I can tell. He can still eat well; it just needs to be modified. Smaller portions of the low-calorie kind. He'll have follow-up appointments with me, so he can't cheat."

It was like a weight had been lifted. The doctor was speaking of the future, a future with Papa in it. I sent up a silent thank you to the universe.

"How long do you think he'll need to recuperate?" Maman asked.

The doctor shrugged. "We'll have to wait and see, but he will need to take things easy. Does he have someone to care for him? The nurse said you both flew in from Paris . . ."

"I'll be here," Maman said. "I was only visiting my daughter. Once he's better, we will be moving to Paris to be closer to family," she said, fervently.

"You're going to move?" I asked. This was the first I'd heard of it.

"We both are," she said. "Papa doesn't know it yet, but it's where I want to be. This proves it. We can spend our twilight years wandering down the Champs-Élysées, or go boating on the Bois de Boulogne. He won't even notice he's taking exercise. A small apartment in the Latin Quarter will do us both good. My chef friends can come and visit." She gave a small shrug like it was no big deal. I fought the urge to hug her. I was so proud of the person she'd become.

The doctor scribbled some notes in the file. "If that's what you plan to do, it sounds possible. I'll see him for the next few weeks, and then sign you over to another doctor in Paris for any follow-up visits. A more relaxed lifestyle is crucial, and if you can find that elsewhere, do it."

"Merci," Maman said. "Once he's strong enough, our new life will commence."

"He should wake soon. He'll be groggy, so no excitement. I'll be back later to check on him."

The doctor did some further checks and then smiled once more before leaving the room.

Maman and I exchanged looks of gratitude. "I thought . . ." My words petered off. I couldn't say any more in fear I'd jinx us and something bad would happen.

"I thought so too," she said. "But he's strong. And from now on, I'm in charge and he will listen. He's not leaving me this way, all alone with him having the last word. Non, non, non."

I gave her a wide smile as the door burst open and in walked Lilou and Henry. Why was he here? Lilou's face was lined with lack of sleep and her eyes bright with tears.

"Go sit beside him," I said. "The doctor has just been and Papa is through the worst."

She broke into a bout of noisy sobs. Through her gulps and shrieks she said, "He's not going to die?"

The journey must have been fraught. Her hands shook, and she couldn't stop crying.

"Come here," Maman said, and Lilou moved to her, allowing Maman embrace her like she did when we were children, with her head on her breast. Maman patted her back and let Lilou expel the grief she'd been holding tight. "He's not going anywhere. But it's going to take time for him to recover and we have to be mindful of that."

"Oh my God, he's going to be OK!" She moved to Papa, and draped herself on the bed, and hugged his sleeping frame tight.

Henry stood off to the side of the room, stiff and straight like a toy soldier.

"I'm sorry," he said to the room in general.

Maman waved him away. "Don't be sorry," she said. "He's going to be OK. I can feel it in my heart."

He braved a glance at me and was met with a murderous glare.

"Henry wanted to come," Lilou said, sitting up next to Papa, taking one of his hands in her own.

"Nice," I said frostily, aware of Henry's scrutiny.

She turned to me. "He's a good guy, Anouk. And so is Tristan."

"Says who?"

She frowned. "Anouk, really? Aren't you happy they caught Joshua?"

I shrugged. "I'm going to get some coffee."

Stumbling from the room, I made my way to the tiny cafeteria, searching for a strong cup of coffee. My thoughts were zigzagging from relief about Papa, to fury over Tristan's double life. Deep down, I knew he'd only being doing his job, but did his investigation have to include kissing me? It was like I had a neon sign on my head flashing, *Take advantage of me.* I didn't want to consider any of that, while Papa lay in the hospital bed.

Instead of giving in to the anguish, I thought of all the things we'd need to do in order to get Papa safely to Paris when he was better. They'd have to sell their house, their car, Papa's business. Find a nice apartment in a relatively humble quarter. I'd concentrate on my family, and forget Tristan ever existed. There was a lot to consider about such a move and especially now with Papa's long-term health.

Taking some watery vending machine coffee back to the room, I was almost pushed over when a group of doctors ran past with cries of *Excusez-moi!*

I leaned against the wall, to let them pass. Nurses followed quickly behind. When they turned into Papa's room, my heart seized. Without a thought I dropped the cup and raced in after them. Maman and Lilou were clutching each other, their eyes wide with fright.

Doctors were leaning over my papa, working furiously with the paddles.

"What happened?" I asked though I knew the answer. No one spoke as we watched them try and revive Papa, his ox-strong body being pulled upward by the force of the shock they were giving him to start his heart.

Henry was just inside the door on the phone. He spoke brusquely to someone in a low voice. "You said to call. He was, but he's just had another heart attack . . ." He paused and listened to whoever was on the other end. "Yes, they need a specialist here urgently, or else. If he stabilizes get him to Paris . . . Yes. OK. When? I'll tell them." He clicked off the phone.

It was like being caught in a nightmare. The doctors were speaking quickly to one another, doing compressions on his chest. Was he dying? My eyes welled with grief and an utter feeling of helplessness.

Henry came up behind me. "That was Tristan. He's found a cardiologist – one of the best he said. He's flying him in as we speak."

I nodded mutely. Could Papa wait that long? What could the cardiologist do that these doctors couldn't? I joined Maman and Lilou. We leaned against the window and clutched hands. All we could do was wait and hope the cardiologist would have some magic cure. *Please hurry!*

A thousand *if only* scenarios raced through my mind. If only I'd listened to him. If only I'd made him visit Paris earlier. *If only* must've been the saddest two words in the world.

Almost two hours later, we were delirious with worry as Papa barely clung on to life when Tristan strode in with an elderly somber man. The man introduced himself as Doctor Carmichael, and went straight to Papa. The other team of doctors came in and spoke in hushed tones while Doctor Carmichael nodded.

"We're going to move your papa to surgery," Doctor Carmichael said. "I'll do my best."

There was no time to question him. We offered up thanks and watched as they quickly moved machines, and sorted out wires, so the bed could be wheeled out.

Maman leaned over and whispered in Papa's ear. She kissed him gently on the forehead, while Lilou and I waited to do the same.

"Je t'aime, Papa." His skin was warm to the touch, and smelled of the lavender soap he used. I stood out of the way, and held my hands over my mouth as if it could stop the anguish from pouring out. What if I never got to kiss his warm cheek again? Hold those big, sturdy Papa hands? I pushed the thought away, and instead thought of him waking up, thought of making soup for him while he healed. They'd move to Paris, and we'd all care for him.

They pushed the bed, and the machines from the room. The empty space it left was almost grotesque, as if he was truly gone from us for good.

Tristan motioned for me outside, and while I wanted to ignore him, I couldn't after what he'd just done. His jaw was clenched as though he was nervous. "Doctor Carmichael is the very best in his field. He's got his own team with him, and feels confident from the briefing he can save him. I'm going to stay here, in case he needs anything else."

"Thank you." Words evaporated as I stared into his eyes, my grief reflected in them.

"I'm so sorry, Anouk. For everything."

"I know." It would have been rude to voice my opinions so I kept quiet. And who cared. In light of everything it suddenly seemed so insignificant. All I wanted was my papa to be given one more chance at life.

"He's going to be OK. We will make it so." Tristan's eyes clouded. "My parents . . ." He swallowed hard. "I couldn't get there in time. They were gone . . . and I was too late. But this time, things will be different. Whatever he needs we can get it . . ."

My heart tore in two. This was like reliving his own personal nightmare, and yet he'd still done it, tried valiantly to save my papa, when he could have just wound up his investigation and left. "What you've done, we appreciate it more than I can say."

"I have a lot of apologies to make to your family once everything has settled."

Exhaustion settled heavily in my limbs. I wanted to sit down, and wait. I didn't want to think of anything else. "I'm going to the waiting room to lie down for a while. But thank you, again."

He raised his eyebrows. "I know it's not the right time, but will you ever forgive me? I'd like to be friends, or . . ."

The real world came crashing into my subconscious. "Won't you leave now? Go undercover again and wake up in Brazil, or something?" There was zero point offering friendship when what we had was based on a lie. I knew absolutely nothing about the blond man standing in front of me. And I didn't think I wanted to. Trust was important, and he'd broken it in so many different ways. In order to protect myself I'd have to walk away. It was the right choice. As I drifted away, my heart was heavy. Why did it have to hurt so much?

Chapter Twenty-Nine

A few weeks later I was back in Paris, eagerly awaiting the arrival of my parents. Papa's surgery had been a success but he was still on bedrest. The doctor approved his travel on the stipulation he didn't move much once he arrived. I was excited to see them, and help Maman search for an apartment to rent. Their house was up for sale but the property market in their village wasn't exactly thriving, so in the meantime they'd find a rental in the Marais, the quarter Maman loved for its fresh food markets and bohemian style.

There was a knock at the door, so I raced to answer it. Instead of my parents it was a courier holding a big box. "Anouk?"

"Oui."

"Delivery."

I took the box, which was heavier than first appeared, and opened it.

Inside was the Henry Miller typewriter we'd argued over at the flea market on the Seine. Perhaps it hadn't been the one the Postcard Bandit used after all, and I was grateful his grubby paws didn't mar Henry Miller's legacy. There was with a ream of paper and a neatly typed sentence.

"*I miss you.*"

It was bittersweet. I missed him too. There was no return address so I couldn't send it back. I placed it on the side table and sighed. Would I ever be able to forget those brilliantly blue eyes . . .?

Lilou called from the balcony. "Let's take a walk before they get here. My nerves are jangling with excitement."

I laughed, ready for a distraction from the typewriter, and followed her into the glorious day. Summer was putting on a fine show. The air was fragrant with flowers spilling over planter boxes in balconies above. Red carnations and yolky daffodils, and an abundance of trellised roses met us at every turn.

Lilou wore a black and white striped dress that swished around her thighs. An American company had put in an order for her Je t'aime bracelets: silver links connected with a mini padlock in ode to the Love Lock Bridge that was no longer. I proudly wore one on my wrist, loving the symbolism. I'd always thought my sister needed guidance, a helping hand to set goals, but I just hadn't been listening.

She'd known she'd find her path, the same way she knew she'd find the right kind of love one day, and she wouldn't settle for anything less than the best, but in the meantime she really lived her life, by enjoying every minute of every day.

"Where are we going?" I asked.

"Ice cream in the passage Dauphine?"

"Oui. I love it there." The passage Dauphine was a cobblestoned laneway off the Rue Dauphine. The streetscape was beautiful. We'd trip down the uneven stones in our heels, our necks craned up to take in the ivy climbing the rustic walls. It was postcard pretty, and had a number of bistros and cafés we loved, including one that sold homemade ice cream in the summer. When ice cream is churned properly with the best ingredients it tastes nothing like the bulk sugary supermarket brands you find everywhere. It was one of life's greatest pleasures, taking time to enjoy the magnificence of summer with something to cool you down.

"Tristan keeps asking after you. He's never going to stop," Lilou said, turning to watch my reaction.

"Don't respond. That's one way to make it stop." Lilou was still firm friends with Henry, chatting constantly by email and Skype, and often he passed along messages from Tristan.

She gave me the Lilou look, as if I was too silly for words. "Anouk, can't you give him a second chance?"

Kids' laughter peppered the bright day, their clamoring footsteps echoing between the buildings. "What for? I don't see the point." The lie caught in my throat.

"That is the biggest load of rubbish I've ever heard! You've been walking around with those moony eyes, and long face, like your whole world has ended. You can't lie to me because I can read you like a book."

I sighed. "Lilou, he was all set to send me to jail . . . Who does that to someone they supposedly have feelings for?"

"He said at the market that day, when you fought over the typewriter, he told you to run. He risked his career saying that much to you."

I thought back to that day. Did he? How foolish I'd been thinking he was the robber! "I don't remember that. But I was alluding to *him* that he should run. And what does that make me? A hypocrite in the world of antiques."

"So you'd let the first man who really loves you lose you, over his job, which is protecting antiques, the things you adore most?"

We came to the café and took a table out the front. "He doesn't love me."

"He does; he told Henry. And Tristan quit his job! Just like that. He's been offered security work, in Paris. Gustave, the guard you so admire, hired him because the owner keeps leaving the building unlocked. That's how you got in that night."

I inhaled sharply. "Why did he quit?"

She gave me a dazzling smile. "Why do you think?"

"He can't quit and expect that will change my mind."

281

She shrugged and took the menu from the wooden holder. "Apparently . . ." she drew out the word ". . . it was the first time he'd ever let his feelings get in the way of a job. And that was the death knell. If he can't separate the two worlds, he can't commit to it properly. It's time, he said, for a new life, a *real* life."

I made a show of reading the menu. I didn't want him to quit his job because of me. Hadn't he said he thrived on his job? But was that even true, or just part of the back-story of Monsieur Black who was in fact fictional?

"I hope he knows what he's doing," I said softly.

What would he do with his life? It was one of those careers I thought might make a person feel lost if they had to give it up. Did this change things? I ordered my ice cream, Violette, and wondered about him. The man he really was. The one who lost his parents, who had no siblings, no ties, except that job, and now he didn't even have that. Perhaps he could create the man he wanted to be . . .

"I'll have the Sabayon," Lilou said, giving the waiter a saucy smile. "He's cute," she said, watching him walk off. "So, if you happen to see Tristan can you be nice? He saved our papa, in case I need to remind you. Really stepped in when no one else did. That makes him a great man in my eyes."

It suddenly dawned on me; an intense pain flickered in my chest. "Did he get fired, Lilou? Is that what happened?"

A flash of guilt crossed her features.

"Lilou, tell me."

She sighed dramatically. "I'm not supposed to tell you, but if it's the only way to get into your steely heart, then so be it. Henry told me that Tristan's superiors said if he used the plane for personal reasons, he'd get fired. Well, he chose to use the plane, twice! Once to get you there, and the second time to send the cardiologist, *which* he had to pull a million favors to get the man to agree to go. His bosses weren't happy but they couldn't stop him. And then he quit. Henry told me when he threw down his badge he had this huge smile on his face, like he was free of that life and he was goddamned happy about it. But it was you. He was thinking of you and what might be."

"I can't believe he did that for us." It was one thing to quit, but choosing to leave a career in order to save someone's life, well that was something else entirely.

* * *

Back home, an hour later, our parents arrived. Maman pushing his wheelchair through the door with a few knocks and bumps and cries of "careful!" from Papa. He didn't need it long term, just long enough to recuperate, and keep any exertion to a minimum.

After effusive greetings and lots of hugging, Maman and I set off to see some apartments. The first one was too small, a bedsit really in the upper Marais. "Maman, you couldn't fit the wheelchair in here."

The next was bigger and better, suited to their needs, but the agent said they'd had lots of interest and people were now offering above the advertised price.

"We'll keep looking," Maman said.

The third apartment overlooked the Musée Carnavalet and its manicured hedge gardens. The balcony led out from the living room, and was wide enough for Papa to get out in his wheelchair and have plenty of space to turn.

The balustrades were full of hanging pots, ready for Maman to work her magic, plunging her hands into the fertile soil, planting herbs, and salad vegetables for her cooking.

"This is the one, Anouk. The kitchen is perfect. That island bench is big enough for the chefs to sit around . . ."

I couldn't hide my smile. Maman was flushed with happiness. "It's beautiful; the afternoon sun streams right in. Once Papa is back to himself, why don't you think of opening a cooking school? Something boutique?"

"Do you think I could do it? What about those who've had training in patisserie, and fine dining – things I know little of? They'd probably call me an imposter."

I tutted, running my hand along the smooth granite of the bench. "Non, Maman, you're catering to a different clientele. Ones who want to learn the traditional ways, the best ways for everyday meals. Family meals, meals for celebrations."

"Once Papa is better . . ."

She'd do it. I knew how to recognize the quiet determination in the women of my family now.

"Have you got the paperwork?" Maman asked the estate agent who'd been on the phone outside.

"Maman," I said, "Don't you want to see more first?"

"I'm sixty, Anouk. I don't have time to waste!" She cackled and the sound bounced around the room.

* * *

The long, hot days tired Papa out so easily. Even on bedrest, he was gray, so we took pains to keep quiet and tiptoe around the apartment while we sorted their new life in Paris.

Movers had taken the boxes to their new abode and we were meeting them to unpack, and then coming back for Papa so he could go from one bed to another.

It was so much fun having my maman here, happy, making plans. I couldn't wait for Papa to get better so he could enjoy Paris too.

I was lugging a box of delicate items downstairs. Maman didn't trust anyone with her kitchenware, so we had to take it by taxi ourselves, all eight boxes of it.

Putting the box carefully on the pavement I arched, stretching my muscles. I was counting down the minutes until I could flop on a chair and enjoy a cold glass of wine.

"Moving?" My body tingled, and I spun to face him. The real

284

Tristan wore washed-out denim jeans and a tight white tee. He appeared younger, maybe because he was a little more ruffled. His hair was windblown, and attire casual. It suited him.

"No, not me. Maman and Papa are moving to the Marais," I said, struggling to keep my voice in check. He was breathtaking to stare at. How could I have forgotten the sheer presence he had? My body betrayed me. My legs were jellylike, my hands quaking with nerves.

"I wanted to visit him and see how he was, but thought it better to ask you first." He gave me a half smile, flashing his beautiful white teeth.

"He's doing great. A few more weeks and he'll be up on his feet." I looked up at him, couldn't stop myself. "Tristan, I know you lost your job because of what you did. I'm so sorry. I know, well I *think*, you loved your job. I feel responsible."

He waved me away. "I've spent the last fifteen years with no fixed address. That takes a toll. And when I let my emotions get in the way of my job, I knew I'd made the right choice."

"So what will you do?"

"I'll spend my days getting lost along the boulevards, and wear a geeky hat, and some really bad shades, and then when summer is over, I'll start as head of security at Cloutier Auction House. Gustave's been showing me the ropes. I think I'll be happy there."

"You really are staying in Paris for good?" I stood stock-still, not daring to breathe until I heard his answer.

"There's this girl, you see, and she doesn't know it, but she's stolen my heart . . ."

I smiled and gave him a playful shove. "Stolen? I don't think she *steals*."

"You're right she doesn't steal." He laughed. "But if she's willing to give love a chance, and leave her soup bowls to gather dust, I think I can help her out."

Oh God, he'd heard everything and still he wanted to be in my life, with my quirks and all. Could I give my heart away again? What if it got broken? Staring into Tristan's azure eyes, I thought maybe I could try. Life was for living, and because of what Tristan had done Papa would have the best chance. I could feel something like hope settle over me.

"Maybe the girl might give you a chance. You never know." And with that he took me in his arms and kissed the very breath out of me.

Epilogue

Over the next few months Tristan's eyes lit up like stars when they saw me, those full lips of his twitched because he wanted to plant kisses all over me. I'd given in to the sensation of falling in love. It was like jumping off into an abyss. I was weightless, butterfly-bellied, and thrilled all at once. How could this be real? I hadn't ever felt this profoundly love-sick before. Some days I couldn't eat; my nerves fluttered and my thoughts grew hazy just thinking of him.

"What do you say?" he said, giving me that slow saucy smile of his. "Can I finally scream to the world that we're in love?"

I smiled. In light of the events, I'd kept our relationship under wraps, and I was treading carefully, going slowly before tumbling all at once into this heady, passionate love affair.

"You can scream it to the world if you want."

With a few quick strides he was at the balcony, and wrenched the doors open. "I LOVE ANOUK! Is anyone there? I love Anouk, and one day, she's going to marry me!"

I gasped. "I forgot how American you are! Get away from those doors right now!"

He dissolved into laughter. "I mean it," he said, taking me in his arms, and smothering me with kisses. "One day I will marry you and you can take out an ad in the marriage classifieds, bigger and better than anyone else's . . ."

I bit my lip to stop myself from laughing and said mock seriously, "I'm not sure about your brash American ways."

"You looked to the left."

"So?"

"That means you're lying."

"I love you."

"You looked to the right."

"Oui, so what does that mean?"

"It means you love me."

"A little."

"Liar."

I laughed and pressed my lips against his, reveling as tingles raced through me at his touch. I wanted to stop time and spend eternity kissing him, the American who'd stolen my heart, because I let him.

Acknowledgements

I want to thank the women in my family who, like Anouk and Lilou, have shown me what quiet determination can achieve. Without their guidance I wouldn't be the person I am today. I know anything is possible, if you only believe in yourself.

Acknowledgements

Loved *The Little Antique Shop under the Eiffel Tower*? Then turn the page for an exclusive extract from

THE LITTLE BOOKSHOP ON THE SEINE . . .

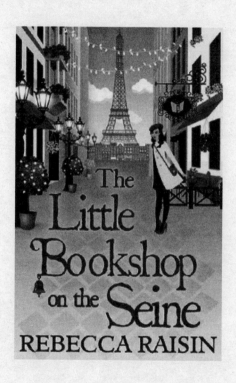

Chapter One

October

With a heavy heart I placed the sign in the display window.

All books 50% off.

If things didn't pick up soon, it would read *Closing down sale*. The thought alone was enough to make me shiver. The autumnal sky was awash with purples and smudges of orange, as I stepped outside to survey the display window from the sidewalk.

Star-shaped leaves crunched underfoot. I forced a smile. A sale wouldn't hurt, and maybe it'd take the bookshop figures from the red into the black – which I so desperately needed. My rent had been hiked up. The owner of the building, a sharp-featured, silver-tongued, forty-something man, had put the pressure on me lately – to pay more, to declutter the shop, claiming the haphazard stacks of books were a fire risk. The additional rent stretched the budget to breaking level. Something had to change.

The phone shrilled, and a grin split my face. It could only be Ridge at this time of the morning. Even after being together almost a year his name still provoked a giggle. It suited him though, the veritable man mountain he was. I'd since met his mom, a sweet, well-spoken lady, who claimed in dulcet tones, that she chose his name *well* before his famous namesake in the Bold and the Beautiful. In fact, she was adamant about it, and said the TV character Ridge was no match for her son. I had to agree. Sure, they both had chiseled movie star cheekbones, and an intense gaze that made many a woman swoon, but my guy was more than just the sum of his parts – I loved him for his mind, as much as his clichéd six pack, and broody hotness. And even better, he loved me for me.

He was the hero in my own *real-life* love story, and due back from Canada the next day. It had been weeks since I'd seen him, and I ached for him in a way that made me blush.

I dashed inside, and answered the phone, breathlessly. "*The Bookshop on the Corner.*"

"That's the voice I know and love," he said in his rich, husky tone. My heart fluttered, picturing him at the end of the line, his jet-black hair and flirty blue eyes. He simply had to flick me a look loaded with suggestion, and I'd be jelly-legged and love-struck.

"What are you wearing?" he said.

"Wouldn't you like to know?" I held back a laugh, eager to drag it out. So far our relationship had been more long distance than anticipated, as he flew around the world reporting on location. The stints apart left an ache in my heart, a numbness to my days. Luckily I had my books, and a sweeping romance or two helped keep the loneliness at bay.

"Tell me or I'll be forced to Skype you and see for myself."

Glancing down at my outfit, I grimaced: black tights, a black pencil skirt, and a pilled blue knit sweater, all as old as the hills of Ashford. Not exactly the type of answer Ridge was waiting for, or the way I wanted him to picture me, after so many weeks apart. "Those stockings you like, and . . ."

His voice returned with a growl. "*Those* stockings? With the little suspenders?"

I sat back into the chair behind the counter, fussing with my bangs. "The very same."

He groaned. "You're *killing* me. Take a photo . . ."

"There's no need. If you're good, I'll wear the red ones tomorrow night." I grinned wickedly. Our reunions were always passionate affairs; he was a hands-on type of guy. Lucky for him, because it took a certain type of man to drag me from the pages of my books. When he was home we didn't surface until one of us had to go to work. Loving Ridge had been a revelation, especially in the bedroom, where he took things achingly slow, drawing out every second. I flushed with desire for him.

There was a muffled voice and the low buzz of phones ringing. Ridge mumbled to someone before saying, "About tomorrow . . ." He petered out, regret in each syllable.

I closed my eyes. "You're not coming, are you?" I tried not to sigh, but it spilled out regardless. The lure of a bigger, better story was too much for him to resist, and lately the gaps between our visits grew wider. I understood his work was important, but I wanted him all to myself. A permanent fixture in the small town I lived in.

He tutted. "I'm sorry, baby. There's a story breaking in Indonesia, and I have to go. It'll only be for a week or two, and then I'll take some time off."

Outside, leaves fluttered slowly from the oak tree, swaying softly, until they fell to the ground. I wasn't the nagging girlfriend sort – times like this though, I was tempted to be. Ridge had said the very same thing the last three times he'd canceled a visit. But invariably someone would call and ask Ridge to head to the next location; any time off would be cut short.

"I understand," I said, trying to keep my voice bright. Sometimes I felt like I played a never-ending waiting game. Would it always be like this? "Just so you know, I have a very hot date this afternoon."

He gasped. "You better be talking about a fictional date." His tone was playful, but underneath there was a touch of jealousy to it. Maybe it was just as hard on him, being apart.

"One *very* hot book boyfriend . . . though not as delectable as my real boyfriend – but a stand-in, until he returns."

"Well, he better not keep you up half the night, or he'll have me to answer to," he faux threatened, and then said more seriously, "Things will slow down, Sarah. I want to be with you so much my soul hurts. But right now, while I'm freelance, I have to take whatever comes my way."

"I know. I just feel a bit lost sometimes. Like someone's hit pause, and I'm frozen on the spot." I bit my lip, trying to work out how to explain it. "It's not just missing you – I do understand about your job – it's . . . everything. The bookshop sales dwindling, the rent jacked up, everyone going on about their business, while I'm still the same old Sarah."

I'd been at this very crossroads when I'd met Ridge, and he'd swept me off my feet, like the ultimate romance hero. For a while that had been enough. After all, wasn't love always the answer? Romance aside, life was a little stagnant, and I knew it was because of my fear of change. It wasn't so much that I had to step from behind the covers of my books, rather plunge, perhaps. Take life by the scruff of the neck and shake it. But how?

"You've had a rough few weeks. That's all. I'll be back soon, and I'm sure there's something I can do to make you forget everything . . ."

My belly flip-flopped at the thought. He *would* make me forget everything that was outside that bedroom door, but then he'd leave and it would all tumble back.

What exactly was I searching for? My friends were getting married and having babies. Buying houses and redecorating. Starting businesses. My life had stalled. I was an introvert, happiest hiding in the shadows of my shop, reading romances to laze the day away, between serving the odd customer or two – yet, it wasn't enough. In small town Connecticut, there wasn't a lot to do. And life here – calm, peaceful – was fine, but that's just it, *fine* wasn't enough anymore. I had this fear that life was passing me by because I was too timid to take the reins.

It was too hazy a notion of what I was trying to say, even to me. Instead of lumping Ridge with it, I changed tack. "I hope you know, you're not leaving the house when you get home. Phones will be switched to silent, computers forgotten, and the only time we're leaving the comfort of bed is when I need sustenance." A good romp around the bedroom would suffice until I could pinpoint what it was that I wanted.

"How about I sort out the sustenance?" he said, his voice heavy with desire. "And then we'll never have to leave."

"Promises, promises," I said, my breath hitching. I hoped this flash of longing would never wane, the sweet torture of anticipation.

"I have to go, baby. I'll call you tonight if it's not too late once I'm in."

"Definitely call tonight! Otherwise, I can't guarantee the book boyfriend won't steal your girlfriend. He's pretty hot, I'll have you know."

"Why am I jealous of a fictional character?" He laughed, a low, sexy sound. "OK, tonight. Love you."

"Love you, too."

He hung up, leaving me dazed, and a touch lonely knowing that I wouldn't see him the next day as planned.

I tried to shake the image of Ridge from my mind. If anyone walked in, they'd see the warm blush of my cheeks, and know exactly what I was thinking. Damn the man for being so attractive, and so effortlessly sexy.

Shortly, the sleepy town of Ashford would wake under the gauzy light of October skies. Signs would be flipped to open, stoops swept, locals would amble down the road. Some would step into the bookshop and out of the cold, and spend their morning with hands wrapped around a mug of steaming hot tea, and reading in any one of the cozy nooks around the labyrinth-like shop.

I loved having a place for customers to languish. Comfort was key, and if you had a good book and a hot drink, what else could you possibly need to make your day any brighter? Throw rugs and cushions were littered around seating areas. Coats would be swiftly hung on hooks, a chair found, knitted blankets pulled across knees, and their next hour or two sorted, in the most relaxing of ways.

I wandered around the shop, feather duster in hand, tickling the covers, waking them from slumber. I'm sure as soon as my back was turned, the books wiggled and winked at one another, as if they were eager for the day to begin, for fingers of hazy sunlight to filter through and land on them like spotlights, as if saying, *here's the book for you.*

Imagine if I had to close up for good, like so many other shops had in recent times? It pained me to think people were missing out on the real-life bookshop experience. Wasn't it much better when you could step into a dimly lit space, and eke your way around searching for the right novel? You could run a fingertip along the spines, smell that glorious old book scent, flick them open, and unbend a dog-eared page. Read someone else's notes in the margin, or a highlighted passage, and see why that sentence or metaphor had dazzled the previous owner.

Second-hand books had so much *life* in them. They'd lived, sometimes in many homes, or maybe just one. They'd been on airplanes, traveled to sunny beaches, or crowded into a backpack and taken high up a mountain where the air thinned.

Some had been held aloft tepid rose-scented baths, and thickened and warped with moisture. Others had child-like scrawls on the acknowledgement page, little fingers looking for a blank space to leave their mark. Then there were the pristine novels, ones that had been read carefully, bookmarks used, almost like their owner barely pried the pages open so loathe were they to damage their treasure.

I loved them all.

And I found it hard to part with them. Though years of book selling had steeled me. I had to let them go, and each time made a fervent wish they'd be read well, and often.

Missy, my best friend, said I was completely cuckoo, and that I spent too much time alone in my shadowy shop, because I believed my books communicated with me. A soft sigh here, as they stretched their bindings when dawn broke, or a hum, as they anticipated a customer hovering close who might run a hand along their cover, tempting them to flutter their pages hello. Books were fussy when it came to their owners, and gave off a type of sound, an almost imperceptible whirr, when the right person was near. Most people weren't aware that books chose us, at the time when we needed them most.

Outside the breeze picked up, gathering the leaves in a swirl and blowing them down the street in waves. Rubbing my hands for warmth, I trundled into the reading room, and added some wood to the fire. Each day, the weather grew cooler, and the crackle and spit of the glowing embers were a nice soundtrack to the shop, comforting, like a hug.

The double-stacked books in the reading room weren't for sale, but could be thumbed and enjoyed by anyone who wished. They were my favorites, the ones I couldn't part with. I'd been gifted a huge range from a man whose wife had passed on, a woman who was so like me with her bookish foibles, that it was almost like she was still here. Her collection – an essential part of her life – lived on, long after she'd gone. I'd treasure them always.

Wandering back to the front of the shop, the street was coming alive. Owners milled in front of shops, chatting to early-bird customers, or lugging out A-frame signs, advertising their wares. Lil, my friend from the Gingerbread Café, waved over at me. Her heavily pregnant belly made me smile. I pulled open the front door, a gust of wind blowing my hair back, and fluttering the pages of the books.

"You take it easy!" I shouted. Lil was due any day now, but insisted on working. Times were tough for all of us, so Lil had to work, but claimed instead she wanted to spruce things up before she left. Nesting, her best friend and only employee CeeCee called it.

Lil tossed her long blonde curls back from her face. "If I take it any easier, I'll be asleep! Besides, how are you going to survive without your chocolate fix?" The wind carried her words to me in a happy jumble.

"True," I agreed. "I'll be there as soon as my tummy rumbles." It was torture, working across the road from the café, the scent of tempered chocolate or the yeasty smell of freshly baked bread wafting its way to my shop. I'd find myself crossing the street and demanding to be fed, flopping lazily on their sofa, while they flitted around making all my food dreams come true. The girls from the café were great friends, and often gave me a metaphorical shove in the back when they thought I should step from the comfort of my shop and try something new, like love, for example.

They'd set me up with Ridge, knowing I wouldn't take the leap myself. When I'd first met him, I couldn't understand why a big shot reporter from New York would be interested in a girl from smallsville. It wasn't that I didn't think I was good enough, it was more that our lives were a million miles apart, and the likes of him were a rarity in Ashford.

My girlfriends hadn't seen it that way, and *literally* pushed me into his arms, at a dinner party the night of the infamous man crease fiasco. I wouldn't say that's when I fell in love with Ridge, my face pressed up against his nether regions after a 'fall' on the uneven deck, but it was pretty damn close. My so-called friends had orchestrated the night, including the 'whoops' shove in the back from Lil, so I toppled ungraciously towards Ridge, landing on my knees at his hip level. My breathing had been uneven, as his sweater rode high, and jeans had slung low, giving me ample

300

opportunity to scrutinize the deep V presented to me. My lips a mere inch away from his tanned flesh, until he scooped me up, before I almost licked his skin to see what it tasted like. I had this strange burning desire to see what flavor he'd be. That's what reading too many romances does to a girl.

Recalling the evening still provoked a blush, because it was so unlike me. I mean, imagine if I *had* flicked my tongue against his exposed skin? He would have been running for the hills before the entrée was served. But that's the effect he had over me, he made my mind blank, and my body act of its own volition, including a thousand scenarios I'd never have entertained with any other guy. Dumbstruck by love was a real thing, I'd come to learn.

Lil's boisterous laughter brought me back to the moment. "See you soon. I'll have a chocolate soufflé with your name on it."

"You'd tempt the devil himself!" I joked and gave her a wave before stepping back into the warmth of the bookshop.

My email pinged and I dashed over to see who it was from. That's how exciting my life was *sans* Ridge, an email was enough to make me almost run, and that was saying a lot. I only ran if chocolate was involved, and even then it was more a fast walk.

Sales@littlebookshop.fr

Sophie, a dear Parisian friend. She owned *Once Upon a Time*, a famous bookshop by the bank of the Seine. We'd become confidantes since connecting on my book blog a while back, and shared our joys and sorrows about bookshop life. She was charming and sweet, and adored books as much as me, believing them to be portable magic, and a balm for souls.

I clicked open the email and read.

Ma Chérie,

I cannot stay one more day in Paris. You see, Manu has not so much broken my heart, rather pulled it out of my chest and stomped on it. The days are interminable and I can't catch my breath. He

walks past the bookshop, as though nothing is amiss. I have a
proposal for you. Please call me as soon as you can.
Love,
Sophie

Poor Sophie. I'd heard all about her grand love affair with a dashing twenty-something man, who frequented her bookshop, and quoted famous poets. It'd been a whirlwind romance, but she often worried he cast an appraising eye over other women. Even when she clutched his hand, and walked along the cobbled streets of Paris, he'd dart an admiring glance at any woman swishing past.

I shot off a quick reply, telling her to Skype me now, if she was able. Within seconds my computer flashed with an incoming call.

Her face appeared on the screen, her chestnut-colored hair in an elegant chignon, her lips dusted rosy pink. If she was in the throes of heartache, you'd never know it by looking at her. The French had a way of always looking poised and together, no matter what was happening in their complex lives.

"Darling," she said, giving me a nod. "He's a lothario, a Casanova, a . . ." She grappled for another moniker as her voice broke. "He's dating the girl who owns the shop next door!" Her eyes smoldered, but her face remained stoic.

I gasped, "Which girl? The one from the florist?"

Sophie shook her head. "The other side, the girl from the *fromagerie.*" She grimaced. I'd heard so much about the people in or around Sophie's life that it was easy to call her neighbors to mind. "Giselle?" I said, incredulous. "Wasn't she engaged – I thought the wedding was any day now?"

Sophie's eyes widened. "She's broken off her engagement, and has announced it to the world that *my* Manu has proposed and now they are about to set up house and to try immediately for children—"

My hand flew to my mouth. "Children! He wouldn't do that, surely!" Sophie was late-forties, and had gently broached the subject of having a baby with Manu, but he'd said simply: absolutely not, he didn't want children.

The doorbell of her shop pinged, Sophie's face pinched and she leaned closer to the screen, lowering her voice. "A customer . . ." She forced a bright smile, turned her head and spoke in rapid-fire French to whoever stood just off-screen. "So," she continued quietly. "The entire neighborhood are whispering behind their hands about the love triangle, and unfortunately for me, I'm the laughing stock. The older woman, who was deceived by a younger man."

I wished I could lean through the monitor and hug her. While she was an expert at keeping her features neutral, she couldn't stop the glassiness of her eyes when tears threatened. My heart broke that Manu would treat her so callously. She'd trusted him, and loved him unreservedly. "No one is laughing at you, I promise," I said. "They'll be talking about Manu, if anyone, and saying how he's made a huge mistake."

"No, no." A bitter laugh escaped her. "I look like a fool. I simply cannot handle when he cavorts through the streets with her, darting glances in my bookshop, like they hope I'll see them. It's too cruel." Sophie held up a hand, and turned to a voice. She said *au revoir* to the customer and spun to face me, but within a second or two, the bell sounded again. "I have a proposal for you, and I want you to *really* consider it." She raised her eyebrows. "Or at least hear me out before you say no." Her gaze burned into mine as I racked my brain with what it could be, and came up short. Sophie waved to customers, and pivoted her screen further away.

"Well?" I said with a nervous giggle. "What exactly are you proposing?"

She blew out a breath, and then smiled. "A bookshop exchange. You come and run *Once Upon a Time*, and I'll take over the *Bookshop on the Corner*."

I gasped, my jaw dropping.

Sophie continued, her calm belied by the slight quake in her hand as she gesticulated. "You've always said how much you yearned to visit the city of love – here's your chance, my dear friend. After our language lessons, you're more than capable of speaking enough French to get by." Sophie's words spilled out in a desperate rush, her earlier calm vanishing. "You'd save me so much heartache. I want to be in a place where no one knows me, and there's no chance for love, *ever* again."

I tried to hide my smile at that remark. I'd told Sophie in the past how bereft of single men Ashford was, and how my love life had been almost non-existent until Ridge strolled into town.

"Sophie, I want to help you, but I'm barely hanging on to the bookshop as is . . ." I stalled for time, running a hand through my hair, my bangs too long, shielding the tops of my eyebrows. How could it work? How would we run each other's businesses, the financial side, the logistics? I also had an online shop, and I sourced hard-to-find books – how would Sophie continue that?

My mind boggled with the details, not to mention the fact that leaving my books would be akin to leaving a child behind. I loved my bookshop as if it were a living thing, an unconditional best friend, who was always there for me. Besides, I'd never ventured too far from Ashford let alone boarded a plane – it just couldn't happen.

"*Please*," Sophie said, a real heartache in her tone. "Think about it. We can work out the finer details and I'll make it worth your while. Besides, you know I'm good with numbers, I can whip your sales into shape." Her eyes clouded with tears. "I have to leave, Sarah. You're my only chance. Christmas in Paris is on your bucket list . . ."

My bucket list. A hastily compiled scrappy piece of paper filled with things I thought I'd never do. Christmas in Paris – snow dusting the bare trees on the Left Bank, the sparkling fairy lights along the Boulevard Saint-Germain. Santa's village in the Latin Quarter. The many Christmas markets to stroll through, rugged up with thick scarves and gloves, Ridge by my side, as I hunted out treasures. I'd spent many a day curled up in my own shop, flicking through memoirs, or travel guides about Paris, dreaming about the impossible . . . *one day*.

Sophie continued: "If you knew how I suffered here, my darling. It's not only Manu, it's everything. All of a sudden, I can't do it all any more. It's like someone has pulled the plug, and I'm empty." Her eyes scrunched closed as she fought tears.

While Sophie's predicament was different to mine, she was in a funk, just like me. Perhaps a new outlook, a new place would mend both our lives. Her idea of whipping my sales into shape was laughable though, she had no real clue how tiny Ashford was.

"Exchange bookshops . . ." I said, the idea taking shape. Could I just up and leave? What about my friends, my life, my book babies? My fear of change? And Ridge, what would he have to say about it? But my life . . . it was missing something. Could this be the answer?

Paris. The city of love. Full of rich literary history.

A little bookshop on the bank of the Seine. Could there be anything sweeter?

With a thud, a book fell to the floor beside me, dust motes dancing above it like glitter. I craned my neck to see what it was.

Paris: A Literary Guide.

Was that a sign? Did my books want me to go?

"Yes," I said, without any more thought. "I'll do it."

Want to read on? Order now!

Dear Reader,

We hope you enjoyed reading this book. If you did, we'd be so appreciative if you left a review. It really helps us and the author to bring more books like this to you.

Here at HQ Digital we are dedicated to publishing fiction that will keep you turning the pages into the early hours. Don't want to miss a thing? To find out more about our books, promotions, discover exclusive content and enter competitions you can keep in touch in the following ways:

JOIN OUR COMMUNITY:

Sign up to our new email newsletter: po.st/HQSignUp

Read our new blog www.hqstories.co.uk

🐦 : https://twitter.com/HQDigitalUK

📘 : www.facebook.com/HQStories

BUDDING WRITER?

We're also looking for authors to join the HQ Digital family!
Please submit your manuscript to:

HQDigital@harpercollins.co.uk

Thanks for reading, from the HQ Digital team

If you enjoyed this wonderful romance then why not try
another feel-good story from HQ Digital?